# THE TERRA AUSTRALIS UNIVERSITY FOR ALCHEMISTS

## JADA MCKINLEY

*For anyone caught in the blizzard.*

# A Note from the Author

Hi everyone,

Before you begin *The Terra Australis University for Alchemists*, I want to share a few notes about the content of this book. *TTAUFA* is a New Adult romantic fantasy set at an academic institution for military recruits. This novel contains on-page violence, death, sexual content, drug use, explicit language, and mature themes, including discussions of politics, mental health, religious trauma, suicidal ideation, and active addiction. **Reader discretion is advised.**

Last but not least, TTAUFA is, above all, a story about people. And it was important to me that this world reflect the diversity of the real one. *The Chronicles of the Phoenix* series centers characters of varied races and backgrounds and includes LGBTQ+ relationships as part of the narrative.

If any of the above gives you pause, it's okay to close the book here. Otherwise, I welcome you to Terra Australis.

**— Jada Mckinley**

# THE TERRA AUSTRALIS UNIVERSITY FOR ALCHEMISTS

By Jada Mckinley

# PART ONE
# GENESIS

# CHAPTER 1

I run the pad of my index finger along my gum line. Soft tissue going numb as I tongue bitter-flavored grit beneath my lip, its taste shadowed by the tang of liquid iron.

Phlegm congeals in the back of my throat, and I hike up the skirt of my dress. Pink-tinged saliva dripping into the toilet as a chortle breaks the sound of labored breath, the harsh bang of a steel door a warning for the blinding flash that follows.

"Hey?! You can't—"

"Shhh. It's for the obituary," Sam says, issuing another flash before sliding her Leica into the pocket of her sundress. "Even though I've never seen someone *on the verge of death* squat in stilettos."

I climb down from my perch to flush the handle behind me, eyeing the dropped baggie that's been whirled down with my spit.

"Did you bring my medicine?" I ask, squeezing my nostrils shut as blood soaks through the fresh wad of toilet paper.

"Nope. Just came to watch you bleed out." She ushers me forward to adjust my bangs, mocha spirals defying Sam's every attempt to twist them into submission. "On the bright side, I escaped before the college years. Bet you fifty bucks he mentions the good ol' days. A hundred if he gets a half chub while he does it."

"Alright, I don't think Runsson's that bad."

"He literally douches with raw milk."

"And who told you that?"

"The bacteria that crawled up his intestines and rotted his brain into thinking hitting on his student is acceptable." Sam rolls her eyes as I swat away her hands. "Relax. I'm being nice because he hasn't kidnapped you yet."

"Stop saying that. He's not going to *kidnap* me."

"Abduct. Kidnap. Tah-may-toe, Tah-mah-toe. We'll be three thousand miles apart next year. You insisted on going it alone, so no more giving the benefit of the doubt to losers. You could be lured into a van with a half-eaten, expired candy bar and the promise of a good back scratch."

Well, that's not entirely true.

We were all set for Boston when Sam had been plucked off USC's waitlist and woken me up with window-shattering shrieks. Timidly asking me over her celebratory dinner at Angelo's what I thought she should do about it.

Mom told me I have to stop lying to spare people's feelings, but I don't think gritting my teeth and bearing it is the reason for this unwarranted separation. I blame Dad's documentary habit for her career choices, and I attribute Sam's impressive senior thesis on human rights violations in Congo to her admittance.

The thought of Sam in a war zone, using a camera for a shield, is my worst nightmare come to life. But everyone else seems to think it's a noble profession. So who am I to tell her she can't?

"Please stop. I haven't been explored by anyone except Dr. Reeves, and I wouldn't get into a suspicious vehicle for anything less than a king-sized candy bar."

Sam chortles, sliding into a posh accent. "All right. No betting on half chubs by royal decree." She curtsies in front of me but quickly grows serious. "Now hurry. You're up soon."

"Oh. I changed my mind. I'm not doing it." My feet drag toward the row of sinks on the opposite wall, and I avoid my reflection, twisting the knob in front of me. A spurt of water shoots up from the intense pressure and sprays my silken dress with scalding droplets.

Sam paces back and forth, fingers digging into curvy hips as if they wish to throttle me. "What do you mean you *changed your mind* and you're *not doing it?*"

I chuck the wad of blood-soaked tissue into the nearby wastebasket and stick my face under the cooled-off stream.

"Yes! Minus the first four words!"

"Bee, I didn't stick on polyester and broil in the sun for over an hour for you to be taken out by a nosebleed." Sam pinches blue fabric between her index and thumb for emphasis, holding it as if it's a ticking bomb.

"You did that for your opening address. Which was fantastic! Do you think a round two would be too much to—"

"Shiloh Brooklyn Benson, get your ass moving. *Now.* Or I'll move it for you."

The cautious grin I'd dared to let grace my lips, falls flat.

Full government name means Sam's about to get vicious. A trick she's plucked from my parents and has somehow made scarier.

Treating me like a child isn't necessarily her fault.

When you spend years speaking for someone and expertly filling the silences they leave at odd places, it's disarming when they find some semblance of their own voice. Even still, a flash of irritation writhes within my veins and makes me itch.

I wait for the water to run clear before I scoop up the bag Sam's plopped on the counter beside me, digging through its contents until I reach a familiar orange bottle.

Three chalky ovals fall into the palm of my hand and I guzzle them down, starting a countdown in my head. In exactly ten minutes, my medication will minimize the stress that's managed to build and crest until the tension now feels so palpable I could snap at the waist.

Until then, this bathroom is my sanctuary.

I switch off the flowing tap while coming to the conclusion that I've morphed into a melted popsicle. One of the character treats I'd beg for from the ice cream truck as a kid. The gumball eye somehow located near its mouth from lack of proper refrigeration.

Okay, maybe my eyes are still in place, but I *am* molting to some degree.

Sam stops pacing and opens her clutch, rooting through for what feels like eternity. She pulls out a pen Mom gifted her, with an assortment of small crystals scattered on it like polka dots. Thumb pressing the golden plunger in repetition as it creates a springy noise.

She hands it over, and I press the end exactly as she'd demonstrated. *Click, Click, Click.*

"It'll have to do," she sighs. "Let's go."

"No, I don't want to!" Nausea turns my intestines into molten lava. Stilettos sliding across slippery tiles as Sam steers me toward the exit, grasping anything in sight to slow us down. "I'm serious! They were already pointing at me."

"Because the decaying look is trendy this year."

I frown. Sam's referring to the purple bruises that form under each eye, only made darker by shadows cast on them by heavy lids and thick lashes. My color today is paler than normal. Chestnut skin losing its golden undertones and settling on something close to gray.

"I'm kidding. You worked hard for this. Don't let peons you won't even remember in a few years steal your moment."

"It's not stolen if I never take it to begin with. Wait, let me go! You can't force me onstage, Samantha!" Though she intends to do just that. *Kicking and screaming.* "Alright, so, apparently you can. But at least grab my cap! *S*-seriously. At least—" At the last second, her manicured hand snatches my mortarboard off the counter.


IN THE BLINK OF AN EYE, I'm seated back onstage and clicking the pen with reckless abandon, every so often casting a sideways glare at Sam, who's all of a sudden interested in Mr. Runsson's college years.

Below, the freshly mown lawn is flooded in a sea of polyester. Four hundred students, swathed in blue, fidgeting atop padded folding chairs as the sun bakes them like sardines.

The rest of us onstage squint against the blinding daylight, scanning the bleachers for our parents as the crowd blurs into thousands of tan blobs.

"Bee," Sam whispers.

"What?!" There's slightly more agitation in my response than she's anticipating, cringing at the unfamiliar vitriol in my voice.

*Click, Click, Click.*

"He said your name."

My body runs on autopilot as I dig through my purse.

Crumpled at the bottom is a folded piece of paper with all the words I scribbled in the early hours of the morning.

I'm unable to process the walk to the podium or what Mr. Runsson whispers to me, smiling brightly and outright assuming it's some compliment he feels responsible to give.

Warning gurgles infiltrate my bowels as I register a lingering touch on my lower back. I arch away from searching fingers, unfolding my speech and flattening wrinkled paper until it lies flush with the stand—triple-checking I've marked dots and slashes between long sentences.

"Hello... *everyone.*"

Every sensation feels turned up a thousand levels.

My voice booms in the mic too loudly. The tassel hanging from my mortarboard smacks me in the eye. Static reverberates in the speakers and triggers tinnitus as I move my mouth backward a few inches. Blinking away swimming stars and pushing aside sweat-drenched bangs.

"I'm Shiloh."

Ashley Abbytt stifles a smirk from the front row, flanked on each side by two carbon copy brunettes. The bleach-blonde slaps her chest with the side of her hand and everyone beside her bursts into giggles, furthering her barbarous imitation with harsh grunts as guffaws grow louder in response.

"Let's see if she's still laughing when her husband has her washing skid-marked, hole-ridden, boxers but never changes a diaper in his miserable, cheating life," Sam mutters to a lanky boy from the robotics club.

Ethan's eyes widen when she rises to her feet, pointing towards the front row like they've been marked for death.

"Do it again, and I'll fuck you up!"

The crowd breaks into murmurs. Clutching their pearls and whispering about participation trophies as if Sam isn't the smartest person onstage. "Don't look at me like that! You know what you're doing!"

Luckily, she's good at ignoring people. Sam claims that it's the best trait she's inherited from her adoptive parents.

*Click, Click, Click.*

"Ms. Davis, please be seated. One more outburst and you'll be removed from the premises," Mrs. Stanley says.

Of course my principal takes issue with Sam while turning a blind eye to the front row. The same blind eye she's turned as I've pried hot pink bubblegum from my curls for years now.

"But they were—"

"Ms. Benson, get started."

Sam plops into her chair, and I scratch out half of my speech in the same instance. Cutting it down to its bones as I swallow against the sandpaper in my mouth, lowering the microphone and shuddering out a breath.

"Um, okay. I guess I'll start with a book of poems my Dad used to read to me when I was younger? His favorite one talks about getting lost in the woods in a snowstorm on the darkest night of the year."

*Click, Click, Click.*

I squint into the sun as a drop of sweat creeps down my spine.

"I'd always tell him it was the worst in the collection. That stories leaving someone without a proper ending aren't something I want to read. But he'd look at me with this frown and say, 'Bee. Every story, every person, gets the same ending. The only differentiator is if you're brave enough to trek to new heights on your way there. His journey is what you're upset about. It wasn't kind to him.'"

"As a child, I didn't understand that. How could someone brave a snowstorm alone when the woods are so alluring? The journey didn't have to be so hard. If I'm being honest, I've put research into hypothermia to rule out freezing to death. You're in pain and shivering, confused and scared, and eventually it makes sense why Robert Frost went another route and said fire was the way to go. At least it's quick, right? And you feel something when it all ends."

There's the sound of nothing but my voice, and the dry wind that blows around us on this hot summer day, feeling as if I stand under a heaven held blow dryer as people steady their stoles to keep them from flying away.

*Inhale. Exhale. Inhale. Exhale. Speak slower.*

"Anyway, I went in pursuit of a new answer. Figured history is as good a place as any to understand what it is to hike. To rationalize climbing Mount Everest and going higher than you intended, because you still have time. And in my studies, they said that Hannibal had a cry against impossible feats on his walk through the woods. *Aut viam inveniam aut faciam.* In Latin, that translates to mean, 'Either I will find a way, or I will make one.'"

"Maybe a war general isn't the place to look for comfort. But for some reason, his words echoed for centuries and we're still around to listen. We've all been walking the paths of impossible choices since we were old enough to make them. But today, we'll begin walking on our own. Trekking outside of the pathways our parents and our trusted guides have helped us travel. And my greatest hope is that any roadblocks we face as individuals, we'll push aside together as one. So that the barriers that slow us down are cleared for generations to come."

My vision's slightly blurry, but my family's closer than I'd realized. Cheeks tingling as Dad pumps his fist in the air. The people nearby chuckle when he yells, "That's my baby! You tell 'em, Bee!"

Mom yanks him back into his seat. Sending around a sheepish smile and burying her face in his shoulder. Without a doubt, her bronze cheeks have gone ruby red.

I switch the pen to my right hand, the object heating slowly like the surface of a lit stovetop.

"My fellow graduates, no matter where we go next, we get to ask ourselves... **Quis sum ego vere?**"

*Click, Click, Click.*

The heat from the pen grows so intense, I place it on the stand. Staring toward the large monitors with my face on them.

Blood dribbles from my nose onto the top of my silken dress, a steady red stream flowing down my chest and pooling in the cups of my bra.

I stumble backward, body wading through a thick blanket of energy that crackles and pops around me. Time moving to the tune of unsure whispers as someone screams my name and I collide with a row of faculty.

Multiple sets of hands make to catch me but I bat them away in my attempt to flee. Escape slowed by espresso irises filled with dread, camera clutched in her hands a shield from the inevitable.

As I turn to look for what's frightened her, the podium explodes. The sheer force of the blast blowing me backwards.

The base of my skull strikes a sharp surface and tingles spread through my limbs as horrified screams ensue. Shrieks of clamoring students, keening along with them, battering my eardrums.

The Universe bursts into stars and vibrant colors.

Then, there's nothing left at all.

And I wonder if I've gone to sleep at last.

# CHAPTER 2

Ahummingbird thunks against the glass wall leading to the backyard. Its green-feathered body reorienting itself when it reaches the feeder on the patio, skinny tongue lapping up sugar water as small wings beat at its side.

It's the same one as yesterday.

And the day before that.

And... the day before that.

The strip of magenta on its neck highlighted by the setting sun as it twists its beak side to side and eyes my curled-up form.

The bird hovers until I give it a little wave, massaging away phantom pain from the base of my skull.

I stretch too far and my blanket falls from my lap, gathering the cashmere pooled around my feet as I glare at the clunky black band around my ankle. A green dot blinks every three seconds, tormenting me more than my lone visitor ever does.

*You're a criminal,* the light screams. The device vibrating with aggravation each time I step outside to pour sugar water for my guest.

"I'm not. I didn't do it," I mutter toward the taunting glow.

*Perhaps I am crazy.*

"Didn't do what?!" Dad yells, dropping a half-constructed Ferris wheel onto his pile of blocks.

He's spent the past few weeks 3-D printing a small society in our basement and has decided to assemble it in the kitchen to keep a better eye on me. Monopolizing every inch of our island's fifteen-foot-long surface with odd bubble trains and eclectic-looking vehicles.

I push a curl behind my ear. Frustration making the feeling of anything against my skin harder to bear as I wave a shackled ankle in the air.

Dad runs a brown hand atop his overgrown fade, and when that doesn't soothe him, massages closed eyelids with his thumb and middle finger. "We've been over this."

He's right. And several months ago, I'd agreed.

But after twelve weeks of house arrest, I can't stop thinking prison might allow me more freedom.

The second we'd gotten back from the police station, Mom had been in hysterics. My phone and laptop were the first to go and by midnight I had everything taken. In protest, I've remained inside my own space with a singular sleeping bag because to accept her reaction as reasonable feels like an admission of guilt.

"You don't think it's cruel for them to lock me up and throw away the key?"

Dad emits a chuckle that rumbles in his belly. "Cruel'd be a belt to the behind because you forgot to thaw a pack of frozen meat. We built you a movie theater downstairs?"

"So we're just going to pay people off until everyone forgets?"

"You don't know what you're talking about."

"I do. I checked our bank statements from your laptop this morning."

"One. Stay out of my office. We told you, no phones and no laptops. Two, stay out of my pockets because it's not *our* anything. Mom and I are covering medical expenses regardless of who's at fault. It's the right thing to do." Dad shoots me a pointed glance, and I fall face-first into fluffy pillows in an attempt to indulge myself with a light smothering. "Did you steal the roof of my town hall? Where are they supposed to convene for grievances?"

"In the privacy of their homes," I mumble into the plush white sectional.

"*Sheeeeit.* That's cold," Dad audibly sucks air through his teeth. "Real cold."

"Have you ever been victimized by one of your blocks?"

"Yes. And I still managed to abide by humanitarian law."

"Daddy, they're toys." Even still, my cheeks burn with embarrassment.

"To *you.* Dude's got a block family to look after and no opposable thumbs. Now what?"

"Take it back."

"No. Look at him! C's for hands, and his wife just gave birth to twins he can't hold properly." I grimace when Dad waves the yellow block-headed man around. Covering his smiling mouth as if I've silenced the plastic piece. "Come on, Bee! He told me he fell off the table and it won't happen again. Who'll help him if not us?"

"Fine, sicko. Put him down. Slowly. And no one gets hurt."

Dad sucks on his cheek to hold in a laugh and I dig into the lumpy pockets of my shorts, chucking over stolen blocks one by one until the roof is in his hands.

"I'm telling Mom she should rethink her marriage choices."

"Yeah? While you're at it, let her know our offspring is a Klepto."

Dad pauses to ponder his words.

"Then again, so is she. All my sweaters have gone missing." He says this fondly. As if he looks forward to waking up to half his closet given away in one of Mom's spur-of-the-moment donation extravaganzas.

*Clutter* is not in Jessica's vocabulary. Evidence of this is in the minimalist manner in which Mom keeps the house.

With modern light fixtures and tall angular ceilings, our home has all the makings of being cold and lifeless. So bright inside that sometimes it hurts to blink.

Before me is a glass coffee table and plush Persian rug, ambience accompanied by a grandiose television playing the Discovery Channel on the lowest possible volume. Bloodshot eyes more interested in the blue flames dancing in the electric fireplace below.

As meticulously compiled as it all seems, there's a lived-in quality easily felt in its bones.

When looking close enough, there's a ripped seam where my dog Baker, who's long since passed from old age, chewed up the corner of our couch. And one deep breath fills my nose with the scent of sandalwood from crackling candles and the mouthwatering aroma of pork simmering in the crockpot.

With the clatter of a ridiculously loud keychain, the front door unlocks and Dad's already grinning at the sound. Stretching tattooed arms above his head and avoiding my gaze on his way out the door.

Reality sets in again as I remember the front entrance to our home is entirely off limits with the screeching shackle on my leg, and that everything in my life has separated into two distinct segments.

Dad pre-explosion made me smiley-face pancakes every morning with copious amounts of maple syrup. He kept his clothes ironed every day and his hair lined up every two weeks. He wore long-sleeved dress shirts and a crisp white coat to work, and his shoes were always polished.

People would sometimes even allude to the fact he was handsome.

Or, more than allude. There'd been many student-teacher conferences where they'd hit on him outright. Even with the solid gold band that always rests on his left ring finger.

Dad *post-explosion* is on an indefinite hiatus from the lab, desperately needs a fade, wears wrinkled basketball shorts as if in uniform, and hardly ever smiles. Today's considered a good one because he hasn't spent it scowling in silence. Small flickers of the old him are almost enough to follow Dad outside, scared he'll throw eggshells down when he has time to remember he hates me.

I rise to stretch my joints as well. Feeling as if the walls around me cave in an inch when Mom enters. Arms overflowing with brown paper bags and smelling of hyacinth flowers.

I rush to take a few from her and bring them over to the counter.

"You look different," she says, pressing her palm to the crown of my head and kissing my temple with lipstick I know will leave stains the color of Chelan cherries. The observation's almost funny coming from her, a slender frame that wears heels to have any inches on me.

I wipe away the residue with the back of my hand, noting quietly that it must be a Friday. She feels a little more emboldened to wear a red lip to work by the week's end.

"It's my spine compressing from lack of use."

"Okay? Unnecessary."

Mom fidgets with the wedding ring resting on her right hand, a line forming between furrowed brows as my eyes graze her left, where she's missing her ring finger.

"Sorry," I mutter.

She shrugs, sniffing the air as she nears the countertops to stir shredded pork. "You eat today?"

"Didn't you hear? I cook basically all the time now."

She rolls her eyes at the half-truth.

My skills consist of burning toast and smiling my way through eating it. And yet, it's still better than starting my mornings with a frowny face of blueberries.

I unload milk and vegetables from the bags, careful to organize the fridge as best I can, small tasks as helpful as I can be at the moment.

"Cast's off. Sammie's looking good as new," Mom says, leaning against the countertop while I stifle a flinch.

A SWAT team raided the Davises' home shortly after the ceremony, destroying Sam's photography equipment in the rough searches, claiming she was a suspected person of interest. With my phone revoked, she hadn't been able to call me, so she called Dad and yelled at him instead. When I'd wrestled the device away, she'd hung up instantly.

That was the last time we'd spoken, which hadn't been much of anything.

"Dad's taking her to move in. One of us has to stay with you, but..." I tune out the explanation, gut stirring as Mom says the words *has to* while wringing her hands.

I'm careful not to crack the eggs. Sliding them into an acrylic container, placing them in the fridge and throwing the styrofoam carton in the recycling bin with a rough *thwack*.

Dad returns, adding to the stack of groceries before they escape to the pantry to refill cereal containers.

I reconfigure items in the freezer by myself, singing to help me ignore the beastly sounds coming from the walk-in. After everything's been squared away, I pad over to the front door. Ignoring the vibrations on my ankle while I snoop through the mail Mom's hidden in her briefcase.

She must suspect that I've been too quiet because she peeks around the corner to check up on me. Smudged lipstick and all, she still looks beautiful in her creamy button-up and dark brown pencil skirt. Auburn ringlets slicked into a tight ponytail at the nape of her neck.

I pull a face when she re-tucks her blouse, scrambling to do up her top that's come unbuttoned.

"Why is there lipstick on your collarbone?" I ask, flipping through mail faster as she approaches. "You've been home all of two seconds."

"Should we do the birds and bees again?" She purses her lips, hands pressed to flushed cheeks as dazed eyes attempt to focus. "When you love someone, yada yada, someone sips nectar… things get pollinated?"

I shudder, gaze falling on a thick white envelope with a Veritas shield stamped into the corner.

Mom's bronze hand darts for it and I yank it behind my back. Twirling out of her grasp and putting immediate distance between us while she stalks forward, a catlike clarity in the amber orbs that narrow down at me. "No bees or birds! Just this, thank you very much."

"We shouldn't do this tonight," she sighs.

In the back of my mind, I know she's right. No good information ever comes from a university in a small envelope.

When I got my acceptance to Harvard, it was accompanied by a large pack of red confetti—*Class of 2029* littering the kitchen floor as Dad lifted me on his shoulders like I was a sack of potatoes. But I can't seem to stop myself from tearing into the thick stationery with the final remnants of hope, hands trembling as if holding a surefire crystal ball.

My eyes flicker over a few sentences before I squeeze them shut. The words *regret* and *rescinded* etched into my retinas, no matter how hard I attempt to blink them away. I suck in shaky breaths, razor blades in my lungs as my ankle continues to vibrate.

"We're handling it," Mom whispers.

"Handling what? For who?!"

"For *you.*"

"I didn't do anything!" I rub out a stab of pain that centers in my forehead. Vision blurring at the edges as I narrowly hold on to my composure. "I'd never hurt anyone!"

"We said we believe you." Mom's voice is strained, motioning toward what was once a formal dining room and now holds only plush furniture and a grand piano I haven't touched since before this all began. "Why don't you sit and—"

"Do I look like I give a *fuck* about a piano right now?! Honestly! Let's all be serious for one goddamn minute!"

I don't make the conscious decision to snap, and at my core, I feel bad about it. But my body does the work for me and it's about time I let my glass mind work in my favor.

Mom's lips fall open in shock, at a loss for what to say as Dad rounds the corner.

"Who the hell do you think you're talking to? It can't be me, and it's definitely not your mother. So let's figure it out. *Quickly.*"

"I'll let you think on it," I all but spit.

He inhales sharply, a tight pinch to the corner of his mouth that means he'd cuss someone out if only he had less self-control.

I steel myself as Dad counts down from five, seeking to spiral me further into the abyss. Water through a cracked dam I'm trying desperately to hold together with willpower alone.

*"Room,"* he whispers when he's reached zero. So eerily reserved that my stomach twists in knots. "Now."

"Fine." And because I'm already acting like a cunt, I commit to it. Tearing up the letter and leaving the scraps on the ground.

"Clean it up!" he yells as I walk away, itching at the scars on his forearms. "I swear to God, Shiloh! If I have to, you won't like me in the morning!"

Mom throws him an incredulous glance, hand resting on his fingers until he ceases his scratching.

"Well I don't like you right now!" I whirl on my heels, glaring up at him and pushing the upset behind a feral wall of rage. "So do something for once besides being a passive-aggressive douchebag because the frowny faces aren't cutting it anymore!"

Dad releases a strangled laugh. Brown eyes flooded with emotions that make my heart sink faster than his anger ever could. "I can't look at you and not feel embarrassed this is who I raised."

"Henry—" Mom starts.

"No! Someone explain to me why my daughter, who is the most intelligent little girl I've *ever* met, had enough narcotics in her system to tranquilize a fucking racehorse!? Explain why I can't take a piss now without wondering if she's sneaking off to dig out a hidden crack pipe in my sock drawer! It's not normal behavior!"

"It was just edibles and my prescription."

"Lie *one* more time. You're about to let your mouth write a check your ass can't cash."

Mom shifts in front of me with a frantic glance, tiny frame attempting to shield me with her own as if his words are anything but an empty threat.

Dad's never raised a hand to strike me, and he certainly won't start now, but the mere suggestion tells me his anger has never been more prevalent for the thought to so much as cross his mind.

The flood of rage dissipates to a dull ache as quickly as it had rushed in, replaced entirely by grief. Dad grunts when tears roll down my cheeks, abruptly turning his gaze toward the ceiling and refusing to so much as look at me.

I blink back wetness to clear my vision.

*I'm not stupid. I'm not crazy. I'm not stupid. I'm not crazy.*

I'll repeat the mantra as many times as I need to absolve my actions.

If I have to live in lies, they can live with the person they created.

"Get out of my sight. Maybe in the morning you'll have grown up and realized how much we've sacrificed to allow you this awful life in this big-ass house you're so desperate to escape."

Mom kneels, picking up the scraps I'd torn with a detached stare and Dad shoots me an unforgiving glare, melting beside her as her shoulders begin to shake.

I run up the glass-encased staircase, unable to spend a second longer near the fallout. Knocking over a flower-filled vase during my escape.

My socks slide across hardwood floors, past the gym and the art studio. Mahogany doors and brightly lit hallways bleeding together until

I reach my bedroom at the east end of the third story, scrambling to shut and lock the door behind me.

Inside is when I can finally catch my breath. Murals of the nighttime sky Mom painted for me the only thing left of my pre-explosion room.

I drag my sleeping bag across the empty hardwood and into the corner. Crawling into it and shutting myself inside the welcoming embrace of darkness, aching desperately to sink deeper into permanent unawareness of existence instead of some half-lucid state that only lets me fantasize about it.

But mere hours later, reality comes crashing in as it always does.

Brutal and unforgiving.

Instead of the nihility I claw at, life takes form in the shuffle of heavy footsteps, molding itself into the shape of armed bodies in military fatigues. And only now, beyond a reasonable doubt, do I know that this post-explosion nightmare never ends. And I am owed nothing to weather the storm to come.

# CHAPTER 3

My bedroom door flies open and the snapping of its lock stirs me from oblivion. Sleep-crusted eyes blinking harmoniously with the shuffle of thick boots on empty flooring.

A blow to the head thrusts me into reality, and I shoot upright, vision slanting and correcting itself before my assailant raises his rifle.

"Hands where I can see them! Try *anything*, and they're gone!"

My only thoughts are of what will allow me to keep my fingers while I soak in every detail I can.

Five figures are outlined by slivers of moonlight that stream through cracks in my blinds. They stand in a V-formation and wear all black, with the exception of the blue and green patches on their shoulders.

The barrels of their rifles jut forward, and the same man with a thick accent yells, "Hands up! I won't say it again!"

Urine gushes down my thighs, and my hands shoot up. I refrain from calling out his contradictory instructions as my empty palms twist toward the gunmen, his pale finger stroking the trigger at the sight.

The next command is issued by a curious voice in the back of the group. The woman's southern twang is cautious, but less riddled with anger. "Stand slowly, and we won't shoot, hun."

I unfold one leg, then another, moving at the pace of a snail as I rise.

One red dot is trained on my kneecap, another aimed at each hand, and one trained directly over my heart. I can only assume the last one is dead center on my forehead.

The leader's finger twitches again. "Now turn and place your hands behind your back." I do as he instructs, using all my strength to stiffen instead of convulse.

Boots pound across the empty flooring until a cool material is placed around my wrists, and their leader pushes me into motion. Two soldiers walk ahead of us, and two behind. His hand gripping my arm so tightly the blood stops flowing, twisting my rotator cuff at an angle where my shoulder dislocating is not a fear, but an inevitability.

I stumble as pain lances through my tendons, and he drags me until I regain my footing. Silent because to protest is a bullet in my back.

Through each step, I lose hope until I spot Mom at the end of the staircase. Noting she's unharmed, but seemingly discombobulated, frizzy ringlets springing up at odd angles as amber orbs widen to saucers.

When we reach the bottom of the stairs, Dad is kneeling, hand-cuffed on the floor, eight agents surrounding him with red-lasered rifles pointing at his head and hands. It seems like overkill, but most of them cringe away from so much as meeting his gaze.

"Finger on the trigger, Valdez. Kill shots for that one."

In response, Agent Valdez bashes the barrel of his gun into Dad's jaw, leaping back when Dad retaliates by spitting blood on his boots.

"I said don't bleed him!" the red-faced soldier roars in my ear.

"We had a deal," Dad rasps, face swelling as he scans me for wounds.

"Deal's off. We're bringing her in."

Mom tightens her robe as she steps between them. "I'm going with her. Okay? You'll wait here. They won't allow you in the facility."

*"They?!"* Dad seethes.

"Momma?" I whisper as softly as I can so the gunman on my arm doesn't press his steadily twitching index. "What facility?"

"Get your hands off my daughter."

The man gripping me appears ready to protest, but Mom doesn't give him a chance. Even though she's a foot below him in height and half his weight soaking wet, he backs away when she bares her teeth—allowing her to tuck me into her side as we exit the house.

Time passes in a blur.

Through tinted SUV windows, I can hardly see where we're headed, but it feels like only moments have passed when we reach the location and pull into a nondescript garage.

Mom tells the soldiers I've soiled myself, and I'm thrown into a white-walled shower guarded by a woman who refuses to speak to me while having full access to stare at my naked breasts. Cringing in the corner as she switches the cuffs to the front of my body so it's easier to scrub.

When I'm clean, I'm escorted to a freezing interrogation room like cattle ready for slaughter. Bangs plastered to my forehead and soaked spirals dripping every so often onto my white cotton t-shirt.

As always, the trusty ankle monitor is still attached above my foot. Angrily blinking red to warn me that I've stepped out of bounds.

The observation makes me laugh aloud. An off-key croak that bounces off the walls of the barren room just before the door opens.

"Hi," Mom whispers from beside me, surveying the rumpled man who enters.

The agent clears his throat, sliding into the seat across from me and ignoring her greeting. Hands gripping his cup of coffee like a lifeline, as I notice deep bruising under ocean-mist-colored eyes. He tosses back a full head of curly hair that's salt and peppered with silver strands before meeting my gaze. "Hello, Ms. Benson."

"Hi." I survey the manila folder he's placed between us, using the one scrap of knowledge I'd managed to overhear from the soldiers in the hallways. "Are you... Adam?"

"I'm Agent Creen."

The light audibly flickers overhead, and he blows on his steaming coffee to pass the time. Angling away from Mom like her presence is a poison that's sure to spread.

"So who's—"

"The American Defense Division Against Magic. It's a branch under the U.D.A.M."

My hands fall limply on the cold table. Silver chains clanking against steel as he awaits my reaction.

"Is this a joke?"

"Far from it. You're here because you're in direct violation of Addam's Safe Haven Act. At approximately nineteen hundred hours, you admitted to openly accessing the internet while on probation."

"What do you mean she—" Mom's voice catches, and she bends to inspect my ankle. "Is this *bugged*, Steven?"

Agent Creen laughs without humor, and the tune carries a thousand words he doesn't say.

Mom cringes away from his stare, and I grab her hands, clasping them in my own as I peer toward the man who makes her seem almost frail in his presence.

"Magic?" I ask, the light above us flickering again. "You're accusing me of... witchcraft?"

"Alchemy," Creen corrects. "Your people consider the words witchcraft and vampirism taboo."

Mom squeezes my fingers, and I lean as far back from the table as I can get, but the chains that lock my cuffs to the surface only allow for so much distance. "This isn't funny. I want to go home."

"I can promise you, no one finds this funny." Creen frowns, looking over his shoulder at someone through the double-sided mirror. "In fact, you're set to be deported to your homeland. Effective immediately."

"My homeland? I was born in Phoenix?" I yank at the chain attached to my cuffs, and Creen's coffee topples over, splashing on the manila folder between us as Mom flinches.

There's a knock at the door, and he rises to answer it. Mom's voice a whisper while she rubs small soothing circles on my wrists.

"Calm down, Bee. He's trying to help you."

I attempt to catch a breath as he returns carrying a fistful of paper towels, meticulously cleaning up the splattered coffee as if to stall his next words.

When Creen's seated again, his voice remains passive and calm. "You're not legally a citizen."

Several moments pass before I can speak and not want to claw out of my own skin. "I know this world's rewinding rapidly, but it doesn't work like that."

"It does," he sighs. "Addam doesn't grant jus soli to Alchemists."

"But I'm not an Alchemist? I'm Pre-Med, majoring in Chemistry! Momma, just tell him that—"

She's suspiciously silent as I pause.

"Mom...?" I twist my wrists from her grasp, heavy chains clinking against the tabletop like a gavel on a sound block. "This is a *m*-misunderstanding."

"It's not. Your hearing is set for May." Creen's next sentence is a whisper for only us to hear, speaking through gritted teeth. "I suggest you act grateful to hear that before the situation is above me."

"May was three months ago?"

"Next May. That's the first date everyone will be available to hold a hearing with the amount of discretion needed."

The world begins to melt and distort as I ask, "What about my parents?"

"I'm sorry, Ms. Benson." Creen avoids my gaze, and to his credit, looks displeased as he adds, "This plane ride's for one."

I'm sorting through my belongings in the garage when Mom attempts to plead her case once more. Unlikely to reach an innocent verdict with only ten minutes left of my time at home.

I gather the last of my things and brush past her into the house. Stopping in the kitchen to shove fistfuls of Dad's blocks into my pockets at random, the rage a red inferno that blazes over all my good sense. I dig through Mom's purse next, stuffing her favorite lipstick into the depths of my bulging sweatpants.

When I make it to the living room, I drop to my knees in front of my suitcases, rolling each sweater as tightly as I can in silence.

"We were going to tell you," Mom says, sinking to her knees beside me and re-folding everything better the second time.

"When?" I ask, shaking out her folds and shoving things in by myself.

"After graduation. Then, the incident happened, and we decided— As your *parents,* we decided we needed to wait until the dust settled. Then you could decide for yourself."

"Brilliant execution, Momma."

"Bee, we don't have time for this. I need you to listen to me." Mom launches forward to cup my face, forcing me to meet her eyes and speaking rapidly as if time plays on fast forward. "We wanted you to be sure of who you were before the world told you who you should be. We wanted you to question. To *dream*. We only ever wanted to give you choices, never strip them away." She points to my heart, and her words become frantic. "That's who you are. Hold on to that. Don't let a ring, or a stone, or a name, or the people there tell you what is true. You are kind and brilliant and giving and I love you with my whole being. Please believe that."

"I can't believe anything you say to me anymore?"

Her face crumples at my words, and I have to look away. Mom has the sort of face that makes you feel like you're always wrong for going against her. No matter what she does.

I turn the heat to Dad, who's been silently observing it all, rising to my feet to meet his empty stare.

"How *c*-could you?"

In retrospect, it feels stupid to not have made the connection. To realize my meds weren't for chemicals in my mind, but unknown secrets hidden in my body.

"You don't understand."

He's right.

I don't understand, and I never will.

How could any explanation he gives be sufficient?

"The pills were to slow down your progression. It takes time to form the pathways and make them connect. You turned thirteen... and I had to make a choice, Shiloh. There wasn't another way."

"There's always another way," I whisper, a low moan of horror vibrating in my chest. "You had no right."

"The change is dangerous," Mom says. "You needed to be as strong as you could. It burns you out if you're not careful. And your Dad, Shiloh, you know he loves—"

"Stop saying that! He doesn't *love* me, he *violated* me! He sat there and judged me all summer long when he made me this way. It's all his fault! All of it!"

"You don't know the first thing about love if you think I wouldn't do it again," he whispers. "There's no line I wouldn't cross to keep you safe, and if you can believe nothing else I say, believe that."

The funny thing is, Dad sounds so sincere I almost do.

But lies have found home on his tongue.

I can't speak for fear of crying, so I work on closing my suitcases, overstuffed and difficult to zip from my shitty folding job and frantic movements.

When my endless jumping proves itself unhelpful, I begrudgingly step aside and Dad kneels with caution. He zips the bursting luggage, full of sweatshirts I've stolen from his donation pile, sliding my suitcases over to me and lengthening the handles so they're easier to wheel.

"Steven's waiting outside," he rasps, clearing his throat before he's able to speak again. "I'll fix this. You'll be back home before—"

"You can't fix this, Henry. I'm not some obscure illness you ruminate over in the lab. I'm your daughter? At least, I was?"

"You still are? You're not clear-minded right now, and I'm begging you not to leave things like this. Just hear us out."

"I've heard you out, and I'm taking the advice given. I don't need to be told anything else to know in my heart that I'm done. With the both of you."

My hands tighten on the handles of my suitcases, and without a look back, I trudge through the front door. Off toward whatever new life awaits me.

# CHAPTER 4

The flight attendant passes me another glass of champagne while Agent Creen slumps forward in his plush cream armchair, drooling on the mahogany tabletop in front of him.

The classical loop blaring from the overhead speakers gives me space to think, and at some points, spiral into worry. I slip my hands over my chest. Curious if the tenderness of the tissue is anxiety, or if my body will progress a bit more now that it's free of Dad's medicine.

"Is getting plastered before you're about to step into a new country the most productive use of your time?" Creen muses as I lift one arm to check for a lump.

I jump, spilling half of my flute and dropping my hands from my discreet breast examination. "You're awake?"

"Yes."

"Why didn't you say that?" he cuts off the sound of progressive piano chords and I emit a sound of protest. "Hey! That was Ludovico!"

"I've experienced enough. We're landing soon."

I hiccup in response. Glancing at the vast sheets of ice below us through the circular airplane window, churning stomach leaving me regretful of the extra helping of soft serve I'd stress-eaten.

"Where? There's nothing down there."

"You think we fought to get to the moon but left a mass body of land all on its own?"

"I don't know what to think anymore."

"How about the truth?" Creen stirs his lukewarm coffee, taking a sip as something darkens his eyes. "It was the nineteen-fifties when Udam first found proof."

"Of?"

"Human evolution that exceeds what we're capable of understanding. Your people are... *particular.* They're good at hiding secrets right under your nose and violent when you challenge their private affairs." His lips twist in revulsion. "When Udam first discovered them, some countries wanted to break bread and others felt Antarctica was land they should have a say in. Staking claim to uninhabited portions too close to the Alchemists' liking."

Creen cracks a bitter smile, and I stir in my seat. "They believed that even past their borders, every inch of the continent was theirs. Up to the point of contact, they allowed explorers and bases as they saw fit. Thought it was more imperative to maintain secrecy. Making sure we never came close to their lands by manipulating wind speeds and creating canyons to prevent widespread continental exploration. As soon as they couldn't deter exploration, attacks began. For every one of their soldiers to fall, so did hundreds of our men."

"Our men?"

"To them, it's Alchemists versus the human race as a whole. *Our* men versus theirs."

He chuckles, and I shoot him the dirtiest look I can muster. "What's funny? You started it."

"If you think I was kicking it in the fifties, I must be aging like a milk carton." Creen winces. "What I find funny is that the first time the world came together for anything, it was for invasion. Mankind will always love an enemy more than a neighbor. It was against many people's will, but it was too late. Once one country challenged, all of them issued a challenge. They believe in the oneness of people."

"So a bunch of innocents suffered the consequences?"

"For the patriots who died around the globe, it was a heavy price to pay. Their families never knew what led to their deaths." Creen fiddles with the cup on his table until the flight attendant replaces it with a steaming hot mug. "When the dust cleared, Udam lost. Unprepared for how badly they would. The only thing that prevented further retaliation was working together. After seeing what they were capable of, every country agreed."

"To what?"

"To anything it takes. Whether it be hundreds of warheads or preventative nuclear action, it would be done."

"There's nothing preventative about a nuclear approach. No one will survive, and if they do, they'd wish they hadn't."

"Believe me, the fallout from a nuclear bomb would be less damaging than millions of them unleashed on our soil."

*Hiccup. Hiccup. Hiccup.*

"I wonder if Oppenheimer knew he'd become Ares. Do you think Gods suffer in the afterlife?"

"Why?" he asks. "Hope that he's burning in hell?"

"I don't believe in hell. I just wonder if there's cosmic consequences for people who operate without thought for the suffering of others."

"Someone else would've done it if not him. Where would we be then?"

"No telling where we'd be, but I know where he led us." I finish my sixth champagne flute, hiccuping as alcohol settles in my empty belly. "No. I don't want him to suffer, but we all know he created the world's most sinister timer. The countdown starts when enough powerful people disregard the ones they see as beneath them in their ambitions."

Creen signals to the flight attendant that I'm cut off from further drinks while I clink my empty flutes.

One of them shatters as I clack the fragile glasses together and she clucks her tongue in disapproval, sweeping the shards onto her tray.

"*Oh.* I'm sorry, ma'am. You've been so nice. Send my parents the bill. Then, tell Dad he owes you a *looong* vacation. He's good for it."

Her annoyance dissipates as I sloppily scribble down Dad's credit card information, underlining the word *Centurion* as Creen grimaces.

*Hiccup. Hiccup. Hiccup.*

"That being said, the threat worked. By that point, they were done fighting too. Not left without the scars of war. They lost some of their most valued leaders. People they saw as not just political figureheads, but their Fathers and Mothers. Holy in a sense."

Indignation flickers through me, a branding iron buried deep in my belly. "Why not let them live in peace like they did before you arrived?"

"There were already whispers of the land before the secret war. No matter how outlandish it sounds, it was bound to happen again and they don't *want* to be discovered. It became part of Addam's agreement with them that we would hide the continent from... ourselves. You know how to satiate curiosity? An unassuming story. Science and progress belong to no one, so we allow only science to be done here. Restrict and deflect. Control the variables where you can. Let people visit when and where it's regulated and voila. You guard a secret nation and prevent yesterday's mistakes from bleeding into tomorrow."

"You can't hide an entire country forever. The past has a way of becoming the present more often than people like to admit. Transparent knowledge of our mistakes is all we have to prevent making them again. If you segregate populations and hide past transgressions, people will *other* them. They'll make them their enemy no matter what the truth is?"

"Again, they segregated themselves." Creen fastens his seatbelt and motions for me to do the same as the airplane rattles in our descent. "We're not the villains in this story. Addam is the only branch that's allowed Alchemists to so much as touch our soil."

"Do you know all the shit your squad leader said to me when we were in that SUV? He called me a demon. A *freak*. An alien. Every name in the goddamned book." Creen's silent as I slump into my seat. "There was no kindness in his eyes. No inkling of empathy. Just the decision that I was different and I had to go because *he* had the gun and the laws behind *him*. Never mind the fact that he had an accent himself."

"Becker's a transfer. He has and will continue to be reprimanded for his behavior." Creen swirls the dregs of his coffee. "But an Alchemist is never unarmed unless they're *unarmed*."

"Right." *Hiccup. Hiccup. Hiccup.* A moan releases and I swallow back bile. "Please don't make me go there. I don't want to."

"This isn't a punishment," he sighs. "Consider your time here training on how to blend in and a break for me to figure out the paperwork."

"I can blend in back home."

"Sober up, Ms. Benson. You're sloppy." A stray water bottle hits my thigh with a rough thwack. "The truth to getting back is simple." Creen ticks off his fingers, listing my tasks like a drill sergeant. "You act in a manner that's befitting your country. You're—"

"*My* country?! I'm being kicked out!"

"Day and night, I've advocated to get you this freedom. This is the product of my labor. Does that not count for something?"

"What does freedom mean to you?" I raise my leg and wave around my cuffed ankle.

"It doesn't matter what it means to me. This is as close as you'll get so cut me some fucking slack and drink the—"

*Hiccup. Hiccup. Hic—*

He issues a glare so scary that the third hiccup stops in its tracks. I crack open the water bottle and chug in silence.

"What you need to know is our world is not ready for any of this to come to light. So they're going to teach you to control yourself because it's in everyone's best interest that Terra Australis stays hidden."

"Terra Australis?"

"Your country of citizenship. We're nearly there."

As the jet lands on the tarmac, I can see why a seatbelt was so desperately needed. The landing strip is coated in ice, and it feels as if we slide for miles before the plane comes to a screeching halt.

Creen unbuckles himself and walks to the cargo hold, opening a compartment that's stocked full of winter attire, carrying an armful over and dropping it into my lap.

Taking that as my cue to get dressed, I shove the black beanie over my curls and slide my arms through the sleeves of an oversized puffer, pulling the gloves on last—lined with cashmere and cozy on my hands.

By the time I turn around, Creen is in a matching outfit, along with the same gray sweatpants. He grabs my ankle, a pair of sharp scissors in his hand, snipping off my monitor before moving to grab my suitcases.

Creen returns with my luggage and a pair of mountain boots. I shove my feet into the oversized footwear, three sizes too large to be functional and entirely too difficult to fasten with my gloves on.

Or, honestly, I'm too drunk.

As I move to rip them off, he bends to finish the buckles with nimble fingers, the tenseness in my shoulders leached away as he rises.

"You said they're teaching me stuff?"

"University. We made contact with the Dean and she made a last-minute exception for your admittance."

I ruminate on all of this as he works to deboard the plane.

"So, my only goal here is to blend in?" I call up to him as the flight attendant pries open the door.

"Your goal is to be perfect and report your findings. Perfect Grades. Perfect Attendance. Perfect Behavior. The model American."

"Report my findings. Like a spy?"

"Observer," he corrects. "Addam will be more lenient if you have information to share about the current climate. We haven't been briefed on the state of their society in nearly two decades. Whatever you glean in your time away will be liquid gold."

"These people are helping me... and you want me to invade their privacy? The thing you just clarified they value the most?"

"Yes. Because if you fail to do so, if you misstep again like you did at graduation, it's unlikely you'll be back. In fact, I'm doubtful you're around at all. This isn't child's play and it isn't negotiable." I frown as he adds, "I want you to understand something. There are single days of my life that changed me fundamentally as a person. And you have no idea what difference a year can make. Life has a funny way of erasing the person you were as it writes your story. So play the long game. Be the one to remember, you can't lose."

"You can never guarantee a win."

"I'm talking about losing yourself," he whispers.

The door to the plane bursts open and a sobering blast of air hits me, so chilling it causes an immediate shiver down my spine.

We've landed at South Pole Station.

Off in the distance, the buildings are boxlike and metallic. Instead of flat on the ground, they're platformed on man-made structures with little underneath, huge floodlights illuminating the dark path toward the station. My breath creates clouds in the air as I waddle down, the atmosphere so cold it's slightly painful.

"We have a little longer to go. The entrance you're taking is too far for a drive in a Snowcat. For now, we'll stick to flying." Creen jerks his thumb toward a shiny red helicopter in the distance.

WITH EACH JOSTLE OF WIND, I struggle to remain optimistic. Endlessly searching a sheet of ice in the darkness. "Agent Creen?"

"My name is Steven. You're Agent Creen-ing me half to death."

"I figured we're still on a last name basis. Unless we're friends now, then I guess I'll start calling you Steven. That seems more appropriate."

Creen gives me a once-over, seeming to choose his next words carefully. "You look exactly like your mother. And you have your father's everything else."

"Umm... Thanks?"

"It wasn't a compliment. I'm audibly working through why looking at you enrages me."

I nod. Cheeks burning as a black speck reveals itself well before my eyes should be able to make it out.

Several hundred yards away stands a simple stone archway, balanced by itself in the middle of vast nothingness. Headlights of the helicopter illuminating the darkness as we make our descent.

We jostle and thunk against the ice below us, and Creen wastes no time opening the door as the blades of the aircraft wind down.

He offers me a hand, guiding me down the steep ledge while I hang on for dear life. Creen may not be a friend, but he's the last tie to some semblance of the world I know.

"Agent Creen?" My breath puffs in the frigid air as a shiver travels down my spine.

"Yes, Ms. Benson?"

"I really don't want to go."

"I know." He squeezes back softly against my death grip. "Let's grab your things and I'll show you something."

Creen unloads my luggage from the helicopter, taking both handles in his free hand and tugging me forward.

The archway only seems to grow bigger as we approach. Towering above us, forty feet in the air.

I step forward without him, reaching out to touch the rough stone.

It's as dark as iron and appears to sparkle when I squint.

"Would you like to do the honors?" Creen pulls a flint wheel lighter from his pocket, blinking away snowflakes that catch in his lashes. He opens the lid and sparks it, my eyes drawn to the flame like moths.

I take the silver rectangle and shield it from the cold winds around us. Firm in the knowledge that there's only one thing fire's meant to do.

When I place it against the stone, the reaction is instant. Flames ignite and travel over the archway, wrapping around it in spirals until it's encased and glowing. The structure glistening vibrant shades of orange and yellow as it interacts with the surrounding atmosphere.

I step back several feet to take it all in. The once dim area bathed in a warm glow.

The air within the arch warps from refraction. Carved into the stone, a phrase inked in black. Invisible to the eye before, but now a sharp contrast to the rest of the arch.

***Unus fit duo, duo fiunt tres, et de tertio unum fit sicut quartus.***

"One becomes two, two becomes three, and of the third... comes the one... as the fourth?" My brows crinkle as I try to concentrate. "Jung?"

"How do you feel about Jung?"

"I have my issues with some theories, but he had points. We all want to be whole."

"Freud?"

Creen gives me as long as I need to answer. Gnawing at my cheek, rocking back and forth from heel to toe. "He thought about sex too much for me to not feel suspicious. But I do believe people fall in love with an archetype of their parents. Or, the exact opposite. Whatever you think you deserve. Though I don't think they harbor hatred toward the other one. He was repressed and it bled into everything he did."

"So who's better?"

"Whoever expanded on their research and developed anti-depressants."

Creen barks out a laugh, the wind turning the tip of his nose red. "Jung's thinking originated with the Axiom of Maria. That's what's actually set in stone."

I prod at the surface of the warped air, noting it has the resistance of jelly as Creen steps closer, rolling my suitcases beside him.

"You're not going to push me in, are you?"

"If I pushed you in, you'd end up just on the other side. Not in Terra Australis. You have to choose to step through."

I drop my hand from the barrier. "I could choose not to?"

"You'd spend the year on a military base in the freezing cold. Your ankle monitor would be strapped back on, and you'd be miserable. I'd also be responsible for staying here too. So, yes, you *could*, but if I've gotten to know anything about you, I'm certain that you won't."

"I step through, and I'm there? That's all it takes?"

"We were told it has two rules. One, you know of its existence. You're stepping through with the intent to get there. Two... is an open heart. Your intentions need to be in the honest pursuit of knowledge, not to do harm to the people inside. This is the entrance humans would use if allowed. It was intended for like-minded individuals."

I take a deep breath, cold enough to scorch my insides, squeezing my eyes shut before opening them again. Creen's ocean-mist-colored eyes tense with what might be worry.

"Ms. Benson, a walk through the woods feels impossible sometimes, but there's still a destination to be gotten to. Bells to be heard."

"You watched my grad speech."

"It's my job. But I'll admit, it's not every day you're tasked to keep tabs on a selectively mute genius."

"I'm not a genius."

"When you were taken to the hospital, after the explosion, your MRI revealed reduced gray matter consistent with chronic use of alcohol, cocaine, methamphetamines, *heroin,* you name it. Pick your poison."

"I—"

"So, are you not a genius, or are you attempting to burn it all out?" My lips part, and he raises a hand to quiet my rebuttal. "I don't like liars. If we're going to do this, then we need to be upfront with each other."

"Do what?"

"I know a thing or two about surviving a treacherous journey. The walk isn't so lonely when you have company." He grabs my hand, thick gloves encasing the fingers that ball into fists. "But you need to get through the first roadblock alone. Can you promise me that? You'll walk and walk and keep on walking? No matter what throws you off course, you only look forward until we meet again?"

For a moment, I try to remember the girl who wrote that speech for graduation. When in the early hours of the morning, all the outside voices were quiet. That girl ached to believe she could take chances. Claimed that she could walk without a guide.

"Okay."

"Okay," he agrees, releasing my fisted fingers.

I make to hand him back his lighter and he waves me away.

"Keep it. You can return it when you're home."

I stuff the rectangle into my pocket, hoping his optimism isn't misguided and wondering if I have a home to return to. Or, just a lone trek through the woods, and a promise he'll be somewhere on the path waiting for me when it gets too cold to remember.

Creen places the handles of my luggage into my hands, and I notice the stone archway is slowly cooling. Words coming out choppy as I rush to get them out. "Listen, I know you didn't want to be responsible for me. But, for what it's worth, I'm sorry for whatever my parents—my *mother,* must have done to you."

"Your Mother and I are past the point of apologies." There's an indistinguishable flash of agony in his irises that I wish I knew how to soothe. "But I hope you and I aren't. I'm sorry for how this panned out. If you can find a little faith to spare on Addam, a little time to right this all, know you can bet the last of it on me."

I chew on my cheek, and he seems to understand when the most I can muster is, "I guess I'll see you around then?"

"I'll see you. Goodbye, Shiloh."

"Bye, Steven."

We exchange smiles before I turn, leaning closer and closer to the wavering boundary. Then, before I lose all nerve, I jump through the arch with an open heart.

"Remember—" Steven's reminder is cut off as I'm sucked into the brightest light imaginable.

Directly into a new world.

# CHAPTER 5

What happens isn't painful. At least, not at first.

It's an array of colors as the world bends and twists on its axis. It's the feeling of being wrapped in a warm blanket and tossed through the stars at the speed of light. It's a trillion sensations in a fraction of a second that equate to every nerve ending exploding inside me.

One moment, I step through a great arch of flaming stone, and the next, I slam onto cold pavement with the breath knocked right out of me, groaning as my gray luggage set slides across cobblestone. It takes a few breaths to regain my senses, or remember I'm alive at all. Testing out each limb to make sure nothing is broken or missing.

After confirming my wholeness, I roll over, eyes sliding open to face the brilliant blue sky of what appears to be mid-afternoon.

It's chilly here, but the bearable kind. The type of weather you'd expect as Autumn takes its first breath.

I sit upright, taking stock of where I've materialized. A large landing of dark circular cobblestone surrounded by great oak trees.

A whole forest of them wraps around me as far as the eye can see. Leaves of vibrant oranges, yellows, and reds falling gently against the soft brown soil near their roots.

Men and women in military regalia surround the clearing, standing at attention. Not speaking and certainly not acknowledging my rough arrival. Their black suits are ceremonial in nature. White sashes across their chests and serpentine pins placed over their hearts, the scales patterned like a chessboard.

In the center are three different flags I can't quite make out.

"Next time, bend your knees." The thoughtful suggestion is almost eclipsed by the whoosh of flapping wings. Scrambling to my feet, I search in the direction it comes from until my eyes land on the culprit, a screech escaping as a small woman plugs her ears. "Stars above, you've got a set of pipes on you!"

I stumble backwards, tripping over one of my own suitcases.

The woman emits an audible wince at the harsh sound my head makes as it smacks the cobblestone.

*Great.* I'll be taken out by head trauma and Agent Creen will assume I lied, offing myself the first chance I got.

"Ouch," I moan.

I've seen a horse before.

Of course I have.

This white beast isn't anything I've ever experienced. With shimmering wings that sprout from its back, seven feet on either side of its six-foot-tall body. I rise again, dusting off my white puffer and nursing my pride at having made a fool of myself in front of dozens of strangers.

"What's with the dramatics?" she asks from atop the beast, a sun-browned seraphic face growing agitated the longer I stare. The woman wears riding boots and fur-lined leather. From the pants to the top, to her slim-fingered gloves—everything about her looks expensive.

I yank off my gloves and stuff them into my pockets, rubbing my hands over my eyes.

"I—" My voice cuts off as my tongue ties.

*Inhale. Exhale. Inhale. Exhale. Speak.*

"Is that a pegasus?"

The stranger crinkles her dark brows. "You're screaming over Sunny?"

"*Sunny?* That's its name?"

"Sunny's a filly. She's harmless." The pegasus snorts, irritated by the label and almost bucking the woman off her saddle. "Maybe a little temperamental. Going through a bit of a growth spurt. She's in the home stretch now."

"A *growth* spurt?" My eyes widen. "How much bigger do they get?!"

"She'll be full-grown by year's end. She's getting her flights in now to prepare to join the others in a few weeks." The woman leans forward to scratch Sunny's neck. "Shiloh Benson?"

"Yes? Who are you?"

"Professor Laroche. You're late to the party. Move-in day was last week."

"Did classes already start?" I frown.

I don't know what I'll be studying, but I'll be damned if I fall behind so quickly. Not when Agent Creen stressed the importance of my success.

Blend in. Stay out of trouble. Report to Addam come May.

Simple.

*Easy.*

"No. You're just in time for the Welcome Ceremony."

"Is it optional?" She fixes me with an odd look as I grimace. "I just, um, don't really do well in public settings. So I don't think—"

"It's required," she deadpans, twisting her hands in a flicking motion.

The bags rise and turn before being aimed toward Sunny, stopping just shy of hitting her.

The straps she has on her hind unwind to grab the suitcases, slithering like snakes and tightening to hold them firmly in place.

"I recommend closing your mouth. We have flies in this forest that fester and multiply inside of you. They eat through your stomach lining until they make their way out through your belly button." I'm quick to clamp my lips together as Laroche guffaws. "I'm having fun. Now *up, up, up!* I'm a busy woman."

"We're going to fly there?"

"No. We're going to stay here and stare at one another." I blink at her, and she sighs. "Yes, dear. We're miles away from campus. Would you prefer to walk?"

I drag my feet closer to Sunny, something about knowing she's a baby making me hesitant. "You're sure?"

"I've been Professor of Flight longer than you've been alive. I know what a pegasus is capable of."

I find that hard to believe. She appears to be in her early thirties at most. But I don't want to offend her. So I nod in agreement, gently raising my foot to hover over the shimmery wing.

The moment I do, Sunny boosts me into the saddle with no care for my rough landing.

"She's so warm," I observe aloud, her coat hot to the touch under my palms.

"Some say fire runs in the blood of a pegasus."

Without warning, Sunny takes off.

I jerk my arms forward to wind around Professor Laroche as she chortles. The three of us pounding over cobblestone and into the soft dirt as we gain speed and eventually launch into the sky. Insides bottoming out as gravity tugs at the weight of my internal organs.

Sunny releases a neigh, dipping before increasing her altitude.

I can't help but look down. Can't help but scream again as we fly at rapid speed over a sea of multicolored foliage. Professor Laroche calling out directions every now and then.

Only five minutes ago, I thought this kind of thing was a fairytale. The idea of a Pegasus against the laws of nature itself.

But as we break through a mist of clouds in the sky, I forget how odd it is. On to the next impossible thing.

At first glance, it's a small golden speck, but soon enough it's a sprawling campus unlike any I've ever seen. "Whoa."

"Welcome to Aurelia, Shiloh Benson. With any luck, you'll spend the next four years here."

I don't have the heart to tell Laroche I'm not very lucky at all.

"Woah," I repeat again.

Because what else can someone say at the gates of paradise?

Terra Australis University is situated near the Transantarctic mountains. A circular campus with enormous golden gates that catch each sun ray that finds its surface.

The main building in its dead center is the largest, drawing my attention due to its angular lines and points. As if a pentagram has been laid flat and had its top point removed, the sides made out of pale gray stone. It has to be five stories high. The roof formed from crystalline material—I can only guess they're large slabs of diamond.

Other buildings I can't put names to are scattered all around. Connected by paved walkways and surrounded by the greenest grass imaginable. Each unique and ethereal in its own way.

Toward the front of the main building is a flag post. A banner waving wildly, high above in the changing winds. In the center is a black Ouroboros, glistening against the matte white background. Still so crisp and brilliant that I wonder how it stays so clean in the outside conditions.

When I ask Laroche, she sighs, "They change it out twice a week."

"Twice?"

"Forbid that white be stained, there'd be anarchy."

As Sunny flies over the gates, she dips lower, veering to the right. No slowing in her descent. I squeeze my eyes shut, prepared to be a splatter of goo on the cobblestone.

When a few seconds pass, and every limb still seems to be intact, I peek one eye open.

Sunny landed so gracefully I hadn't even felt the impact.

She turns her head, and I could be wrong, but I've never seen a horse look so smug.

"Touche, Sunny... *Touche.*"

The pegasus bows her head in recognition of my props, and I'm floored.

As I slide off, Professor Laroche unwinds my luggage, floating the bags to the ground and ignoring curious stares. Some toward me, but most towards the sparkling creature to my left.

"Is there a dress code?"

Every student who passes looks copied and pasted from a catalog. A high-end magazine full of models wearing immaculately fitted clothing, not a wrinkle in sight. They dress in neutrals with pops of yellow, blue, red, and green thrown in. Their outfits consisting of ties, pleated skirts, and cashmere sweaters.

In comparison, I look like a frumpy marshmallow. Puffer coat swallowing me whole and causing my arms to stick out as if ready to fly alongside Sunny herself.

"Wear what you like. If you feel you're missing anything, ask for it." Laroche dismounts, eyeing a group of young men who are bothering a gray-haired staff member in a button-up shirt and apron, pushing a cart of supplies and attempting to escape—a bit too frail to outrun them. "I'll be right back, watch the little one."

I think she's talking to me until the pegasus grunts in agreement.

*Okay then.*

"I'm sorry, Sunny. You're beautiful. Nowhere near a beast or anything. I promise. Also, you're the best at flying I've ever seen." She snorts at the facetious compliment, pulling off my beanie, then tilting her mouth out of reach.

"Stop! Wait!" I jump upwards a few times until I'm able to snatch it back. In disbelief I'm getting bullied by a horse. "It wouldn't hurt to be nice, ya know? You're my first friend here. I think. Or, not a friend, but an acquaintance?"

I wipe pegasus slobber off the beanie and shove it back over my curls as Sunny stares down apprehensively.

"Unless you're offering friendship, then I wouldn't mind that. In fact, I'd be honored."

When she tilts her head closer, I realize she's waiting for me to plead my case. A palpable awkwardness in the sudden quiet.

Sunny shuffles her hooves and slumps her wings, heavy hesitation in her eyes, which doesn't surprise me. She's a white mare with wings, and today I embody the spirit of Bibendum.

"Right... So, I don't have a lot going on for me at the moment." She turns her head side to side, taking in my words. "But, it'd make me feel a lot better if we part on good terms. Equals? No harm done?"

Her eyes seem to glaze as they meet mine, and I wave my hand in front of her face.

"Hello?"

*Christ, did I just talk a pegasus into a stroke?*

Before I can acquire help, Sunny's eyes refocus. Wings extending high above and dropping to the ground.

She does it a few times, the wind blowing my hair back until I realize she wants me to compliment her show. So I do.

In response, she nuzzles my outstretched palm with her hand. More relaxed than she'd been before.

She leans her head down, and I take it as my opportunity to scratch between her ears, fur softer than silk and akin to shined pearls.

"You really are beautiful."

Sunny attempts to snatch my beanie again, and I duck my head, stepping away from her teeth. "Do they feed you?!"

Laroche approaches us, visibly relieved by what she sees. "Thank the Universe! I was afraid Sunny might stomp you out before I returned."

"Why would you leave us alone then?"

Sunny's wings tremble from holding back her amusement, feigning innocence as I cross my arms.

I think I'm starting to understand her in the short time we've had together.

I have no doubt she'd stomped on multiple caretakers. For no other reason than they were invading her personal space.

"Take this," Laroche says, tossing me a cream colored envelope from her satchel. "It's your room assignment."

"Singles?"

"For New Bloods? Not a chance." Laroche snaps at Sunny, who now refuses to lower her wings for her to mount. "Damnit, Sunny! I've got no time for this!"

"Look, kid, if I were you, I'd listen to Laroche."

Sunny appears irritated with my suggestion.

I tilt my head toward the Professor who waits with narrowed eyes, tapping her foot impatiently as Sunny's wings flap for takeoff.

*Without Laroche.*

"Don't you dare!" Laroche yells as Sunny trots forward, refusing to let her mount. "No flights for you if you leave me here! *Grounded,* I tell you! *Earthbound!*"

Sunny flaps her wings, deep in thought and looking at me once more.

"At least back to where you picked her up from, or that's not very nice."

The mare huffs, begrudgingly lowering a shimmery wing as Laroche mounts, shaking her head in confusion.

"Professor, can we talk about this room situation?"

"Can't talk. Too much to prepare for tonight." Laroche taps Sunny's hind, and her wings flap, the pegasus leaning forward to yank off my beanie before they gallop away in a running takeoff.

"What?!" I shout as she rises into the sky. "I thought we made up!"

Laroche waves down at me, and they leave as fast as they'd come. More than a little sad, I don't know when I'll see the baby pegasus again.

I tear into the envelope as fast as I can, reviewing the sprawling map of campus and a gray stone building labeled for First Years.

I scramble to grab my suitcases just to find out pulling them up steep cobblestone steps is no simple task. And by the time I make it to my floor, I hate every ounce of clothing I'd felt the need to shove inside. The sound of music thumping and giggles catching my ear.

"Let me have this one thing," I plead into thin air, walking past several silent doors. "If you're real, give me this one thing."

My room's exactly where it's coming from.

I ruffle out my curls that have been flattened by the beanie, swiping my bangs into place and managing to knock before I fully convince myself it's safe.

The music's too deafening to hear the gentle raps of my knuckles, loud belts blocking me out from the other side.

I break out the key that's been folded in with my papers, cracking the door open and peeking my head through the narrow gap.

A tall man stands with his back to me, hips gyrating and belting at the top of his lungs.

Snaps echo around the corner, keeping him in beat with his moves.

He points a finger toward the left side of the room, a few golden rings on his hand, and moonwalking backward as he sings.

His voice is better than anything I've heard on the radio back home, remarkable in its deep timbre. What's harder to grasp is that he elevates several feet in the air while he dances, shaking shoulder-length locs as if he leads a rock band.

The music's a funky synth song I've never heard before, and a girl I can't see yet, giggles heartily. As if he's the most captivating man to grace this planet.

He does one last spin, and I think I understand why.

Chocolatey orbs meet mine and widen like a deer in headlights, the loud beat going quiet with a flash of yellow from his fist.

Without warning, he falls with a rough thump. Similar to my own landing in Terra Australis, hitting the floor hard enough to prompt a wince.

"Sorry!" I yelp.

"Babe!" The girl's voice fills with worry as she rushes to peer down at him. "I told you, you were going to tire yourself out!"

He glares at the ceiling, voice deepening from his carefree performance only moments ago. "I was distracted."

Her head swivels side to side, sandy blonde waves whipping around her shoulder as she faces me. The girl has a fresh tan that doesn't seem plausible for a place so chilly. Face sun-kissed and smattered with dozens of freckles.

Hazel eyes fill with surprise, and pink lips form a circular O-shape as I let the door creak open. Observing one another until she breaks the tension with a terrifying assertion.

"You're the Arsonist?"

Her boyfriend props himself up on his elbows, long legs splayed across the floor. I make out a simple bronze star pinned above his heart. Placed directly next to it—a golden Lion.

He seems to shake out of his embarrassment as he rises, scratching the stubble at his jaw. Now that he's firmly planted on the ground, he appears to be a centimeter shy of six feet and perhaps the most symmetric man to grace this earth.

Everything is naturally straight and angled on his face, teeth white and bright against brown lips that curl in a diplomatic grin. I'd think they were veneers if they didn't look so natural, a voice for radio and a face for every billboard in Times Square.

The handsome pair exchange a wide-eyed glance as if I'm a new species under a microscope.

"Hi. I'm Shiloh."

Clothes are strewn everywhere like a high-end department store has burst open inside, and she turns away, flitting about the room to clean up the mess of her stuff that's crept over to my side.

"Sorry for all this! Jace gifted me a new wardrobe as a present for our first day. I have *too* many things now."

She stuffs massive handfuls of lingerie into her drawers, my eyes wandering toward the now barren area that appears to be mine to claim. There's a twin bed made of iron with a fluffy white duvet on top. A wooden desk beside it with a singular cactus plant on its empty surface.

I roll my suitcases over to the desk and pick up a cream colored note card with a simple message near the plant.

*It's been said that Cacti are low-maintenance gifts.*
*Just prickly enough to break the ice.*
*Have a year to remember, Ms. Benson.*
*— Dean Alvarez*

I SIT on the edge of my bed, setting the oddly worded notecard down.

"Sorry to interrupt."

"Not an interruption. We were expecting you! I'm Suede Audere. This is my boyfriend, Jason Honestus. As you can probably tell, he loves to moonwalk. He's a show off."

"That was amazing, I've never moonwalked like that." I unzip my white puffer coat, a fireplace going on the opposite wall that has the room feeling nice and toasty, as alive as the heartbeat in my own chest.

Jason grins. "If you have an affinity for Air, you'll learn quickly."

They sink into her bed, sitting side by side and staring at me with expectation.

When they don't say anything, I clear my throat. "Arsonist?"

"Dean Alvarez gave me your background," Suede giggles. "I've never been friends with a criminal before."

A long stretch of silence fills the air.

"What?"

"Well, Jace and I went to the registrar's office because I was supposed to have a single, but Alvarez was waiting for me, all creepy as she is."

"Creepy?"

Suede mutters something under her breath. "She said she felt like we should be roommates. Me being from the Triangle, and you being from, well, not here *or* the Triangle. Neither of us are very common at a school like this."

"And she said I'm a *criminal?*"

"She informed me that you have some issues. But honestly, as long as you're not blowing our people up, I don't mind." I frown as she adds, "Your Mom and Dad live in Addam Territory? I've never heard of that before. Jace hasn't either."

"Did she tell you guys why?"

"She wouldn't, but she assured me Suede was safe," Jason sighs. "My father seemed to be okay with it. So, by all means, this situation is fine with me. You seem normal enough."

"He's hovering in case you aren't. We're still deciding."

"Oh. And you're not from here either?"

"I've lived here with my Mom for a while. I just got back from visiting my Dad and brother. Summer vacation and all."

"You said the Triangle. Like, the Bermuda Islands?"

"No." She raises a brow. "I mean, the *Triangle.*"

"I didn't know there were other places like this."

"We have an Island occupied by Alchemists. Short flight too when there's Air affinities onboard."

"You can't teleport?"

"No. Can you?" she asks.

"I came through the Arch of Maria. That was teleportation, right?"

"Our borders are centuries old. We don't do blood magic anymore."

"Oh," I say, unsure what else to add.

My eyes land on the box of chocolates on her dresser, and Suede pops up, quickly offering them to me before sitting back down.

I take two, closing the glass container and slipping the first in my mouth. "Sweet tooth?"

"When I'm stressed," I admit, covering my mouth as I chew around the candy. "I've survived off champagne and ice cream the past twenty-four hours."

The chocolate bursts with peppermint filling so powerful it makes me cough.

"Strong, right? They make your shit smell like mint for a week." I blink, swallowing the half-chewed chocolate and banging on my chest as Suede adds, "I don't know about you guys, but I could eat an early dinner."

"Sure. Just let me change first," Jason says.

"Thanks, but I should probably stay in to unpack my stuff."

Suede looks disappointed, and Jason says, "Don't worry about that. The staff will handle it. You should get some food in you."

"White button-downs?"

"Yeah. The cleaning crew come and tidy our rooms once a week. They also set up all of our stuff to our liking." Suede's portion of the room has been decorated with seashells flecked across her wall. The beach theme includes a golden duvet with patterns of the sun stitched into it. Her desk full of multicolored beakers and test tubes, some brewing with steam as we speak. "They must have gotten your aesthetic from your parents. Your side is so... *modest,*" Suede says.

"Oh."

"I'm disappointed someone didn't carry your bags up for you. Was no one stationed at the entrance when you arrived?" Jason asks.

"It's fine. I *w*-wanted to do it myself."

"Let them unpack for you. Even if you do it, they'll go fold it correctly anyway."

Suede claps as my shoulders sink. "Then it's settled! We'll get food now. Poor thing. They must have starved you, you look emaciated."

"Okay. Sure! How could I say no?"

*Really. How?*

# CHAPTER 6

As close as the cafe is to our dorm, it takes only seconds to realize no walk with Jason Honestus is a short one. He's changed into a lavender sweater, paired with expensive black dress pants and leather shoes to seal off the look. Students leap for the chance to introduce themselves as he passes, and I have the sneaking suspicion that, even if he wanted to hide, people would still seek him out.

In a sense, he's saying, *Look at me! I know you're going to anyway.*

When Jason opens the door to the dining hall for Suede and I, it's impossible not to tilt my head up and ogle the ceiling. The glass-roofed cafe is contained inside a rectangular building made of so many windows it could easily be a mega-sized greenhouse.

Dozens of food stations are sprinkled throughout the building, each offering a variety of different cuisines that prompt my stomach to rumble. Familiar scents swirling around us that ease my worries about the type of food we'll be required to eat.

It seems as if everyone had the idea for an early dinner, hundreds of Alchemists buzzing with excitement in anticipation of tonight's events.

Suede and Jason leave me at the soup station without much fuss. A giddy skip in my roommate's step as she swats at her boyfriend, pointing towards an empty table in the far corner.

I nod, waiting in line with my arms crossed over my chest, catching a waft of fresh spicy citrus.

The boy fidgeting before me is all limbs, knees and elbows, with circular golden glasses that pop against deep brown skin.

The sides of his head are close-shaven with a mop of dark coils on top, and I can't describe him as anything other than awkwardly model-esque. Increasingly tic-ridden with every nervous shift of his shoulders, adjusting his frames as he reads from a leather-bound journal.

One nosy peek around his arm shows the text written is near-hiero-glyphic scrawl. I debate saying anything at all, but my curiosity gets the better of me.

"Excuse me?" I tap his shoulder, and the touch seems to startle him, doing a triple take before slamming his journal shut.

"Sorry. Am I standing too close?"

He adjusts his glasses as they slip down his nose bridge, taking a step forward and bumping into the back of the woman before him.

She shoots him a dirty glance. Then, upon taking him in fully, averts her eyes as if he has the plague.

He's as put together as can be. Tucked inside a gray and white argyle sweater vest with khaki pants that are pressed with precision. His eyes grow wary when I part my lips, as if afraid I'm going to say something harsh. One small look of terror filling me with the innate urge to hold his hand. "No! *No*, I'm behind you, so that would be my fault. Hi. I'm Shiloh."

"I'm... *Russ?*"

"Are you?"

"Yes." He stuffs his journal into the worn-down leather bag he carries, smile fading as his gaze sweeps back and forth. "Have you been bribed to speak with me?"

"No?" I laugh until I realize he's serious. "Has that happened before?"

Russ shrugs and we move through the line getting the same thing. A heaping serving of broccoli cheddar soup and a small loaf of sourdough.

The red-headed server fills my bowl, ladling in a pour that gets a slight mess on my metallic tray.

His gloved hands wipe up the splash of soup that seeps out of my dish with a napkin until it's perfectly leveled, looking displeased with himself.

"Don't worry about it. Thank you, this looks amazing." The corners of his mouth tug downward as Russ and I walk away, staring after me as if I've grown a second head.

"What did I do wrong?" I whisper, walking toward the beverage station. "Sorry, I'm not from here. I—"

"Where are you from?"

"Arizona."

He frowns, minor hints of recognition in his eyes. "Your last name?"

"Benson."

Russ repeats my name to himself and his eyebrows knit. "You're from *Addam* territory?"

"It's a long story."

"Make it shorter with others. Okay?" He sucks on his lip, nostrils flaring. "People here don't particularly like outsiders."

"They'll probably assume I'm from the Triangle, right? Or some other Alchemist island?" I noticed it immediately. Suede and I have a similar manner of speaking, compared to the way his mouth naturally morphs words. But Russ's face twists in confusion, head cocking to the side until I continue. "Or, maybe no one else is thinking that deeply into accents."

"Accents?"

"You're all so enunciative. Always going for the most correct way to pronounce something. Always lingering on your vowels to make sure they stick. Elocution is the better word."

I inflect my voice to try to talk as he does, and it takes all my effort to not stutter, almost painful to speak so meticulously.

Russ chuckles, and the sound gives warmth to my insides as his stress dissipates. "You mean, we talk like know-it-alls?"

"Oh... I don't think my foot could be any further in my mouth."

"No. You were being funny. And, back there? He was trying to make it perfect for you and thought you were dissatisfied with his work."

"Should I apologize? Or clarify? Or—"

"Hey, you're okay. I swear." His brown eyes soften, adjusting his glasses with an abashed look on his face. "Professions here are a source of great pride. It's the polite thing to let people perfect their craft." Russ sounds like a travel guide. Citing knowledge that's ingrained in his head, spouting facts relayed so many times they've become second nature.

"So, I shouldn't say thank you? Ever?"

"There's no desire for thanks when giving to our country. It dilutes the purity of our sacrifices." As we wait our turn in the drink line, Russ begins to ramble. "I used to talk people's ears off while they were working. My Father would write who I should and shouldn't talk to in permanent ink on my arms for events. That's how they found out I needed glasses. The first few times, I couldn't read the lists. But, I was also five and he writes in cursive."

I can't tell if he's joking, but I don't think he is.

A younger man with dark skin and a soft face fills our glasses with chilled ice water. Russ meets his eyes and offers a gentle smile before he moves on to the next person in line, so I do too.

The staff member returns our smiles with a megawatt grin, bowing his head before moving on to the next person.

"Would you want to sit with me?" We ask in unison.

Russ clears his throat. "Sure. Where are you sitting?"

"Over there." I point to the table where Suede and Jason are already enraptured in some animated discussion. "Don't worry. They seem nice. But, between you and me, I think she might not love my presence. I sort of took up space in her room last minute."

"With *Jason?* Jason Honestus?"

"Yes...?"

Russ turns away and I struggle to keep up with his long stride. Beelining for our table where Suede and Jason are doubled over in laughter. He swoops in, sweet shyness momentarily shadowed as he sets his tray down with an audible smack.

"On my name, stop doing this or I'm calling home!"

*"Wha I dew now?"* Jason mumbles through a mouthful of mashed potatoes.

"You know what you did," Russ seethes, slumping into his chair. He turns to me over his shoulder, embarrassment flooding his eyes. "I apologize. My brother is an idiot."

"For thinking you'd have enough tact to introduce yourself properly?"

I slide into the chair beside Russ, and he says, "I have tact! I have plenty of tact!"

"If you did, you wouldn't have stormed over hurling baseless accusations. Shiloh, this is my little brother, Icarus Honestus. Icarus, this is Shiloh Benson. No, I did not bribe anyone, and you can't prove I ever did."

"Icarus?" I take a seat beside Russ, and Jason raises his brows as if to say, *Proper, huh?*

"I'm a grown man," he seethes toward Jason. "And I prefer Russ," he mutters to me.

"And I'd prefer to eat my first meal of the day in peace." Jason stuffs another piece of roast in his mouth, words muffled again by his food. "Yet, I'm being accosted and accused."

They hurl insults back and forth, but it seems in good nature, reminding me of my pre-explosion family at dinner time. Usually, Sam debates Dad on something both of them already agree on, but love to argue over anyway.

I tear a chunk of bread from my loaf and dip it in the perfectly balanced chowder.

As I stuff my mouth, the door to the Cafe opens, diverting my attention to the two people who enter. Eyes gravitating to a man with olive skin and ink black waves.

"Who's that?" I cough, swallowing my bread half-chewed.

The man's lips curl into a carefree grin, leaning down so he can catch the words of the girl at his side, dimples forming in both cheeks.

He manages to have several inches on her, and she herself is nearing six feet. A pretty brunette with glossy black tresses, warm olive skin, and inquisitive dark eyes.

"Ezra," Russ frowns. "Dean Alvarez's son. To his right is his girlfriend, Josephine White."

"Ex-girlfriend," Suede corrects. "Last I heard, they were broken up."

She shifts closer to Jason and pats his knee. I can't help but smile at the instant attentiveness he shows her, throwing her his undivided attention as if anything she says is the most interesting thing he's ever encountered.

"Babe, I forgot to tell you. She said Icarus looks like he starches his pants every morning. Then, asked if adjusting his glasses is a nervous tic." Russ glares, and his brother's gaze darkens. "She proceeded to suggest that if he wore less sweater vests and stopped mouth breathing, people wouldn't mistake him for a pervert."

Jason rubs her back in contemplation. "Then, I'll talk to her about it."

Russ grits his teeth as Suede kisses Jason's cheek. "I knew you would. You're such a good big brother."

"Guys, we've talked about this?"

"Icarus." Jason's tone doesn't give the sense it's up for further debate and I attempt to steer the conversation away from Russ as everyone slides into uneasy silence.

"They don't look broken up. They look engaged."

"Why would you think that?"

Ezra and Josephine have gigantic rubies on their ring fingers, rocks so shiny they seem to throw off light with each flick of their wrists. "I mean, those could be promise rings, but that's a pretty large promise."

Russ adjusts his glasses before he says, "Alchemists wear our wedding rings on our right hands. Your parents don't do the same?"

Jason raises his left hand into my sightline, showing off the rings I hadn't paid much attention to before. A thick gold band with edges sharp enough to cut steel is on his ring finger. A yellow gem runs through its middle, embedded into its center. Two digits down, a gaudy golden Lion rests on his pointer finger, purple amethysts for its eyes.

"My Mom. But she's missing her ring finger."

"Right." Russ chokes on a piece of sourdough. "We're... all left-handed. It's the only way."

"For the most part," Suede offers, seeming to have warmed to my presence. "That's not, like, a rule or anything."

"For the most part?"

The brothers follow her gaze to my right hand, and I switch my spoon to my left, stirring soup until my appetite fades, the liquid sitting heavier in my belly.

I eye the pair again, and the man's dimples have fallen away. What remains is a scowl shadowed by high cheekbones and the curve of a strong jaw, full lips pressed together in agitation.

Ezra murmurs something under his breath, and Josephine cranes her neck, searching gaze downright lethal.

"*What are you staring at?*" she mouths.

Well, nothing now.

Shit. I've never looked away so fast. I might have whiplash.

"Maybe they are back together. What-evs. His brother's hotter."

In response, Russ's mouth twists in disdain.

"Do you know him?" I ask.

"Bennet lives on the Islands," Russ says. "And fair warning, Dean Alvarez is—*Ooof.*"

He grunts as a foot seeks him out beneath the table, ears popping as Jason swiftly changes the subject.

"Are you guys excited for the ceremony?" he asks.

Suede grows giddy while I grow accustomed to knowing nothing. "I wish you could be there."

"Me too. And I know I've already said this, but if it doesn't take..." Jason casts a downward glance at both his brother and girlfriend. "There are still places for you here. No state schools."

This seems to offend both of them in different ways. Suede stabbing her salad with a fork as Russ slumps in his seat.

Jason now speaks to me directly. Probably because I'm the only one at the table not glaring at their food. "You're already dressed for it," he says, referring to the white sweater and black leggings I'd slid into before dinner. "You must be ready."

"Yeah," I mutter.

Because, in a way, he's right. Whatever comes next, I must be.

# CHAPTER 7

According to Russ, the first day of the school year is the longest for first years and faculty alike. Tonight's ceremony is *technically* tomorrow, and with only twenty minutes left until midnight, the witching hour is almost upon us.

Russ looks dashing in a black suit fit for a prince, and Suede almost regal in one of the many outfits Jason provided for her. The white dress sits high on her collarbones and dips low on her back, long blonde hair covering most of her exposed skin.

Side by side, the pair have me second-guessing my sweater.

"Never gets old," Suede sighs, chin tilted toward vast twinkling galaxies. With each passing moment, the sky reveals more stars. Streaks of color wavering as if the Northern Lights have traveled over to say hello, ultimately deciding it was better to stay and shift shades at will.

"It's manufactured," Russ mutters, fiddling with his black wax candlestick while looking sick to his stomach.

Suede points her unlit candle at him. "It's not manufactured?"

"The sky ceilings out several thousand feet upwards. This whole ecosystem is held together by blood magic. Everyone would freeze to death without it."

"*Manufactured* makes it sound fake. It's a window of the cosmos in its current state. Our borders act as a super telescope." Suede rolls her eyes as we near the main building. "Don't mind him. He's being grumpy and rude because he has a *top secret meeting* after this."

"Sorry," Russ concedes, mustering a smile when I nudge his arm.

Droves of students dressed in black and white pass us as we file into the crowd, moving toward the grand entryway as a pack. A looming man lights each candle that passes into the building, shock coursing through me when I notice it's the tips of his fingers that are ablaze, no lighter to be found while flicking stray embers onto our wicks.

We march single file through dimly lit halls, immediately met with the echo of drums. A haunted beat that loops enough to get lost in the sound. The instruments are operated by figures in black cloaks lining the stairwells upward, from each hand shimmering soft golden light.

Russ offers me his free hand as we ascend, focusing on putting one foot in front of the other after our fingers clasp.

"It's meant to be friendly. They're walking with us."

I nod, allowing myself to relax until we reach the Great Hall.

With long marble benches and bright gothic arches, the room is comparable to a chapel in that it seems a holy, yet sterile, space.

Starlight pools through the ceiling, casting a milky glow through the refracted diamonds, accompanied by radiant candlelight from hundreds of New Bloods piling in. I'm sandwiched between my friends just as the heavy wooden door swings shut.

The faculty onstage are shrouded in white cloaks, chatter dying down when one among them rises to her feet.

She's tall, with hollow cheeks and a cold gaze. Forgoing her cloak for a pure white turtleneck tucked into slacks of the same color. A silver Ouroboros pendant hanging around a slim neck as her hair fans a silky platinum halo around her head, cut blunt at her chin and tucked behind each ear.

"Fern Alvarez," Russ informs me.

There aren't many similarities between Dean Alvarez and her son.

Her skin is pale as bone, and her lips are thin and pink. His wavy black hair a direct opposition to the pin-straight tresses on her scalp.

She has a face so ageless I wonder if she's old enough to be in charge of anything. Or, have a son that's older than I am. Which, in turn, leads me to notice no one onstage looks a day over forty.

Laroche stands off to the end, hands restless and legs wiggling with the urge to be on pegasus back. When she notices me watching, she pretends to take a dagger to her throat, small grins playing at our lips.

"Welcome to Terra Australis University," Dean Alvarez says, introducing herself formally. She has a dimple in one cheek that matches her son's, pink lips curling crookedly to the side as if hiding a secret, the uneven smile making her more human.

"Here you will spend the next four years honing your craft. Wielding power that many have died to find and live to honor. But I won't sugarcoat it for you. Some of you won't be chosen." I glance at Russ, and his nostrils flare slightly. "Some of you will not be able to harness its power. In which case, there are places for you in our world, but they won't be at this University."

Mumbles of concern echo around the room, though none of them sound surprised.

"Harness *what's* power?" I ask.

Dean Alvarez places a glass bowl on the table, prepping ingredients before she's presented with a smooth, ivory colored box.

As it's opened, there are audible gasps of astonishment. A noticeable shift in everyone's demeanor after we're shown what's inside.

A fist-sized black stone with swirls of purple.

It has its own continuous heartbeat, pulsing with energy as if the fabric that holds the stars together has been bottled and stuffed inside, leaving me with the overwhelming feeling that the stone's as alive as we are.

"The Philosophers' Stone. A fragment of the soul of the Universe."

"Anima mundi?" I ask.

"Exactly. Tonight, we hold the hand of God and demand it gives us a speck of itself in return. It's a two-way street, of course. Gods don't take demands lightly."

"And it's just us?"

"No. Dean Alvarez will take the stone to the other universities starting next week to do their ceremonies. Full guard in tow. She'll be gone for a few weeks. It's the only time the stone leaves the premises."

*"Ever?"*

"Ever." Dean Alvarez nods toward Professor Laroche. Without her riding gloves, I notice she has a shiny yellow stone on her finger wrapped within a copper colored coil. She twists the Stone upward and places it gently into the bowl. "It's the only thing capable of creating the prima materia for the ceremony. The only thing that can forge our rings."

"What happens if it doesn't choose you?" Suede sinks lower in the pew, and Russ adjusts his glasses. *"Oh.* That's really comforting, guys."

We turn our attention back to Dean Alvarez as she calls the first students up.

A brutish boy with greasy blonde hair shoves his way to the front, eager to be first in line. He engages in quiet conversation. Picking out objects as she instructs, throwing them into the bowl and setting fire to its contents. It blazes brightly, melding everything into a milky white liquid before he sticks his hand inside.

Everyone holds their breath. A tangible feeling of anticipation when the liquid begins to glow. Light fills the room until, all at once, it dies—followed by an audible squelching snap.

The boy's screech is Earth-shattering. Yanking out his hand as the prima materia dissipates, fingers protruding bones and bending in misshapen angles.

I fix Russ with an accusatory stare as I withdraw my hand from his grasp. "They'll get him to the infirmary, and he'll heal up... *Probably."*

"So, is he human?"

"No. We're all Alchemists." Russ frowns. "But no ring means he can't access magic. He'll be sent to a state school, solely for academics."

It's a while before there's another rejection. A redhead ripping her hand out of the crystal bowl before her bones can shatter.

She's dragged away in hysterics, massaging her fingers while crying out that there's been a mistake.

I pick at my polish, only looking up again when there are several murmurs of excitement. Everyone straightens to catch a glimpse of the next man to walk up the steps, a ragged breath escaping against my will.

His every feature is sharp and deadly.

High cheekbones, gaunt cheeks, and dark brows stand out on pale skin, tone underlaid with a healthy flush of pink. His hair's white as fresh fallen snow, braided in a simple plait that falls just past his shoulders.

*Not a man,* I correct. *A God.*

Carved not of flesh and bone but of chisel and ice.

He's tall and lean underneath the simple white button-up and brown pants he wears. Gaze sweeping the room for some invisible threat, mouth twisting as if in pain, before evening out.

He has two women at his side who share his face. Both wearing silver dresses that move like streams of water. Tresses braided in intricate updos peppered with black diamonds.

There are noticeable differences between his sisters.

One has the same snow white mane. Half an inch below him in height, and his twin in every sense of the word.

But the violet-tressed one is nearly five inches shorter with fuller lips and softer features. Cherubic face without a speck of makeup and carved of silken marble.

She's dangerously beautiful, and when I look toward Russ to see if I'm making it up, he appears sort of pained at the sight of her. An odd stir in my gut until he glares at his feet.

The siblings share the most unique irises I've ever seen. Obsidian black with differing amounts of gray swirled in, the girl with violet hair rolling the palest of the three.

One by one, they forge their rings, everyone eager to see what they get.

The softer sister frowns when the bowl before her doesn't immediately respond, prompting me to hold my breath until light explodes through the cracks of her fingers, flickering rapidly until she drops the stone and raises both middle fingers to her brother.

She curses him out where they stand, and he stiffens when she storms past him with a nasty shoulder check, leading the charge out of the ceremonial space, her siblings quick to follow her.

"The triplets all got fire affinities," Russ murmurs, turning his head to watch them leave.

"Jace said their father's declaring their betrothal to anyone who'll listen. It's a done deal," Suede says, tilting her head toward the tall blonde who takes her brother's hand before the door swings shut.

More rings are forged, and more hearts broken.

When it nears our turn, we carry our candles to the stage, slowing down to let everyone pass us.

Even this close, the process is extremely private.

Suede places her candle on the table, and I can't hear a word she says, her free hand twirling a piece of sandy hair to soothe herself.

The bowl's contents light up, and Suede grows still as stone, shoulders dropping in relief.

Tears gather in the corners of her eyes when she lifts her left hand in front of her face. A heart-shaped yellow crystal nestled into a spiky silver band that mimics thorns on a vine, turning to us with wide eyes before she's ushered off the stage, refusing to sit down, which earns her some stern looks.

Russ goes next, and a million ping pongs bounce within my stomach lining, hard to concentrate on anything besides making sure this frail boy makes the cut.

As he bends, he adjusts his glasses to keep them from sliding down his nose bridge, whispering something into the bowl.

Then, without hesitation, he drops his hand into the light.

The bowl emits a flashbang of bright white as the liquid dissipates. A ring forming so fast I wonder if it was already waiting for him in the cosmos.

Russ raises his hand to the sky in wonder, heaving a sigh of relief. It's a thick golden band, the texture of bark, holding a square emerald in its center. I can't help but clap, and the professors nearby look wildly impressed as he steps off the stage to wait near Suede.

Dean Alvarez turns to face me, and my excitement leeches away in an instant.

"Shiloh Benson, please step forward."

I take small steps until I'm by her side, surveying the table in front of us. The crystal bowl is nearly empty once more, only containing the pulsating Philosopher's stone that rests at its bottom.

"Thank you for the cactus, Dean Alvarez."

"It's not for you, but take care of it anyway." She motions for me to set my candle down, placing a heavy hand on my shoulder.

I stiffen so rapidly that she emits a chuckle, swiftly removing her icy fingers. "Pick a crystal."

"Does it matter which one?"

"Your choice."

The table is scattered with hundreds of small gems. From rose quartz to topaz, to plain old rocks. I have no attraction to any of them, and I wonder if it even matters. It doesn't seem likely for a cosmic gift to hinge on whether I prefer an Amethyst or an Emerald.

I eventually decide on my birthstone, sliding it into the bowl until it clunks softly against the Philosopher's stone, vibrating against it in the empty glass.

"Pick a coin."

There's a stack of assorted coins in a wooden box. Too many, of all different shapes and sizes. I assume it's the metal that will form my band, but again, I don't think it matters.

My fingers sift through them, pulling one out and examining the small circle in my palm. It's so dingy, I have to hold it in the candlelight to see the inscriptions, soon realizing it's a dirty penny.

A noise between a laugh and sigh escapes my lips as I toss it into the bowl. Metal clunking against the Philosopher's stone and vibrating at the bottom against the diamond, cracking the gem into bits and pieces.

She hands me a needle, and I prick my left index with it, heart rate quickening as blood pools on my hand.

I follow her instructions and squeeze my blood on the stone, watching it sizzle and pop against its surface, sucking my finger to staunch the flow.

"Familiar with Latin?"

"I can read it better than I can speak it."

"Repeat after me and place your hands on the bowl. Offerimus haec elementa."

***"Offerimus haec elementa."***

"Responsum Petimus."

***"Responsum Petimus."***

A slight breeze picks up around us and I look for an open window, but it appears to be the stagnant air around the table beginning to shift.

The Dean pours a goblet of water into the bowl, then takes a handful of soil and sprinkles it atop the water. Floating bits swirl around inside, the liquid growing cloudy with filth.

"Take your candle, and light the soil."

I do as she commands. The flame wavering as I turn it on its side, brushing it onto the soil.

As soon as I do, the contents in the bowl meld into a milky white mixture. So thick and pasty I can't see the stone any longer.

"What now?"

"Ask it anything you want. The stone has knowledge of all you seek."

My heart flutters in my chest as I lean closer to the prima materia, noting it smells like the absence of smell, as if ingesting this strange liquid could erase all my senses.

"Quis Sum Ego Vere?" I ask, inserting my left hand into the brew.

There's a vibration of energy as my fingers ensnare the Philosopher's stone. It becomes weightless as it absorbs the penny and diamond chunks, but the elixir stays dull, blinking and sputtering light as my hand stays submerged in the cloudy mixture.

In the prolonged silence of held breath, I drop the stone with a splash, raising my hand in front of me.

Prima Materia drips down my arm and dries immediately as mumbles break out across the hall.

*There's nothing on my finger.*

I'm not mangled, but I don't have a castor ring either.

"What should I do now?"

"It rejects, or it accepts," Dean Alvarez replies, the liquid slowly dissipating into the swirling air.

"Could I try again?"

"The Universe gives many second chances, but only one to craft a ring," she says. "How unfortunate... Pack your things and come to my office later. We'll have to call Addam. Tell them they should collect you."

"But Russ *s*-said there's another school?"

"Ms. Benson, you have been living in a foreign nation for most of your life. You are not to step foot off this campus during your probation year. I thought I made that clear in your welcome packet?"

"Oh. You don't think you could make an exception? Just once?"

"No," she replies dryly.

We watch my elixir swirl away, bubbles brewing in my gut as my insides seek to empty themselves.

*How have I failed before I even started?*

*Will they really keep me on base, or was Steven bluffing?*

What I do next makes no sense, and when I think about it in the days to come, I still feel puzzled by my actions.

It's as if the thought has been planted in my mind.

No, resurfaced from the day of graduation.

The shift I felt when I grasped the pen in my right hand. The pulsating, boiling energy I had no name for but comes easily now.

*Power.*

I bring my right hand to my mouth. Biting into my palm until I taste iron and pulling it away as blood drips down my lips. Eyes wide open, I reach my hand into the near-empty bowl.

Faculty members launch forward to stop me, leaping backwards as my right hand encases the stone in the final remains of the milky mixture. "***Mendacem memorem esse oportet,***" I whisper.

Blood drips down my chin, hand trembling against the rapid vibrations of the stone.

A cracking sound occurs, and I don't let myself think about if it's my hand. I only grasp the stone tighter.

Light streams through the spaces in my fingers, stone sizzling my blood and stitching my wound back together, soaking up each speck it can.

It's so bright I don't only close my eyes, I look away. As does everyone else. The glare as blinding as gazing directly into the sun.

There's a tightness in my chest. Energy dispensed down my arm in a million little lightning bolts, connecting nerve endings I'd never known I had before burning them in its wake. Until finally, it grows so intense, I'm sure my fingers will snap. Tension pushing and pulling as if every atom is on the verge of ripping apart.

At the last moment, the energy ricochets through the rest of my body. An electric buzz that makes my hair rise with static, air snapping and crackling around me.

I wade through a dense blanket of matter until, at once, it stops—curls dropping to frame my face once more. Magic finding a balance in the core of my being, wrapped right around my sternum like a blanket.

The all-consuming energy leaves behind a warm feeling of peace.

I release a soft sigh, licking blood from my chin before it can crust to my face, the liquid a little sweeter than I remember.

The stone falls with a heavy thud into the empty bowl, cracked glass shattering on impact and prompting me to jump a foot into the air.

With a shaky breath, I lift my hand, relieved that it's still intact.

However, that isn't what draws gasps around me. Or, what draws in the faculty onstage, who crowd around to examine it.

Nestled onto my right ring finger is the most beautiful object I've ever seen. A circular-shaped crystal that pulsates with swirls of blood red energy.

The band forms from iron, winding around the stone and coated in scales of thick black Obsidian, glistening in the moonlight like glittering reptilian skin. Four diamonds scatter across the band like leaves on a vine, somewhat dull and empty compared to the shimmering stone.

Through the thicket of faculty, I search for Suede and Russ, catching small glimpses of their faces.

Suede's mouth forms an O, eyes glued to the shimmery gem on my right hand while Russ mutters to himself.

Dean Alvarez's gaze saps away every speck of peace left within me.

There's only one emotion that could do it so quickly. Embedded so deep into her eyes, there's no mistaking her thoughts. The same thing I saw in Sam's eyes on graduation day.

*Fear.*

Laroche shoves past everyone, parting a walkway for her to approach. She reaches upward to grab my hand and pulls it close to her eyes, releasing a snort as the rest of the faculty shifts warily. "Fashionably late, but you know how to keep the party going. I'll give you that."

"Professor—"

"Sit, Ms. Benson. And stars above, let the girl through! It's a ring! Nothing you haven't seen before."

I cradle my hand to my chest as everyone scurries away at her demand, endlessly grateful for Laroche and unnaturally possessive of this little piece of jewelry. As if it's a living, breathing thing, with a heart-beat of its own.

My friends exchange mystified glances on the way back to our seats, and I decide on making an escape back to my room.

Russ grabs my hand, looking warily toward the exit. "We're not supposed to leave early."

"You're in societal operations tomorrow morning, right?"

"Yes, but—"

"Okay! See you then!"

I twist out of his slackened hold and bolt for the exit, heads turning as I run down the aisle like a bat out of hell.

Dean Alvarez calls my name until I burst out of the ceremonial space, stumbling into the violet-haired triplet who lurks just outside the door, hidden in the shadows.

We collide and twist before impacting against unforgiving stone.

Tumbling down several dozen steps as the girl takes the brunt of both our bodies, somehow stopping us from continuing to skid down further.

"Motherfucker," she grunts, pale face twisting as my bony elbows dig into her rib cage while scrambling off of her.

"Oh. I've—*Oh!* I'm so sorry! Are you okay?!"

She sits upright, eyes narrowing on my ring before I slip it behind my back.

A deep gash has formed across her cheek, and scrapes run up and down both limbs, delicate dress ripped and shredded down the back.

I'm unscathed yet dying of embarrassment. The smell of sweet almonds making my jaws clench as blood beads on her wounds.

"Stars be damned! How didn't you—"

My heart races as she leans forward, grinding my teeth and pressing my tongue to the roof of my mouth in case she punches me in the face, scraped palms blocking my head as she issues a few small sniffs.

When her fist never makes contact, I pat my sleeves, finding a loose thread and biting at it. I rip off a strip of fabric from my own shirt and dab it on her bloody cheek, angry red welts blooming on her previously unmarred face by the second. "*S-sorry.*"

What comes out next is a rapid stream of consciousness that I don't remember half of.

My inconsolable explanation shifts her gaze from murderous to extreme confusion to careful consideration in the span of several silent minutes, settling on a blank acceptance as I pull the fabric away to examine her cheek.

"I— I'm—I *h*-have to *th*-throw up."

"You are going to *throw up?*" She blinks, taking stock of how close my mouth is as I shove the scrap of fabric in her icy grasp. "Right now?"

"Yeah." I clear my throat against rising bile, stumbling to my feet. "Shit, I'm so sorry. Are you okay? Do you want me to help you to the infirmary? Or your dorm? Or, you can punch me if you were still thinking about it, but let me get ready first."

"No." She winces as I bend to help her up, squirming out of my grasp as if I'm contagious. "Stop touching me! I'm *fine!*"

"Okay. Sorry." I blink up at her as she stares down her nose. Cheeks prickling as I survey her beautiful gown that's been torn to shreds in our slide. "I have to go... Sorry. *Again.*"

"Wait!" she yells, leaning over the spiral staircase as my tennis shoes fly down several flights. "I know you didn't mean to! It's—We're good!"

The moment I burst into fresh air, my mind clears a bit, aware I should go back upstairs and offer my help once more.

But I barely make it to the rose bushes before my warning becomes truth. Well-balanced soup, chocolate, champagne, and ice cream not nearly as pleasant when it all comes back up.

Although it does taste inconceivably minty.

# PART TWO
# NYMPH

# CHAPTER 8

I skip breakfast to get to societal operations early and arrive at an empty lecture hall. The seats are placed in a radial row arrangement, and the spot where the professor will be located is in the center. A raised platform for them to walk around and see every student's face at a moment's notice.

It's almost sterile inside.

Not a speck of dust floating in the chilly air, or crooked chair in sight. Every tabletop shiny, as if someone's taken toothbrushes to dark wood, spot-cleaning surfaces until they've become black mirrors.

I make my usual rounds, scoping out a designated safe zone while twisting the ring on my hand. Since last night, it's never ceased vibrating with a low hum of energy. A consistent feeling that's as natural as my own heartbeat, unnoticed unless I pay close attention.

Already, the thought of parting with it feels terrifying.

The instant possessiveness I have, somehow even more horrific.

In the middle of my ruminations, someone places a hand on my shoulder, and I yelp—jumping several inches into the air. "Shit!"

"Sorry! I didn't mean to sneak up on you." Russ offers a timid smile, and my swirling belly settles. "Where are you thinking we should sit?"

"In the back."

"Is the podium traumatic? Suede informed me of your—" He clamps his mouth shut at the look that must be on my face, reluctantly following me up toward the seventh row.

We pick the seats near the aisle and pull out our notebooks as the room fills up with New Bloods. "Is there a library I can study in? I didn't see one on the map."

"No."

"No." I frown. "On... a college campus?"

"Efficiency. Our books and supplies are provided and placed out for us before we arrive. The next day, they're placed as you've left them. Leave a pen, and you'll see it's in the same spot you positioned it the day before. It's so you don't have to carry around your things aside from your notes. You can take the texts back to study, but usually people don't want to lug them around."

"Any records on family trees? I'm trying to see if I have any extended family here. Or, um, at least get some background on my own."

"That'd be at the Library of Veritas. We can go together if you want. I can call a car service for this weekend."

"I'm not allowed to leave campus. I'll get expelled."

His brows raise, and he adjusts his glasses. "Expelled?"

"Dean Alvarez wrote it in my welcome packet. In about fifty different ways."

"Interesting. New Bloods aren't supposed to leave campus, but it's usually not an expellable offense. On holidays, everyone goes home?"

"Not me." I shrug.

"How much did you know about us before you arrived?"

"Nothing. Do you have a website?"

I'm only halfway serious, but Russ says, "We don't use the internet. Some of us have electronic devices, but most send letters. Our mail system is advanced."

"How do you get your news then?"

"Same as you, I assume? Radios, television, newspapers... different channels report what's going on in each of the territories and outside the border."

"You all know about the countries outside of here?" An unexplainable sense of relief has me relaxing my shoulders.

"America most of all, because of our alliance with Addam."

"Okay," I concede. "I'm still not sure how I feel about no internet."

"We protect our anonymity and our children first. Online digital spaces breed toxicity for youth. I saw a story on cyberbullying once. I personally would have killed myself as a child." I tilt my head, and he shrugs. "We value in-person communication and entertainment. Less room for misunderstandings. Leonusver is home to the best entertainment in our country. You should come see the state choir if we can get you permission to leave campus. My people love to sing."

"Honestly, social media's a hellscape. I guess it'll be sort of nice to log offline."

"Is it as bad as they say?"

"Um... I think it's better left unsaid, actually. I've left that life behind me."

"That's not fair."

"Russ, I'm embarrassed. Mortified would be the better word."

"Come on. It'll give me some insight into what Children of Addam are really up to."

"Okay? Uh, I once watched a bodybuilder, with fake tan dark enough to rival our desktops, eat ten burger patties and wash them down with mayo. In the next video, he was arguing his taxes shouldn't be used to give *brokies* free lunch. And the brokies in question were impoverished children. I then rage-watched twelve of his videos, including an extended street interview where he asked underage girls their body count at a carnival. So, in turn, I just made him more money."

Russ gapes, and I twist the textbook in front of me to get a clearer view of the byline. "Moving on. Who's Geber?"

"Could... be... anyone. Most authors write under the pen name Geber or Maria."

"Why?" My cheeks prickle as he throws me a small smile. "Sorry for all the questions."

Russ waves away my concern. "Alchemists are private people. We have three founder bloodlines now, but Maria's was the fourth. She died when the borders were cast. It's another way to honor her."

I pull out a pencil to write notes on everything I've learned so far.

"So, who are the founders?"

Our hushed conversation is interrupted by heavy footsteps and a cane dragging across the hardwood.

"Professor Silas Martin," Russ whispers.

I recognize the pale, looming man who lit our candles before the ceremony. A thick, scraggly gray beard, shaved head, and eyes so dark they look black. There's no youth in his gaze, dark eyes landing on me as if he could pluck a needle tossed in a thousand haystacks.

Professor Martin steps up to the podium, wasting no time with pleasantries as he cracks open *The Future of Alchemy*. His wrinkled hand clad in a gaudy and gothic silver band, nestled into it, a chunky and dull red crystal.

"Ancient civilizations have searched for the answers we have managed to unlock. From the Mesopotamians, to the Egyptians, to the Romans. They've picked up hidden bits and pieces of our history, and many have come close. The common denominator? All have come up empty-handed."

I hear too much all at once in this quiet room. A boy two chairs away from me scratches his arm, my ears amplifying the sound of nails dragging across dry skin. I inhale sharply, the monotonous tone of Professor Martin not as helpful as it could be.

"Alchemy as we know it began when our ancestors found a way to unlock their natural abilities using the Philosopher's stone. Something that, until that point, had only been hypothesized and alluded to. The same stone that crafted the very rings you see on your fingers today."

Professor Martin slaps the book closed with a hard thud and the sound of pens against paper stops just as fast. I scribble in his last few words before promptly setting my pencil down, noticing Russ never picked his up to begin with.

"I expect you to memorize this book by year's end. You should be more accurate than an index. Down to the paragraph. Down to the line." Overachieving Alchemists nod their heads as I stare down at the thick textbook in front of me. "You should understand the ways you can serve your community. What jobs are available to people of your status, and the importance of your work here. We'll start with mid-level entry positions and work our way up to the important things."

"I thought all our jobs would be important?" A woman asks. "T.A.U. graduates get first pick when we enter the workforce. That's what my mother says."

"A high rank does not guarantee you something respectable. Do you want to spend the next three hundred years supervising sanitary workers?"

I crane my neck in Russ's direction. "Did he say three hundred years?"

"When we start using magic, our bodies begin healing quicker. Our aging slows down when our brains are done developing."

"But, *three hundred?*"

"Some go longer if they're more powerful. My father's been around for decades and looks hardly ten years older than Jason does. My parents are mated, so my mother's aging slowed alongside him."

A pit forms in my stomach. "Our lives are abnormally long?"

"Does that bother you?" Russ laughs.

It's a peculiar question, and I decide not to investigate the answer. Instead, wondering how old my parents are. They've aged normally my whole life. Although, according to Mom's timeline, they haven't used magic my whole life. "Wait, what is mating?"

"Blood magic," Russ says, lowering his voice when Professor Martin glances our way. "There are two blood magic spells we still allow to be done. The ring ceremony and the mating of souls."

"But what does it do?"

"It's a marriage contract with the Universe. It's unbreakable even after death do you part, and then it calls you to the other side. It takes a strong soul to stay after their mate has passed."

"Why would anyone want to do that?"

"Why wouldn't you? Two hearts, two minds, but souls that bleed together for all of eternity. The stronger it gets, you feel what they feel. Eventually, you'll hear and exchange thoughts. It's been said that the founders could even share their power with their mates. The first to do it, were lovers named Castores and Anoush. Castores was dying of old age and Anoush mated with him on his deathbed. Said one lifetime was not enough. He was *pained* the last few years he remained, but he could feel his mate's presence inside. Never to part again."

"Can you do it with anyone?"

"You have to have a soul tie. You can only mate once, though, regardless of how many matches you find."

"How do you—"

"There are many given signs from the Universe, but it's intimate to know for certain. For instance, if you blood-share during... the act, it's evident. Or, so I've heard." I grin at the goosebumps rising against his skin, eyes falling to the desk.

Russ is a romantic at heart, it seems.

A boy with full cheeks and kind eyes is speaking when we tune in again. "Do not go against or interact with foreign governments. We are only allowed magic in lands occupied by Alchemists under the Antarctic Peace Treaty."

Professor Silas Martin spins in a circle, eyes landing on me. He then cuts his gaze slightly to my left. "What happens if we disobey that rule? Icarus?"

"I didn't raise my hand."

"Which I find interesting. Your brother would have been the first to chime in. I see the stories of who takes after your Father aren't fables." Professor Martin gives him a once-over as giggles ring out from around the classroom. "I inquired because you seem to have the answers to all these questions and do not need to listen."

Russ adjusts his glasses as everyone observes him, casting me an apologetic glance before he answers.

Yesterday, he hadn't reacted oddly to my Mom missing a finger. He'd reacted oddly because, for all intents and purposes, I should be missing a finger too.

Technically speaking, I should have gotten worse.

"If you use magic in front of a human who is unaware of our world, you are committing treason. The sentence is the loss of your finger. If you use magic against a human, to harm or injure *anyone* inside Udam territory, it's considered a declaration of war. Your sentence is death."


WHEN I ARRIVE AT FORMULATIONS, my mind's still reeling. No wonder that man kicked me in the head. *I'd* have kicked me in the head.

Who had my Mom used magic in front of? Why would Addam grant my parents more access to the human world afterwards? If she had been in danger of exposing it, wouldn't that have led to her exile? Not a lifetime stay and a chance for her daughter to repeat her mistakes?

I beeline for Suede's table in the front of the laboratory, taking note of the gigantic goggles magnifying her eyes to a near ridiculous degree.

"What?" she asks.

"Nothing."

"Listen, Arsonist—" Suede slides the goggles onto her forehead, irises returning to a normal size. "I've been waiting for this class since I was pushed from the womb."

"I believe that. How do I look, twin?" She gasps as I slide on my goggles too, pink lips forming an O.

"Hello all!" A short man with swollen red skin so pale it's translucent walks into the room. "I am Professor Hari Agarwal." I shrug in response to Suede's grimaced confusion. "Please open Chapter Fourteen."

Suede and I unstack the books at our table. *The Alchemical Glossary* and *Elixirs for Beginners.* I flip through the textbooks until my eyes fall on the chapter in question, labeled, *Self-Transmutation.*

"Today we will focus on changing our eyes, but eventually..." Professor Agarwal looks up to the clock impatiently. When it shifts to three, so does his appearance. "You'll be able to do so much more."

It starts out small.

The intense green of his eyes shifts to a deep brown, twinkling with mischievous possibilities as elasticity returns to his drooping skin and the rusty red atop his head morphs to black—a gelled swoop of thick hair in its place.

What was once translucent skin, full of blue veins and age spots, evens out to a warm, radiant brown. The energy shifts as he stills in front of us. A smile pulling his lips upwards in a devil-may-care grin. "Transmutation elixirs are my favorite. Back in my day, I used to get into a lot of trouble always looking like someone else."

"Why would *you* want to look like anyone else?" A woman blushes.

Agarwal shakes his head in good nature, walking to his desk and casually sliding a ring onto his right hand. "I was a little boy with too much free time and no friends. Aside from my lovely wife. We've been mated since we were you youngins' age. She saw my potential, ladies and gentlemen! Pimples, scrawn, and all."

All of the inappropriate fantasies in the room burst with a palpable deflation of tension and a few audible grumbles.

"Enough about me!" Agarwal fishes into his pocket, pulling out an amber colored bottle and uncapping the rubber topper. He hovers the dropper over each eye, splashing in a few drops of the clear liquid. When he tilts his head, his eyes have returned to the shiny green he walked in with. "Can anyone tell me what causes this type of reaction?" Suede is the first to raise her hand. "Ms. Audere?"

"Some sort of thermochromic and photochromic pigments? They react and change color in response to changes in temperature or exposure to certain wavelengths of light."

"Correct!" Professor Agarwal walks over to the window and opens the blinds. Sunlight streaming into the room, blinking rapidly as sun rays hit his face. The pigment in his eyes breaks down, a natural deep brown within a few moments. "If I had more time to brew, this would have held up to my standards. Regrettably, I had to whip this up within minutes. It reacted positively to the warmth of my eyes as was intended, but reacted negatively to the UV rays and heat from above..."

And so forth, he begins his lecture.

Agarwal's probably the most informative teacher I've ever had. More importantly, he explains things so articulately, I don't feel lost. Breaking down each small component, so not one person needs to pepper him with questions by the end of his hour-long lecture.

Instead, we gift him a round of applause.

"Remember, this requires accuracy! Don't be overeager or you'll leave with melted eyeballs."

Everyone begins at once, intent on being the first ones to finish.

"It's go time, baby!" Suede slips down her goggles. "You won't slow me down, right?"

I flip through the beginner's elixir book in awe. "If people had access to this everywhere, you guys would save the world. Eczema could be cured based on the information I have in my notes alone! And look at this!" I point to a recipe toward the back of the book. "No pain concoction!"

"Don't recommend. That one makes the world too shiny." Suede slips her goggles back up as I dog-ear the page. "And what would be the benefit in handing off our advancements to outsiders?"

"They could pay you guys?"

"We're swimming in gold. We give it to Udam for specific imports. Though that's the extent of our coin usage."

"What?"

"I know Children of Addam get pickpocketed by their government. I understand your shock."

I side-eye her as I pull out my pen. "How does your government work exactly?"

"The higher rank you are, the jobs you get, the more access you have to things."

"So, status is your currency?" I attempt to pop my ears as Suede's ring glows a soft golden yellow. The voices of those around us growing dim. I can hear her soft spoken voice more clearly now, and I guess that everyone else can hear ours less.

"Think of gifts. You give gifts and expect to receive nothing in return. Later, you receive something because your friend remembers when you gave to them. And they give you what you need because they understand what you need. Not equal but equitable."

I momentarily fidget with the band of my goggles. "So, Jason gives a lot?"

"He gives everything he is. People are fine that he lives in luxury. They receive much more from his family than they give back. But even those who contribute near nothing don't go without basic necessities."

"How do you keep track of everything?"

"IDs keep track of our consumption rates, but it's not money. The founders and state accountants make sure resources are allocated appropriately."

"And you have no homeless here? No hungry people?"

"There's not a single person without a living dwelling with regulated living conditions. With clean water and proper food allocation.

That's all a fundamental right. Barbaric otherwise! Could you imagine?"

Suede shudders, and I slump in my seat.

"So what's with the Honestus family?"

"The Honestus family are one of the founding bloodlines. Royalty."

"Russ is royalty? Like, a prince?"

"For all intents and purposes. In shorthand, he's a son of the founders. And since we have an elective Monarchy, their family is favored to take the throne next. Actually, there's never been a time before now that Lions haven't taken the fourth since the borders rose."

"But the way people treat him...?"

"That's another story for a different day. But there's a limited decision pool and it's his duty to serve. There's only a Chalybe now because when the country was electing, after the war, Cairo—"

"Their Dad?"

"Yes. He was the only Honestus of Sureblood left. Lions almost went extinct protecting this land. They went to the frontlines for their people."

"Sureblood?"

"It's used in founder families to know who keeps the namesake. Cairo wants Jace to take the throne and Icarus to take the Father's seat of Leonusver. He plans to retire soon. Lions refrain from full life terms. They believe it's fair to turn leadership over generationally."

"This is more layered than I realized."

"That's not even the half of it. Audere's aren't *no names,* but our contributions tend to fall on the latter half of society. At least, they did. I'll change that."

"No names?"

Suede cracks her knuckles. "There are millions of us. Not everyone has an honorable family name. It's probably why you've managed to fly under the radar."

"I've managed to fly under the radar?" This is news to me, but I'm grateful for it.

"No one knows you're from Addam territory. And even then you're a—"

"A what?" I frown.

"A low name?" Suede winces. *"Benson.* Ben's son. Low names are always suffixed that way."

"Is that maybe just my Dad?"

"No. When couples get married, they take the more distinguished surname."

"Oh. I guess it doesn't really matter."

"Yeah, I wouldn't worry too much. You can grow as high as you want through marriage or service." Suede twirls a piece of her hair as she lapses into silence, sound crashing back in as she says. "Maybe we should get back to work?"

I'm not done asking questions, but Suede is done answering them, seemingly a bit more subdued than when we'd started.

We get to work on our elixir, and it's clear that, although it's a beginner course, the information within is anything but. Relying on the notes from our lecture more than the text itself.

"I went too light on the binding agents," I insist, squinting into my microscope. "The patterns are off."

Suede and I press our heads together, eyes narrowed in on our creation. It's almost as clear as Professor Agarwal's but not quite.

Suede waves him over anyway, and he squints down with interest. "This is great! Who wants to try first?"

We point at one another simultaneously.

There'd already been one pair to try. Both men were sent to the infirmary with bright orange lashes and itchy eyeballs.

Agarwal shakes his fists in mock outrage. "Where's the bravery?!"

"Sorry. It looks cloudy, Professor."

"And I, like, *love* my eye color and really value my eyesight," Suede tacts on. I try not to laugh, but one escapes anyway.

He takes the clear vial from us, shaking it around. "What pigment is it supposed to be?"

"We agreed on purple." Agarwal nods and, without hesitation, drops splashes into both eyes. "If we blind our Formulations professor, I'm *never* coming back," Suede whispers.

His eyes shift in an instant. Red and blue swirled at random in both irises. Agarwal takes the mirror laid flat on our desk and examines them. "So close!"

"My fault," I admit aloud.

"There's no fault to be had in my lab, Ms. Benson. Mistakes are integral to progress. Isn't failure invigorating? What a rush! I'm second-hand high! Or... maybe that's the chemicals." He points to the back row of the classroom. "Open the window, Geoffrey! I'm about to pass out!"

"Yes, sir! Also, my vision's gone black and white."

I can't help but laugh as Agarwal pats my shoulder. A wink that tells me he'd watched me make the mistake and let it happen, walking away to attend to Geoffrey as Suede claps.

"That's the only elixir he tried!" She lowers her goggles and rubs the palms of her hands together in anticipation. "Alright. Let's go again, Arsonist! You're handy after all."

# CHAPTER 9

A scream rips through the sky, and dozens of chins lift upward—a flock of black pegasus rolling through puffs of fluffy cotton above. Professor Laroche leads the charge with several students on her tail, and one of the boys comes unseated, hanging on by a muscular wing the more he attempts to control it.

"This isn't funny!" he screeches as everyone guffaws, pants sliding down his thighs until he flashes us his full ball sack.

Laroche whistles in warning when they reach his ankles, circling back to the end of the line. The boy emits every expletive in the book as she forces him on the back of her own stallion.

I take to looking for Sunny, as I've done every day for the past week.

"I bet Jason's itching for more flight time with Jupiter," Russ says.

It's been the main conversation topic around campus. His brother bonded a stallion on his first flight. One hour-long ride, and the pegasus was his. Unheard of to bond so quickly, if ever at all.

Full-grown pegasus are nearly twice as large as Sunny. Eleven feet high with gossamer wingspans of twenty-five feet wide. Once I got over my initial fear, the prospect of being a pegasus rider is enough to make me sad New Bloods aren't considered ready for flight. According to

Russ, with only several thousand in existence, the chances of bonding one are slim. Loyalist families usually snatch them up.

As we walk past the stables, I spot a violet braid swinging in the distance. The triplets gathered together as the one I'd injured raises the hem of her shirt.

A sinking feeling floods my chest as she reveals a side full of deep purple bruises. A jagged cut scabbing across her right cheek, mouth twisting in pain as her brother prods her side.

Every time I've had the urge to check in on her injuries, my brain threatens to spill out alphabet soup, and then, another helping of actual soup from my belly. It seems too late to say anything and have my concern sound genuine. But my curiosities get the better of me.

"Hey, who's that girl? I ran into her right after the welcome ceremony and I—"

Russ collides with a staff member, the bin of matches she's holding flying into the air. The three of us scramble to pick up the boxes, and when we rise, the triplets are gone. My teeth biting into my lip so hard it's a wonder it's still attached.

"What girl?"

"Never mind," I sigh. "Have you used your ring yet?"

"A little bit." He clenches and unclenches his fist. "To be honest, it doesn't make much sense to me. Earth affinities believe that controlling the ground we walk on means they're the strongest."

"What's wrong with that?" Russ smiles bitterly, and a flash of upset rips through my belly. "You're strong, Russ. You have a caring heart. That's the strength I value the most in this world."

"And if I want to be strong in that way?" He glances at his brother and Suede, who walk hand in hand ahead of us just out of earshot. Jason picks up his girlfriend, powerful and sure of himself in every step he takes. Throwing her over one shoulder and placing one hand on her ass to hold her pleated skirt in place. Sandy blonde waves flow in the wind that nips at his heels, laugh echoing as if the forest and mountains are made solely to amplify his glee.

"We could take roids? I'll try anything once. As long as it's not smoke, PCP, or bath salts."

"You can't be serious?"

"Well, I'm joking about steroids, but on Saturday mornings my sister and I eat edibles and watch the Discovery Channel on silent. We get close to the TV and pretend we're at the aquarium." He frowns, and I scramble to add, "Never mind. Imagine my guns juiced up."

I bump him with a bony shoulder, flexing my twigs for arms until there's imaginary definition.

Russ's resounding chuckle is as warm as sunshine. The same full-body laugh as his brother.

Yet, it's quieter and tapers off much too quickly.

We approach the furthest section of campus, directly behind the main building. Before us is a flowing river containing large ice chunks. On the other side, the tallest thicket of trees I've ever seen, blocking the view of anything behind it.

A single bridge is situated in its center, connecting the two pieces of land. Dozens of trees have been twisted to arch over the flowing water, hundreds of interwoven vines for handholds, an intricate arch of greenery above it all. Blooming roses dangle overhead, giving it the look of a wedding arbor. Romantic enough to stand below and seal your fate to another, yet no one pays it any mind as they clobber over the swirled wood structure.

"Race you!" I abandon my ogling as I take off running over the windy bridge, ignoring the flowing water underneath.

Russ hesitates a singular second before bounding after me.

We run side by side, and I kick my legs into overdrive to keep up with him through the winding dirt pathway and thicket of tall redwoods. No room for Russ to be saddened as our screeched laughter takes over the forest, countless New Bloods shooting us odd looks as we blow past them.

We've traveled half a mile when Russ catches my arm, arguing about who won when we clear the forest simultaneously. I'm intent on gloating until the site ahead brings me up short, mouth falling agape in wonder.

The Arena is an open-air stadium of ice and earth in pristine condition. The circular structure has rounded arches and tall columns ascending five levels upward. With ginormous white statues of Lions, Tigers, and Bears lining each side, spouting water from their mouths.

"You've gotta be kidding me."

"Did I forget to mention my family owns this?" Russ squeezes my shoulders as we walk under the stone Ouroboros hanging above the entrance tunnel. Divided into fourths, there are enough seats for three hundred thousand audience members to sit and observe. Easy to make out that a quarter of the Arena is dedicated to each element.

In the Fire quadrant, the floor and railings are the deepest black I've ever seen. The benches a strange material that glow like heated coal. A blend of orange and red that could leave you mesmerized for hours watching them brighten and dim.

The Water quadrant is styled after the sea. With walls a deep blue and images of boats that seem to move through the painted waves if you stare hard enough.

The next section to catch my eye is Air, because it looks the most alive. With wind that blows yellow flags the color of sunshine around. The bleachers cast a soft golden glow and the benches aren't nailed in, only hovering in place and ready to be used.

Last is Earth. Whose bleachers are made of ginormous white stone slabs and whose walls are covered in floral from floor to ceiling.

In the center is a circular patch of land. The lawn divided into the same four sections, each the size of its own football field, with symbols of the classic elements on steel flag poles.

Suede and Jason catch up while I stop to survey the architecture.

"One of my first memories is of my parents taking Icarus and I to watch Ludi Bellorum," Jason says.

"What's that?" I ask.

"Biennial Tournament, the first Friday of May," Russ says. "Everyone gets four days off to celebrate or travel here and back to their homes. Unless people volunteer to work, things go completely automated. It takes some preparation."

"So it's a big deal?"

"Tickets are acquired in a lottery because everyone wishes to attend. Some even camp out to watch the projectors outside if they are unable to acquire tickets. Everyone else watches at home."

"Since you're an Imaginifer now, there's no chance you're not captain, baby," Suede says, leaning her head on Jason's arm as a soft breeze ruffles her hair.

"It's a title," Russ explains as my brows furrow, scribbling the word in my notepad and wondering if any of this is good enough for Addam. "When we were at our welcome ceremony, twenty Bronze Stars were tapped in. They teach this class. Our advisor's only here to make sure we're not killing each other."

Jason wraps his hands around the railing of the stadium as he leans forward, a new ring on the pointer finger of his right hand. An Ouroboros with shiny checkered scales eating its own tail, the mark of an Imaginifer.

"So what are the rules?"

"Capture the flag, and you'll violently die trying." Suede sighs.

"Oh. Wow. *Fuuun.*" I say. "Is it, like, a... cultural thing?"

"Sort of. There are two games. One for first and second years, and another for third and fourth. The first game happens at sunset, and then the main game starts after a short intermission. Both go as long as it takes," Russ says.

"Who chooses teams?"

Russ tilts his head thoughtfully. "The Dean selects the captains. In our case, the captains stack the team with the other Imaginifers. New Bloods are left out all the time."

"I won't," Jason declares. "When I'm captain, I'll make it fair. That's what practice is for."

"Will it be fair when you get in the match and command them to hand you their flag? The game would be over instantly with a Lion in the ring."

"I'd never do that? That's not in the spirit of the game."

"This game is archaic. I can barely stomach watching. Two years ago, a girl was hung from vines off the Earth quadrant's flagpole. They kept her up as decor in game two."

My eyes widen, and Jason waves away my concern. "It's pride that kills people. Not the game. It's only when you refuse to give up your flag."

"What student would walk away from a flag? What captain would advise that?" Russ asks.

"I wouldn't ask men to die for Ludi Bellorum."

"You wouldn't be happy with them either," Russ mutters. "Some would prefer death to your disappointment."

Jason scratches at his jaw, heading towards the Imaginifers while the three of us are swept into the crowd with the rest of the New Bloods.

Dean Alvarez walks onto the field of the Arena wearing a black turtleneck. Her platinum hair parted down the center, tucked behind both ears with not a wisp out of place. She has a shiny blue castor ring on her finger now. Whereas, during the Welcome Ceremony, she hadn't worn anything but her Ouroboros pendant.

Twenty Bronze Stars stand opposite us, grouped up by color. Five in red, five in blue, five in yellow, and five in green. All standing at attention, like war generals. The only three I recognized are Jason, Ezra, and his girlfriend, Josephine.

The crowd screams like madmen when our Imaginifers raise their hands in the shape of the Ouroboros, stomping their feet so hard the ground shakes. The crackle and buzz of energy in the air almost intoxicating enough to want to join in.

"First Years, we welcome you to the Arena!" Dean Alvarez shouts, raising a hand until the chants taper off. "You have all crafted rings. You have all been given a start. But it is up to you to choose where you reside. To reiterate a fact many forget, the affinity doesn't choose your course of study. You do. The Founders were able to wield all four elements. *Five* if you're a true believer. Maybe one of you could be so lucky."

Everyone laughs, and I'm suspicious I don't get the joke.

Russ is ahead of me, leaning down to whisper in my ear. "A Gold Star Earth affinity wouldn't be able to warp air better than a New Blood on their first day."

Hope blooms in my chest. "But not impossible? I could switch affinities?"

"You could try," Suede offers from my other side. "But not Air though, we're pretty full."

"Alvarez is making a joke. I couldn't burst a glass of water if my brother's life depended on it."

Suede frowns. "But some say Maria could—"

"The founders were powerful, but they didn't bend Aether. That's a legend."

"Aether?" I ask.

"The fifth element," Russ says. "Someone could crash planets together with that type of power. Trillions of innocent organisms left to the whims of a singular person. For an Aether bender to be born would be as if the Universe flipped a coin and let its fate rest in their hands."

A chill runs down my spine at the thought.

"Icarus is going straight to doomsday scenario. Hypothetically, after years of practice, could an Aether bender maybe do that," Suede says.

"After years of practicing *crumpling planets?*" Russ asks.

"The scope of its possibility is outside the realm of our knowledge."

"I know the possibilities. They'd be a God walking among men. Eventually, if they had the power of the founders, so could their mate. I'd recommend they'd be put down if that were the case, and I don't believe in capital punishment."

"How did the founders bend all four if it's near impossible to do anything outside of our affinity?" I ask.

"The stone gave them all four in reward for discovering it. But never again will it give that much. To dare touch it on its own is... Death."

My eyebrows skyrocket upwards. "Death?"

"It strips you of your life for daring to take more than what is offered. That's why it starts breaking your fingers. It warns you to let go before it's too late."

I grimace, and he lapses into silence, turning to face Dean Alvarez once more.

"You've been sorted into your respective groups, and your Imaginifer will seek you out. If you want to try your hand at another station, another affinity, be my guest. We'll reassign you."

The crowd disperses as people break off, and Suede's swept away by Jason in the shuffle. Russ clears his throat, angling his head toward the direction I see an argument brewing.

Ezra stands in front of Dean Alvarez, locked in an intense discussion and throwing unsettled glances towards the two of us. She points to Russ and I, snapping her fingers in his face several times.

It's only when Ezra turns away from his mother, a heated stare dead-locked on me, that I take a step backward.

As he approaches, he doesn't look like he's willing to extend a helping hand. He looks as if he has the intention of chopping one clean off.

"You're mine for the year." Ezra's voice has a smoky timbre and reverberates in his chest, eyes glaring down at my stone to double check he isn't being deceived.

"I thought that I could pick my affinity?"

"So pick. If you're late to my lesson, I dock three points from your daily report," he says, brushing past me on his way toward the fire quadrant.

"I don't understand why he's upset with me. Do you think it's because of graduation? His Mom told him?"

"I don't know. Would you feel better if I spoke with him? Tell him you're nervous about being here? I'm sure it's a misunderstanding."

Russ's voice is so earnest that my chest warms in response. He has a knack for little bursts of softness that make me think he's too caring for his own good.

"It's okay. I'm just gonna head over before he docks me points."

"You'd better go then." Russ winces. "He's scribbling angrily in his book."

I gasp, hurrying after my Imaginifer before I'm late to his lesson.

# CHAPTER 10

I find myself surrounded by a sea of red stones, sitting on the lawn as Ezra lectures with dimples on full blast. So relaxed, I wonder if I've hallucinated his ire.

"When you're comfortable, you can pick up a flint ring." He raises his arm to reveal a textured band beside his castor ring, a lit cigarette balanced between his fingers until he takes it into his mouth to free his hands. Puffs of miasmic smoke waft down as Ezra twitches his fingers, a spark flying out between the bands—grabbing and twirling it until a tornado of flame whirls against his palm before dissipating.

"For now, you'll carry a matchbook in your pocket. They're easier to practice with, but less convenient if you're ever in need. You'll look ridiculous trying to scramble for one in a sparring match."

He pulls a box of matches from the grass at his feet.

Everyone whoops as he tosses them out, catching the sacred prizes like keys to paradise.

When he's about to set the box down, I raise my hand, and when he ignores my hand, I clear my throat. "Ezra?"

"Sir."

"Sir...? You forgot me."

Ezra takes a drag from his cig that seems to last for minutes before responding. "Did I?"

"Yes."

"And you are?" He checks his roster for my name, which is odd because he's already docked me three points for being late.

"*Sh*-shiloh Benson."

"Sure about that? Sha-sha-sha-shiloh?" A freckled boy inquires as the other New Bloods break into chortles.

Although Ezra doesn't laugh, a flash of satisfaction flickers in his gaze—reaching his hand into the box at an agonizingly slow pace, capturing a matchbook, then flicking it in my general direction.

It lands behind me with a squelch, buried an inch deep into the mud pit. Sparks of embarrassment shooting through my limbs and heating me from the inside out.

"Why would you—"

"He said fetch, bitch." The woman closest to me shrugs. "Shouldn't be an issue. We all know you lap up the attention."

"What?"

"What? What? What?" She chirps my question back to me three times in different yet grating tones.

"Enough," Ezra mutters. The energy shifts around us as he drops the box full of matchbooks into the grass.

"Can I get a new pack?" I ask, shoulders sagging as I release a ragged breath.

"One per student. Per lesson."

"But there's more in the box?"

"We have an odd number of people in this group. You can watch since you don't want to use the matchbook allotted to you." The remains of his half-smoked cigarette dissolve in his grasp, eaten away by fire.

"I mean, I never said that, but okay. Do I still get points for watching?"

"Is watching participating?"

"No?"

"So what do you think?"

"I—"

"This class is training, and this quadrant is not for the weak," Ezra says, no more dimples to be found. "Inside this arena, you earn your place. You pull your own weight. Don't like it? Go home to cry to your mothers about it. Not to me, or the other Imaginifers. Are we clear?"

The voices around us chime out, "Yes, sir!"

"Great. Let's have some fun. Hit the bleachers, Benson." He rises as the excited chatter of students grows. Everyone breaks into pairs, and I'm left by myself, grinding my teeth so hard it's a miracle they don't shatter.

I pull my matchbook from the mud pit and blink away frustrations. A glob of thick soil encasing the small rectangle, wiping it clean on the grass and shoving it hastily into my pocket.

In the Air quadrant, Suede's showing off her moonwalk for Jason's group with far less rhythm but way more excitement. She's half a centimeter off the ground, but her partner seems to be impressed.

I rise to get a better view of the Earth affinities next, eyes sweeping the northern section of the arena for coily curls and oversized glasses, heart sinking to hell when I finally spot him.

Russ is surrounded by three students who double over in laughter as he searches the grass for his glasses. Every time he almost grasps them, a weed sprouts, flinging them farther away. His carefully pressed khakis steadily collect grass stains until my feet carry me toward the Earth quadrant on their own volition.

I feel possessed as I approach, watching them taunt the shyest boy I've ever met.

*Russ,* who wouldn't smack a damned fly to save his life.

Who keeps to himself and is so afraid of people that *he* apologizes if they step into *his* personal space.

I near the one laughing the hardest, using both hands to shove the large man as hard as I can. Enough force and anger to send him stumbling, fists clenched as his ring vibrates with energy.

I assess him quickly: deep brown coils, warm brown skin, a full-lipped grimace, and a crooked nose that twitches as he meets my gaze. It's slightly off-center, as if someone once broke it clean in half—the singular thing on his face that could mar his beauty.

Even still, his eyes don't fill with the evil I'd imagined on my march over. A flicker of regret filling them before he steels himself.

I pay no mind to the girls at his side for longer than the second it takes me to notice they're there, pulling my mud-stained matchbook from my pocket and drawing out a match as quickly as I can.

The moment I spark it, I feel its presence like an old friend. The flame flickering back and forth as I hold it between my fingers. "Okay, let's try that game again. This time I get to stand in for Russ."

A girl with thick lashes, a few feet away, appraises me with a nod of approval. Motioning for me to take a deep breath as Russ finally finds his glasses, setting them back crookedly on his face, a large crack embedded in the lenses as he stumbles over with wide eyes.

"Nope! No games! Everything is fine! Nothing to see here!"

"Is it?" The man spits on the grass near Russ's feet. "You're a stain on your namesake, and you certainly don't deserve to keep it if you need your bitch to save you."

"Tristain, come on. Enough is enough. I get it."

The boy pauses to consider Russ's statement, and I step between them.

"Fine. Just *s*-stay away from him and we don't have a problem."

Tristain chuckles, amusement filling his gaze. "Do you know who you're talking to?"

"I know a bully when I see one." I back against Russ, attempting to shield him with my body. The flame flickering wildly as Russ steps out from behind me, pulling me under his arm and attempting to soothe my trembles and diffuse the situation. "Now walk away! Or else."

"Or else wha—" Tristain topples to his back. As if an invisible rope has been tied to his feet and yanked backward. He's dragged across the grass several yards and lifted by his ankles.

"Or else nothing now," Jason says, standing on my other side, his ring glowing with bottled sunshine.

Russ groans as his brother flicks Tristain around like a weightless rag-doll. The boy grappling to be free of the invisible force latched around his ankles, fingers wading through the thin air. "Humor me, Shit Stain. Why shouldn't I cave your lungs and watch you implode?"

"Jason, it's fine," Russ whispers, the flame on my match sputtering as the wind picks up around us. "Let's all calm down."

"I—" Tristain chokes out the singular syllable before he's throttled by invisible hands.

"Say my name before you speak to me."

"Jason Honestus," Tristain sputters, spit flying from his lips. "I was *joking*. Tell him, Russ!" My mouth morphs into a grimace as he attempts to use Russ's nickname.

"His name is Icarus Amias Honestus!" Jason growls, the sound so blaring that all activity on the field stops. Any sense of playing down the situation leaves Russ, who quiets in an instant. "And my brother is not your punchline! You wanted to act tough in front of the other New Bloods?! Wanted to prove you could torment an Honestus without consequence?!"

"I save Honestus' blood in my veins," Tristain chokes out. "You can't kill me!"

People in the gathering crowd shift uncomfortably at the statement, and so do I.

Jason releases an unhinged cackle completely unlike his warm chuckle. The sound as cold as the frigid winds that blow outside of the borders. "You think that entitles you to anything other than to brown-nose my Father? Let me be clear to everyone, here and now!" His voice booms louder as he sneers. "You have a *drop* of the blood of my family. To which you should be grateful, or I would have snapped your neck on sight! For decades, your blood has been soiled by low names. Which is evident from your behavior today. You're a diseased branch on a nearby tree, *Korovk*."

People nod in agreement. Even the Earth students are quick to rally behind Jason's decree. The hiss of their words egging this on.

"And what should one do with diseased branches before their sickness spreads to the rest of the forest?" Jason doesn't give Tristain a chance to answer, tightening his grip with each word. "Cut. Them. Off."

Tristain gurgles as air crushes his windpipe, clawing desperately at an element he can't manipulate. Brown skin going purple as he gasps and flounders.

My hands fall to my side, clenching around my match and snuffing the flame. "Russ...?"

"Stop." Russ clasps his hand on his brother's shoulder. "Jason, it's fine. *Stop.*"

Suede comes to stand at her boyfriend's elbow, doe eyes filled with horror. Not sparing one look toward the choking man. Only focused on the rage that flashes in Jason's eyes, her words a quiet whisper for only the ears of our small group. "Babe, you proved your point. If you kill him, you won't be happy with yourself tomorrow."

Russ retreats as Jason stirs at her voice, allowing air to fill Tristain's lungs. He remains hanging upside down with bloodshot eyes, gasping like a fish as he regains oxygen.

Russ avoids my gaze, wiping smudges of dirt from his cracked frames as his brother turns to survey the damage done.

Ezra approaches with caution, daring to get closer to the situation than anybody else will. "Jason."

"Ezra."

"Would you mind setting the boy down?" Jason raises a brow at the request. Content to keep Tristain hanging upside down until all his blood pools in his skull. Ezra raises his voice slightly, so more can hear him ask. "If you could find it in your heart to be merciful to such disrespect?"

Jason huffs out a laugh, dropping Tristain on his head. He falls with a heavy thud onto the grass, wincing as he curls into himself, massaging his skull that took the brunt of the impact.

"Thick ass brain." The girl with long lashes mumbles from the side, having gotten closer to us without my knowledge. Her hands are so shaky that she clasps them behind her back.

Ezra approaches Tristain and helps him to his feet. "You good?"

He nods to himself, avoiding the gaze of the girl glaring from my side.

"Listen, Shit Stain—" Jason spits directly on the boy's shiny boots. "I'm a fan of prescribed burning, and Icarus is my only family here. Don't forget it. Because you won't get another chance with me."

Ezra pushes Tristain toward where the four of us are grouped together. His gaze focused on the grass as Ezra claps him on the shoulder, body tensing under the weight of his hand. "Yes, of course. I'm sorry."

"Glad we've all come to an understanding," Ezra rumbles.

The girl at my side rolls her eyes, storming off as soon as Tristain is in the clear.

He runs after her in an instant. "Osira! Sira, wait!"

Dean Alvarez watches with intensity, and I'm reminded for the first time I'm supposed to stay out of trouble as her eyes narrow.

Ezra turns his back on us, head swiveling to observe the gathered crowd as his voice carries in the wind. No other sound but the gentle breeze and labored breaths of frightened New Bloods.

"If you've all forgotten, it'll be me who reminds you. An Honestus doesn't forget a friend or a foe. Loyal to them, they're loyal to you. Make an enemy? Well then, that's when the stone sets. Congealed with the blood of their opposers!" People appraise Russ warily as he stands behind the shoulder of his brother. "If that's not enough, I'll let everyone in on a little secret. Jason Honestus is an understanding man. *I,* on the other hand, am not. Alvarezes have been loyal to the Honestus family since the unity bells rang. I will not hesitate to show how far that loyalty goes the next time this boy is touched. Are we clear?" When no one moves a muscle, a dark chuckle escapes him. "*Are we clear?!*"

The air seems to grow hotter around him as he waits for a response. And everyone, regardless of what section they're in, nods.

"Good. Get back to work. Anyone with an Earth affinity laps the Arena four times before they leave. This quadrant is dismissed for the day."

Jason chuckles as the Imaginifers in green freeze with widened orbs. "You too."

People break apart in a hurry. Green ringed Alchemists scrambling to run the perimeter of the arena. Those who linger watch Ezra storm over to me, his large hand digging in my jean pocket. I choke out a labored breath, stepping backwards as Russ steadies me.

Ezra's fist clenches around my muddy matchbook, waving it in front of my face with a sneer. "You've lost casting privileges for two weeks."

"Two weeks!?"

"You're right. Make it three."

"But—" Russ claps his hands over my mouth, cradling me in his thin arms. I'm well aware of how childish it is, but I do it anyway—slobbering against his hands at the audacity.

Russ emits a disgruntled noise as my tongue pokes at his fingers.

When enough spit has seeped between the cracks, he grunts, releasing me to wipe it on his khakis. Though I resolve to remain silent as Ezra continues his lashing.

"Three weeks, Benson. You don't make threats with weapons you don't know how to control." Ezra's stride is long, and his jaw is clenched as he walks back toward the fire quadrant. My gaze following his long stride, noticing the violet-haired triplet watches Russ intently.

"Are you okay?"

"I'm fine." His nostrils flare. Unclear whether it's because of our defense of him, or his lack of ability to defend himself. "I'm sorry, Shi. I didn't mean to get you in trouble."

"What? It isn't your fault?"

"It's completely my fault."

Jason runs a hand over his face, eyes sweeping side to side as if daring another threat to approach. "Fair warning, I'm speaking with Father. Today."

"You swore you'd stay out of it."

"I agreed to let you handle it on your own. Now look at what's happened? People have gotten too comfortable. Those closest to us most of all."

"What's the point?"

"Icarus, when our conversation is through, expect a call from him."

"I wouldn't hold my breath," Russ mutters.

"You won't have to." Jason grips Russ's head when he won't meet his eyes, straightening his broken glasses. "Understand me here and now, brother. You have the blood of Lions who learned to write within you. Men and women who commanded their own narratives and made sure their children were born to the purple. We will not allow people to test if you still can. Not after what our family has given for these *ungrateful* hyenas that claim to love us, yet took the first chance to attack. Father should have never"—Jason inhales sharply, staunching his steadily building anger— "Yes. This ends tonight."

Russ clamps his mouth shut as his brother claps him on the shoulder. A smile already back on Jason's lips. I stare up at him with wide eyes, taking in how quickly he's flipped.

It's only the four of us left by now, so I let my question spring free. "Did you have to—"

"Yes." His voice is flat, eyes surveying me with aporetic inquisitiveness.

It's unintentional when I take a shaky step backward, yet it leaves a tension in the air. The small action hanging between the four of us like a thick curtain. My retreat spurring a flicker of upset that he quickly wipes away. "You know what they used to scream to my ancestors when someone would dare to insult a Founder family? What each person in the land would beg of us?"

"No."

Jason squints as if there's an accusation layered in my whisper. "*Damnatio ad Bestias.*"

"Oh."

"I'm disappointed my way of defense wasn't pretty enough for you, Shiloh. Or that you'd feel afraid of me when I've given you no reason to be. But I will never be sorry." He grabs Suede's hand, rubbing it between his own as he talks. "Instead of judging my methods, think about what you would've done with your magic if I hadn't stepped in to do it for you."

"I was only wondering if we could have—"

"There is no *we!*" he yells. And this time, I stay still as stone.

Jason leans down to meet my gaze, lowering his voice and inhaling sharply. "I've always known only some of us have to make choices that appear ugly. We're not all born Lions, right? Sometimes you're born as a soft-looking girl who cries wolf. Begging to be saved and is frightened that the savior appears scarier than the beast who'd attacked her."

Suede gently tugs him away, but she's clearly on his side, rolling her eyes when I glance her way.

"Am I on to something, Shiloh? If I were the prince of long-told fairy tales, would you be entirely okay with my choices? Would my actions be less *terrifying?* How quickly would you justify them without knowing the workings of my inner mind?"

"My Dad—"

"Look me in my eyes when I tell you this. I don't give a *fuck* that you have a Black daddy who holds his temper when flagrantly disrespected. I will not allow my brother to do the same and have people think it's open season for trophy hunting."

"Both of my parents are Black?"

"And I'm sure your Mother shows off the blue in her veins quite often," he snorts. "Let's agree to steer clear of one another from this point forward. I refuse to waste my breath explaining myself to anyone. Least of all to you."

"Jason, wait. I'm sorry." He brushes past me, exiting the arena with Suede in tow. "Russ, tell him I didn't—I thought Tristain was going to die because of me."

"First off, you aren't responsible for the fallout of a fight instigated by several grown men." Russ tilts my head up to better look into my eyes, reeling over my own idiotic comparisons that helped no one in the end. "Lions hold ourselves to higher standards than Tigers or Bears ever will. We're twice as scrutinized for our shortcomings, and you were... a mirror of his worst fears."

"I know! I didn't mean that the way it came across."

"Trust me, I saw exactly where your heart was, and that makes all the difference in the world. But I also know my brother. He'll need time to see that too. And also to admit he could have handled that better."

"Condemnation to Beasts?" I whisper.

Russ slings an arm around my shoulders as we walk toward the exit.

"That's a more literal sense. As a rally cry, it's a phrase my family holds close."

"Signifying?"

"Long ago, when someone would commit a crime, they'd tie him up and throw him in a pit with lions to meet his fate. The animals would leave nothing behind, and neither should the Honestus in an attack on the peace and unity of our nation. In times of difficulty, we are expected to know the way forward. Our people ask for help, and we step in to do what no one else will. Opposing our word is the greatest crime of all. It's an unforgivable act."

# CHAPTER 11

Several weeks have passed since Jason suggested we 'steer clear of one another' and I've remained silent and out of his way upon realizing an Honestus doesn't make *suggestions*.

Russ has temporarily become my roommate, Suede's time spent largely with her boyfriend while he's icing me out. And after banishing the second son to her bed for mouth breathing, and crushing me with his limbs at night, I'd be okay with how the semester is going if not for my casting reports coming back with large red zeros on them.

Ezra might as well draw smiley faces with how smug he appears to hand them over.

My gaze falls several yards away, eyeing my main sources of interest in the time I've spent warming benches.

*The triplets.* Who I've finally put name to while watching them spend just as much of it taking refuge by the fire pits.

Josephine seems content to let the Sapienti's teach themselves, and if their reputations hold any inkling of truth, leaving them to their own devices is the intelligent choice.

When Suede begrudged me a tight-lipped gossip session in Formulations, she'd told me Nox Sapienti notoriously sleeps around. The Bear has an itch for older women he can't help but scratch and they say it must be why Solara is so icy.

Two weeks ago she'd set fire to the classroom of a Professor when she caught them in the act. No surprise when Ms. Molina was seen hauling her bags into a trunk last weekend.

No one's heard from her since.

Nox always sits on the right of the fire pit. The white haired man fiddling with a piece of wood, shavings flying into the flames as Solara throws in silver for fun—turning up the heat until her fancy jewelry melts.

Sky, the girl with violet tresses, is a mystery to us all.

Suede says she avoided the public eye even more skillfully than Russ had growing up. There's no rumors to decode because there's not an inkling of information to twist.

She peers up from her sketchbook and I wave my hand in greeting.

When she doesn't return it, I pretend to be scratching my head.

"If you're not going to pay attention, my time is better spent elsewhere," Ezra says from beside our unlit stack of wood.

"Sorry," I murmur, ripping up a blade of grass beneath my leg and pulling my knees to my chest. It's my first lesson after being benched and I'm already blowing it.

"The first thing you need to understand is that most of the elements are allies. They seek souls who align with their frequencies. Air affinities are stubborn. It's what prompts Air's desire to befriend them. To teach them what it is to know how to waver. It's also the most protective of all elements. It fills our lungs daily and needs no thanks for its sacrifices."

Ezra pulls a matchbook out of his pocket, tossing me the rectangular object as he adds, "Earth affinities need stability and connection. If not for gravity, they'd float away and spiral into the ether based on thoughts alone." I part my lips and he shoots me a glare that tells me commentary isn't welcome, so I fish out a red tipped stick and wait for him to continue. "The human race damages the Earth and it allows us to live upon it still. Does not judge us as much as it should. For that reason, there's lots of reckless and impulsive Earth affinities. However, the most tenderhearted of souls are thrown in the mix too. People who need the ground to soften for them each time they fall. With the cushion of unconditional love, it's harder for them to break."

"Water affinities are ever-changing, adaptable wildcards. Never think you know them. They'll always surprise you. Continuously change their course to what is most honest in their heart. Water makes up our life's blood but it especially honors people who seep through any crack to become exactly who they need to be."

"And Fire?" I ask.

"Passionate beings consumed by our emotions and desires. A blazing inferno that never quite seems to end." Ezra runs his hands through his wavy locks, a wild look in his eyes. "Fire is a part of you in a way the other elements are not. Fueled by the electricity inside your soul. We all have something we'd be willing to burn the world for but it's against our nature to unleash every bit of what lies within us. We'll never bear that much of ourselves."

"We could scorch the Earth?"

"Yes in theory, no in practice. Not many have had that type of power, and if they did, what's left for a pyromaniac to burn on a scorched planet?"

"Is that why Addam is terrified of us?"

"Addam isn't terrified, they're strategic. We choose to communicate with them because they're reasonably tolerable and seem to have sway among Udam."

"And how do you feel about Udam?"

"How do *you* feel about them?" he asks.

I feel as if a hum of understanding thrums through my bones.

If Udam believes in a scorched Earth, it makes sense they'd rationalize a nuclear response. Hoping they'd be the Phoenix to rise from the ashes while reality would likely mold them into roaches who outlive. Scurrying in pipes underground amongst the sewage of ghosts they'd shit on when they could still see the sun.

"I've come to terms with the fact it was built as a shield over buttons and that there's no going back. But the threats are like a loosely strung guillotine above my head."

"Great to hear you're catching up to the rest of us who live in reality, Dreamer."

"I've always lived in reality?" I frown. "But reality weighs heavy on my fingers now. How can any of us go on ignoring it?"

"There's no ignoring it. There's deciding what you'll do and where you'll go when the blade drops. It's no use staring up to watch a guillotine quiver if you're certain of where your loyalties lie?"

"If Udam struck... you're saying you'd push your button and allow innocents to face your retaliation?"

"Our enemies aren't innocent."

"How could a kid be your enemy? There's no child in this world who has access to a button, neither do most of their parents. And honestly, you don't need to be innocent, or even a good person, to avoid being subjected to war. There's a limit to what you can do to another human being. Even if they're awful?"

"In fairytale land, sure. But the reality is, leaders choose to barricade their borders with living beings all the time. Avoidance of civilian suffering will always be the weakness they count on when they ask people they've struck from a fortress, not to blow their house down."

"Yeah, well, unfortunately we've gotten so comfortable with the game we've had to create rules. The least you could do is abide by them."

"Look, for the most part, we'll play fair. Innocents wouldn't be the target but casualties *are* an inevitability when the target's hidden. So, yes. I'd light up their skies to protect my own. Every. Single. Time."

"That's it then? Their crime, sentence-able by death, is being born on the same continent as someone who abused their power? Who decided it's okay if unrelated flesh burns in their rage?"

"If you don't want to be caught in crossfire, don't allow incompetent men to steer your ship in battle."

"This planet sails through space! We're all on the same ship?! One day the oceans will rise to fight back and the Earth that provides without judgment will have nothing left to give. Who will you blame then? Will it still not be your problem or are you hoping you and your children are dead before strangers face the consequences of our mistakes?"

"These borders will hold until the sun eradicates the Earth we stand on. Maria's lifeblood flows within them and my people will remain as one. That's the type of certainty that comes with loyalty. I sleep like a baby. What about you? How do you sleep at night?"

"Terribly," I admit.

How can there be limits? How can I not give my loyalty to those who know nothing of the agencies that control things behind the scenes? How can I not weep for people who cry out centuries from now? How can anyone, across a sea I hope will one day have bridges, be my enemy?

"Sleepless nights tend to come when you don't have allegiance or faith in your country." Ezra shrugs. "Get on with it."

"What do I do?"

"Use your stone to channel your power. Hold all the energy, then restore it back to yourself. And, fair warning, don't try this without wearing a ring. If you were to attempt to, you'd implode yourself... *Usually.* I've heard you survived your attempt to press your button. Must be why you've had such a change of heart about it."

"You don't know anything about my heart if you believe that."

"Light the match and stop wasting my time."

"But—"

"Light. The. Match." I drag the head across the striking surface and the crackle of the tip catching fire echoes around us. A flame dancing on the end as the scent of sulfur hits my nose. "What do you feel?" he asks.

"My chest feels tight." The inside of my nasal cavity begins to itch and Ezra snatches the match from me, hand encasing the flame until it's smothered out. "What? What's wrong?"

"Your control. Magic doesn't start there." He narrows his eyes, grabbing another match for me. "Have you heard of Vena Amoris?"

"Sort of? It's why your wedding ring is worn on the fourth left finger. Because it's connected to your heart. But it's been disproven."

"No, it's been taken by people who have no knowledge of our ways. It does connect to your heart. In your case it's a little different but I'll assume it works the same." Ezra sparks the new match on his pant leg, tapping the unlit end against my ring. "Grasp the energy *here.*" His eyes travel up my arm to my chest. Warmth following the trail they make across my limbs. "Let it travel to your heart. Then, allow it to ricochet back to your hands." I grab the matchstick but he keeps hold of it, fingers surprisingly soft against my own. "Keep the flame. Let it go when I say."

"What if I level the arena?"

"You won't." Ezra releases the match and scoots away from me slightly.

"That didn't look very confident."

"You won't," he repeats as my eyes slide shut. "And open your eyes." I peek one open, the flame flickering back and forth. Ezra observes me with an unlit cigarette in hand. "You command the flame. Being frightened allows it to command you."

"Could you not light that then?" He grimaces, sliding the cigarette back into its pack and offering a small grunt of agreement.

I take a deep breath of clean air, imagining pulling the flame. Imagining it traveling down my fingertips and through my veins, scorching arteries and blood vessels in its wake.

The fire stills at the end of the match.

Although it doesn't move, warmth spreads from the tips of my fingers and swirls inside my arm. Electric tingles twining themselves up every nerve ending. Past my elbow, to my shoulder, and finally into my chest.

My ring vibrates in elated agreement as heat fills my racing heart. There's a sense of devoted loyalty in my grasp. The same thing I felt when touching the Philosopher's Stone.

"It's mine."

"Now let it ricochet," Ezra whispers. "Controlled."

The warmth ricochets out, faster than anticipated.

When energy hits my hand again, the response is instantaneous, the stick disintegrating within my grasp.

At once, my hand is encased in fire, ring pulsing brightly within the flames.

"Light the wood and snuff it out. It's about intention."

I clasp my hands together and pull them away. A rope of fire dangling between them. My eyes glued to the mesmerizing and morphing glow. It grows thicker and brighter between my palms. The blaze inching up both forearms until I frown.

The cloth around my wrists burns to ash and the flame seems to want to explore me. Inching upwards as I lean forward, grasping the wood in the fire pit. It burns in an instant but doesn't stop spreading, scraps of my hoodie falling to the grass in pieces. "Ezra?"

"Dismiss it."

*Will I accidentally send it into the grass? Scorch my friends in the process. Leave burnt bodies in my wake. Level the whole damn place? Will it be another repeat of graduation? Will I burn them like I—*

"Dismiss it!"

"I *can't.*"

"Yes, you can." He frowns. "It bids *your* desires. It's an extension of yourself."

"I can't! I don't—" The flames reach my shoulders and I release a strangled cry, moments from my clothes being nothing but ash.

Ezra clasps my hands within his own and I feel a strange pull as the fire is drawn away. Spiraling up his arms in glowing ribbons of orange and red, his hoodie going up in flames instead.

Alarmed screams ring out from all over the quadrant as people nearby dive for cover. A human torch holding my hands as all I can do is watch.

Ezra exhales the flames through his mouth. Fire pouring from his facial orifices and roaring flames so incendiary they could reach clouds above.

Is this all my fire? Is some of it his too?

All I know is he keeps the blast aimed upward. Saving me from finding out what it would have done to the field itself. And more importantly, the bodies on it.

In an endless blaze of glory, the fire is extinguished.

Ezra clenches my hands in a daze.

Unscorched.

*Unburnt.*

Olive chest glistening with sweat and containing old runes I can't place, dragons covering his body. Their depictions stretch over muscles that bulk and tense each time he shudders.

"Ezra! Ezra, are you okay?!" I crawl toward him as fast as I can. Cupping his cheeks and zeroing in on hazy eyes that slowly regain lucidity bit by bit, wondering if he might keel over at any moment from being charred internally.

He nods, shaking like he's chilled to the bone.

Josephine pushes through the gathered crowd, eyes filling with relief before she fixes me with a scathing glare. Her lips part before Ezra shakes his head.

"I'm fine. I'm good," Ezra rasps, appearing light-headed.

Drunk and sobered in an instant.

Even though it seems as if it pains him, his lips curl upwards, the first attempt at a smile I've seen him take in weeks.

"I'm so sorry. What can I do to—"

"What the fuck were you doing, New Blood? Trying to show off?" Josephine kneels down, physically pushing me away from him before rubbing her hand on his bare back.

"No? Of course not. It was supposed to be a small flame."

"Yeah right," she sneers. "You're lucky. You could've killed him!"

"Killed him?"

"Am I not speaking English?" She frets over Ezra and I scoot backward, pulling my knees into my chest. He turns to survey me, eyes tense with pain but softening for the briefest moment.

"Last one standing here looking lost gets sidelined," Ezra rasps.

Our audience scrambles away like a stampede of fast moving cattle.

Josephine stays, eyes like daggers in my chest. I'm no mind reader, but her most probable thoughts are fantasies of my death at her hands.

"You're fine," Ezra mutters. His chin rests atop her head, patting Josephine's back lightly.

When I meet his eyes again, they're strangely calm, forgetting to be angry with me in his tired state. "We'll pick this back up next session."

# CHAPTER 12

"I still don't understand." Jason hands his brother an ice pack and Russ presses it over the bump still growing on my forehead, a byproduct of passing out cold after tasting Suede's sleep sap. It was embarrassing enough in front of Agarwal and twenty New Bloods, but recounting the accident again is a special kind of torture.

"I miscalculated," Suede groans for the fiftieth time, elbows on the lunch table as she sulks over her untouched tray of pasta. "Don't you feel terrible for her, babe? Look how sad and fragile she looks right now. Like a baby bird with broken wings! You love baby birds."

"Did you hit your head too?"

"Suede," Russ interrupts. "Can I speak with you? *Privately?*"

"No." She sniffles, dabbing at dry tear ducts with her shirt sleeve. "I'm going through trauma. My brain's blocking out the events that led up to the accident."

Jason smooths a hand along the back of Suede's skull, gently bringing her temple to his lips. When he mouths something, she cracks her knuckles, shrugging slender shoulders and refusing to meet his gaze.

Russ's hands tighten on my ice pack, and I wince.

It isn't going to kill me, so there's no use making a fuss about

Suede's scheme. Even though it feels like my skull has been cracked open and pried apart. "It was an accident. We're good."

"Looks badass, Shiloh. I've heard fire affinities take bruises as a badge of honor," Jason says, seeming to think a month pretending I'm not here, and an enormous forehead knot, is enough of a punishment.

"That's what I thought. Who doesn't look cool with a forehead bruise?" I ask.

"Wow! At least one good thing can come out of—"

"Enough! Or I'll have you take that shit. When you stand up, maybe you'll finally have a backbone!" Russ snaps, his tone more frigid than it's ever been. My eyes widen as he swallows a large bite of tofu and chucks the ice pack on the table.

*"Icarus."* Jason holds Russ in a bone-chilling stare that halts conversation for minutes on end. My friend's shoulders sinking as he's the first to look away.

I squeeze Russ's hand under the table and he squeezes mine a little tighter.

"How's Jupiter?" Suede asks, attempting to break the tense silence.

"Alright."

"What's going on with Jupiter?" I ask.

"Jace has to force him into the sky recently. He's... sad about it."

"I'm sorry." I frown, wondering if the same thing is happening to Sunny.

Jason's face still sets in a hard line. Clearly not wanting to talk about pegasus or anything else at the moment. From the way his mouth pinches, I don't think he knows how to navigate being mad at his brother or being annoyed with his girlfriend. A war brewing in his mind as Suede tries again.

"Any closer with your Father?" she asks.

"No." He twists his Imaginifer band before scratching at his stubble.

The title is something that can't be stripped from him by anyone but the Sovereign himself, but Jason was taken out of First Year Casting and informed Ludi Bellorum's been axed too. A joint decision between Mr. Honestus and the Dean.

"I don't see how your participation in Ludi Bellorum wouldn't be great for optics."

"Maybe too good," Jason mutters. "Lions command from the head of a table, and march with their soldiers to battle. We don't petrify atop a copper throne. Only men like that would make her a Dean."

My eyes dart to his ring, shining the softest glow possible.

Over the past few weeks, I've realized he shields most things he says from prying ears.

I imagine it comparable to flexing muscles in my arms, lifting them above my head, and never setting them down. What he could do a few decades from now is unfathomable.

"You deserve it more than anyone else." Suede sniffles, *actual* upset now filling her eyes. Which may have more to do with his brush-off treatment than Ludi Bellorum.

Jason frowns, rubbing her back as his pinched expression wanes.

"Come here," he rasps.

Russ and I are a team against the onslaught of near pornographic tonguing that's begun on the other side of the table. A shaky whimper releases from Suede as Jason pillages her mouth and fists her sandy tresses to better sweep her tonsils. An earthy coconut scent flooding the air until Russ appears as if he's just sucked on a lemon. "Stars above, I think he's about to swallow her."

"She's about to swallow him back," I whisper, feeling sort of bad about it, but it's the sheer truth.

I tilt my head, and honestly, the embrace would be kind of hot if it weren't so horrifyingly up close and—yep. *Nope.*

Russ and I shudder in unison.

"Never a dull moment around here, is there?" he asks.

As if on cue, the liquid in our dishes begins to rise. So minuscule a movement I think that I imagine it, a tiny bead of water breaking from the still surface of the soup in front of me.

I lean closer to inspect the phenomenon. Dozens of tiny droplets warping and whirling in the air.

Russ inspects his drink just as intently, whispering his brother's name in a deathly serious tone as Jason unlatches himself from Suede's mouth.

"Someone's burning out," Jason says, eyes sweeping the cafe as he pulls Suede into his lap. Her body curls up in an instant. "Icarus—"

"I've got her."

"Burning out?" I ask.

Russ shields my head just before his protein smoothie explodes.

It coats his face and fixed glasses in tan sludge, the scent of peanut butter and bananas filling the air. "What's burning out?!"

The desperate cry to follow emits from a table full of New Bloods. A small framed first year clutching his skull, banging on his temples with closed fists as blue light shines from his left hand.

When his fists aren't enough, he leans forward, smashing his face against the oak tabletop as people scream in horror. His friends scrambling away and leaving him to fend for himself.

Over and over again, he bangs his head.

Midnight black sludge spilling down his face, pouring from not only the deep gash on his forehead but from his nose, eyes, ears and mouth too.

"Kill him!" Jason demands, voice booming from across the cafe as horror roots in my belly.

"What? No, help him!"

"He can't be helped, and he's not from Leonusver. He's sitting with the residents from Ardengris." His tone fills with frustration as the boy continues mutilating himself. My view of him warping as Jason's ring glows brighter.

"It doesn't matter where he's from! Look at what he's doing to himself!" I rise from my chair and slam into a thick barrier around our table. A solid wall of air keeps me from reaching the boy whose screams turn to wailing sobs. "Jason, drop it!" I bang against unyielding air, squinting to peer through the wavering barrier as the boy raises his hands and a girl with long blonde pigtails cries out, jerking in her chair.

"Blood bending," Russ whispers, her limbs contorting at an odd angle.

"We need to—"

"No. *We* don't need to do anything. *You* need to sit down. I'm protecting Leonusver residents, and you're putting people at risk!"

I finally notice the wavering air around a large section of the Cafe—not just our table.

Jason shields half of the people inside the building.

In another section, fire has sprung across the floor and risen to the ceiling. A firm barrier between the screaming boy and what is happening behind it.

What is left, in the middle of the cafe, is where it all happens. A Gold Star Water affinity with a strawberry blonde pixie cut crawling under tables, yelling at people to move.

She wastes no time, rising to her feet and pulling a dagger from the waistband of a New Blood, stabbing the boy straight in his carotid.

Inky blood spurts from the side of his neck like a geyser.

My knees can't seem to hold me upright anymore. I sink into my chair, watching the boy's awful screams turn to gurgles, hand clapped over his wound to staunch the flow of blood. Strangely enough, he's nodding, eyes lucid as she keeps him from falling to his knees.

I muffle a scream, tears springing to my eyes when the boy's body goes limp. Lifeless blue irises staring at the ceiling while black goo spurts from his neck, glowing ring cracking and disintegrating off his hand.

The Gold Star, who's covered in blood, thrusts him into the arms of his betrayers before she walks away. A relaxed aura inside the Cafe as chatter resumes as normal. People already working on their meals again by the time Jason's barrier drops.

As soon as it's down, I run.

"Wait!"

"Let her cool off, Icarus," Jason demands.

My tennis shoes thump against the ground, leaving my bag and food strewn across the lunch table as Russ continues calling after me, running and running until I've gotten outside and slammed directly into Ezra Alvarez, Josephine right at his heels.

His brows furrow in sheer surprise, steadying me while I shake, unable to stop the tremors in my hands.

"Don't *t*-touch me! Don't—" My sentence is choked off, incapable of finishing my thoughts through the flood of tears streaming down my cheeks.

"What happened?" Ezra brushes away my bangs to inspect the bruise and nasty gash deep on my forehead, tilting and turning my face. His voice is soft, and so are the hands that grip my jaw while trying to assess what is wrong with me.

I push him away, and when I can't get the words out fast enough, he attempts to walk past me and see what's happened for himself.

"Don't *g-go* in there!" My hands grasp his forearm, heels digging into concrete as he effortlessly drags me along with him, outright carrying me as I hang off his arm.

"Give me a name," he demands, an eerie calmness to his anger.

I shake my head rapidly, Ezra's gaze sweeping through the windows as we get closer. "You don't understand! We have to get out of here! We have to go! They killed him!"

Ezra tilts his head, and I choke out what's happened. His tense shoulders relax the farther I get into the explanation, warm eyes hardening to his regular indifference. "That happens."

"It *happens?*" I jerk backwards, and Josephine looks increasingly annoyed as I scramble away from both of them. "It *happens?!*"

He rubs a hand down his face in sheer agitation. "How has no one told you that it's a possibility?"

"I don't know! Maybe because I was put on an unwarranted probation for three weeks!?"

"You don't need to be in casting to know the stakes, Dreamer. It's common knowledge you're informed of before you ever put on a ring."

"No one told me." I wipe my eyes and nose with the sleeve of my oversized crew neck. "No one tried to help him."

"There is no help but a quick death. If you wouldn't be willing to do that for a stranger, you are weak. If you couldn't put a knife through the heart of someone you love, then you are as cowardly as they come. It is true mercy to kill someone before they lose themselves completely."

"To what?"

"Burnout. Stage one is Cortex Fracture. You're in pain, and you can't remember why. Stage two is Synaptic Breakdown. Your brain misfires. You harm others. You're a wounded animal with burnt blood and no humanity left. What do wounded animals do?"

My brain has a hard time centering itself, comprehending the death I'd just witnessed as *mercy* instead of *murder.* And I must take too long to think, because Josephine grows irritable.

"Stars above, do you suffer from mental retardation?" The question shocks the devastation from my system and makes me numb all over. Eyes flickering back and forth, unsure if I've heard her correctly.

"What?"

"Are. You. *Sloooow?* Seriously. I want to know before I hurt your feelings."

"Josie," Ezra cautions. "Apologize."

"For what?" She fixes him with an innocent stare, and he traces his tongue against his cheek. "If I were trying to offend her, I would have asked if her ring's on the wrong hand because she confuses her rights and lefts. I would have asked if she didn't understand the word *dismiss*, because she's cognitively aged three. I would have asked if she spends her spare time licking windows that have been freshly cleaned with brain corrosive chemicals instead of studying. She's now the lowest-ranked fire affinity in her year. These are honest concerns."

A heavy silence follows her rant. So thick I could wade through it.

"I'm not stupid."

"No shit. You're too duplicitous to be stupid. I asked if you're slow, so I can talk to you like you're slow. But, I'm starting to think that's not the case. I usually tolerate the disabled, but you have a slap-able face."

"Enough! I mean it. Right now, Josephine." Ezra fixes her with a stare that could melt ice. A silent exchange between them, that he appears to win as she releases a held breath.

"Fine. I'm sorry if you felt offended by my line of questioning. Someone should've diagnosed you sooner."

She doesn't pause to gauge my reaction. Instead, looking up at Ezra as if to say, *Look, is that better?*

His face twists in disdain. "You used to be better than this, White."

This is the first time I've ever seen it. A flash of pain, a sense of being bothered, and she covers it up by looking through him. "I'm the same person I've always been, except you think you're too good for me now."

"That's not remotely the case, and you know it."

Instead of a verbal sparring match, she emits a noise of dissatisfaction, shoulder-checking me on her way back to the dorms.

"Do you have to blow shit up everywhere you go?" Ezra asks.

*"Me?"* He pulls a cigarette from his pocket, lighting it with the tip

of his finger, stuffing it in his mouth and taking a long drag as the smoke wafts into my face.

The action makes me snap. Jumping to snatch the stick from between his lips. Throwing it onto the ground and stomping it beneath my tennis shoes. I feel only a minor pang of guilt as a staff member comes by to sweep it up. "What is wrong with you sick fucks!?"

He raises an eyebrow, stooping until there's a breath of space between us. "When you start using magic, your prefrontal cortex is over-stimulated, and it misfires when you're emotionally unstable. It's permanently rewiring your neurons and synapses. The simple truth is, that boy's body couldn't handle the change. There was *nothing* to be done. It's something you accept long before you come here." Ezra clenches his hands and can't stop himself from adding, "I've known Josie since we were in diapers. She would think harsh things, but under normal circumstances would have the self-control not to say them."

"I'm so sure."

"You don't appear to have the best self-control either, so I would have some sympathy for her."

"Sympathy? I'm not any of those things, Ezra. And even if I was, so what!? To experience the world a little differently, gives her the right? Fine. I'll happily wear that badge, but your loser girlfriend is a bigot, and she'll have to live with *that*, and so will you."

Ezra avoids eye contact while he pulls out another cigarette.

At least this time he angles the smoke off to the side.

"How do you prevent burnout?" I ask, peering through the windows and observing my friends huddle together in conversation at our table.

"Give up magic. Otherwise, uncertainty is the price that comes with power. We get maybe a few a year, and by the time you're twenty-two you're usually in the clear."

"So Jason's okay?"

Ezra chuckles darkly. "Founder kids don't burn out. Worry about the Honestus boys a little less. They're going to continue thinking they have a claim to you if you let them."

He walks past me, into the cafe, and I make a break for the dorms.

The boys scream, and the sound of a forehead cracking open racketing inside my brain.

I don't notice she's in my room until I'm sliding off my sweater. Releasing a shriek when Josephine clears her throat, and holding my crewneck against my braless frontside before sliding back into it.

"*Ew.* Don't flatter yourself. Not one person is looking at your tits and thinking anything besides what mosquito got to you twice."

"How did you even get in here?!"

"These flimsy locks practically beg people to break in." She plucks Suede's stuffed elephant off her mattress and rolls her eyes, throwing it back on her pillow with a heavy thud.

"Get out!" I yelp, hurling a fluffy pillow at her that barely makes an impact.

Josephine directs me to sit on my own bed. Unfazed as I plop at the edge with a wary gaze. She surveys my desk and sweeps up a bag of chocolates Russ left for me, opening them and popping one into her mouth. "Do you hate sheep?"

"What are you talking about?"

"Do you despise people who stare and mock you? Hope the whole flock goes extinct?"

"Do you?" I frown. "Despise people in general, I mean?"

"I don't have enough care for people to despise them. I just think they'd be much better off stuck inside docile mammals. Your turn."

"Sheep are led, so I try not to despise them."

"*Try,*" she emphasizes. "They can survive by themselves, you know."

"Wild sheep." A fleck of nail polish chips under my thumb. "The rest have been bred and domesticated for wool production. Now they need shepherds. And, even wild ones get trapped with a flock mentality."

"Go on." She pops more of my candies in her mouth, intrigue in her eyes.

"Well, sheep herd together to protect from predators. Realistically, they could walk off a cliff if they're in a pack. More natural than self-isolation. I suppose they feel it's better to, um, go down together than be picked off one by one."

"Correct. They don't dream of being free, they yearn that others are herded for company. They don't pound their hooves to rattle the ground, they bleat until shepherds are forced to put them down. I've lost the will to care about what happens to flocks. They bring it on themselves."

"You don't take any issue with breeders and predators?"

"Survival of the fittest. People need sweaters, and tigers need to eat."

"The world doesn't have to be like that."

"If you're not stupid, don't play it," Josephine all but spits. "Lions, Tigers, Bears and Sheep. Apex predators and docile prey. None of them are so dangerous as wolves. I'd watch out for them if I were you, little lamb."

"Are you a wolf?"

"I'm asking the questions. Tell me something, Shiloh Benson. What separates us from animals?"

"Our... complexities. Our reasoning. Our empathy. We can understand the meaning of being finite. We can voice our worry. We can do something about it. And when you take those things away..." I trail off, and Josephine smirks, nodding her head as I shake mine back and forth.

"Congratulations. You're not a lamb after all."

"What's left to be? I'm not some jungle leader or nefarious wolf."

"An Ethologist such as myself. Green, but to no fault of your own." Josephine dusts off her skirt as if something has been settled inside her before she pockets the rest of my candies. "I'll warn you once more, window licker. Purely as an act of good faith because I'm positive you have a severe case of the tizzies."

"Oh. My. God. You need to leave."

"And you need to stay away from Ezra and stop batting your slutty eyes."

"How can you understand what sets us apart and still be the most unkind, *bitter* person I have ever met?"

"Candy dissolves in the rain. Cry about it elsewhere, Skeeter Bites."

"You're in *my* room!"

"And look at that, I still don't owe you kindness!" She walks forward and stoops to my eye level until I cringe backwards. "I know when someone wants what's mine."

"This is about a man? You know how many men are outside right now that don't reek of nic and tobacco? You can have this one. Just leave me alone."

"A man is the least of my ambitions in this life. I'm not sorry for calling it like I see it. So stay out of my way, or you will be."

"Don't—" Josephine knocks over the cactus on my desk, cracking the pot ever so slightly before shoving past my roommate, who stands in the doorway with wide hazel orbs. I guess she's decided to return from her long stay in Jason's den.

"Did she take your candy?" Suede frowns, readjusting the strap of her yellow duffle bag, bursting full of clothes.

"Yes," I mumble, flopping face-first onto my bed. "And I'm not talking about it anymore, or I'll start crying."

"I still have those minty ones?"

"No thank you."

"Alrighty. Suit yourself."

# CHAPTER 13

I show up to First Year Casting in the most flame-retardant piece of clothing I brought with me. The wool sweater is ugly and scratches with each turn, itching my forearms so much I contemplate stuffing it in my backpack for safekeeping, pretty sure I'd ripped the tags off Dad's donation for this exact reason.

But, if I've learned anything from Josephine, it's that no one is hesitant to point out they've mistaken my tits for mosquito bites.

As I'm double-knotting my laces, three bodies plop down in front of me, casting shadows on my white tennis shoes. The familiar faces staring down at me are those of the other Imaginifers.

"Hi."

"Hi...? I'm Shiloh."

"Bridger Emerson." The one who'd greeted me replies with a wink. He's devastatingly handsome with a slit shaved in his left eyebrow and deep brown eyes and skin.

"Mai Black." He motions his head towards the round faced woman with a fringe cut tumbling an inch past her shoulders, hair dyed a navy blue so dark it may as well be black. She tips her head in greeting, a shiny silver nose hoop piercing her left nostril.

"Arlo Romanov." Bridger tilts his head toward the long haired brunette that observes me warily. I turn mine side to side. Ezra's nowhere in sight. "He's not here yet."

"Oh. Are you saying I should tuck into a tight ball?"

Bridger chuckles but I'm only halfway joking. I'd gotten forced to dunk my face in toilet water exactly two and a half times before Sam had learned to fight and I'd learned to take hits.

"Funny, New Blood." Mai surveys me, a feline smile on her lips. "We've heard a lot about you."

Arlo breaks his silence next, suspicion lacing his voice. "What's your deal?"

I glance toward my castor ring. "You're talking about this?"

Bridger takes my hand. His calloused grasp is firm, but gentle, as he pulls it closer to examine. "Hell of a rock, Little One." The other two nod in agreement, leaning in close to my stone as a tingle hits my cheeks.

The tone of which he says *little one* is as non-condescending as someone can get about my malnourishment.

As if it's only ironic and he thinks of me as something bigger.

Bridger meets my eyes, drawing my knuckles to his lips. The softest kiss placed directly on my ring as we exchange grins.

"*Cuck,*" Mai coughs under her breath.

Despite her insult, his smile remains warm. An intense interest that isn't innately sexual, but flirtatious all the same.

"Have you thought about switching Imaginifer's? Ezra and I are buds. It shouldn't be an issue."

"Emerson," Mai starts.

"I'd love to if you don't mind." I attempt not to sound too eager to cling to his offered safety and it's as hard as asking the ocean to stay still. "But you have even numbers. I don't want to mess up your group dynamic."

"Not an issue." Bridger squeezes my hand as a heavy gaze lands on my back. A warm blanket from the glares of Ezra and Josephine, both more frigid than normal.

Ezra blows a smoke cloud in my direction. "Didn't I ask you guys to stay away from her?"

"Doesn't ring a bell."

"Then I'll tell you this time. Benson's off limits."

"Me and the little one have decided for ourselves, as people do. We're going off on our own now. Right?"

"Yep." I chirp, internally screaming for him to sweep me away and run. "Bridge doesn't mind odd numbers."

"Bridge?" Josephine rolls her eyes. "How... *familiar.*"

"I formally decided to drop the R," he says.

"When?"

"When you did. Gave this one an all access pass." Bridger's lips twitch with a stifled grin. "Integral question to our newly formed alliance, sweetheart. Would you rather be the peanut butter or the jelly?"

"Mmm, I'll take Jelly. You can be crunchy peanut butter. It's better for you."

"I'm smoother than that. What about the runny kind? Isn't that healthy?"

"I'd have to Google that."

"What's a *Google?*" Bridger frowns. "Never mind. You'll teach me later."

"Get up," Ezra demands, his backpack thudding against the dirt.

Bridger rises to his feet, dropping my hand in the process.

His fingers twitch at his sides, raising them to flaming horns before he charges.

Ezra sidesteps him and Josephine out of the way and she groans Bridger's name, breaking away from the match forming in front of her.

There's a playful glint in their eyes the longer I observe.

Especially Bridger. Dark irises glinting with devious energy, hands throwing off embers as he makes the first leap.

As they collide, I decide this reckless boy with a kind heart will someday be a good friend of mine. He doesn't dress flashy like all the other men here. Boots more scuffed and clothing made of denim and cotton. After a few minutes of knowing him, I could swear up and down he lacks a cruel bone in his body.

The men scramble and roll, daggers drawn from seemingly thin air. A flurry of fists and fire that consumes my every sense.

Their weapons clash as they hop to their feet, each already having drawn deep cuts. The metallic scent hangs heavy in the air shadowed by cedar wood and oranges.

The sparring match is over before I know it. The weight of heavy disappointment in my chest as Bridger charges Ezra one last time, a bull catching sight of a red curtain.

Ezra's reach is strong and fast, putting him into a headlock as they scuffle. Bridger tries to escape but his fire is snatched away and dissipated into nothing.

"*Flame Thief!*" Bridger spits in Latin.

Ezra laughs, unable to hide a full dimpled grin and scrambling for so long I wonder if Bridger might pass out. "Cede, motherfucker!"

"Fine! I Cede! I Cede!"

Ezra releases him in an instant. Their combined laughter echoing around us. I can't help but join in as the large man hurls insults.

Every time I stop laughing, Bridger's incredulous face brings stitches to my side.

The only one who's *not* amused is Josephine.

My laugh only tapers off when I find Ezra's gaze. His outward appearance relaxed, but brown eyes tense.

"I was rooting for you, Bridge."

"Don't worry, I'm coming back for you."

"Perhaps bulk up a bit more," Mai suggests. "The calves could use some work."

"No one be fooled by the underdeveloped calves, I'm packing." Bridger lets his arm fall like an elephant trunk and we burst into laughter until everyone besides Arlo looks annoyed.

"You're an idiot," Josephine seethes.

"Oooouuu. You want me so bad," Bridger says, pretending his fingers cast a spell as Josephine rolls her eyes. "You can't stand how bad you want me. We're about to tongue-kiss, naked."

"In your dreams."

"We do depraved things in my dreams, Mrs. Emerson." He catches her hand as she stalks past, brushing his thumb across her right ring finger.

Josephine blinks rapidly before yanking away from him, flipping me off as she passes.

It plants a gleam of victory in his eyes and a seed of curiosity in my head. Bridger crouches next to me as he says, "I'll see what I can do about your grade. No promises, but I may be able to give you some extra points for—"

"Get to your own kids," Ezra orders, the both of us ignoring him as we continue our private exchange.

"You and Ezra?" I wince.

"Love him like my own blood, but don't let him fuck you," Bridger grunts, rising to leave along with Mai and Arlo.

I'm unsure if his advice is figurative or literal but my insides warm regardless.

Ezra nears to squat before me, the scent of Tobacco clinging to his sweater. "Look at Audere."

Suede currently lingers on the outskirts of a group in the Air quadrant, silent and composed—posture slumped as she picks at a stray speck of dust on her skirt.

"Now look to your right." I use my peripheral vision on a group of pissed off Fire affinities that clump together. "There's sharks in the water, ready for new blood. They don't like people receiving special treatment they haven't earned. Stay away from Imaginifers."

"Oh."

Ezra straightens to his full height. "Get up. You're behind."

I swallow hard as I scramble to my feet, struggling to keep up with his long strides. The smell lingering in his wake with every step.

"Have you ever thought about quitting smoking?"

"Have you ever thought about minding your own business?" Ezra casts me an odd look as I smile. "What's funny?"

"You blow smoke in my face constantly. It feels like my business."

"I don't need your concern."

"Just tell me what would make you stop," I sigh, itching my wool bitten forearms.

He laughs to himself, thinking long and hard before he says, "Do something that surprises me and they're done."

"Really?"

"No one surprises me. More often than not, people are exactly who you think them to be at first glance. I doubt you're the exception."

"Ezra, I'm not a boogie man in your closet? I could show you I'm not a danger to—"

He stops mid stride and I slam into his back. "I'm unclear where you got confused but I'm *also* your Imaginifer. I don't need to be shown a damn thing besides you controlling your magic."

We make it to the fire pits without further incident, picking up right where our first lesson left off. "Last week you started off strong."

"Then what made me lose control?"

"You didn't lose control," he sighs. "You refused to accept it. To be afraid of the flame, is to be afraid of yourself and what you truly are. No one can ignore a blazing bonfire once it erupts. Once you accept that, you can never go back."

"I'm not afraid of myself," I insist, tilting my chin up in defiance.

"You are." Ezra places his elbows on his kneecaps, leaning toward me from where he sits on a rock mere inches away. "What is fire meant to do, Dreamer?"

"Burn."

"What is its *only* other alternative?"

"To get snuffed out."

"You have a flaming soul of fire that will burn or be extinguished. Your choice. Don't waste my time or your own again. Light the damn match and accept that it's yours."

Taking a deep breath, I repeat the steps and order my match to my beck and call. Except this time, I accept it as part of myself. Imagining pulling it from inside my soul. My essence the gasoline I use to spread this small flame.

Energy twirls through my veins, scorching arteries and blood vessels in its wake as the fire stills at the end of the match.

Electric tingles twine themselves up every nerve ending. Past my elbow, to my shoulder, and finally into my chest—my ring vibrating in agreeance.

A feeling of heat in my racing heart.

A sense of devoted loyalty in my grasp.

*Mine.*

I let the energy flow into my hand and suddenly it's blazing. My match disintegrated. The orange red glow becomes a whitish blue flame dancing on my fingertips.

The brilliant glow should melt anything it touches. I sense its heat as air ripples near my fingertips, tickling and licking at me like a pet.

I gasp as I watch it, chest rising and falling over my quick breaths, a pyromaniac at heart.

"Hot," Ezra whispers.

"What?" It wavers at my surprise.

"Your flame." He swallows roughly. "Cool it down. You're burning too brightly. It'll wear you out fast."

*Inhale, exhale, inhale, exhale.*

The flame dims to an orangish red but I still hold the feeling inside me.

In this moment, it isn't anything to be scared of. It's energy. Neither good nor bad. I get to choose if it harms or it doesn't. Because it's *me.*

I spend the entire class relighting the same piece of wood until it's charred and disintegrated to nothing. Going through an entire pack of matches until he's confident I can dismiss a flame in my sleep.

"Letting it go is not as hard as I thought it'd be." I speak mostly to myself. Ezra hasn't spoken more than a few sentences the past hour.

"Great. Now we focus on giving it away and you're caught up enough to run courses." Ezra rises and I follow him to an empty patch of the field. "This is essential."

"It's different from what you do?"

He raises a small ball of fire in his hand. "Yes."

"How?"

"Catch and I'll tell you." He underhand tosses the glowing orb and I grab it with both hands, cradling the fire in my palms as it responds to new ownership, a weight to the element that's simultaneously light as air. "I gave that to you, Dreamer. And if I wanted to, I could take it back. I can take any fire I want."

I observe the object in my hands.

It responds to me. It feels like mine. But I don't doubt him. Not after the way he absorbed my flames.

"But, you won't?"

"No. You're going to give it to me."

"How?"

"Here's the deal. I'm going to hold out my hand. I'm not going to *take* the flame, I will receive what you throw me. Do you understand?" I shake my head as he continues. "If you throw a flaming fireball at me without the intent to pass it. You're going to burn me. Now make it cool as can be, like a lightbulb and pass it towards me."

My lips part as I clutch the ball tighter in my grasp. "I'm not doing that."

Ezra raises his brows. "You're not doing that?"

"Why can't you take it again?" He takes a step forward and I take a step backward.

"That's not the point of the exercise."

"What is the point?"

"For you to learn control." Ezra takes another step forward, moving towards me until he's a few inches away. I have to tilt my chin up to continue staring at his face. "That's the key. Think of it as an extension of yourself. If you are sharing a piece of yourself you get to control how it reacts.

I worry at my lip as his gaze traces its edges. "You don't get scared of hurting someone?"

"Being scared is senseless." He holds out his hand, palm facing upward, fingers wiggling in challenge. Deep brown irises a pit I could stumble into, ready to consume me if I let them.

I hover mine above. Placing the orb in his grasp and willing it to cool to candlelight.

Ezra's face remains stoic. Giving no indication of feeling anything as I sense the jumping nerves under each lick of my fire. "Are you okay?"

"Tickles," he admits. "You're not burning me so that's a good sign."

On his instruction, I rip my hands away, the tingle of power gone as soon as I break contact.

A gust of air escapes as I exhale a sigh of relief.

Ezra releases a shudder, shaking his hand as the flames dissipate, seeming to have been more worried than he let on.

After a brief pause, he snaps to attention with rapid fire instructions.

He teaches me how to make shapes, like small fire stars I can throw.

For some reason they don't singe his clothes as they should but he curses when they touch his arms.

He also teaches me how to create a whip of fire that immediately becomes my favorite.

Starting with a ball, I fashion the shape into a snakelike whip, making the temperature that of a lightbulb.

I hurl it forward, the fire snaking around his arm, a solid rope of soft glowing light that I still firmly control.

If I wanted to, I could make it hotter and hotter. So full of heat that it sears off his arm.

Instead the whip gives a gentle caress, snaking up to twine around him, binding his arms and flicking at his nose.

He wrinkles it at the ticklish gesture and a soft laugh escapes when I pull it back, the snake dissipating as I command.

Ezra nods curtly, in indication that we're done. "You can control your flame now."

"That's it?" I frown.

"It was fast," he admits begrudgingly. "I couldn't do that when I started. It took me weeks. Takes most people weeks."

Before I can respond, there's a gentle shake of my shoulders. I grin when I notice it's Bridger, his backpack slung over one shoulder and a playful gleam in his eyes.

"Want to come back to my dorm and teach me about *Google?*"

"Yeah." I rock back and forth from toe to heel. "Then, you can teach me—" Ezra throws me a heated glare and it's a stroke of luck that the Earth quadrant was dismissed minutes ago as Russ comes into view. "Actually... I forgot, Russ and I are going on a date tonight."

I place his hand on my waist, meeting his eyes and silently begging him to play along.

"Damn Icarus. Got that dog in you."

Bridger nods in approval, dapping him up like a long lost brother. A wide grin on my face until Russ replies, "Yes. I do have, uh, a *dog* in me. But we don't want to publicize—*Ooof.*" I elbow his stomach and he grunts, glasses slipping down his nose bridge. "On second thought, it could get serious tonight. We're excited to explore this budding relationship in a consensual and supportive manner."

I release a strangled laugh, standing on my tiptoes and clapping a hand over his lips.

"Isn't he silly?" I ask. "Come on... baby? Walk me back to my dorm?" Russ nods up and down, licking my fingers as we walk away. "Ew?"

He grins, patting my hip. "So, *baby*. When's our first date?"

"You're never letting me live this down, are you?"

"Can't. I see you and everything shoots straight up."

"Icarus Amias Honestus!" I dodge him as he attempts to land his mouth on mine, lips landing on my stomach instead, blowing raspberries until screeched laughter expels.

He hurls my body like a sack of potatoes over his shoulder on full display. And as we exit the arena, I notice Ezra is still watching. Along with everyone else in the fire quadrant while I plead to be set down.

"You will pay for this!" I grumble as we reach the safety of my room.

Russ tosses me onto my bed with a rough thud. "I know! How am I going to explain our breakup to my Mother?! She'll be heartbroken!"

"How would she know?" As if on cue, a device in his pocket rings. "Oh. I'm sorry."

"It's alright," he says, declining a call without pulling it from his pocket. "We'll make out in the courtyard once or twice. Then, we'll start an argument in the soup line to sell the better off as friend's story." Russ declines a second call with frightened eyes. "How would you feel if I touched you intimately in public?"

"I'm sorry, *what?*"

"Throw this dogged man a bone," Russ pleads, falling to his knees before me. "People already think I'm a loser. If I lose you this quickly, I'm a pussy who couldn't do sex right."

"Jesus, fine. You can smack my ass."

"Grab...?"

"I guess? And it wouldn't hurt if you said it was big. You know, to like *really* sell it. Maybe pitch a tent if I back up? I heard guys can make that happen pretty quickly. Mostly in situations they shouldn't."

"I need more male friends," he sighs.

I lean over to kiss his cheek. "And no making out. My first kiss will be when I'm in mind-melting, world ending, Universal sent *love*. Full stop. And then, after many dates and growing tits, I'll lose my virginity with sexy lingerie and silk sheets and music and flavored—" Russ puts me in a headlock and we wrestle one another to the floor, bursting into guffaws when we're a tangled heap on the rug.

"Flavored what?" He frowns.

"Actually, it's none of your business. It's *my* fantasy, not yours."

"Right."

# CHAPTER 14

"I'm not actually going on a date tonight. You know that right?"

"It's called having fun," Suede says, lining my lips and swiping a coat of clear gloss atop the neutral shade. "A little mindless distraction never hurt anybody." She ties my hair into a low ponytail with a white ribbon, styling me in stilettos and a blood-red satin dress that may as well be magic. It has a slit up one side that practically meets my hip bone. And for once, my boobs are full with extra padding on the cups, the dress hugging curves that I was unaware I could possess. Cheeks rouged with maroon and lashes coated with mascara that widens my eyes impossibly.

The mirror has always been a jagged knife in my own psyche. Never coming away from it feeling anything less than worse about myself. But right now I feel desirable. Years of name-calling on the back burner for the truth that resides in my own reflection.

Somehow, Suede's made me look like a woman.

"I can't believe I lied about going on a date with Russ."

"He's excited that everyone believed you," Suede giggles.

It's the truth. Russ had a skip in his step all day, saying if people thought he'd pulled me things are surely looking up for him. "Would going on a date with him be such a bad thing?"

"Russ is handsome," I sigh.

"Exactly. And now that you've admitted it, you *are* going on a date. Jason and I demanded he be here in an hour."

"Suede."

*"Whaaaaat?"*

"No chance." She glares at me through the mirror. *Glares!* "What?!"

"He's better than Alvarez and you think he's hot."

"Thinking isn't a crime and I value more than what's on the outside. Why would I spend my time pining over a man who looks through me and has a stabby girlfriend?"

"So there's no interest there?"

"I can't keep up, are you trying to pimp me out to Russ or to Ezra?"

"Both? Neither? I don't know! I'm trying to get you laid so you stop antagonizing me about talking to the staff."

It's almost comically relevant when Suede rises to answer a knock at the door, picking the note card off the tray and shutting it in the smiling staff member's face without acknowledgement.

"Thank you!" I shout to him through the heavy oak as Suede tears into the fancy card stock.

She waves the card in my direction. "You've been summoned by the Dean."

"Do I have to go?"

"A summons isn't a suggestion here." When I nibble at my pinky nail, debating the validity of her statement, she pulls my hands from my mouth, handing me the envelope and patting my shoulder in good nature. "Go. Get it over with. I'm sure it's nothing."

"You're sure?"

"Forty percent. But better safe than sorry."

*"Oh."*


THE DEAN'S office is located on the same floor where the Welcome Ceremony took place.

Admittedly, I'm creeped out on the journey upward. Heels echoing in empty halls lit only by flickering sconces on the wall. Swooping to the corner office until I come upon a large rectangular door of midnight black—silver plaque in the center reading ***Dean Fern Alvarez*** in large imposing letters.

I knock against the door to alert her that I've arrived and notice it's slightly ajar. The sound of piano coming from inside the room. When I twist the intricate knob, fashioned in the shape of a serpent, the heavy door opens to reveal purgatory.

If I could imagine death, and the judgment that comes after, her office is its waiting room.

Sterile, cold, and lacking any personal items to distinguish her taste.

A desk of black marble sits at its center. Around the size of a standard kitchen island.

The oversized leather chair placed behind it is empty.

Also empty, are two angular chairs in front of it.

The room's gray cement floor is devoid of carpet. Making the sound of the piano more haunting than the notes that play.

Large windows fill up one wall, bringing light to this dark space, the entire starry cosmos visible behind it.

I discover none other than Ezra Alvarez is responsible for the soft melody, seeming to be lost in a trance until I clear my throat.

My presence startles him, hands fumbling on the keys as he turns my way. Chocolate irises dragging head to toe until he mutters, "I'll never know a minute of peace in this lifetime."

Ezra pulls out a cigarette and heads toward the wall of windows. Sliding open an eight-foot-tall sheet of glass and leaning forward, placing his elbows on the windowsill. His fingers twitch until the cigarette is lit, taking a long and shaky drag.

"Hi." I wince. "Why are you here?"

"Why are *you* here? Don't you have a date with a Lion?"

He gives me another once over, eyes tensing as they drag along the curve of my hips and the swell of my breasts—lingering on the slit up my thigh.

I fumble with the clasp of my purse, pulling out the creamy stationery with his mother's handwriting as a shield.

Ezra barks out a laugh as I approach him, pointing to the identical envelope he'd left atop the piano.

"Do you think we're in trouble?"

"I'm sure the answer will become clear soon enough," he deadpans.

"How long will we have to wait? I have a date that I'm supposed to be on soon. You heard him. Next level for us tonight. So, ya know what that means. He's going to... fuck... me?"

I look over my own shoulder for an escape route as Ezra says, "Yeah. I'm sure you're aching to be fucked respectfully."

"Consensually and supportively," I correct with flaming cheeks.

*Kill. Me. Now.*

"Right."

I approach the open panel, settling on the obvious as we peer toward the sky rather than each other. If only to ease the tension so thick I can wade through it with a butter knife.

"The stars." My face tingles and I'm grateful for the dimly lit office space, even more grateful for the shade of my skin. Both working in tandem to mask the blood that always rushes to my cheeks. "They're beautiful here."

I expect a snarky reply as he exhales another drag, but his next words are genuine. "My people believe they hold souls. After all, energy can't naturally be destroyed. Only transferred, stored, and dispersed. After death, souls pick stars and wait."

"For what?"

*"Wait for me in the stars, when we meet again, we will run together to the light,"* Ezra says this in Latin then repeats it in English. Each time the words roll off his tongue like a hypnotic spell. "It's something you say to people you can't imagine another lifetime not loving."

"So, the light is...?"

"A transfer of energy. Souls bound through something deeper than blood to the next life." He turns contemplative while ashing his cig against his palm, dusting the soot outside. "We used to believe we're all fragments of the Universe experiencing itself over and over again. Until eventually, everyone has come to a higher state of being. When all stars burn out and there's no more experience to be had."

"Used to?" I tilt my chin toward the stars above, full of souls waiting in earnest to meet their next experience, twinkling for their loved ones as if to shout that they're inside.

"Couldn't prove it. As many answers as we've found, for good reason, there are secrets the Universe keeps to itself. It has to in order to protect us." Ezra's dimples pop out and I have the strange urge to trace them, hands tightening on the windowsill instead. "Wouldn't we all off ourselves if we knew there was a safe place for us to run to? Away from the challenges of human existence before we decide to try again?"

"Depends. Sometimes I think that the price of sentient living is too high to pay. But there are bells to remind me. There's reasons—"

"Are you about to tell me everything happens for a reason? Because there's trillions of ways your life could go and none of them are predetermined by some higher being."

"No. I was saying you find reasons good enough to remain when senseless things happen, or you wait for them to present themselves. Billions of people firmly believe there's an after already. They're still around. There's something to that."

"Faith isn't fact. The fact is, we stick around to make use of the sure things we have here. The something you see is uncertainty."

"I think it's hope." Ezra turns his back to the stars, arms crossed over his chest as he observes me. "What? Belief isn't about what's true or false. If you carry something with you, think it enough times, live your life as if it's true, then it's more powerful than a fact could ever be. It's manifested to tangible lived reality. Have you ever argued with someone about their belief in God? You won't win unless their faith is already shaky or they learn to believe in something stronger. Eternal life is the end all be all."

"Are you religious?" Ezra asks.

"Would that be a problem?"

"According to you, there'd be no point in continuing this conversation."

"My best friend, sister actually, was adopted from China by a couple who couldn't have biological children. And her father, for lack of better word, always claimed to be *God-fearing*. But he'd still come home from work and yell, and scream, and... other things. So, she'd spend every weekend at my house and most weeknights too. Then, still want to attend church on Sundays. My family made it this whole thing. Tried out a new one each month. And my driver, Vincente, is Catholic. I'd surprise him every now and then. Play piano for his congregation. So, churchgoer... *technically*. Religious? The jury is hung."

"What grand revelation are you waiting on?"

"I'm not. I just haven't finished the Bible. What if there's something in there that makes me change my mind?"

"The first book wasn't enough for you? Lot's wife may as well have been Orpheus. Is Hades a King you'd bow to?"

"I'll never bow to a King. But it's interesting that you've read up on religion and think I'm idiotic for wanting to do the same. To turn every stone for the people I love. It's okay to have questions?"

"I want to make it crystal clear that I've never thought you were an idiot? You don't have to lack intelligence to be sucked into a cult. All it takes is exploitability. Which, you don't lack."

"Am I exploitable or accessible? I haven't kneeled at an altar, I just sing songs and throw money in collection? Trust me, I've been in *cult-ier* places." I wave my hand around the office, and Ezra laughs. "What?"

"Without fail, your people slap God onto every form of currency because they are ruled by one thing. And judging by the fact that you have a personal chauffeur, you haven't just kneeled to their King, you've rolled before their puppet masters and done tricks like a dog."

"*Oh.* Wow. Okay. I'm... having an *awesome* time tonight. You, sir, must be *really* fun at parties!" I pat his shoulder, and Ezra stiffens at my touch. "So... personable. I imagine you and your girlfriend sit in the corner, pointing out which New Blood to bully that day?"

"Would you have to imagine because you're not invited to them?" I laugh and Ezra sighs, reeling back his annoyance. "This doesn't bring me joy, Dreamer. But yes, I find vindication in knowing what lies I allow to be forced down my throat and made to swallow. *God* will never be one of them."

"What's your belief then?"

"Control of self and subjects. On the islands, we hold a festival for Yule. And when December comes around, we don't tell our children there's a diabetic red-coated elder sliding down our chimneys because it's just not true. And guess what? They're still happy to celebrate in the morning. So why teach them to accept something so fictional to behave themselves? Tell them they need to be good because you're their parent, you acquire their gifts and food and that's the end of the discussion."

"Except, it's not? It's necessary to believe in something larger than yourself to maintain your humanity. Using faith to subjugate human beings on the pathway to salvation is what is *delusional.* Or, misguided, maybe? I think those people are really scared to not exist. They yearn for eternity so badly, it's easy to sell out their neighbors with the promise of receiving it. And they're convinced that when they reach it, they won't suffer for what they've done on Earth because their horrors will be forgiven. They believe it, Ezra. They're not evil, they're—"

"Cowards?"

"Frightened. Fearful. Hurting others because they live without a love that can't be rescinded. My parents say to give grace to people who've sold their love for human beings away out of self preservation. It's a harder life to love everyone. It breaks you a million times over because not everyone will love you back." I tilt my head in contemplation. "My original point was if you're still alive right now, and believe in an afterlife, it's not uncertainty that keeps you breathing."

"How do you feel about the threat of damnation? Could that keep someone from slitting their own wrists?"

"Damnation for taking your own life is not a belief that equates to an eternity of peace. If I entered gates and left gentle souls behind, I'd spend the rest of my eternity mourning or I wouldn't be myself anymore. There's extremists, but you can't account for outliers when speaking so generally about the human race. To stay alive, with the promise of a waiting paradise, is to believe in a better now. A better here, and better future, for everyone. And most importantly, that you'd want to be a part of building it in any way you can before you rest. The issue is the ways people go about doing it. Some people's better makes this place a worse existence."

"What if we experience while we can and then crumple to nothing? If only believers keep their humanity, what about Atheism, Dreamer? How do you communicate with the unfaithful?"

"Well, I have to acknowledge my bias. Energy isn't destroyed so I can't fully get behind the phrase, *crumple to nothing.*" Ezra chuckles, motioning for me to continue. "Shocker. Maintaining belief is even more imperative for an Atheist. If you believe we have this one place and one life and you don't wish to make this world better, what would be the point of experiencing any of it at all? The things you did, the material items you owned, all of it would be for nothing. Oblivion would rip any ounce of its existence away. Some may argue it's good to live in the moment but when all moments are erased, what's left? What impact have you had on the world? The people, the lessons, the art, the inventions, the progress of existence... you do it all for *them*. To be here, just to make it worse, is plain evil."

"Some people are just evil."

"Some people are selfish and believe their selfishness serves others. Or they're sick and disturbed. Or, they're in pain and decide others need to share their burden to stay alive. There's no point to evil for evil's sake. That'd be the worst plot ever written. If that's the case, the Universe has a faulty pen."

Ezra rubs his face and appears much older than his twenty-one years. "Not everyone gets to make big waves in this lifetime. Will they have lived for nothing before their end?"

"No. A butterfly can't make art but it's naturally beautiful enough to be art itself. It can land on the nose of a surgeon, seconds away from stepping into oncoming traffic, who'll save countless lives through their lifetime."

"That's called a short lived lucky accident."

"It's called a purposeful existence. The most special thing you can be is a caterpillar that was brave enough to learn to fly. No matter how unthanked and unrecognized you are by the masses, the surgeon will never forget. I wouldn't need a grand legacy if I got to hold a caterpillar through metamorphosis."

"You have a lot of faith in caterpillars." Ezra closes the open panel of glass, sealing us off from the chilly air sweeping inside.

"And you have none?"

"Wait until you're face to face with someone who's beyond belief for better. Watch how fast they take everything you have to give them and more. Your hope will be hard to maintain."

"And that someone is?"

"A novelty collector. They'll sweep up the cherished butterfly you prayed to protect. Pin their delicate wings to boards and hang them behind glass until they disintegrate. Then, they'll search for more. Because *that* is what evil men do. If they're honorable, they'll claim it's for science. For a just cause."

I gnaw at my lip, turning my back to the stars too.

Ezra surveys the shift in my gaze, jutting his chin toward the piano, a silent question in his eyes.

"Since I was seven."

"Ten."

"Does your Mom play?" This blacked out piano with intricate silver accents is top of the line. Too nice to be mere decor for her office.

He sighs heavily. "Know anything off the top of your head?"

"Everything." When he raises a brow I pick at my fresh coat of nail polish, stopping before a chip can form. "In the least annoying way possible."

He smiles a soft dimpled grin. "Is there a non-annoying way to say you know everything?"

"I meant the chords are already in my head. If I hear it, I can replicate it."

"Perfect pitch? Interesting." Ezra sweeps his hand toward the piano bench and I follow, sitting as far away from him as possible. "I want to hear something you've made."

"How do you know I've made anything?"

The keys before me are made of real ivory and I brush my hands against the surface of the naturals, used to the smooth surface of plastic and not the slightly textured feel. My fingers stroke the sharps and flats made of dark wood as he says, "You can't look at a piano the way you are now, and not have attempted to teach it something new."

"I haven't played in a long time."

"You never forget."

I clear my throat, shifting so I'm perched in the middle of the bench.

The sides of our thighs press together and I scoot forward until I'm as close to the piano as possible, wobbling at its edge.

Ezra scoops me up with one arm and I stifle a soft gasp. Large hands sliding off my stilettos one by one, placing them on the ground and holding me in the crook of his left elbow. When my feet are bare, he scoots the bench closer to the pedals in one swift motion. I release a shuddered breath and he sets me at his side.

"Play."

I close my eyes as my fingers caress the keys, deciding it's familiar enough to stay like this.

Yet, even with my lids clenched shut, I sense his searing gaze.

I allow my body to decide for me, starting the piece with a minor major seventh chord as Ezra shifts from beside me.

My fingers slide into several soft chord progressions that carry into the open space before taking the song into a frenzy like state. Notes rising upwards and yearning for an answer, building and cresting higher and higher.

As I play, I'm aware of one thing, the sensation building inside me.

Pianos are the only good feeling I've ever felt stem from my belly. Their music that of many butterflies that burst and take flight inside me, remembering why I always turn to it when I'm lost.

When my stomach is in knots, music unbinds them with ease.

The minutes long piece feels like only seconds when my fingertips strike the final chord, ending the song incomplete. It doesn't make sense but it's exactly as I'd written it.

As if more is meant to be said, yet nothing else can be.

My eyes fly open from the trancelike state I'd been under and there are questions within his gaze I can't make sense of.

"*You* composed that?" Ezra asks. "What's it called?"

"Henry's Song." I suck my teeth. "It's melodically similar to something *m*-my dad used to hum."

"Hum?"

"He hums when he's stressed out. Or, when he's trying to solve a difficult question."

"Did you have a question in mind when you were composing? Or is this a concentration tool?"

I pause for the briefest moment. "Why."

He scratches the back of his head. "I need to know."

"Ezra." I meet his gaze. "The question was, *why?*"

"Did they answer?"

"Who?"

"Who do you think?"

My brows crinkle. "You're asking if a higher power answered me? Why would I have theorized the meaning of existence with you if they had?"

"I don't know how they could leave you without a response. That was the most truthful anguish I've ever heard."

My breath catches in my chest. "I think... the great why of life is only answered with death as payment. And music, it's the beating heart of this Earth. The most alive thing about this planet. So the piece was pointless and the question is rhetorical."

Ezra's eyes soften as his hands stroke the keys to play the final chords again.

A few notes are wrong but the gist of its melody is correct, stopping abruptly just as I had.

The palpable tension I swam through earlier grows thicker as our hands lay side by side on the piano keys, hitting stray notes with each tentative flex of our fingers.

As I rise to leave, Ezra's hand catches my wrist. No words spoken between us but his eyes tell me he hadn't decided to do it, his body made the choice for him.

With a singular tug I'm between his thighs and the piano. The smallest flicker in my chest as his dimples set in deep when he frowns.

Everything about Ezra dwarfs me and he may reek of cigarettes, but the warmth of his body draws me in closer. Overdriving my sense with the need to be kept inside a stoked campfire. One that has the capability to burn a forest down if left unattended.

"Ezra." His tongue sweeps his lower lip as if to taste my temptation.

"I'm still trying to figure you out, Dreamer. I don't understand your game."

"I don't *n*-need to be figured out. I'm not a problem to be solved." My words catch in my throat as his fingers trace along the slit on my thigh, nails digging into his broad shoulders as I tremble. "And you can't seriously think you're going to kiss me."

"I'd rather meet oblivion," he murmurs.

Our words are bolder than the way our bodies shake, registering that some part of me is raw enough to let him.

*Alone* enough to want it.

Pained enough to take any relief to what feels like a gaping wound in my chest.

I accept the warmth of body heat. The strength of calloused fingers tilting my chin up, being more gentle than I knew he was capable of. Eyes that usually fill with disdain, holding only the soft echo of reverence within them.

For one endless second, I imagine Ezra Alvarez could do for me what faith does for believers.

But a throaty chuckle stirs me from my thoughts. Reminding me that one moment without ache will never measure up to my belief that worship is reserved for something far less tangible than the comfort of his hands. And it will be gifted to someone when reverence is far less fleeting on both ends.

When I see the mouth that made it, I leap backwards, ass smashing against piano keys as Josephine leans against the open door jamb—a cream-colored envelope stuffed under one arm.

Her claps echo loudly as I adjust my dress. The sounds a blasted cannon bringing me closer to death with each boom inside the empty space. "This is great," Josephine declares. "Truly."

Ezra grimaces. "This isn't as it appears."

"Is that so? Because, it appears as if a battering ram is straining through your zipper. And I'm positive Skeeter Bites nips are crudely pointing at me under all that padding. It's disturbing actually. My clit's never been more shriveled in my life. I'm self-sterilizing at the site."

*Fuck. My. Fucking. Life. Kill me. Shoot me. Let me die!*

Ezra and I stay still as stone.

"You aren't an Ethologist. You're a meretricious insipid viper, aren't you?" My stomach twists and I physically flinch backwards. Every word a blade hitting bullseye on my worst fears.

"That's *n*-not true."

*Inhale. Exhale. Inhale. Exhale. Speak.*

Before I can manage a sentence, she lashes again. "Save it for someone that cares, you home-wrecker."

Disgust finds its home in my belly as I walk away.

After a few paces forward, I stop, darting back to grab my stilettos and scrambling away once more.

"Dreamer."

"What?!" I pause near the doorframe, leaning as far away as I can from Josephine as an eerie calm washes her face that's far worse than her anger could be.

I don't know what I expect. Maybe for him to say he'd initiated it? Or, anything at all in my defense.

But, Ezra only shakes his head. Eyes cold and uncaring as every piece of me that wished to know him is erased.

"You can't ignore the Dean's summons."

I choke out a near deranged laugh. "Yeah? Well if it's important she'll put it in writing. Clearly, she knows how to do that."

They lapse into eerie silence and I use the chance to bolt. Running down the stairs and away from the screaming match that begins behind me.

# CHAPTER 15

A whistle blows loudly, signaling for everyone within the fire quadrant to gather round. It's been one week since my disastrous other woman stint and all excess energy has gone to avoiding my Imaginifers. Seeing how effective I've been, I wouldn't be surprised to find out Ezra and Josephine have done the same. The only thing that's prompted me to attend First Year Casting again at all is my agreement to be perfect with Creen.

Even if I'm unclear how much longer I can walk by myself.

"Maybe we should head out," a voice to my side suggests. It takes me a second to notice, due to the shuffling of the crowd, but I'm the closest to the triplets I've ever been. The deep velvety rumble belongs to Nox.

"This class is useless anyway. White might as well have been a piece of furniture when he was off coddling the airhead," Solara mutters. "Clueless. How do you almost torch the place with a simple release?"

They look to Sky for additional insight and she seems to be ignoring them completely. "Is this boring you now too?"

She shrugs, fiddling with the braid placed at random on the side of her head, an intricate afterthought rather than having any functionality. The rest of her hair flows unbound past her narrow waist. All three of them dressed in black and brown leathers with accents of silver.

Nox and Solara side-eye one another, something unspoken between them as Ezra bellows, "Alright everyone, today you run the courses!"

Our Imaginifers stand in a pack toward the front.

Well, most of them do. Josephine stands slightly off to the side, even though Bridger keeps attempting to include her into conversation.

"When we were in your shoes last year, all anyone worried about was being the best. Putting one another down to psyche out your competition. Well today, we take over for you. You cheer on your teammates or you shut your mouths when your quadrant members are on the ropes. Prove you're capable, not that others aren't. Are we understood?"

"Yes, sir!" we scream in unison.

"Then, as always, let's have some fun."

The crowd cheers in response, getting wary looks from the other quadrants—more rowdy than anyone else by a long shot.

"Gather into lines. Four at a time!" Mai orders.

The air is pierced by another ear-splitting whistle that vibrates my eardrums. At once, I'm shuffled into formation along with the rest of the groups as the first line prepares themselves. "Go!"

Four men take off running as if their lives depend on it. Boots squelching through the mud pit and slowing their strides.

The brunette with the longest legs arrives first. Fumbling for his matchbook and drawing out two sticks before stuffing the box back into his pocket. He places one match between his lips and lights the end of the rope with the second, bending fire to travel up the length of the thick braid of nylon.

Without hesitation, he uses the rope to ascend the wall of steel.

"You morons can't do any better than this?! I would've been twelve feet under by now!" Bridger screams, malice in every syllable.

The man's steel-toe boots are rubber on the bottoms so they grip on easily, climbing as if it's no more difficult than inhaling breath.

While impressive, the true feat is his control of the fire under tense conditions. The way it eats away slowly at the rope, not disintegrating the nylon until he reaches the top of the wall.

"The last one of you back licks the underside of my boot clean!" Arlo shouts. "I have a dog so there's shit residue in every crack. Bon appetit."

When the brown-haired man reaches the top of the wall, he straddles it, taking the match from his teeth and swiping the head on his pants.

He morphs a ball of fire, gaze focused on a shiny red target below him. When he's holding something the size and shape of a flaming football he chucks it downward with as much force as he can.

"Boring. Nauseating. Waste of existence," Josephine yawns.

The man doesn't wait, propelling himself off the ledge head first toward the ground.

I hold my breath until the fireball lands, breaking the surface of the target seconds before his skull does.

He falls into the newly formed hole and it swallows him whole.

The men behind him follow suit. One by one letting the Earth consume them.

Staff members standing off to the side, climb to the top of the structure, tying new ropes to the four posts atop the wall.

It takes a few minutes before they're out of the way and back to their original positions. Then, the whistle is blown again.

*Cough. Cough. Cough.*

The hacks to my side are stilted. As if they're fake or horribly stifled. I can't tell which.

"Are you trying to get my attention?" I whisper, peering at Sky from the corner of my eyes.

"Your attention?" She raises her brows. "If I wanted that I would have taken a sledgehammer to your ribs. No?"

"Well, I didn't ask if you wanted to get even. But, if it'd make you feel better, one rib would be fine. Am I allowed to take a shot first?"

"It's fascinating. I've never met someone who's gotten the chance to make multiple first impressions and has used each and every one of them to act like a creep."

"I'm just making conversation?"

"Okay. Let's converse. What's my first class of the day?"

"Architecture with Professor Farber."

"In my free time?"

"You sketch on the bridge."

"Favorite ice cream?"

"Pistachio...?"

"So, when you just pretended not to know what I meant, is that a normal thing you do?"

"You're also keeping tabs on me? I could say the same."

She scoffs. "Please. I am only watching my back to make sure the coast is clear. At any moment, a five foot girl who insists on being my shadow could knock me down another flight of stairs."

"You look great by the way! Healed up well. Not even a scar."

Sky crinkles her nose as if she smells something gross. Gray eyes trailing from the ribbon pulling back my curls to my bunny tied tennis shoes in clear assessment.

I stand straighter and she releases a small huff of air, the sound halfway between amusement and exasperation.

"Any other commentary on my appearance?"

"Your hair's cool. Purple's an awesome choice. And I like your— I mean, the leather's crazy cool. Were you made in some, like, cool people store? Mrs... *Cool* girl."

Her eyes narrow to slits. "I don't think I should dignify any part of whatever that was with a legitimate response."

My shoulders sink, turning to face the course as one ripped woman plows through the first obstacle within thirty seconds. "Please don't."

"You weren't paying attention to the lectures on your banned weeks?" Sky's tone isn't mean, but cautiously bored. As if I have a singular chance to catch her interest before she gets vicious.

"Ezra chose the furthest section from the bleachers and Josephine's was close to me but she was purposely speaking low so I'm still catching up on some things."

"So, you went spineless amidst a lovers spat?"

"How do you—"

"Before you arrived, Josephine told Emerson you're a man stealing slut who molested Ezra. They argue rather loudly."

"Whoa! Hold on, I'd never *molest* anyone. That's a heinous accusation."

"Yeah?"

"Yeah! And slut's have names too!" I notice her boot is unlaced as we shuffle forward, squatting down to double knot the laces as I rant.

"I'm Shiloh. It's nice to meet you. And, just so you're aware, I didn't steal anyone's boyfriend or perform unsolicited sexual acts. I'm single, I'm a virgin, and I've never even seen a penis in real life but it was poking *me,* not the other way around. His hands were on *my* hips and my nipples aren't crude or sterilizing to look at. So I don't understand how someone's clit could shrivel at the sight of them? I wear a B cup when I'm on my period. I'm sure someone's into that."

Her eyes widen at my unprompted overshare, reaching out a near translucent hand to help me to my feet.

"Hello Virgin. I'm Sky Sapienti."

Her handshake is cold enough to burn. Sky's castor ring a wavy cut band of silver, stone off centered and crooked. She eyes the ring on my right hand but doesn't address it.

"My brother Nox and sister Solara."

Sky tilts her head toward her siblings and their silence seems to entice her, smile dancing on her lips as their heads remain unturned.

"People call them the incest twins behind their back, but no one would ever dare say it to their faces." Her smile grows as Nox tenses. "In fairness, I don't think they fuck. Or, at least, I haven't seen proof of it. But I'm not with them all the time. Guess we'll never know until the babies pop out with malfunctioning hearts and deformed faces." Sky shrugs as Solara grits her teeth. "Sorry Caveman hasn't proposed yet, Sol. He's got a few years left to plan something big."

"You're certainly nowhere close to a viable choice. I can see why you'd be upset."

"I'm not arguing about who's viable for our brother to wed and bed. Congrats on the impending nuptials. You prepared for that Caveman? It'll be like all the other women you blow through. Just close your eyes, you won't even notice a difference."

"Good thing I've already dealt with the discrepancies from inbreeding," he deadpans. "At least my own child won't be a headache."

An unmistakable flash of hurt floods Sky's eyes and she glares at her boots in silence.

Before I can stop them, words gush from my mouth in a wave of red. "In my opinion, sleeping with your sister *currently* is more embarrassing to a family than someone doing incest in the past. The only discrepancies between you two, is that she's someone to actually respect. Not men who touch their twins. Maybe Josephine should point the finger somewhere else."

Sky's lips part in shock and it isn't until I've said it that I remember how many people eavesdrop on the founder's children, sharp intakes of breath all around us as Nox's hands shake.

There's an immediate switch within him. Some snap behind obsidian orbs that can't be taken back. "I don't touch my sisters. Anyone spreading that vicious rumor further than this field will meet a worse fate than what I'll give you for such insinuations."

His gray swirled irises darken to a bottomless black pit, staring into mine with rage growing by the second. As the sun bathes me in its light, there's nowhere I can hide from his increasingly murderous gaze, but I steel myself not to take a step backward.

"That was fucked up. I'm sorry. I meant—"

"I do not care what you *meant.*" My heart thunders, threatening to leap outside of my chest as Nox leans past Sky. Face mere inches from my own. "You're this close to finding out what it will cost you."

"Caveman." Sky frowns. "Chill out. She apologized."

"You've said more than enough, Sky." He leans closer as I release a breath of air and lock my shaking legs. "And you? One more word today and you're done here, Shiloh Benson. In fact, see yourself to the back and away from my sister. *Now.*"

Nox straightens up, turning to face the obstacle courses with white knuckled fists.

I pivot toward the back of the line and Sky tugs me back by my shirt tail, clearing her throat before the whistle blows again.

"Caveman's all talk. He's not as insufferable as he wants to appear. Got me a shiny pink bike once. It's give and take with neanderthals."

Nox cuts her a glance that she actively avoids meeting and our heads turn toward the sound of splitting stone.

The brown haired man from earlier runs out of the ground. Shirt on fire, dagger in hand, but generally unscathed.

He nears the Imaginifer's and throws his knife in their direction.

I hold my breath as it buries itself deep into the bullseyes on the wooden panel. *Millimeters* from Mai's ear.

She's unflinching as she pulls it out, throwing it back.

He catches the dagger, squeezing until blood drips down a silver blade onto green ones.

Mai issues a nod and he roars in victory, banging his chest and celebrating alone as the others among us refuse to cheer for anyone who finishes first.

I clap my hands and he turns toward me. Everyone staring as if I have three heads until my claps taper to nothing.

I dig into my pocket for my matchbook, proceeding to stick two matches behind my ear as the first finisher appraises me up and down, the smallest of smiles on his face. I smile in return and Sky asks, "You interested in him?"

"No? Ezra said to support our teammates."

"I'd suggest throwing support elsewhere. I know a creature with an idea when I see one."

"Have you heard things?"

"Grayson Belloc is squeaky clean. Family friends with the Sovereign. It's his associates that clue me in. When you come across a group of men, who always seem to have rumors circulating, it's good to steer clear."

"Rumors?"

"Bastard babies, assault, violence, you name it. It's always the nice guys in the bunch of creeps that are the most vile. The ones lingering around the dark, but appear to be bathing in light. They're either okay with darkness as long as it doesn't touch them or..."

"All their darkness rests inside?"

"Exactly. They're better at hiding it. That's more sinister than the ones who get caught could ever be."

I nod, avoiding Grayson's curious gaze and readying myself for the course.

We move into our starting block. Eyes glued to the ropes getting situated in front of us with only two goals running on repeat in my mind.

*Get up fast. Jump down quickly.*

When Mai blows the whistle, I take off. Feet flying out from under me and eating shit as the Sapientis run forward, thunderous footsteps shaking the ground I rest on.

The laces of my shoes have been tied together. Too focused on the course to be aware. I undo the knots, lacing them sloppily while the girls behind me giggle, a wink issued from the taller of the two.

By the time I make it to the wall, white sneakers bogged with mud, Nox is the only one left on the first obstacle. The only unburnt rope directly in his path.

He wavers on top at my approach. Hands clenched on steel and glaring back to the Imaginifers, eyes flashing with unbridled rage.

"No words of encouragement for the girl?!" Nox yells, referring to the brutal insults the Imaginifers have hurled with every run. At everyone but myself so far. But then again, I'd been purposefully tripped and fallen behind. What's the point? I'm humbled enough.

"Worry about yourself Sapienti," Mai says from off to the side. "Or your sisters I hear you are... *fond* of."

Bridger throws her a look of annoyance and she wiggles her fingers, symbol of the land on full display. To cause harm to one of our instructors would mean an audience with the King himself.

"Wonder why that is?" Nox sneers. "What about you is so fucking interesting, huh? So manipulative, that you've bashed in my sister's face and she didn't slit your throat on impact. Is it the Lions that make you feel so emboldened? If so, allow me to set you straight here and now."

The crowd behind me laughs as I climb. An instant decision in his eyes as they meet my own.

When I pull myself to the top, I barely manage to prepare for the blow. Pressing my tongue to the roof of my mouth and clenching my jaw just before a size thirteen boot clocks me square in the face.

There's a flood of pain but I manage to hold on, pulling myself up even farther.

"Sapienti, stop!" Bridger gapes as Arlo holds him back. "She doesn't mean any harm!"

When Nox reels back and clocks me for a second time, no amount of willpower can keep me up.

I'm done for.

Falling back the way I'd come. Twisting and turning, twenty feet to the ground and landing face first with a harsh squelch and thud.

Audible winces stagger through the air as I moan, crawling out of the mud inch by inch with fingertips that are still ablaze. When I get to the grass, I turn over to catch my breath, unable to inhale properly.

"The next person to speak on my betrothal will meet their end. Are we understood?!"

Everyone bows their head and Mai blows the whistle as Nox goes over the wall.

I sit upright powered by sheer adrenaline, spitting blood and wiping mud from my spotty vision.

My fingers dig into the ground as I work to calm myself, dismissing my fire—the rush of energy I'd gathered parting with it.

I scramble to my feet and sway a few steps as shouting ensues between the Imaginifers.

"Russ!? Icarus Honestus!" I sob his name as the world swirls. My equilibrium thrown off when my vision darkens in one eye, slipping in mud and hitting the ground again with a heavy thud.

Murmurs of annoyance surround me as staff members surge forward to soothe me. Putting a hold to the next run as they shield my balled up body from prying eyes.

An older woman with gray curls uses her apron to clear gunk from my damaged eye. "It's okay, Ma'am. Don't cry. We will help you."

"Icarus. Only *h*-him *p*-please?"

They call for Russ and he seems to hear them over all the shouting, voice laced with fear as he runs from the opposite end of the Arena.

There are thumps of boots slamming against the ground and the scuffle of several men fighting until Ezra's blurred features come into view, sporting a busted lip and a face tensed with dread.

Russ shouts so viscerally that people not already knelt, fall to their knees. And I can't hear what Ezra murmurs to me as he scoops me up, but I know I dream of snow falling through barren tree limbs.

# CHAPTER 16

I wake tucked into bed with a glass of water beside me, bolting upright and grabbing the crystal cup on my desk. I chug the room temperature liquid, rivulets of water trailing against my chin as I slap down the empty cup with a heavy-handed thud.

Suede looks up from her card game, motioning toward my chest.

In one fluid motion, I yank my covers upward. Adjusting the tube top made of bandages that's drooped to my belly button under the weight of melted ice packs. Russ uses the fire poker to break apart logs, the crackle of fresh wood filling the silence. "Did someone hurt you?" I ask, noting his splinted thumb with a small frown.

"That's not important. How are you feeling?"

"He hurt himself," Suede laughs. "Broke it on Ezra's face, *defending your honor.*"

"What about this situation is amusing to you?" Russ asks, raising a protein drink to his lips.

Not for the first time do I notice his weight gain. Gaunt cheeks a little fuller and clothing a little less baggy from eating twice as much now. When he isn't eating, he's on a run. And if he isn't running, he's lifting weights. "Say something constructive or say nothing at all."

"Okay. Arsonist, there are things about our world that you need to understand."

"Talk shit get hit? No, I get that. I should have kept my mouth shut."

"More like, don't disrespect founder families."

"But the way people are to Russ is fine?"

He flinches. "We're talking about you."

"Am I in the twilight zone? That's the complete opposite of—"

"His dad influenced them to do it!" Suede blurts as Russ curses under his breath.

"What?"

"They love him as much as they do Jace. They thought they were helping him become a man."

"Russ?" I stare in shock toward my friend who's gone tight lipped.

"My Father... said I was born with a golden spoon in my mouth. Told the Loyalists that, until I graduate, I'm treated like everyone else. Worse even. In order to recognize what my birthright has granted me. Who I would be without my name."

I cringe as his eyes turn apologetic.

I've always thought of Russ and I on the same level. Made of that same thing that others find off-putting and different. But apparently, I'm just the loser who'd blindly believed him.

"I don't hold it against my people. It's my duty to protect them and I was weak. I am not prone to dominating a space but one day I will get my territory and I'm to *earn* respect. If I can't, then I was never a true Lion to begin with."

"And Jason?"

"My brother's always taken his duties seriously."

Freshly chugged water whirls in my belly as my tongue traces over a scabbing lip. "Is this why people treat me this way? They think I'm disregarding orders from the Father of Leonusver to... get ahead?"

"I—"

"Why didn't you tell me the truth? I could've prepared myself?!"

"I'm sorry. Okay?" Russ adjusts his glasses. "After welcome week I was lonely. But it will stop now. The more respect I earn, the more they'll come back to heel."

"How could you just let them all think—"

"I made a miscalculation. I didn't realize you'd interact with the Sapientis. They keep to themselves. There was really no reason to bring it up. Nox is the only one who would take it that far."

"Some girls tied my shoes together for helping Sky with her laces!"

Suede waves away my concerns. "That's just childish antics. You were sorta being a kiss ass and Nox has the right to respond however he wants to public disrespect. You have to learn to take your hits somewhere, right?"

"Oh my God," She looks at me expectantly. As if her vague explanations should be enough. "Show me the laws. Right now."

"The founders *are* the law?"

"They can say and do whatever they want to whoever they want? You know how difficult it is to stay in the lines when the boundaries aren't clear? Can people even leave this place if they don't agree?"

"Of course people can leave. But why would they?"

Suede rises and picks up a newspaper, throwing it at my feet. Next, she pulls a tablet from her nightstand, switching it on as she flips through new channels before sliding it across the hardwood.

"What's with this strange accusatory attitude? Do we have anything negative to say about your homeland?"

"Yes. *Frequently,*" I murmur while raising the newspaper, eyes skimming over local headlines.

The front page is a feel good story about an uptick in grain production. I flip through page after page as she taps her foot, brows raised when nothing suspicious leaps out and bites me.

Suede seats herself back on the rug and I turn down the twenty-four hour symphonic orchestra, made available courtesy of House Chalybe. Migraine worsening as violins blare through the speakers of her tablet at a bone rattling frequency.

"The rules are simple. If they have the surnames Honestus, Chalybe, or Sapienti, *or* they wear a Lion, Tiger, or Bear pin, they're off limits. If you carry yourself tactfully then it's not difficult. Would you ask your parents to explain themselves to you? If you knew they kept you from harm's way by their word?

"Yes...?"

She rolls her eyes in response. "Only a Child of Addam would act like this."

"Act like what? I'm not a mindless fool who can allow myself to be ordered around without question anymore. That's what got me here." Suede goes red in the face, an angry blush creeping over freckled cheeks. "I, um, was talking about myself."

"Whatever. I don't get hurt from stones thrown from glass houses." She cracks her knuckles and sniffs. "Your shitty parents lied to you your whole life and you had to blow people up to see the truth. So you're right. You were a fool."

"My parents aren't shitty people? They did their best and you're way off base."

"I'm off base? You come from a world that treats people like you as second class citizens. It's disturbing what I've seen on the news. Tell her Icarus!"

"Suede?" He frowns. "That's not—"

"Fine. I'll say it. The truth is you're unbearable half the time. You're entitled and never want to handle the consequences of talking back. This country is peaceful and you bring war upon yourself by being obnoxious and weird every chance you—"

*"Enough!"* Russ snaps.

It's as if all the air has been sucked from the room as he takes a deep breath to relax his tense muscles. "Look at how quickly we've divided. Amplectere Silentium, Amplectere Fortitudinem."

"Embrace Silence, Embrace Strength?" I ask. "What's that from?"

"My father says it before every event." Russ adjusts his glasses. "We don't sit and explain every step taken to protect our people. There is not one country in the world that has come as far as ours has. It's not perfect by any means, but it counts for something. I'm sorry I did not guide you as I should have and I'm appalled that your parents did not inform you of this before attending school here. *They* are supposed to guide you in the right direction."

*Maybe they did,* I think.

"We don't question our leaders. Ever. At least, not publicly." He huffs out a breath, rubbing his neck to work away the stress and tension in his shoulders. "Now you know, and we leave it at that. No one else will harm you, I swear on my name."

"What's the damage?" I mutter into the silence, skimming my hand over my torso.

Suede plays with the carpet in her hands, not looking upwards.

"Asleep for a few hours. Probably healing a nasty concussion and cracked ribcage. And your face... has seen better days."

My hand feels for my swollen cheeks and I grimace. Both of them wincing as I caress another scab, skin still raw from someone scrubbing the mud out of my wounds.

"I tried my best," she insists. "They were using the infirmary for brews today."

"Brews?"

"Birth control. Young men were... impregnating people." Russ grimaces. "Only taking credit for the children from their marriages. It was getting unsustainable. But to be fair, a lot more take it by choice. I do and I will continue until marriage."

"Really?" Suede asks. "Aren't you exempt? And celibate?"

"It's best practice."

"If I was impregnated now, I'd drink the Syrup of Dite and it'd be the stars' problem." His nostrils flare and Suede squares her jaw. "Come on, I'm joking! Clearly."

"I think I missed the part where killing Lion Cubs is funny."

"Stars above, you're the one who made the elixir readily available."

"But—"

"My Mom always told me that any explanation before the word but is a half truth, and anything afterwards to bend over and prep your asshole cause shits about to fly straight out."

"Did your mother actually give that advice? Because it's dumb. *But,* is a necessary and powerful conjunction when you're dealing with any conversation of nuance."

"Okay, Mr. Language Expert."

"Pregúntame cualquier cosa, en cualquier idioma, y lo entenderé. It all bleeds together."

"Great! Insulting my intelligence again?" His brows furrow as she turns to ignore him. "Whatever. Russ is baby pushing—"

"Suede, that's not fair, and you know it."

"—because he would see his nephew as his child as well. Families here are closely bound. Which is why they are on top of their brews. The offspring of founders aren't as celibate as they *pretend* they are. While simultaneously judging from high horses."

I huff through a stitch in my side, and when I look up again, I realize they're waiting for my input. "Oh. I don't have an opinion."

"Sharing an opinion in private is fine," Suede says.

"Probably shouldn't. Second class citizens aren't as smart."

"That wasn't what I said?"

"*Riiiight*, you were just insinuating I should shut my mouth and be grateful you don't treat me like one. That I'm *handy* after all?"

Her lips fall open. "I didn't—That was a compliment! Because people were calling you a bimbo!"

"Great. Very helpful."

"Fine." Russ narrows his eyes, patience wearing thin. "Yes. Jason will break up with you if you suggest to him what you're suggesting to me now."

She flinches. "That's not what I was—"

"Yes it was! You seized the opportunity to grill me as a test run. So listen to what I'm telling you," Suede swallows roughly as he says, "In her pregnancy with me, my mother did not leave bed *once* and I was still premature. There have been countless lost on the birthing bed. Too many swaddles buried. We refuse asking her to miscarry again for our freedoms."

"I wasn't suggesting that."

"Good," he snarls. "Because her sacrifices are recognized. It is our time to step up. And yes, that also falls on our wives."

"Babies are all I'm good for?"

"Of course not? My mother could only carry two. None of us blame her for that. But being *infertile* and being *unwilling* are different issues entirely. Do you understand what it could result in if the Honestus family dies off?"

"What about the Korovks? They've been carrying the bloodline since—"

"You're insinuating we give centuries of history to people we occasionally mix with to carry *drops* of Lionblood?" Russ' lips curl in disgust and it's the most insulted I've ever seen him. "Even if we would consider that, none of our extended family will be bowed to as they bow to our children. Which is why my Father cleared our future with the other houses. Jason and I's first four offspring are considered Sureblood. To regrow our tree from the *nothing* they left us with. Now ask me what happens if we don't follow through?"

"What happens?" I whisper when Suede falls silent.

"My father takes a second wife. My mother cried for *weeks* when he made the deal for himself too. It'd be cruel and it will never happen if I have anything to say about it." Russ shrugs, a silent war brewing in his head. "You want me to be the bad guy, when I am suffocating inside. Because you know I won't betray your doubts until I have no other choices."

"I don't have a choice! Jason and I can't live without one another."

He rolls his eyes. "For the love of—"

"You don't understand, Icarus!"

"It's you who doesn't understand! To be a ruler is to have millions of children. My Father has always said that. Jewels are the blanket over the horrors we face. It's not sunshine and rainbows. It's sacrifice, day after day. I can assure you, most rulers in this world wouldn't piss on their subjects if they were on fire."

"But—"

"We'd give our own lifeblood to staunch flames and we have before. If you make your people pay the price for your crown of gold you should not have put it on in the first place. You were meant to already have been rich with knowledge to afford its heavy price. And when you don't have knowledge to pay for it, that's when people suffer. Ruling is the gravity of millions atop the crown of your head, trusting you have the strength to hold it together. The gravity my brother was born to hold as the first son. Hold it *with* him or leave."

"But—"

"No buts because shit's about to fly straight out. You're selfish and you're the polar opposite of everything an Honestus is. Marrying my brother isn't your future."

Suede bursts into heaving sobs, her fear of losing Jason bursting to the surface along with them.

My heart sinks to my stomach wondering if I could survive feeling so deeply for another. And as the sobbing drags into minutes, I decide that I don't think I'd want to.

"I'm *n*-not trying to *b*-be *s*-selfish," she chokes out. "I want to be a part of your family more than anything."

Russ pulls her into his arms rocking her against him. "I know."

Her apologies come out as a blubbered unintelligible mess.

Russ and I lock gazes as he kisses the crown of her head, unable to prevent the softness within him from seeping out.

They dive into whispers that I tune out for privacy sake until her sniffles quiet to nothing, and as the two of them make up I pull my covers to my chin and unwrap my chest.

Russ releases Suede and takes off his zip-up, throwing it towards me.

I slip it on and let the duvet fall down, throwing him a look of appreciation he doesn't return. His mind elsewhere as I realize I wouldn't want to know the weight of the crown either.

Suede sniffles, wiping her raccoon eyes and blotchy cheeks with the sleeve of her shirt. "Ezra left a note." I grit my teeth as I grab the notepad that's facedown on my desk.

Consider yourself lucky to be alive, Dreamer.
Monday. The Arena. 8 p.m.
You're late and you'll see there's worse punishments than Sapienti gave you.

"What's it say?" I toss Suede the notepad and flop back down as she reads. "Sheesh." Suede scrubs at her runny nose as she curls into Russ's side. "Look Icarus."

I grab a pillow off my bed and scream into the feather-filled object until my voice goes hoarse.

As I gingerly pull it away, something dawns on me.

Even bleeding and battered, I feel stronger than ever.

# CHAPTER 17

Ezra smokes a cigarette, walking across the empty field of the Arena as if he has all the time in the world. When he nears, he ashes it on his hand, letting the remnants fall into the grass before he comes to a stop. "Head in the clouds, Dreamer?"

"I'm firmly grounded and you're late."

I scramble to my feet, raising a golden pocket watch Russ gifted me to stay on schedule. It dangles from freshly painted fingers and I watch the minute hand tick to fifteen minutes past eight.

"New clothes," he says, attempting to hand over the hulking duffle bag he's slung over one shoulder. I refuse to take it.

"What's wrong with my own clothes?" My voice takes on a defensive tone I dislike.

"Allow me to demonstrate?" I don't know what I'm necessarily agreeing to, but I give a cautious nod yes.

Ezra fists the front of my oversized sweater, pulling me against his chest.

The second I'm in his vicinity, he pushes me back.

He does this three times until I'm trapped under his arm. The crook of it locked around my throat. "Get out of my grasp," he whispers.

I attempt to slip away but each time I do his hands grab another portion of my sweater until I'm fully wound in his arms.

The tips of my toes barely brush the ground, the back of my head pressed into his chest as heat radiates on my backside.

"Let me go." He spins me away from him and I gasp, "You smell like tobacco." It's the only thing I can think to say. Head aching, and his point thoroughly demonstrated.

"No one in my life minds."

Again, he offers me the duffle bag. Again, I refuse to take it.

*"Why?"*

His tongue traces his bottom lip, eyes hardening with contempt.

"When you're dressed like this—" He motions his hand toward my outfit consisting of sweatpants and a sweatshirt. "Someone can overpower you in a second. You're small."

"And you're judgmental for a man who towers over everyone. You've never felt like anyone could hurt you. I don't need people looking at my body or picking shit apart."

"You don't know what real hurt is. I know a spoiled brat when I see one."

"You don't even know me, Ezra?"

"I don't desire to know you," he all but spits, nearing me until I have to tilt my chin up to meet his gaze. "You play with fire in a game you know nothing about, and I'm only helping you because it's the quickest way to be rid of you."

"I'm done playing."

"Great. It's best that you bow out permanently before the real players step in."

"So, I'm good enough to touch in the dark, and not even two weeks later, I need to burn at the stake? Do you get off on mixed signals?"

"I don't trust Children of Addam. I never will. The end will come and it won't resolve itself in rainbows after a long storm. It's swept through by fire and ice and rebuilt by who remains. The only thing that will stay standing after mankind's inevitable reckoning, is the Kingdom that has united as one. You've proved you have no intention of being one of us."

"You think I threaten your survival because I believe differently than you?"

"One is an impossible number to maintain. And you, that's two. Two is death to one."

"Two is *growth* to one. I've been thinking about Maria's axiom. She left an Arch for people to enter! She dreamt of—"

"You know nothing of what Maria dreamt! You were raised by savages in the outside lands!" He leans forward until his warm lips graze my ear. "So here's how this is going to go. Unless you want me to fail you, the next two words out of your mouth are, *yes sir.* Then you will be quiet, amiable, and you won't question what I instruct of you from here on out."

Against every instinct I have, I submit. Swallowing the boiling rage and stuffing it in a box. "Yes... *sir.*"

"Glad we've come to an understanding."

The resounding silence holds an acrid taste but the tension deflates around us both, leaving behind an odd sense of caution in the air.

He hands me the bag on his shoulder and this time I take it. The duffle is ridiculously heavy and there's clothing filled to the brim. I pull out a slinky but durable long sleeve, swallowing my pride and asking, "Where did you get all of this stuff?"

"I made it."

My brows crinkle. "You made it?"

"I invented fabrics capable of withstanding extreme temperatures. Advanced aramid fibers but mine are more gentle to touch. Easier to manipulate and infused with tantalum carbide. They're also protective. A regular dagger won't cut through. Now, take off your sweater."

I inhale sharply as he stares at me expectantly, pulling my sweatshirt over my head and letting it fall to the grass—a tight cami tank top underneath that I'd feel shy to wear in front of even my friends.

My stomach is exposed and the neckline low cut, cursing my habit of going braless as the chilly autumn weather peaks my nipples. I force myself to keep my arms at my side, spine straightened to its full extent as I dare him to make a joke.

Ezra picks up my discarded garment, and with a twitch of his fingers, the *Harvard Dad* sweater disintegrates into ash. I bite my tongue to keep from complaining. But eventually, the words I stifle fly out. "I liked that one!"

He shakes his head, stirring the inky waves atop his scalp. "If you like the rest of your clothes you'll keep them in storage or they'll be eaten away by fire."

Before he can continue staring at my chest, I pull a black long sleeve over my head. The material is soft but sturdy enough to stop a bullet even, sucking in every part of my body it touches as if a second skin. Even though it shows off my figure, it doesn't make me uncomfortable. It makes me feel prepared. And I look... *Good.*

I root through the bag for pants and pull out a pair that feels buttery soft. Made of skin tight, leather-like material.

Ezra stares at me expectantly and I raise my brows.

In an instant, he twists on his heel.

I keep my eyes on his back as I kick off my shoes, sliding down my sweatpants and slipping into the new bottoms. When they button, I clear my throat and he turns back around.

I pull out a pair of boots nestled into the bottom, testing out the platformed footwear by rocking back and forth. They're heavy but manageable, increasing my height by two or three inches.

Ezra pulls a dagger from his waistband and I hold up both my hands in innocence.

He twirls it in his fingers and hands it over hilt first.

When I attempt to spin it like he did, he shakes his head. "Stop before you cut yourself."

I let it rest in my upward facing palms, examining the hilt with a red ruby at its top and carved dragons in the finger holds. "Daggers are our main choice of weaponry. Every life you take with your power you can feel the loss in your soul. As a last defense, you need something man-made. You must feel the weight of your kills. It's our way."

"No." I shake my head, attempting to hand him the dagger. "We're not in the medieval era when people were outside stabbing their neighbors for sleeping with their wives. We can use our words now. Like, apparently everyone thinks I'm a home wrecking, man-molesting, stupid slut bag. It's better than being stabbed, I guess. Though, I wouldn't put it past her." The ghost trace of a dimple is revealed in one cheek and Ezra smooths it away. "Seriously. I don't need this."

He ignores me, pulling a thigh strap from his pocket and fastening the knife to my leg.

"Do all of you really go around with hidden daggers strapped to you?"

Ezra raises the hem of his hoodie and a slightly bigger dagger than my own peaks out of his waistband. It's a black hilt made of snake skin, stark against olive toned abs.

"Fire affinities, yes."

I take a deep breath before straightening my spine. "Okay. What's first?"

"She's every step you take from here on out," he responds, motioning towards two slim figures in the far off distance.

One sandy blonde and one with long violet tresses.

"Why?" I ask, heart speeding and dropping as I worry at my lip.

"Sky's a Sapienti. She'll fight like her brother and apparently doesn't hate you."

"And Suede?" She's several inches taller than I am, and naturally athletic. Lean from time spent surfing on the islands.

But Suede isn't a fighter. She can't be helpful to my training.

Ezra shrugs, taking a drag of a freshly lit cigarette and puffing the smoke in my face.

"Reassuring," I mutter.

As Sky nears, she crosses her arms over her chest, barking out a raspy laugh. I haven't seen her since before the incident with her brother. I have no clue what she believes I deserved in that situation but her eyes are expressionless now. Surveying my healed up face for remnants of his attack that don't linger. "Interrupting something, Cousin?"

*Cousin?*

Ezra grimaces and I shake my head no so quickly it draws everyone's gaze. "Absolutely not. He has a girlfriend."

Sky yawns, setting her bag down. "He doesn't have a girlfriend."

"I never told you Josie and I were dating."

"Yes, you did?"

"You assumed that because you think you know everything."

"*Incestous friend group,*" Suede mouths.

"Audere, you mouthing shit is no better than saying it aloud." Sky appears passively amused as Ezra narrows his gaze. "Stay out of my business, Sapienti."

"I cleared the air."

"No one asked you to do that."

"It was heavy with the stench of the shit you're wafting in her face. Do it again and we'll have a permanent problem." There's a stir of relief inside me as Ezra begrudgingly blows smoke in another direction. "We'll move on now. Get rolling around. Yes?"

I gnaw at my pinky nail, polish chipping in my mouth. "Why is Suede here?"

"Figured she could go a few rounds with me until you feel inclined to step in." Sky sports a crooked grin as Suede's face falls. "What? You thought you were invited along to cause headaches?"

"I'm here for moral support. I'm her best friend. She needs me."

"She doesn't need you and you're not her *best* friend? Her and the Lion are clearly attached at the hip. Where have you been?"

"Yes, she does." Suede frowns, ignoring the latter half of Sky's statement. "I'm meant for stealthy surveillance. Less gory stuff. Air affinities don't do hand to hand combat."

Technically, Suede's right.

In the event of an emergency, all citizens are conscripted into military service as needed, T.A.U. students first in line.

If we're called to serve, the idea is that Fire affinities would be the best soldiers. Air affinities are trained as pilots and spies. The Earth quadrant focuses on defensive techniques, building strongholds and lethal traps for the battlefield. And the Water quadrant would take full command of naval operations. The designated areas aren't set in stone but they sure as hell prepare us for that possibility.

"It's okay, Blondie, I'll take it easy on you. Less *gory* stuff."

Suede pouts, smoothing out her pleated skirt and tucking a sandy tress behind her ear.

"Suede, you don't have to," I say.

"Yes, she does," Sky says, motioning Suede forward with a crook of her finger. Suede walks with baby steps into the middle of the grass field. Sky circling around her until she squirms.

"So, I actually don't think she should—"

Without warning, Sky punches Suede across the cheek bone—fist creating a loud thwacking noise that prompts me to gasp.

Suede stumbles backward, sniffling as she massages her face. "Ouch! Why would you do that?!"

Her eyes swell with tears and I groan.

Jason is going to kill Sky. Then Ezra. Then *me*. Then resuscitate Sky to kill her again.

And lord knows what he'll do with our corpses.

"Cede, Suede."

"I cede!" She sniffles as I shakily step between her and Sky. "Sorry, Arsonist. I'm not really meant to be fighting."

"It's okay. You tried."

"That was trying?" Sky scoffs. "What are they teaching you guys in the Air quadrant while we bleed and prepare for the worst? How to be pretty little flowers?"

Ezra rubs his chin in contemplation. Even he's a little mystified. A Fire affinity would have eaten that punch with no issue.

"I'm a pretty flower?" Suede can't resist a sassy quip in return.

I look over my shoulder, silently begging her to shut her mouth. My presence a little *too* comforting to her.

"You're a useless predictable daisy. Sit down. You'll never cease to bore me."

Suede looks to me for confirmation and I motion my head toward where Ezra has walked off to sit.

Apparently, he has no issue with leaving me to be smacked around.

She plops down in the grass a few feet away from him. Smoothing down her skirt and ranting about how he reeks of tobacco and how rude it is to smoke in people's faces.

I turn to Sky, ignoring the bickering that's begun a few yards away. "Should you be the one training me? Your brother told me to stay away from you in a very... *clear* way."

"You look great by the way. Healed up nicely. Must've stopped by the cool people store." Sky's taken on a new tone, voice so casual and unthreatening that I do a double take. "I'm fucking with you."

"I know. But—"

"Leave Caveman to me and focus on what I'm about to tell you." I suck on my bottom lip, attempting to stop the tremors in my hands as she says, "My brother taught me to fight when I was thirteen." Sky unsheathes the silver dagger on her hip, staring at herself in its sleek reflection. "And I learned about gardening the first time I rolled through the dirt."

She wipes the blade off with her shirtsleeve, pointing it forward until the point taps my jugular. "Do you know how much effort people put into cultivating the perfect flower? Some get more care than others. Some need to be tended to for the rest of their lives. Some flowers are thrown into horrible and harsh conditions, plucked before they've fully bloomed. They acclimate to survive."

"Maybe the world should change so all flowers get to survive it as they are."

Sky lowers her dagger and walks around me, observing my new attire from Ezra. "First lesson, flowers don't get to complain about the hand life deals them. Men and women alike despise a victim. Blame them even more than the perpetrators of their abuse."

"I'm not a victim. I'm—"

"Suffering and wondering why no one gives a fuck?" I shrug and she nods her head. "You know how accessible it is to watch vulnerable people get taken advantage of? News of starvation, mass health crisis, police brutality, homelessness, it all reaches us here. And after a while, no one checks for updates. What's attention grabbing about unchanging hardship? It's pretty bland dinner conversation, don't you think? Makes the Wagyu harder to swallow?"

"My family discusses these things all the time. It's never ruined dinner. I think it's better to eat with people who share your horror."

"People don't want to be horrified, they want... something new. Reminding the general public that the cards are stacked against you, only bores them. They've seen that show a thousand times over."

"What now? I change the channel for their viewing pleasure?"

Sky chuckles as she mulls my question over. "Yes."

"I was being sarcastic."

"I wasn't. You can get away with anything as long as it's entertaining enough. People want to be enthralled so they don't have to think farther than a stone's throw. They'd rather be spectacularly lied to than ever face reality." She tilts her head and my gaze falls to the ground. "Take a coin flip. You toss it up, and it lands. Does it have another side?"

"Yes."

"You speak of reality. I speak of two-dimensional perception. Only one matters to an audience."

"If they only remembered that the coin spins—"

"Watching a coin spin is *boring*. People check to see how it lands. And if the face you choose is kindness, they will spit in it because they can. Do you like to be spit on, Shiloh?"

"How would I know what I can handle?" Sky chuckles and my face heats. "I meant I can wait for society to be interested in the truth again."

"Fine. Be spit on all you want, but people are utterly uninterested when someone allows themselves to be abused."

"No one allows themselves to be abused."

"The coin landed differently."

"Flip it over."

"Society lost that ability with each horrendous choice of reproduction. There's only so much compassion the brain can store now before it's screaming for compensation." Sky steps forward until our boots are toe to toe. Gray eyes narrowed, and narrow jaw squared, until she speaks in only a chilly whisper for me to hear. "I watched you struggle already. I held your hand when you cried. Now you refuse to pay me back the energy I spent attempting to empathize? You were supposed to get smarter. *Tougher.* Unapologetic when you sought out your revenge. That was the contract we agreed on when I decided to focus on your hardships. So get up you good for nothing doormat." Sky frowns when I remain silent, tilting her head slightly. "No? You're just going to let yourself be stepped on? Well, now you've bored me. So guess what? You always deserved it and I won't be watching next time. I'll root for the winners. They complain a lot less and don't disturb my peace."

"We can give people more time."

"Absolutely. You get grace to be weak when your appearance

enchants others. When it preoccupies and enamors without a word uttered from your lips. But eventually, every faithful supporter demands your blood as payment. You always look down, so no one can see your face, and wear big ass sweaters that melt off your body. Your current garments are a few steps in the right direction, but unless you want to show some skin, and do a little dance, your time is up."

"I have to fight or get sexier because people are bored and lack critical thinking?"

"The woes of womanhood, am I right?" Sky finger coils one of my curls. "Though the teeth you bare are not the teeth with which you bite. What resides in your molars, is between you and the tongues that sweep your teeth."

"I don't want to perform."

"You prefer watching?" Her eyes take on a sultry glint, tilting my chin up with a singular finger as her words gush into the air like sweetened syrup rolling down a maple tree. "Do you like what I wore for you? Would you prefer me on my knees or bent over? I'll be anything you want me to be, and I bet you'd melt for it and taste so fucking good."

Sky's tongue sweeps her bottom lip and her last words sound like a plea, "Just tell me how you like it. Show me how I should take you."

"That's a... performance?" Sky drops her hand, stepping back as I ask, "Do you break that one out a lot?"

"On occasion. Not all performances are so alluring," she grins. "Your turn."

"You want *me* to act like that?"

"Seduce me, Shiloh Benson." I fill my lungs with air to create the illusion of a fuller chest and jut out one hip, fluttering my lashes as I hold my breath. "Do you have something in your eye?"

"Just you. My, sexy little, sex toy. So, watch out, because things are about to get... *filthy.*" My words come out strained as I use up the last of my air supply and Sky presses her lips together.

"You know what? We're going to try something else."

"You didn't feel anything? Not even, like, general curiosity?"

"This world's about the male gaze. Were you turned on, Cousin?"

Ezra doesn't so much as look up from his book. Giving me a

thumbs down as I sputter, looking to Suede for help. My roommate finds a sudden interest in her cuticles until I turn back to Sky.

"I can be sexy."

"Can you earn female solidarity? You must remember, support from other women isn't free." Sky switches personalities like a t-shirt, batting dark eyelashes and running slender hands along the curves of her body, pausing on her hips in horror. "Am I gaining more weight than my friends? Do they secretly hope that I am? Is my skin pale enough? But not *too* pale, of course. I can't have anyone looking right through me. They'll notice my rehearsed carelessness takes a monstrous amount of effort. Am I dancing terribly? Singing too loud? Am I taking up the space of a woman who performs perfectly? Will she like me better when I've moved off center stage? When I'm not a threat to her show?"

"Oh..." I trail off and Sky relaxes her posture, voice raspy and sullen once more.

"I know a thing or two about blooming for the eyes of an ever-changing society, that demands perfection, yet prays they never have to give it themselves. You cannot satisfy the insatiable hunger of people who are several sandwiches short of a picnic with *reality*. Therefore, learn to accept that most people are criminally stupid. Then, root deep and grow thorns as you feed them your leftovers and call it a feast. Starving people don't know the difference when they get to eat."

"Thorns?"

"If I had to be a flower I'd be the most useful part."

"Some people think the most useful part is the pollen and nectar."

"What do you think?"

"I think I'd like to exist and not have to prove what parts of me are useful and to who."

"I think solely about a flower being of use to itself. Petals are admired until they wither and age. Or, in worse scenarios, their admirers begin to pluck and crumple them for fun. Thorns... get to prick. Defend themselves and other flowers who share their vicinity. She thinks you need her, when the truth is, limp daisies only thrive when growing next to roses with endless nutrients to share." Suede cringes from my peripheral, Sky having raised her voice so it carried. "Mark my words. Blondie's going to look back at her life one day and realize she's drained and exhausted. Wilted herself in preparation to be plucked. And that crystal vase she clawed for will become a clear cage to watch the world pass her by from her husband's shelf."

"That's unkind," I whisper.

"Kindness is not the face I choose." Sky smacks my cheek lightly and I blink up at her. When my hands stay fisted at my sides she turns her face for easy access. "Someone hits you, you hit them back. Twice as hard. Take and take until they don't dare try it again."

"An eye for an eye?"

"That's for men who risk losing their second one. You pluck both in exchange for yours being the slightest bit damaged."

"If you blind someone they'll still retaliate. Someone has to be willing to stop first. If my eye is just damaged, the corneal tissue is the fastest healing in the human body so—"

"When your eyes are taken you learn you never should have poked a Bear. You know your place. You stay in it. Only those with a death wish lose sight when blinded."

"I'm not a Bear."

"I'll make one of you. Now, roar so they fear you. Stomp so they hear your footsteps rumble the Earth they stand on. You'll give them fair warning and they know that you'll still win because to fight a Bear is to lose a fight."

Sky roars and I jump backward, giving her enough time to spark her fire. She draws dual daggers of silver that catch flame in both of her hands and it's hard to remember she's only training me as I stare into the eyes of a flaming goddess of war. The only thing that could satiate her blood-thirst is my defeat.

"You're ambidextrous," I squeak, backing up slowly as I fumble the match I keep stored behind my ear. "You and Nox."

"You're observant when you're trying to avoid something."

"Can't we just do the obstacle course?"

I spark the stick against my pant leg, and the flame jumps into my left hand, fashioning my fire into a whip of light.

Suede cheers from the side, clapping wildly for me. "Go Arsonist! Kick her asssss!" She winces and touches her cheek, massaging the deep red, fist-sized bloom that's sure to bruise.

*Yes, Jason will have an aneurysm.*

"You're funny, Pax," Sky says.

"Pax?" I ask, drawing my blade with a quivering hand.

"Nickname for sissies back home. You'll earn a better one soon enough."

Without warning, she lunges for me, and I do the smart thing.

*I run.*

My avoidance tactic works at first but Sky's a ruthless machine when activated. She fights like a dance—swift on her feet, steel toed boots gliding across grass as seamlessly as blades on ice.

I evade her as much as I can before she corrals me inside a circle of red hot fire with her. Unable to run as she turns the heat up. "I'll go easy on you this time." Sky coughs, the smoke from burning grass wafting into her face as she tosses her blades outside the ring.

I find out quickly that Sky's *easy* is a solid ass beating. The whip of light in my hand only deterring the worst of her punches.

"I cede!" I choke out when the hour of training is at its end. Spitting blood as adrenaline pumps through my veins, hands shielding me from another punch.

My tongue feels around for a tooth that may be loose while she dismisses her fire.

"You're a piece of work," Sky says, rising to her feet before helping me to mine. Although she insults me, her eyes are fond. Almost—

"Are we friends now?" I blurt.

"You're asking me if we are *friends?*" Sky raises her brows as Suede pops over, bouncing in shiny white tennis shoes, her hair flowing in the gentle winds that help dust me off. "Sure. I'm, like, sooo your friend." Sarcasm drips from each syllable as Sky pastes on a frilly voice, eyes slitted toward the white hair ribbon tying my curls into a high ponytail.

"We might be if you got to know me. Mom says I'm like an onion and when you peel the layers you'll see I'm—"

"Undeniably odd." Again, something flickers in her eyes. A certain degree of fondness that is on the verge of friendship. Even if it's not there yet. "See you tomorrow, Pax."

"Okay. Sweet dreams."

She rolls her eyes before turning to Ezra. "Goodbye Cousin."

He grunts in response.

"*You.* Don't feel inclined to show up again." Sky gives Suede a once over before she strolls away, scooping her bag in one swift movement as she leaves.

"I was here first!" Suede yells before turning to me. Putting on the same frilly voice Sky had and twirling a blonde lock around her finger. "Don't worry about it. She's *soooo* your friend."

Ezra huffs his sixth cigarette of the hour. Not seeming to have the same humor as Suede, his dimpled scowl deepening each time she speaks.

"You're going to want her friendship too," she assures him. "Might as well give in now."

Of this one, I'm not so sure.

He scowls, getting up and stalking off without another word.

"*La Toxicaaaa,*" Suede whispers as soon as we're alone. "I bet you're eating this up, huh? I'm now certain that it's your hamartia."

"Which one of the Honestus brothers taught you that?" I groan, collapsing into the grass to catch my breath. "Tell them to stop."

"I'm having Jace teach me insults in Icarus's favorite languages in case he decides to insult me in Spanish again."

"He's never done that and I'm not—"

"You'll figure it out. I know a thing or two." Suede gives me an exaggerated wink that would stir confusion if I wasn't sapped of energy, collapsing beside me as we stare up at the stars. "Fantasize all you want, but can you do it indoors? Grass makes me itchy. If I'm going to lay outside, I prefer that it's sand."

While she may be onto something about my Hamartia, I'm not thinking about Ezra Alvarez. I'm thinking that I got through another day's walk through the woods.

Every person on this goddamn planet can think me a victim, but all I've done is survive and have the audacity to complain aloud about the journey's bitter cold.

And I'll keep surviving.

And maybe, I'll keep complaining too.

# PART THREE
# CHRYSALIS

# CHAPTER 18

Sky hasn't so much as pretended to go easy on me in training. The proof of my uptick in physical activity is tangible on days I can barely bend my knees as my muscles work to repair themselves. Russ is all too eager to help me up the steps and carry my bag— squeezing my ass like a *dog,* or whatever. So much so, that I've started emitting overly satisfied moans to prompt different reactions.

In return, he's taken to talking through his teeth about how he 'never asked me to be an actress.'

Which really could be a career fallback if Harvard is off the table and Societal Operations continues on a downward path.

Over the past few weeks, in addition to our weekly study sessions, Russ and I have developed a system that I'm not entirely proud of, writing it off as desperate times call for desperate measures.

He keeps up with Professor Martin and I keep up with him as best I can. It's something that can't be helped when our Professor drones on in Latin so swiftly it blends into one solid monologue of indistinguishable exposition.

Among all of us, Russ is the swiftest with his notes. Always right on par, shoving paper after paper my way and emitting a few yawns every so often.

When several papers have begun to pile up on my desk, I sit my pencil down, deciding I might as well take my time with Russ's notes when I get back to my dorm.

A significant amount of it must have passed, because he brushes his hand against my back, a repetitive soothing rub that prompts my return to the land of the living. "What's wrong?"

"Nothing?"

"You were gone for nearly twenty minutes."

The man on my other side throws us a dirty look as we talk, deciding not to dedicate his attention for too long. A combination of Russ's cold stare and having missed something Professor Martin said.

When I shrug, Russ takes the matter into his own hands, sorting my notes apart from his in order to take stock of the situation.

After a quick assessment, his mouth forms a hard line, gaze flicking down toward Professor Martin.

Part of me knows what's coming.

I pick my pencil back up and begin to scribble, showing Russ it's fine as his arms fold over his chest, a tense set to his jaw when he begins to take in the lecture—not just absentmindedly transcribe notes as he always does. "Professor Martin, I'd like you to slow down and restart your lecture from the beginning."

"Russ," I whisper in protest. *Because honestly, what the fuck?*

"I beg your pardon?"

"Slow down and restart your lecture, Professor."

Professor Martin eyes me and I drop my gaze to the desk. "You want me to restart from the beginning? Anything else, *your highness?*"

"Thanks for asking Silas."

Everyone stirs at this.

"It's difficult to understand when you switch between English and Latin at a moment's notice. Pick one. The former."

"*Russ.*" I tug on his shirt sleeve and he ignores my attempts to garner his attention.

He told me once in passing that Latin is spoken in his house frequently because the staff aren't fluent. That way dinners feel more personal, something only the founder families and more well-established loyalists make a habit of doing.

It's evident, as people shift uncomfortably, that I'm not the only one having issues. If any of them are lower class, they'll be struggling to keep up too. Maybe better than I have but nothing compared to Russ's level of fluency.

Professor Martin finds this amusing, adjusting the sleeves on his suit jacket. "I understand you want to see your friend succeed, but I don't pander to—"

"You don't pander or you don't do your job?" Russ asks, leaning his elbows on the desk, hands folded together in front of him. "The job you are in danger of losing should there be a repeat of today's lesson at any point moving forward."

"I'd advise you to calm down, boy."

"And I'd advise you to use my full name when you're addressing me next."

There's an awful drag of silence until Professor Martin says, "Icarus Honestus."

"You forgot Amias, but I forgive you." Russ grins. "Now, I can assure you, Silas. You haven't seen me anything but calm. And I'll remain so. Aren't you thankful? Say thank you."

"Thank you," he whispers.

"You're welcome." Russ drums on the desk with our pencils as the class waits in bated breath, leaning back and placing his feet up as the boy next to him moves his textbook to make space. "Before we start over, you should apologize for wasting my friend's time and for being generally unpleasant to look at."

"I... apologize for wasting your time, Ms. Benson."

"Are you forgetting something?"

"Russ," I whisper. *"Enough."*

Professor Martin sucks his teeth. "I apologize for... being unpleasant to look at."

The classroom erupts into a steady stream of laughter as Russ gives him a toothy grin. "Well done, boy! At least someone got to learn today!"

For the rest of class, Professor Martin teaches in slow monotonous English. A snail's pace. Starting from scratch so that we run overtime. By the end of the lecture I know more about the Terra Australis mail system than I ever have.

As the lecture concludes, Russ rises, slinging his bag over one shoulder.

When he reaches the main floor he whispers something in the professor's ear and claps him on the shoulder, Professor Martin cringing away from his hand.

Russ strolls out of the lecture hall, and I hop to my feet, scrambling down the steps as I jam scattered papers into my tattered backpack. Running through packed hallways and out of the front entrance until I spot him by the flagpole.

"Icarus!" I yell from afar, taking two steps at a time so I can match his long stride. He pauses so I can catch up, face a hardened mask. "Russ, what was that?!"

"What was what?"

"Him calling you boy, was... we should talk to someone about that."

"Why? I'm a grown man. I handled it myself."

"Right. Sorry. But also, no one has to speak English because I'm behind."

"I know my future sister-in-law wants to make me seem like some controlling traditionalist, because she thinks the epitome of feminism is to joke about aborting Black children, but I'm not."

"Oh. Okay, so, *layers.* First off—"

"He was speaking Etruscan and throwing in Latin every other phrase."

"Why would he do that?"

"Because he's a taint. No New Blood is going to say they don't understand their lecture." Russ glances at his wristwatch and pulls a bottle from his bag, cracking open the drink in hand. "After you've learned a hundred languages, they bleed together in your head. I make out most of anything people say." Russ chugs the bottle in his hands and tosses the glass into a recycling bin, pulling a protein bar from his bag next. "He was wasting the time of everyone in that room and of course I'm going to be upset when it comes to you. Jason was right, the disrespect has gone too far. This is—" Russ bites into the freshly unwrapped bar and spits it out into the trash can. "I. Hate. Almonds!"

he roars, kicking the metal bin with each clipped word until it dents and falls over, bursting open on the pavement.

People avert their eyes as they pass us, a nearby staff member scrambling to pick up the mess. Russ narrowly contains his temper, waving them away. "Stop! I'll clean it up! I kicked it over!"

I help him clean in silence, thighs burning from the squat as we rise. "You had a phone call with your Dad last night, right? What did he say?"

"Nothing that wasn't true."

"Are you okay?"

"I'm fine."

"You don't look fine."

"I said I'm—" I lurch toward him, pulling him into as tight of a hug as I can, arms twining around his neck.

Russ is stiff at first, but eventually, he returns it.

Arms wrapping tightly around my torso until it's hard to breathe.

My once frail friend has a bit more mass on him than I remember, but he still has a clean spicy citrus scent that clings to his neck.

I inhale it deeply, nose brushing against his skin, small traces of sweet almonds peeking through the longer I sniff.

He smells especially good today.

"Fine," Russ whispers.

"I'm worried about you."

"Don't be. I've never been happier." I only squeeze him tighter in response. "You have an incredibly strong hug."

"Mom calls it a sticky hug. When I was little, I'd run around with half eaten lollipops. Whenever someone was sad, I'd hug them 'til I fell asleep. I'd get them all sticky with whatever was left of my candy."

"That sounds like you," he chuckles.

"I haven't attempted it in a while. Is it working?"

"Very much so."

"Good. I have as many as you need."

He kisses the top of my head just before a throat clears behind us.

"Russ?" The voice is gruff and awkward, but his face is a lot less arrogant than it was before. Tristain ruffles his coils, brown eyes growing wary the longer they survey us. "I mean, Icarus."

"Yes?" Russ asks, tucking me under his left arm.

"Could we talk? Alone?"

"Anything you have to say to me, you can say in front of her."

"Fair enough." Tristain straightens his posture. "First off, I apologize, Shiloh Benson. I have never called a woman a bitch and I should not have started with you. Or, have started to begin with."

"Then why'd you do it?" I frown.

"I believe I have some things to work on. Though the promise of self reflection is no excuse, it still won't happen again. I swear on my name."

I chew my cheek, nodding in understanding. Maybe there's room to be cautious but I've been on the receiving end of Jason's annoyance, it's enough to grant him leniency as I whisper, "We're okay."

His eyes fill with gratitude, bowing his head slightly before turning to Russ.

"I respect you a great deal, Cousin. I may only share drops of your blood but I know some of the pressures of it still. I also know its privileges. You could treat people like dirt in the cracks of your shoes and you have always been nothing but kind." Russ's eyes tighten, and I squeeze his side until tension slowly leeches from his shoulders. "I am sorry when I had the opportunity I did not return the favor."

"Why should I believe anything you have to say?"

"You're under no obligation to do so, but I look forward to seeing you seated in our home state. With complete respect, you've pushed the envelope farther than any Honestus has ever dared to. Last year, I watched you stand by your Father's side on the news for the first time. Revealing your face to millions who had not yet seen it. We knew you traded your private presence for several political concessions. Including for... people who make little contribution to our society."

Tristain crosses his arms over his chest, leaning forward to add, "The day the Lions spoke to Leonusver, Hiemsternum and Ardengris followed suit. *Immediately*. Because the Lions know the way. They have always known. And it is for your mind, and your heart for others that I declare loyalty to you now." Tristain circles his hands and bows his head, not daring to look up as he awaits judgment.

Russ's face is full of doubt. Not in Tristain's words, but in himself. Wondering if he deserves such recognition. I poke his arm and it prompts him to speak after blowing a raspberry. "I... accept your apology."

Tristain raises his head, shoulders sinking in relief as he reaches to shake Russ' hand.

"One caveat, Korovk."

"What?"

"You will sit at my table now."

Tristain's eyes nearly pop out of his head. "You want me to sit at your table?"

"You are in the forest with me. Hyenas will come back to nip at your heels. You should be surrounded by good people. People that don't turn on you. People who are a good influence."

At this, Russ motions toward me.

"Can Sira join us?"

"Of course. And, feel free to tell your parents. I know they've been displeased recently."

Tristain nods his head rapidly as they grasp forearms.

And that's that. When we part, he's only the first to begin issuing apologies to Icarus. And I can't help but grin through each and every one as my heart swells with pride.

My Russ—a Lion he's been all along.

And his people are coming back to him.

Since Sky banned Suede from our training sessions, she's decided she has just as much to teach me outside of them. Things that apparently the Bear will *never* understand. And since no ideas are bad ideas, I'm currently applying waterproof liquid eyeliner.

I don't find myself too bad at it, hands steady from years of piano.

"Sky's gonna laugh when I show up to spar in a cat eye."

"That's the point! If not her, someone will underestimate you. People fill in the blanks on things they don't understand. Assumptions to ease the confusion." Suede unscrews the tube of her mascara, leaning toward the floor-length mirror to work on her lashes. "It'll be easier to fight when their guard's down."

"I guess, but, I don't think I need help being underestimated. For obvious reasons."

Suede's eyebrows furrow, and I wonder if to her, the reasons aren't so obvious.

Even still, whether or not it helps my training, I *like* the way this looks. Why should it bother me what anyone thinks?

"When it's to your benefit, underestimation is a weapon, Arsonist. People aren't quick to ask me to do anything I don't want to." Suede tilts her head, swirling a lock of hair around her finger as she crosses her eyes. "I read texts on theoretical mathematics for fun. I'm *smart!* You know that, right? You don't think I'm a daisy like she said?"

"No?" I ask, lowering my eyeliner as she huffs from my side.

"They all see one thing." Suede taps her temple with her finger before twisting the tube closed. "But really, all the makeup proves is how great at time management I am for showing up at the same time as everyone else looking ten times hotter." She checks my makeup, nodding her head with approval. "You should continue this, you look like a siren."

"You're onto something. War paint wasn't just camouflage. There was tactic to it too."

"Yes! *War paint!*" Suede makes a gesture around her skull and a puffing sound with her lips, as if to signal a mind imploding in on itself. "They'll never get it! And honestly, that's fine. My roommate and my sexy ass boyfriend do. Great outfit by the way. It doesn't make you look like you're being drowned for once."

My new outfit consists of jeans that are fitted to my body and a long sleeve that's true to size—a white satin ribbon pulling my hair back.

I'm fireproof through and through, so perhaps it's what gives me courage to ask what I'm sure is an incendiary question.

"Was Russ a test run?" Suede cracks her knuckles and I fidget with the liquid eyeliner in my hands. "You know I'd never share anything you told me in confidence. Right? You're my friend."

"Really?" she asks. "Because I've never had girlfriends before. All my friends on the islands are surfers and none of them are female."

"Well, I don't have too much practice either, but I know they do things like get ready together and share secrets." I smile and Suede relaxes slightly.

"In that case, Jace came in me when his brews were wearing off, and I let him. A few times."

She blushes as I gape. *"Why?"*

"It... feels better for him at the end of the month and I was ovulating so I was basically in heat!"

"Oh. My. God."

"I know. Okay? I got my period, so we're fine." She releases a heavy gust of air. "But during our post-orgasm, euphoric discussion, he said he wants eight children. Space out two every twenty years so we can give each of them enough attention with all his other duties." Suede appears as if she's just sucked on a lemon. "Eighty years of children! And they don't go away after?! They multiply and have their own!"

"Did you tell him you're hesitant?"

She forces a smile. "Children are non-negotiable, so I'm hoping when I graduate, I'm willing to bend. We'll have staff and his Mom. It shouldn't be an issue."

"Kids aren't something you bend on." I squeeze her arm gently. "If you regret having a kid, you break, or you break them."

"I could change my mind. It's not completely made up."

"Really?"

She stares at her reflection until I nudge her again. "I grew up on stories of *Jason Honestus,* you know? In pictures and on the news, I thought he was hot, but I dismissed it as... infatuation."

"What changed?"

"I ran into Icarus near the Leonusver estate. Didn't recognize him because he was never in the public eye before last spring."

"Tristain mentioned that the other day."

"He attends events with Jace in his place. Russ avoids them like the plague."

"Oh. Things are starting to make sense."

"Yeah. Also, he called himself *Russ.*" Suede giggles. "We hung out for an hour before I realized. Then, he kept asking to hang out and I was new and lonely so why not. But one day, Jace walked into the room and..." She clears her throat and brushes blush on the apples of her cheeks. "One thing led to another. We kissed in the gardens and he asked me to leave when Icarus found us and freaked out. Besides, Jace was set to be engaged soon."

"To who?"

"He won't tell me. It's still a touchy subject. But he denied his betrothal the next morning and no one in the Honestus household spoke to each other for a month. We had the palace staff exchange our letters secretly for weeks, and we didn't see one another again until Icarus forgave him. By then, I was a shell of a person and he had a full beard when he finally climbed through my window. That night was how we knew the stars wrote our story. Our souls are tied."

"That's beautiful, Suede." A lump forms in my throat wondering what it would be like to love someone so desperately.

To be loved so unconditionally in return.

"I'd love my children. I swear on my name. I'd protect them with my life. Curse myself with each coo for *ever* wanting differently."

"But?"

"I might resent having them. And not knowing how much terrifies me," Suede whispers. "My worst fear is to be a mother. But if I take it off the table, we're done with. If I marry him and don't plan to do it, it would be *evil*. Divorce is not in his vocabulary. He hasn't spoken to my dad since he found out about his infidelity."

"Really?"

"He's faithful in what the Universe plans between husband and wife. He wouldn't force me to carry a child, but we'd never recover in this lifetime if that's the path I chose." I wince and her eyes widen. "I know you think, he's like, the worst. But—"

"That's not at all true? I'm allowed to disagree with Jason, and still like him as a person. It's *his* choice that our friendship is on pause. He doesn't like that I question him."

"Why question him at all? He'd protect you, if you let him." Before I can respond, she rushes to add, "Your life here can be easy, Arsonist. Jace keeps his heart closed off but once he opens it he's the most loving man you'll ever meet. He wishes the best for you. You won him over by caring for Icarus when others refused."

"I can't take an easy life if the trade-off is staying silent when people are in need. I see the pressures from society he feels. Ways that people believe men should act, and I want more for all of them. I do. But I can wish for a better life for someone, and firmly believe continuing the cycle they were born into, is harmful. They have complete agency to break it, and a victim can also perpetuate—"

"Hold on. Jace isn't abusive?"

"I'm aware. The one thing I know Jason Honestus would never do is harm you, Suede. This conversation isn't even about him at the end of the day."

"What's it about?" she asks warily.

"You underestimate yourself. *I* don't think you're a daisy. *You* do. Don't see your contributions as inherently less than, because they aren't physical manifestations." Her eyes widen and I've never seen her so hopeful. So curious if she brings equal value that my insides hurt. "If you want to live with him as your guide, that's not for me to judge. It seems nice to have someone who only wants to take care of you. But love is not a zero-sum game and I am not his to dictate. I don't choose that path, and I don't want to be asked to fall in line beside you again. It makes me wildly uncomfortable every time you insinuate I should. He and I will be equals, or we will be *nothing*. And I will still respect our differences of opinion from afar, as long as they stay his own."

Her eyes fall to the ground. "Okay. We'll respect each other's differences. I will walk this path with him, and I won't break. I will bend."

*How much do the both of you have to bend for love before you're different people entirely? Can you survive what you morph into? Will it remain as pure as when you began?*

Instead of unleashing my explosive thoughts, I pull her into a hug.

Suede stiffens until I pull away from her. "I'm sorry."

"Why?" I ask. "It's okay to be upset."

"I mean about the things that I said when I was trying to be a Lion. I had no business facilitating that conversation."

"*Ohhh.* Well, comparatively, it's not the worst thing that happened to me that day."

"Actually, it is the worst thing. People that are mean to you do it because they feed on false narratives. I'm your friend, and everyone on this planet I love is different than me. So, if you could find it in your heart to forgive my occasional missteps, I'm going to do better." Suede blinks several times, doe eyes staring so intensely a laugh rushes through my insides.

"Okay. Sure. If you're willing to have conversations... I'm willing to see them through."

"Of course I am! And, to butter you up, I ordered those candies Josephine stole. But I used my own inventory ID, so I'll have to wait until next week to receive the order."

"Oh my God, thank you. Russ is trying to convert me and he keeps asking if I liked them. I don't wanna explain the break-in to my new bodyguard."

"I figured. I heard you fumbling through a lie," she grins. "Could I try some, though? I want to ship a pack home to Erik, if they're good."

"You just offered me reparations, and immediately asked to share them with you and your family?"

"My brother's biracial?" she frowns, cheeks flushing scarlet when I raise my brows. "He is! Look! Look at my desk, there's a picture!"

"Suede." I muffle a laugh and she groans, whacking me with a fuzzy pillow until we settle our differences with a fluffy fight. Leaving our room in disarray and feathers strewn all about.

# CHAPTER 19

"I wish I got to enroll in Elsiom," Tristain grumbles, mournfully flicking the string on his hoodie. A brisk autumn chill hangs in the air Jason circulates around our table, and Tristain's made it known every day this week he misses the land of eternal spring.

"I wish you got to enroll there too. Then, you wouldn't be bitching in my ear right now," Osira says, flipping dozens of midnight black braids over one shoulder.

She's the other new addition to our lunch table. Dare I say, even more welcome than the first. Her familiar fan of lashes flutters against the glistening ebony of her high cheekbones each time she rolls her eyes. "Turn that big ass head sideways and glare at someone else, Korovk."

Tristain traces his cheek with his tongue and I eye the sour gummies he's been popping with rapt attention, a notable droop to his eyelids as he chews.

Russ squeezes my shoulder, drawing my gaze back to my homework as he says, "You got one wrong."

"What? *How?*"

"You have to have a second operator sitting in the train now. There was a death in Ardengris last week, so the regulations have changed since then. I wouldn't expect anyone to know it, but Martin will expect it."

Things are beginning to get clearer by the day, but Russ says it's a system you learn by partaking in it, not by sitting in class.

"Osira's father heads the transportation systems. She keeps me in the loop. I'll have to have dinner with him over break."

"Icarus, if you don't visit again soon, my parents will *disown* me."

The two exchange grins and Tristain sucks his teeth, cracking jokes to get Osira's attention back.

Although he has a knack for pressing his luck, he's incredibly funny. Telling stories from growing up and visiting the Honestus estate that make Russ and Jason cringe with embarrassment while Suede and I full belly laugh.

"Are you wearing a new cologne?" I ask. Russ leans closer as I inhale, jaw clenching when my nose nears his neck—that same faint scent that's an addition to his calming citrus.

"Soap, maybe?" I ignore curious glances from Jason and Suede as footsteps thunder closer. Heart in a tug of war with gravity as the Sapientis' approach.

One by one, they drop their trays on the table. Solara sitting next to Suede and immediately digging into her food without a word.

Nox pulls out the middle chair for himself, but Sky slides into it, switching the placement of their trays. He stares expressionlessly at the last seat left, placed directly between his sister and I.

Everyone quiets when he plops into the chair, angling his body so that I only see the outline of his jaw.

Sky kicks its base, but Nox remains firm in his stance, flicking a yellow tablet from his fingers that Sky catches in her mouth.

Jason is the only one who speaks, making formal introductions to fill the awkward silence.

I lean around Nox's hulking frame and Sky shoves a forkful of spaghetti in her mouth, licking sauce off her bottom lip as she meets my gaze. "Stop staring at me, Pax."

"Is this you saying we're—"

"Acquaintances," she finishes through a mouthful of garlic bread.

"I'm so full," Suede whines, pushing her plate away and glancing at Sky's. "They give too much spaghetti."

"And here she goes again."

"What? I'm just saying I can't finish big portions."

"Then *just* don't consume them," Sky says. "That's information you should internalize while you pinch stomach flab in the dead of night."

"I don't have stomach flab?" Suede lifts the hem of her shirt, rising to display the washboard she's gained from years of surfing. "Jace, do I have stomach flab?"

"No," Jason sighs, grasping her hips and tugging her into her seat. "No one at this table has stomach flab. Even if you did, so what?"

"Aww. Don't ever let me."

There's a lull in conversation as Solara and Sky eat hunched over their trays. Nox hasn't even begun on his food, glancing at his sisters every so often while he cuts his steak into slivers, preparing his dish meticulously to pass the time.

"So..." Russ begins. "I think you would love Leonusver, Shi. My mother sent me the keys to my estate, so, this summer you could—"

"Reside in Hiemsternum. There's plenty of cottages for Sapienti loyalists." I don't think Sky means it. In fact, I'm sure she doesn't. She wants to piss someone off.

"Why would she want to live there, instead of with me?"

"Who doesn't want to enjoy snowfall with a steak and red wine at the day's end? To get up and dance, instead of sitting and watching others sing?"

"Russ is Vegan," I explain amidst the growing tension.

"That's childish. You think maggots will hesitate to eat *our* eyeballs?" Sky asks. "There's a natural way of life. We're all meat suits marinating for a feast, may as well give them something hearty."

I wipe my sweaty palms on my jeans. "You don't think you're being a little insensitive?"

"Oh no," she gasps. "Is the Vegan community going to riot? Their supreme leader is right here, wearing leather loafers, along with the rest of them. I think it'll be fine."

"They're secondhand?" Russ frowns.

"Would you like to switch chairs, Sky?" Nox asks, a hand covering the lower portion of his face as if he smells something harsh.

"Did I indicate I wanted to switch chairs with you, Caveman?"

Suede mutters something under her breath and Sky looks her up and down. "Say it with your chest, Blondie, or don't say it at all."

"I wasn't talking to you."

"Weren't you?"

Suede curls into Jason's side. "If you *must* know, I said this table is getting crowded."

"Your shrillish voice makes my ears ring, so I guess we're both unhappy with our seating arrangements."

"Blonde on blonde crime is lethal these days," Tristain says.

"Didn't your cousin publicly hang you?" Solara asks. "What's that called?"

"Water under the bridge. Females hold shit in for years. Let it go ladies. You'll all be much happier that way." He frowns when every woman at the table raises their eyebrows. "What?"

"Who are you calling, *females?*" Osira asks.

"Is that not what you are?"

"No? We talked about this."

"*Ohhhh.* Correct! Listen up newcomers, because I'll only say this once. Your options are her, him, they, dude, by your name, or a smile and head nod. So you all need to figure it out, and let me know. But I'm warning you now, don't switch up on me without two days notice. You'll get your feelings hurt." Tristain yelps as Osira pinches him. "Ouch!? What now?"

"Stop. Talking," she says through clenched teeth. "You're embarrassing the both of us."

"How? You told me to smile and nod!"

"And yet, you're flapping those damn gums and still don't know what an inside voice is. Stupid people are always happier. Let's unpack that."

"How did you guys meet?" I ask, searching for a segue as Tristain sighs, clearly reminiscing over the moment.

"A ball at the palace. The first time we met, she broke my nose almost clean off."

"Do you want to tell them what you did before I stood up for myself?"

"Nah. That's water under the bridge too."

"Just checking." A smile plays on her lips and I decide that one day, when Tristain learns to stop speaking his every thought, they're getting married. And maybe even if he doesn't.

Russ adjusts his glasses and Sky shoots him a dirty look, lips parting as my eyes dart around for something of substance to distract her.

"Cat!" I blurt. "You. Have. A. *Cat!*"

"How do you—"

I reach around Nox, who leans backward again, plucking a stray gray hair on the sleeve of her shirt and holding it up to the light. "What's your cat's name?"

"I wouldn't call that thing a cat," Solara says.

One corner of Nox's mouth curls upward, the only indication he's listening to our conversation at all.

Sky roots through her school bag before pulling out a folded picture. "Yes. I have acquired a cat."

Russ' eyes light with interest. "I didn't know that! I love cats."

"Why the hell would you know that?" He falls silent as she passes her picture around.

"I've always liked animals more than people," Suede says, peering at the photograph.

Sky chuckles. "I'm not at all surprised."

"I think I'll open a sanctuary for marine life one day."

"That's wonderful, my love." Jason and Suede share a smile as he passes Tristain the photo without looking.

"That kitten has a face only a mother could love," Solara mutters.

"You have a face only our mother could love."

"Our mother is dead."

"You get my point."

The photo is passed around to the tune of audible winces until I get my turn. It couldn't have been more than a few months ago, Sky's hair platinum white and braided in a fishtail down her back. She wears a grizzly lined cloak and holds forward a scraggly gray kitten by the scruff of its neck, her other hand clutching a white oak bow.

It's ridiculously small, missing an ear, looks like it may have fleas, and its blue eyes narrow in rage—claws bared and overgrown as it hisses toward the cameraman mid-picture.

"It's... um..."

*"Feral."*

I ignore Solara to survey the kitten longer. "Name?"

Sky sighs as I pass the picture back. "Chewy."

"Because she has a bite taken out of her?" Russ asks.

"Because I found her on a hunt. We left to get firewood, and she had already started in on our dinner. Eating it raw, Veggie Boy. I'm sure you know nothing about that." Sky places a V in front of her tongue and looks purposely lost trying to find the center.

"You know what? He's actually *great* at oral sex, so your insults are baseless. Everyone here, take note!"

My table mates look doubtful as Sky smirks. "Is he?"

"Yeah! He's done it! To... *me*. And I orgasmed. Like, four times."

*"Four?"* Tristain whispers. Osira side-eyes him and Suede giggles as Jason places a hand over her mouth.

Russ turns to me and I sink into my chair at the accusation in his eyes. "Sorry."

Sky chuckles as she twirls spaghetti on her fork. "You should come meet her, Pax. I live on the same floor as Veggie Boy, so the commute must not be too far from your passionate embraces. I'm sure she would enjoy you. The others are unwelcome to experience her."

"Thank the Universe."

"No one asked you, Veggie Boy."

"It's Icarus Honestus to you."

"Well, I'm excited!" I manage to squeak out. "Are the fleas gone?"

"Of course they're gone. Do I look like an amateur?"

The rest of the lunch hour is spent in tense conversation. Jason deciding to facilitate any further discussion topics, and Nox leaping upward when the time comes.

I follow Sky through the flood of students, running out of the cafe and grabbing her arm as her siblings keep walking. "What was that?!"

"Fun." She munches on a fresh apple, its tart scent wafting into the air as she appraises me. "I learned Veggie Boy knows his way around a vulva. Does he ingest your skene fluid too, or is that not Vegan?"

"None. Of. Your. Business."

"Could be?" Several sputters fall from my lips before a laugh reverberates in her throat. "I'm fully fucking with you, Pax."

"When I suggested friendship, I imagined sleepovers and painting each other's nails. Not... you making fun of all of us!"

"Blondie's, *I'm so dainty I'm about to fall through the cracks of a sidewalk* bullshit is what you should be focused on. Not me. She embarrassed herself."

"She's still upset about the daisy comment."

"Fine. Let her be picked. More space for the rest who want to grow."

"And what did Russ do to deserve that?"

"He's annoying."

"You're annoying and I want to be your friend." Sky laughs in my face, pressing a hand to her abdomen as if the action causes her pain. "And how come Nox gets to sit with us?"

She lifts her apple toward her lips again and I snatch it from her hand, throwing it against the cobblestone. The half eaten, green-skinned fruit splattering against the ground and rolling into the grass.

"You owe me an apple. I only like the green ones." Sky takes a step forward and I stumble back. "Growing up, Caveman used to read me stories before bed. There was a goddess of cosmic balance that I would see in my nightmares. A recurring boogie man if you will... Your eyes are haunting. They make people feel as if you're weighing their heart against a feather. It doesn't feel great to stare at an innocent and have them ask you, if you deserve to know them."

It occurs to me that maybe I feel this way too. Looking into my own eyes is a soul ready to weigh my own worthiness.

"I'd never ask someone if they deserve to know me."

Sky motions for me to keep walking and I follow a few steps behind her. She avoids everyone who approaches, giving only curt head nods as a greeting, unlike Jason and Russ who stop for everyone.

She decides to converse on the bridge leading toward the arena, almost bumping into her as she plops down without warning.

Dozens of ice chunks pass under our feet as Sky absentmindedly whittles in the wood with her blade. I wait until she finds the words she's searching for, scratching away her impromptu art project and blocking it from my view. "I need to broach an unpleasant discussion with you."

"Is it that the 'staying away from creatures' advice doesn't apply to your brother?"

Sky frowns. "Nox is an asshole, but he's not a creature."

"Could have fooled me."

"And he has. He has a zero tolerance policy."

"For violence?"

"Of course not. My brother is very violent. But never to innocents." Her ski sloped nose crinkles at the end. "I can't stress enough how little that showed of his character. It's something we've talked about extensively since."

"What was the consensus?"

"I've told you? He's an asshole."

"I could have told you that without extensive conversation." Sky's face takes a lopsided grin as I add, "If you want me to understand, you have to give me more information to work with."

First Year Casting is infuriating. Since the incident, I've only been allowed to observe from the bleachers. And observe I do. Nox hasn't shown up once since he attempted to concave my face.

"Where has he been?"

"Skipping," she replies in a clipped tone.

*Cough. Cough. Cough.*

"Why?"

"Because."

*Cough. Cough. Cough.*

"Because?"

"He asked for you to be expelled. You're still here. So, now he skips."

"At what point am I supposed to believe he's not a creature?"

*Cough. Cough. Cough.*

I squint my eyes, briefly wondering if this is to avoid talking about him. But as Sky hovers chilly fingers over my eyelids, I hear her spit into the rushing river below. A warning glance shot in my direction when she lowers them. "To his credit, he phoned home first and said we were transferring schools."

"Sky, please drink something?" I riffle through my bag and pull out my water bottle. The Bear begrudgingly takes a few gulps before handing it back.

"My Father told him under no circumstances is he allowed to leave. So, he had a meeting with our aunt and told her *you* would have to leave. To ship you to the islands instead." My jaw drops as she adds, "Alvarez informed him you're a Child of Addam and confined to campus for the rest of the year. So he would have to figure out a way to put up with you."

"He's allowed to miss as many days as he wants now?"

"What is she going to do?"

*"Fail* him?"

"She's my father's half sibling. She has no sway over him, therefore, he won't allow her to fail his son." Sky's voice is breathy, the hacking cough gone, though she still appears wary with each inhale.

"If he's avoiding me, why is he sitting at our table?"

"Because I've been a jackass and I'm attempting to course correct. Caveman despises insinuations that he would touch either of us that way. He thinks it on par with assault. With everyone pushing marriage between them, he was unwell." Sky scrunches her nose. "My brother won't hurt you again. We've talked about it, and I believe him."

"Okay. If he says sorry, and means it, then I can move past it."

"He won't."

*"Seriously?"*

"I know." She winces. "Forgiveness is free. Trust is earned."

"Do you know what I'd look like right now if I hadn't started using magic?"

"On my name, if you can move past this, what you get back from me is unconditional."

"Is he worth that?"

"Knowing as little about you as I do, you'll take less than what you deserve and be thankful for it. I will try not to take advantage of that, but I am now. Put your faith in me. Believe me when I promise your safety. I'll take it on as my responsibility."

Sky twists her body towards me, the both of us sitting criss-cross applesauce and having a stare down of sorts.

I press my lips together, gritting my teeth as several minutes pass. "If you try to be nicer to Suede and Russ."

"Why? They're both obnoxious?"

"Because asshole is not a face on my coin."

The Bear stifles a grin and I pick up my water to take a sip. The sweet taste on it causes me to narrow my eyes, wiping away a thought too ludicrous to entertain before it forms.

"Fine. I'll ease up on them."

"Then, okay." I nudge her knee cap with my water bottle and she takes the rest of it. "Only because you hit harder than Nox does."

Sky chokes back the water she's just downed, pointing at me with accusation as she dries her face with her shirtsleeve. "I'm the strongest of the bunch. They deny it constantly, but they'd be abundantly lost without me."

"I believe that."

"No shit. It's true." She helps me to my feet and hands me back my empty bottle.

"Can I meet Chewy now? I have an hour before my next class, and I think it's cute that she only has one ear."

Sky freezes in an instant. "No."

"Okay. I'm free after dinner? We could have a sleepover."

"That won't be possible. Chewy doesn't like visitors." My jaw drops as Sky abruptly sweeps past me and I flip her off behind her back. "I saw that."

"How?!" I yell.

Sky twists on her heel, walking backwards as she whispers, "I'm just so fucking wise."

# CHAPTER 20

Several mealtimes pass before I put Sky's words to the test. If only because I'm done with tossing and turning over Nox Sapienti every night. If everything goes according to plan, I'll be killing two birds with one stone.

If not, what's one more day spent healing in bed?

I trudge to the dessert station, mouth watering at the smell of fresh-baked croissants and warm chocolate chip muffins. I glance through the options several times, pretending to make up my mind until the crowd clears away, nervous I might bother the full-cheeked woman standing ready to plate my food.

She's young and seemingly in her thirties. With a short afro full of springy coils, and a shy smile that forms crinkles around the edges of her eyes. White gloved hands prepared with sharp tongs as I approach the counter. "Hi."

The woman smooths down her black apron. "Hello, Ma'am."

"Could I get a few cinnamon sticks, please? There's not any left on the spice table." Silence follows, the lady staring at me with widened eyes. "Only if it's not too much trouble. I can wait."

She jerks her head, darting away as my stomach bubbles with nerves.

I examine all the desserts and she's back before I know it, placing a metallic tin in my outstretched hand. "I hope this is to your liking."

I pop it open to rows of cinnamon in perfect order, shutting it quickly. "Thank you."

"No. Thank *you*."

"Wait, why'd you say thank you back?"

"Because I thank you for allowing me to serve you?" The response is so robotic it brings a chill to my spine, goosebumps rising on the back of my neck.

"Um..." I lower my voice, gaze darting around to make sure we're by ourselves.

No one seems to be watching us except for Ezra Alvarez. His gaze hasn't left my face since I entered the building.

My friends are too busy arguing. Everyone grimacing as Sky starts her first argument in days, baring her teeth inside our table's silent bubble. I'm unclear what the hell has spurred this type of anger. What causes Jason to rise, face twisted in rage as they go head to head. The subject can't be anything other than Suede or Russ. The two people he gets most passionate about.

I whip my head back to the woman and try to keep my questions quick. "You weren't forced into this job. Right?"

"Forced...?"

"To live and work here, you choose it? You could quit and leave?"

Voicing my worry feels slightly absurd. But is it really? I don't know much about service jobs except that they're not considered appropriate for anyone who graduates from T.A.U.

"We're all free to leave. But, why would we, Ma'am?"

"I don't know." My shoulders slump, abdomen unclenching as I ask, "You like this job? They're treating you well? Benefits and everything?"

"I enjoy cooking. I was worried I wouldn't be placed in this position. Or, that one wouldn't be open to me. I..." She lowers her voice, a soft tremor in it. "I would hate to displease you and be removed from service. I forgot to restock the cinnamon sticks this morning."

"*Oh*. No! You don't need to worry, I'm not going to complain."

Now it's this woman's turn to be relieved. "Your service is fantastic. I can't even cook without burning food."

The woman beams, bowing her head. "Stars above, that is unnecessarily kind. I will carry this with me for a long time. The beautiful lady who sits between Lions and Bears causes a lot of buzz around here. And you always come to my station first. It's an honor, Ma'am."

"You can call me Shiloh. What's your name?"

She blinks rapidly. "Meesa."

"Meesa, if you ever need anything, let me know." I wave the tin in front of me. "I haven't given much to start being gifted with things, so I owe you."

"Well, blessed are the peacemakers," she says. "You will give plenty when you begin work. There's not a student that leaves T.A.U. that doesn't lead us somewhere great."

I smile through the bitter taste of admiration I don't deserve.

*Will I give time and service to this country?*

If the answer is no, everything I accept feels stolen.

She wipes the counter with a rag, sensing my discomfort through no fault of her own. "Sorry, I'm rambling. I should get back to work."

Meesa darts away and I stuff the canister inside my pocket. Unable to think too much about the future because I have a bigger goal in my present, something I have to do while I have any amount of courage in me.

I search for Josephine as I pass Ezra's table and she's nowhere to be found. Since she walked into the Dean's office weeks ago, they haven't spoken in public at all. It's all too much for me to wrap my head around and I don't think I need to anymore.

His chocolate colored eyes never leave me, calloused hands flicking embers onto his empty plate as he mouths, "*What are you doing?*"

"*Enjoy that cigarette,*" I mouth back.

Two birds. One stone. Entertain them all.

Ezra blows smoke over one shoulder, staring with suspicion as I'm handed my breakfast.

When I arrive at our table, everyone is conveniently in a great mood.

Which, fine, whatever.

I ask Sky to sit in my empty chair next to Russ and take her seat, sitting sandwiched between her and her brother. Nox pauses mid chew, face of a God growing stonier by the second.

"Nox?" The name feels heavy on my tongue.

I roll my glass of water between both palms, heart racing like a horse as obsidian eyes lock with my own—sending my body into a full blown spiral. "You asked for me to be expelled."

He swallows his half chewed bite of toast while glaring at his sister.

I can practically feel anger boiling off of Russ. Jason's eyes narrowing as the sound of the Cafe comes crashing in around us.

Sky's gone still, eyes flicking back and forth over each minuscule shift between her brother and I.

She nods her approval, so I continue. "Why?"

Nox sucks on his cheek, leaning backward slightly. "That was the choice I felt was best."

"And now that you've thought about it more?"

"I don't regret requesting your expulsion. As for other things—" I slap him across the face and it echoes against the glass ceiling, the skin of my palms red and irritated from the force behind it.

I shake out my tingling hand, releasing a strained moan from the burning sensation of using every bit of strength within me to slap a cold slab of marble.

Osira's hand wraps around Tristain's forearm as if she might keel over, the pair of them exchanging a glance. The type of look my parents used to give each other. What it means, unknown, except to them.

"Arsonist," Suede murmurs in the dead silence of the Cafe.

Sky said twice as hard.

Two eyes, not one.

His pale cheek is inflamed and pink as he turns to meet my eyes. Full lips slightly parted, an angry welt forming from where my ring has scraped. "I hope you know, that you're a sorry excuse for a man."

I hurl my ice cold glass of water at him, cup slipping from my sweaty palms and bouncing against his forehead, making a large thwacking sound as it soaks him.

*Oops.*

"In fact, you're bitch made, your Mom should have swallowed." I straighten my spine and pretend I'd also meant to throw the golden goblet at his head. "Actually, never mind, because you're triplets and she's dead. So, she's not a bitch, but the rest still stands."

"Jace," Suede whispers.

Jason shifts slightly, leaning forward in his chair, but I hold up a hand in caution.

I can take another hit.

*I've already done so.*

I can take being talked down to.

*I've already done so.*

I can take people thinking me weak.

*I've already done so.*

But if I am to forgive him, Nox will take it instead.

He coughs out liquid that's poured in through his mouth and nose, snow white hair dripping water down his shirt as I add, "What you did to me is not okay. No matter what everyone says to justify it. I would have apologized if you'd let me, because I'd never want to hurt someone's feelings. I wasn't raised to kick someone when they're down, but apparently you were." Nox avoids my gaze. "I've healed up nicely, so the least you can do now is look at me."

Our eyes lock once again.

"I'm told you're better than your choice. So I'm choosing to believe it, even though the facts have shown me differently." *Inhale. Exhale. Inhale. Exhale.* I'm relieved to know that my buried stutter doesn't unearth itself when I say, "Today is the first and last time I forgive a man who beats me into submission. Are we understood?"

He nods as I wait for some sort of response.

"Shi—"

"Not now, Russ," I whisper, steeling my spine. "Glad we're in agreement. Because I don't care who you are or who your father is. I'm giving you respect and trust you have not earned because I have faith in your sister. But faith challenged and shaken is the best way to drive someone insane. And an insane woman will burn your house to the fucking ground. So don't ever let me have misplaced it."

"What do you have to say about my house, Shiloh Benson? Repeat it, so I know exactly what I'm executing you for," Solara says, voice like icicles that seek to impale my brain, fingers dancing on the knife strapped to her hip.

"She acts on my permission. Your brother had it coming," Russ lies. Jason apparently too shocked to seal off our table from prying ears as people around us mutter in confusion.

*The word of a Lion or the disrespect of a Bear. What should they take more seriously?*

"She pays for this!" Solara roars, an inferno blazing within her eyes when she rises to her feet.

"She's under the protection of House Honestus!" Russ sneers. Rising to speak, not only to Solara, but everyone on site. "Anyone else touches her, and I swear on my name you will live the rest of your days without hands!"

The cafeteria breaks into panic, a clear divide between their founders never so evident as this moment.

"Shut up!" Jason yells, the loyalists collapsing into silence once again.

Sky's chuckle shatters the tension like glass. She hooks her boot around the leg of my chair, sliding it closer to hers and slinging a thin arm around my shoulders. An instant shift in Solara's gaze when Sky throws her castor ring in the center of the table.

Nox follows suit. And after a moment of contemplation, Solara does the same. A Lion and Bear lowering to their respective chairs, glowering, but no movement made to rise again.

I'm not out of the woods yet. I'm sure of it. I have one wrong move to make before she slits my throat without any care for the consequences.

"Shiloh didn't mean to say that," Suede whispers. "She's tired. So is Icarus."

"I meant every word."

"So did I," Russ deadpans.

Nox grabs his hardly touched orange juice and I brace for liquid in my face. Instead, he slides his crystal goblet until it touches my fingertips.

"I'll take your toast too if you don't mind. I lost my appetite for eggs, so you can have my food. Or, we can share."

Nox switches our trays and I nibble on his half eaten toast. Solara's hands clenching around her glass so tightly it forms fractures, bursting in her hand before everyone jumps, watery crimson running down her wrist. "You're all idiots."

"Sol—" Sky begins.

"Talk to me when you're a Bear again, I don't associate with lapdogs." Solara rises, shooting me a scathing look before her boots clobber past, blood droplets leaving a trail in her wake.

Sky sweeps Solara's ring into a clenched fist, pale fingers shoving the jewelry into her pocket before tossing Nox his jewel.

It twirls past my eyes as if in slow motion, an intricate band of obsidian and silver, glinting in the morning light.

The castor ring contains barbed accents that snake around it, crystals a deep and shiny red underneath it all. Fractured and jagged, like bolts of red lightning are encased within.

I pull my knees toward my chest and focus on chewing, hard to pretend I'm not on the verge of passing out as black spots swim across my vision.

*Inhale, Exhale, Inhale, Exhale.*

Small talk returns to our table, largely thanks to Tristain and Osira, the Cafe breaking into chatter when Nox has nothing more to say.

Sky takes Russ's unused cloth napkin and throws it on top of her brother's head. "The balls on you, Pax. Good shit."

"Thanks." I sip my peace offering and the fresh squeezed juice is the best I've ever had, rim coated with a sugar glaze I want to gnaw on.

After I down the glass, I turn around to check on the second bird.

Ezra twists his pack of cigarettes in his castor hand, lips turned downwards, a dimple popping in his cheek. When he meets my gaze, the entire pack goes up in flames, ashes falling onto an empty plate before he dusts soot from his fingers.

I sit through the rest of breakfast and eat all of Nox's toast, cold sweats forming on my palms.

Upset burns and twists in every cell of my body but I finish my performance, keeping a smile throughout our meal.

When enough time has passed, in order to not appear like I'm making a run for it, I excuse myself to the bathroom to hang my head in a bowl.

Pax hasn't grown balls.

If I'm being honest with myself, I probably won't grow anything but an ulcer in my stomach lining come the end of this school year. But I've just learned to fake it.

# CHAPTER 21

The fast-paced routine of life is a spin cycle that throws me for a loop. Five-mile runs in the morning, classes throughout the day, studying at night, and sparring under the stars, bleed into one endless stream that flows straight into November. Amongst what's required of me, I've incorporated my own secret missions, stopping past the pegasus stables briefly to peek inside the windows every day—still no sign of Sunny since my ride into Terra Australis.

That being said, it's no surprise to me that after a particularly hectic few days bonding with Osira and Tristain, I'd sleep through my morning run. I go to practice an hour earlier than normal to get in my missed cardio, hands groping at my shrinking breasts while I walk toward the bridge. My properly-fitted clothing beginning to loosen, ribs near visible again.

As I mull over the idea of implants, heavy footsteps approach on the bridge behind me.

"Sky?" Nox stops a few paces away, face growing discomforted the longer we maintain eye contact. "*Oh.* Hi."

He juts his chin in greeting. "My sister mentioned she hadn't seen you in a few days, and I saw you heading into the woods by yourself."

"It's... Monday. Right? We don't train on weekends."

"You could at least be courteous enough to tell people where you are," he deadpans, shouldering off his bag and pulling out a burger wrapped in parchment paper, extending it as a peace offering until my stomach gurgles.

"Are you trying to feed me that?"

"Are you trying to eat it?"

"Maybe. If you aren't planning to."

Nox waves the food, and my stomach grumbles again.

I inch across the bridge to grab the sandwich. Holding my hands out flat until he places it inside them, unwrapping the meal, and outright moaning when there's nothing but the patty and bun, accompanied by a slight splatter of ketchup.

"Are you high?" he asks, peering into my dilated eyes.

"Residually," I mumble, taking a huge bite and turning on my heel to continue my walk.

"On what?" Nox follows a few steps behind me while I inhale the food, heavily aware of how pained he looks to be talking so much. He takes the trash from my hand and shoves chilled water into my grasp.

I chug down the icy liquid, wiping my lips dry with the back of my hand. "Does it matter?"

"Getting stoned. That's what you're doing when you skip out on mealtime?"

"Nobody cares if I'm not at dinner, Nox."

"Are you oblivious? Everyone cares. Merging our tables is not ideal for any of us."

I ignore his pointed glance. "Can I ask you something about Sky's health?"

"A mutation in her cells," Nox answers. "Non-contagious."

"I don't care about getting sick. I'm asking if she's okay."

"She leads a normal life, but her lungs gather too much mucus."

"When she coughs a lot, I get scared that—I don't know. I get scared sometimes."

"A founder's offspring has never burned out before."

"Never say never," I mumble.

His face tenses with a scowl. It's less targeted, and more of a *I worry too,* type of expression. "I check her blood every night before she goes to sleep and every morning when she rises. There's been no change since she began casting. Even still, her medical team and I have come to an understanding."

"And that is?"

"She uses enough magic to trigger the healing and slow age process. Nothing more." My lips twitch downward, and he grunts. "I'd sooner have to strap her down and forcefully remove her finger. Her choices with her body will forever remain her own."

"But—"

"You should focus on maintaining your own health. Uneaten soup and housing chocolate chip cookies is not enough to prevent burnout. And you cannot be doing drugs."

"I'm California sober."

"I don't speak lying drug addict."

"Why are you nagging me? I don't smoke, so I'd never put Sky's health at risk."

"Good."

"And F.Y.I., since you wanna be someone's Dad all of a sudden—" Nox's brows raise, but he remains silent. "You don't understand what it's like to have to think so hard about eating. I'm increasingly frustrated with everyone having snide comments about my body. No one ever knows what they're talking about."

"Noted. I'll have shakes delivered, and the kitchen staff will be honored to do it." He sounds like Jason, the same finality to his demand that leads me to realize it's non-negotiable.

"Nox?"

"Shiloh."

"I don't want to run today," I start as we near the Arena, keeping careful watch of the ground ahead as I skirt over a rock and tree stump. "It's been weeks, and I haven't won a fight yet."

There's a heartbeat of silence before he says, "I'm not sparring you."

"Why? Sky said you taught her and Solara."

"Your eyes are half shut? I watched you stumble over a pebble."

"This is nothing? Give me, like, three—four more minutes."

"You're *slurring.*"

"I have a stutter, you jerk. I also burn through substances inexplicably fast, and your sister is impossible to beat."

I'm picking up hand-to-hand combat, but slowly. Every day, waking up with a new dark purple bruise. It's almost embarrassing to eat next to my sparring partner. Not a single visible mark on her yet.

"I'm aware you have a stutter. You're still slurring. And Sky is a fair match, but she also tells me you refuse to raise a hand against her. You need to go with gut instinct. Let your body decide for you."

"But, I need—"

"No."

"I need—"

"No."

"I need it concise and slowed down!" I blurt. "Okay? Then I can learn better! One lesson I swear." Nox falls quiet at this. "Please? I need to pass First Year Casting. And before you say no again, you owe me one more thing for bashing my face in."

He puffs air into his cheeks, stomping down the steps of the stadium and into the grassy field—headed towards its center instead of the fire quadrant. "One lesson. I'm serious, Shiloh. Don't ask me again." When I remain silent he adds. "And if I find out you're taking anything else, the person who supplied you will be dealt with in the manner of my choosing."

"You're not going to, like, *tell* Sky, are you?"

"Do we have a deal?"

"Sureee." I cross my fingers, and he throws me a pinched glance. "Okay. Yes! Deal."

Nox tosses his bag on the grass as I drop my things beside it, checking my eyes every so often until he finally declares, "I will touch you now."

Before I can respond, he stiff-arms me flat. "Ouch?"

"First lesson. You should have a better center of gravity than whatever that was. Work on core and lower body. No one should be able to get you down with a singular shove." I nod, attempting to rise before he shakes his head no. "Too late. Your attacker would have you pinned. You will stay there and work your way up." He kneels, jutting his chin until I lower myself back into the grass.

Nox leans forward until he looms over my body. Blocking out my vision of anything but him, fingers curled into the grass by the side of my head. "Ready?"

"Yes. How do I work my way up?"

"There are no rules to self-defense, except to defend yourself. You can pull hair, scratch, bite—"

"I can't pull hair in a fight? People would make fun of me... More than normal."

"I told my sisters what I tell you now. People who make fun of any way a woman chooses to defend herself are one of two things. Little-minded, or deceitful. Abusers feed you fables, so they may more easily trap you. The first barrier out of their prison is seeing through deceit."

"What about honor?"

"Honor is a lie told by men who want to be worshiped for their ideals. There's only what you are willing to do and why you are willing to do it. Then, exactly how far you let yourself go with your choices."

"Is that what people tell themselves to justify bad behavior?"

"There's only one thought you allow when you are being hurt."

"What?"

"That you will do anything you have to, to make it home to your loved ones. Your fight becomes as dirty as need be until you are out of danger. Only then do you get to be *honorable*. Worry that your prisoners are treated fairly. Your attackers don't receive your mercy."

"But..." Nox allows me to think for a second, the sound of heartbeats and breath surrounding us. "Lines need to be drawn somewhere."

"You cannot prematurely draw lines before people have tested your boundaries." His voice is soft, non-judgmental. Nox doesn't make light of my insistence, but he does vehemently disagree. "You have power. That's not changing unless you cut it out of you. Learning to push yourself is the option that is left."

Frustration nips at my insides and gnaws at my belly. "Maybe I should. My parents gave up magic, and they're fine."

"You'd rather lose your finger than learn to control yourself? Why?"

"Because to harness power, you lose more than just a finger. You can't *unknow* the top rung. You don't let go unless you're pushed down or you fall... Either way, I refuse to look down five years from now to see my boot prints on the faces of people still climbing. I want people to always be *people* to me. No matter whose team they're on."

"What others did in the past holds no bearing on who you'll become."

"It does, and it's too late." I squeeze my eyes shut as tears sting them, the flood of pain I've held back cracking and fissuring the longer he stares. "I'm sorry. I'm not feeling too good."

"That's called a comedown. Tends to happen after a bender." When I open my eyes, the tears are still flowing. A furious look in his gaze. So much so, that I hope my promise will hold true, because lord knows Tristain will tell on himself. "What's too late?" Nox asks.

"My graduation. I injured a lot of people, and my parents paid to make it go away." He doesn't so much as flinch, so I keep talking, allowing guilt to seep out with each admission. "My principal was blinded by splinters in her eyes. My sister's arms were broken. My teacher was paralyzed from the waist down, and everyone in the front row was... *burned.*" A vicious shudder racks my body. "I thought they were all going to die. And if I know anything, it's that the way I left Ashley, she probably *wishes* she were dead."

I remember Dad running through an entire bottle of whiskey when he came out of his office a week after graduation. Sneaking in to peer at his dimly lit monitors, images of mutilated faces—and surgeons' bills—enlarged on several tabs.

I run from the memories in the day, but my nightmares tell the truth. Every night, without fail, they show me what I did to them.

"I deserve every bad thing that's happened to me since."

"You didn't know, Shiloh."

"That doesn't matter! I'm still to *b*-blame. Clearly, *s*-some part of me wanted them hurt."

Nox is quiet for a long time, and I think to myself, *good.*

He sees why he was right to keep me away from his family. Why, in the end, even my own father didn't know what to do with me.

"Do you read?" Nox whispers suddenly.

"Back *h*-home I *d*-did."

"Okay, well, if you've ever read a story, you know a thing or two about a villain. The person who's created specifically to be the big bad.

And the interesting thing is, as soon as a villain becomes the protagonist, the audience refuses to call him that anymore. They propagandize. Name him an *anti-hero* to make themselves feel better about their support. Because they can't admit only one thing has changed."

"Perception?"

"Exactly. Most people's morals become swayable when they sympathize with motivations and reasoning. When you live inside someone's head, it becomes almost easy to root for someone who murders. Who pillages. Who *conquers* to achieve their ambitions. As long as they give you a good show. But sometimes, there are true observers who aren't so fickle. Though they may fall victim to it, they don't seek distraction, they seek understanding. Live with a moral code and hope to see it reflected in the winner. So, I need to know, when do you give up your support for the person telling the story?"

"When they abuse their power and justify it, I make up my mind."

"Let's speak of reality now. When do you give up on real people? I hurt you, Shiloh. You forgave me for worse than what you did."

"Worse?"

"Yes. You decided I was redeemable for a *choice* I made. It's okay to let go of a singular *mistake* you did. Especially if you were on drugs while you made it. Especially if you put your energy into controlling yourself every day after that. You are a real person. You're not some villain you can close the book on."

"Stop trying to change my mind. I'll never excuse what I did."

"No matter what I say, I know you'll never justify your actions. But that is exactly why you deserve forgiveness. It's time to let them go or you'll make the same mistakes again." Nox wipes away the flood of tears on my cheeks, frosty thumb lingering, brushing back and forth.

The movement is so soothing I close my eyes again, sucking in several breaths, on the verge of hyperventilating until he begins to breathe deeply above me.

*In and out. In and Out. In and Out.*

I copy his breathing patterns until I can form coherent thoughts. "I don't know how."

"It's easy. Just like this." My eyes pop open in confusion. "I've decided to let it go for you. Slaughter innocents. Torture your enemies.

Set the world ablaze. I won't so much as blink." Nox shrugs. "Each step you take from here on out is justified in my book."

"I don't want that? Take it back."

"I forgive you, Shiloh."

"Nox." I scramble to get away and he pins my wrists to the cold grass. "No."

"I *forgive* you. For all you've done and all you'll do. I swear on my name." He lowers his head until the tip of his nose touches my own. I have nowhere to look but into his eyes that harden with firm decision. "I've sworn few promises on my name, Shiloh Benson. Don't ask me to rescind it because my ancestors would shudder at the thought."

The storms in his eyes soften to pools of ink and silver as his promise binds us, his sweet breath a tantalizing caress on my lips.

My mouth waters and jaw clenches at the scent.

It isn't a craving. Not really. It's the rabid hunger of a starved animal, debilitating thirst that can only be quenched by one thing.

I've smelled the scent before.

*Tasted* it.

Licked it from the rim of a barely touched glass of orange juice.

His thumb traces soothing circles upon my cheeks until the tears have all been wiped away, each drag of his fingers an electric burn on my skin.

I release a pained groan, the fragrance a branding iron inside my throat until his hand falls from my face.

Liquid obsidian is ice once more, and pale fingers white knuckle the grass by my ear. Several heartbeats before the scent lessens, counting backwards from ten in my head until it clears of its fog. "You can't."

"I can, and I did," he whispers, voice raspier than normal. "So no more lingering in the past. The question becomes, what's next for you? If you can't forgive yourself, can you at least take a blind leap with me?"

# CHAPTER 22

"What's next?" Nox asks, blood whooshing through my chest as a symphony of crickets chirps nearby. "What do you want?"

"To... *unshrink,*" I decide aloud, gazing up with utter bewilderment. "To not be someone people think they have a right to dictate. To feel safe existing however I am. Even if it's as an honorable liar. Without the worship stuff."

"Then let's unshrink you. Let's make you feel safe."

"How?"

"Fighting with honor is not as noble as stories portray. People who live to tell honorable stories have had years of practice and experience under their belt, in order to throw punches that land above it. The hero's lie has spread through the world like wildfire, but to become a hero, you have to surpass the Bear first."

"They can't be one and the same?"

"Bears maul our attackers without care for pleasantries. It's hard to lie when your opponent doesn't walk away so pretty. From now on, you fight like a Bear and come back to your gentle heart after it's over." I nod in hesitant agreement. "Verbally tell me yes."

"Yes," I whisper.

"Yes, *what?*"

"I'll maul my attacker. Turn off my feelings."

"Even grab hair?" Nox asks, a corner of his lips twitching upwards.

"What if someone grabs mine first?"

He surveys my curls that are tied up with white ribbon, sprawled across the grass above my head, soft blades tickling my neck as I'm pressed firmly into the green field.

"Hair grows back. Take your dagger and slice it directly where they grab. They won't expect you to cut something off yourself. Then, make them pay for the loss. May I?" His hands hover over mine until I nod.

Nox slides off my ring, tossing the small piece of me to the side and watching it roll a few feet away. "If your opponent's smart, they'll pull off your ring first. Once the ring comes off, most Alchemists are toast. The others rely too heavily on their affinities."

He pulls off his own ring now, chucking it in the opposite direction.

As Nox parts his lips to speak again, my hand grabs for his, wrapping around his index finger, skin silken and icy.

He pauses as my thumb trails over the face of the gaudy silver ring, twisting it to better see the roaring bear's head. "It matches Jason's."

"Rings are forged for the father's successor at the founder's temple upon birth. Special to us. To never be taken off our person." I drop my hand, and he clears his throat. "For the sake of time, both rings have already come off. It's a fight for dominance against you and someone who's likely bigger than you. You are only five feet. Correct?"

I clack my steel-toed boots together. "I'm five-foot three."

"Hmm. Today, your attacker is six-two. *Without* his boots. If you can go up against me, anyone smaller should be no issue."

"Okay."

"The first step is distraction. Spit in their face, look to the side as if someone has come, and scream to them for help. Sell the performance. Play with their mind before you strike back."

"Sky roars," I grin. "Makes herself seem insane."

"My sister *is* insane, she doesn't just seem it." Nox wears a fond smile, his intense love for Sky shining through in a way no other emotion has. "After they're distracted, use what's at your disposal."

He grabs the dagger in my thigh strap before I can make a move and unsheathes it, tossing it near my ring. I audibly grumble, and he shrugs. "Should've been quicker to your weapon."

Nox lifts his shirt, and I stare at the blade in his waistband. Hilt made of snakeskin that almost blends into a toned stomach, the color of glistening bone.

"Search for theirs in hidden places. Make sure you disarm them first." I grab his dagger, throwing it in the same direction his ring went. It embeds itself in the grass directly next to the jewel. "Nice aim."

"I have steady hands."

"And now you have nothing but. Eyes first." He grabs my hands and rakes them over his face and eyelids. My red painted nails, for the time being, no longer chipped and chewed.

The tips drag softly atop his cold skin. Any harder and it would be painful for him.

"Nose." He grabs the hilt of my hand and brings it under his nose, showing how I would thrust upwards—straight into my attacker's nostrils to break the bone.

"Throat." He pushes me into the ground, hands grazing my neck as I shiver. "If someone gets close enough and you can't use your hands, you bite." He releases my throat and grabs my hands, pinning them above my head.

Nox leans down until his Adam's apple is exposed a centimeter above my mouth before pulling back again. "Tear into their jugular or go for tearing off an earlobe with your teeth." My eyes widen, and he narrows his, releasing my arms from being pinned above me. "You worry about what, Shiloh?"

"Your prisoners. Not your attackers."

"And?"

"Getting home to your loved ones."

"Good. Moving on, most men will—" He falters, avoiding my gaze. "Men go for the face. At any cost, dodge the first hit. It's always the most forceful. They debilitate you that way."

His knuckles hover over my forehead, then cheek, and finally mouth. "A debilitating headshot is not feasible if you are defending against someone my size. Your reach is not as wide. I'd advise you to go for their eyes, Adam's apple, or kick the testicles if someone is on top of you like I am."

He shows me a few chokeholds on the ground that work best for me. All the pressure points I would need to target for my size and for people of similar stature and above.

When he's through, Nox scoops me against him, rolling us several feet in the grass and dirt until he's on top of me again. I release a ragged breath in surprise.

He yanks my dagger from the grass and sheathes it in my thigh strap, sliding my ring back on my finger next. "In other cases, you may have to use fire to get the upper hand. But in its simplest form, I'm going to show you how to flip me, and you're going to make me cede."

My breath quickens as he hikes my legs up one by one to wrap them around his waist.

"Hug yourself to my torso. As tightly as you can," he commands.

I pull myself up until I'm wrapped as close to him as possible, hanging from his body by my full weight. "Your opponent is capable of less force going in toward their own chest."

Nox curls his fist in, lightly grazing my sides.

The punches he throws are awkwardly angled as I cling to him, forcing him to keep balance with my extra weight.

"Start climbing, and hang onto my arms to do it. It makes it harder to hit you. They might land some, but you keep going and keep it fast."

"*Climb* you?"

"Like a tree." I grip Nox's sides with my thighs, hands digging into his arms as I scooch upward.

He taps my side with the knuckles of his hand, and I tremble at each thump. When I get in the right position, he nods, arms incapable of punching unless he wants to lose balance.

"Do it fast. Jerk and twist my arm. Roll the right way and..." He demonstrates by flipping over until I straddle him. "You're on top. Got it?"

When he rolls back over, we practice the maneuver.

Each time, he progressively hits harder, a more challenging struggle to climb.

Once, twice, three times until I can do it in one swift motion. A real flip that I earn, but not without a wound. A hiss escaping as I massage the place he's punched.

Nox's hand flits to my rib cage. "Are you okay?"

His fingers curl around my side, thumb trailing over the thick fabric for signs of damage.

I peer down at him as he massages the sore spot, and a soft sigh escapes me. The throbbing pain fading to a dull ache. Then, to nothing at all but the pressure of his searching fingers.

"Physical pain is *t*-temporary."

"Okay," Nox grunts. "Now what? In a fight, you believe your enemy will stop to ask you if their punches hurt?"

"Trick question! I'll never hold an enemy. Only the challenge of acquiring a friend." When it appears as if he might flip me over again, I scramble for my dagger, the sharp tip pointed directly over his heart—steel shiny against his all black outfit. "Cede."

"Not forceful enough. I could easily flip you again." His hands grip my hips, pulling me forward until I no longer sit on his waist but on his chest. "Make it harder for me to breathe." He instructs me to pin his arms with both my legs so I do, crouched on top of him as my knees dig into his pressure points. "Hair and throat. *Painful.*"

My left hand wraps in his braid and tugs downward. He's forced to hike his chin up and expose his neck, a wince leaving him, my dagger's sharp blade against his Adam's apple.

"Cede, Nox."

"No." He attempts to flip me, but I tug his braid harder, blade digging deeper until it nearly breaks the skin.

A growl rips from my lips. Knees digging deeper into his arms, moving my toe to dig into his testicles, and using my entire body to pin this large man beneath me.

"I cede," he chokes out.

I release him immediately, rocking backward off of his arms and into his lap as his fingers grip my calf to steady me. "Good work," he murmurs amidst synced stolen breaths, the ghost of a smile on his lips.

"Really? You didn't let me win?" There's an excitement about me that I hadn't had before. Rocking back and forth, waiting for his confirmation.

"Shiloh." His voice is serious as death.

I freeze to survey our surroundings. Sure, that danger is imminent. As I glance down, his hair is as reflective as moonstone. Lips pursed in extreme discomfort when my fingers clench in the t-shirt fabric around his abdomen.

Nox releases a rumble from deep within. Half a groan and half something else I have no name for. A stutter and heat filling my core as I hold my breath.

"Stand up," he commands.

"Okay?"

I offer him a hand that he dismisses while rising. Embarrassment blooming in my chest when Nox crosses his arms, hand pressed over his lips and nose.

I turn my head over my own shoulder, testing out my scent as inconspicuously as I can.

*Nothing.*

I smell of soap and laundry detergent, if not slightly like the grass and dirt we've just rolled in.

"What else do you want to know?"

"Are we fine?"

"As fine as we were to start with," Nox says, picking up his knife and ring, back facing me. "You had an opportunity to attack your opponent..." He slips his ring back on and points his dagger with agitation. "And you stood still?"

"What is this? Reverse psychology?"

"Come." He crooks two fingers to motion me forward, and I stand my ground.

"No."

"I said come here."

"Make me." His fingers twitch, and he throws a glowing orb.

I roll forward, shooting my hand into the air and grabbing it above my head, yellow flames bursting bright blue as his fire switches allegiance.

It dances on my fingertips like flickering candles, and I steady the flames to soft yellow once more as I rise.

By now, he's sparked more, cooling them to a candlelight too.

We lock eyes, circling one another, fingers spread and twitching. "Acquire a castor ring, Shiloh Benson. You don't need those little matches you keep stored behind your ear."

"Yeah. I'll put shopping on my to-do list right next to ingesting human excrement." One side of his lips twitches upward. Lopsided. I realize it's not his natural grin. Or Sky's. It's how Sapienti appear when they're trying not to smile.

"That's what you're up to these days?"

I take the opportunity to let a flame leap from the tip of my fingers. Singeing his black denim pants, smoke rising from the hole that forms.

Nox pats it out, a deep chuckle reverberating in his throat.

"Sorry you can't have fun." I shouldn't be talking. I'm in the driest dry spell that has ever been had by a woman. But my ruse seems to work, his eyes momentarily distracted.

"Dipping tongue inside asshole, and kissing with it, is your idea of fun?"

The question makes my fire flicker and cheeks prickle. "That's not what you do. You'd, um, lick it a little."

"I don't think that's the loophole to virginity you think it is?"

"Times... have changed! Virginity is a construct!"

"Then enlighten an old timer." Obsidian eyes swirl with amusement as he calls my bluff. "What's next?"

"Well, Grampy, you'd first be in the mood. For *rim.*" My cheeks are scorching hot as he nods, awaiting a play-by-play explanation.

"I've never been in the mood for a woman's tongue grazing my hole."

"Wait, no one's eating man ass, I meant—"

"I know what you meant, Shiloh. And you'd be surprised."

Now, mortification really sets in. Suede and Osira would absolutely scream if they found out about this. And I can't so much as stomach the thought of telling Sky. I shake my head back and forth, deciding this portion of our conversation is over as we burst into laughter.

This one moment seems a different time and place entirely. Another version of us, as my stomach begins to hurt from stifled giggles.

Nox's choked laughter is like a gong. Jarring to my system. Electrifying as if he hasn't released its full energy in years. It carries through to his whole body until he manages to taper it back.

I shake my head free of thoughts, prepared for this to be another one of his tactics as my fire jumps to my right hand, growing and slithering up my arm. The both of us still circling as we search for weak openings.

He parts his lips, and my whip shoots out to crack at his ankle, pulling as hard as I can on the solid string of light.

Nox falls back with a heavy thud, rolling and leaning to yank the cord towards him.

I don't heat it fast enough to force him to drop it. Instead, getting jerked forward and banging my chin on the ground. A cut opening as adrenaline pumps in my veins.

Nox flinches as I groan, momentarily distracted.

My light cord yanks off his steel-toed boot, and he rolls backwards in a crouch.

I anticipate the movement, launching it forward to clip him in the eyebrow roughly.

"Shit." Blood pours from the wound, the heavy scent of vanilla permeating the air. Nox dabs at the cut with his sleeve, and I do the same to the raw skin on my chin. Fires dissipating as he wears a full smile that shows his teeth and floats to his eyes.

There's no farce, trickery, or distraction this time.

Nox Sapienti is undeniably beautiful.

"Did the world stop turning?" he asks, looking side to side as I do the same.

"Still turning."

"Because you can remain a good person and still defend yourself unapologetically. Tamed animals go back to their cage eventually."

Heavy footsteps approach, Sky and Ezra conversing tensely as they walk toward us.

When they arrive, Sky squints as she fully takes in my face, staring at Nox with the beginnings of rage. He appears slightly perturbed at the suggestion, yet not fully surprised.

"Sparring," I explain softly.

"No kidding. You did that?"

"If you're proud of me, then yes." She rolls her eyes in response. Ezra's face composed while he takes in the scene. I sniff, noting he still smells of tobacco. "Were you not surprised?"

"Only three today," he mutters. Which I can't complain about. He was going through several packs a day beforehand.

Sky nears, circling to look for my every weakness.

I brace myself and allow her to push me to the ground. The wind immediately knocked out of me. She clucks her tongue as I stare toward the stars. "No. Stay and watch your work in action," she demands of Nox, whose heavy footsteps I'd heard lumbering away.

He gives a reluctant nod of agreement, feet dragging to crouch beside Ezra.

"Okay." Sky smirks from above. "Show me what you're made of, Pax."

I sweep my leg, boot hooking around her ankle and pulling as hard as I can.

It sends her tumbling down, a harsh thud absorbed by grass as her back hits the field.

Sky sits up, and I roll forward, leaping against her. The sound of bodies thudding together, echoing in the air.

We're a tangle of limbs, grappling and hitting until she wrestles her way on top. One punch to my cheekbone. Two, then three. Surely to be bruised and swollen by tonight, better in a few days.

She scrambles atop my ribcage, squeezing air out of my chest, drawing her blade and pressing the silver-handled dagger to my throat. "Cede!"

I suck in a tight breath as Sky presses the blade deeper, taking stock of my options.

The answer comes down to her eyes. No matter how big her bite, my fear turns off as soon as I meet Sky's gaze, almost *rooting* for me to fight back against her.

She may be a Bear, but she isn't as feral as she wants people to believe.

I press my neck into her blade, the edge of her dagger slicing along my throat.

The scent of iron rips through the air, and a few droplets of maroon roll down chestnut skin.

Sky jerks the dagger away when the wound deepens. Blood pooling on the weapon. The second she's distracted, I shove her off of me, scrambling backwards into a crouch.

Sky rolls into the same stance, a new type of interest flickering in her eyes. If she gets me in the same position, she'll go for something new. Inflict some type of pain I can't handle.

*Say something first. Get in her head.*

"Bleeding only makes me stronger. Thanks for the spark."

In some ways, what I say is true. Confidence spikes through me at the fact that I've lasted for more than a few seconds. A strange rush that can only be power as adrenaline thrums through my veins.

Sky raises her blade to her tongue, swiping my blood across her taste buds and ingesting it like a delicacy. It takes everything within me not to go wide-eyed or show a reaction as my heart stutters against my ribcage.

"Mmmmm." She smacks her lips, licking the blade clean and inspecting her dagger for stray droplets. "You taste good. Shall I lick your wounds when I'm through?"

I refuse to move until she does, and Sky nods appreciatively. "What'd you do, Caveman?"

We flicker our eyes toward him, then back on each other.

Still as stone but curious to hear his response.

"Gave her permission she never needed."

"Who knew you had it in you?" Sky muses, sarcasm dripping out like honey.

Ezra emits a dark laugh, and on instinct, I crane my neck.

The second I meet brown irises with my own, Sky takes the opportunity to leap, blocking my left arm from sheer habit.

One millisecond before she realizes her mistake, my dominant hand lands a solid slap across her cheek.

My legs wrap around her body, rolling us several times until she's pinned beneath me. One swift movement, exactly as Nox said, even easier with a body closer to my size.

My kneecaps dig into her arms, and I take the opportunity to rip off her rings. Toying with her flint ring before sliding it onto my right hand.

"Perfect fit." I raise my middle finger, where her wavy ring now rests, as Sky writhes beneath me. "I'll be keeping this. Is that okay?"

This earns me a raspy laugh. "I have others."

"Maybe not. That's her favorite one," Nox interjects so unexpectedly, a breathless laugh escapes.

"Shut the fuck up, Caveman. Don't think I won't rock your shit after this."

After one night with Nox, and countless spent with her, I'm too aware she could do it. A combination of willpower, skill, and the fact that he could only go so hard against her.

I draw my blade and press it to her neck. "Want it back?"

"Keep it. It's touched mediocrity. It's of no use to me now."

Sky copies my motions, pressing her throat into my blade until I jerk it away, sweet iron beading on its edge.

My natural inclination is to toss it away from me.

*Shit.*

Sky almost manages to buck me off, but I stay seated on top, ripping her second blade from her waistband and holding it above her chest until she stills.

"Cede, Sky." My hand wraps and tugs her long braid, the same as I had for Nox.

She spits in my face, and I jerk my head back, wiping my cheek clean with my shoulder.

"You took it so well, baby. Was that filthy enough for you?"

*"C-cede!"*

"No. Bears don't lose fights, Shiloh Benson."

Not Pax. *Shiloh Benson.*

Respect for my name now earned. But what will force her to Cede to me? No choice left for her but to say the word.

A bone-chilling idea crosses my mind as my hands tighten in her violet tresses. Strands that fall past her waist, a clear indication she hasn't cut her hair in years.

"Cede," I whisper.

I can stop. I can let her win. It isn't that big a deal.

*Or is it?*

Sky will come to practice and beat me up day in and day out until I give her a reason not to. Prove that I can't be fucked with. Prove I won't let someone spit in my face without repercussion.

So, is it now or later? Ruminate or get it over with?

Something must shift on my face, blazing intrigue in her eyes at my next move. There's no stalemate to be had now. One of us will win this fight.

"Cede, Sky." My hand that fists her hair loosens, fingers trailing down the braid to rest at its end. I tug it, wiggling it back and forth in indication of what's coming.

Her eyes widen, lips parting in disbelief at the mere suggestion.

"Five... Four... Three... *T*-two...One."

I saw through her braid as she bucks wildly beneath me, long hair now resting right above the small of her back. I pull away with five inches of it, dropping the heavy braid on her chest.

I grab her braid once more, placing my fingers five inches higher— knife right on top. She stills to avoid a slip of my hands, and it takes all of my composure to keep from shaking, hoping she doesn't hear the slight tremor in my tone.

"Five... *F*-four... Three... Two..."

"Stop! I Cede!"

I drop the knife, scrambling off of her as she sits up.

A moan emits from Sky's mouth as she holds the chopped braid in front of her. "You psychotic motherfucker."

"I'm sorry." Nox and Ezra go slack-jawed while Sky curses up a storm. Gaze narrowed on her choppy ends, squinting as if the inches will somehow grow back. "Are you mad at me?"

"What the fuck do you think?!" She raises her poorly cut braid, slapping me in the face with it.

"But—"

"I would've ceded to a nose fracture! That would have been far less violent!"

"How is that less—"

"I'll tell you this once. Don't. Cut. My. Hair. Not *ever* again!"

"I—"

"If you were anyone else, you'd be dead for that! Nod if you understand me!" I nod as she rises to her feet. "I'm done for the night. You vexatious little..." Sky complains directly to her brother. Shooting insults so quickly I can't keep up which ones are for him, and which ones are for me, grabbing her bloody knife and shoving it in her holster.

Nox rises swiftly, falling into step with his sister. My ears straining to eavesdrop the farther they walk. "It's always a crazy one, Caveman."

"Sky," he murmurs, tugging at her free-flowing tresses, waist-length and swaying in the gentle breeze. "It was a trim."

"I didn't ask for a trim!" she shrills.

I've never heard her sound so feminine.

"You don't think you're being a little unreasonable?"

"No! I think you're being a big bitch!" Sky smacks Nox with her braid next, and he snatches the piece, shoving it deep into his pocket. "Don't pretend as if she's pulled the idea from thin air!"

Nox slings an arm around his sister's shoulder and guides her away, throwing me a nod of approval. Her complaints fade the farther they walk, raspy chuckles coming sooner than expected.

I grab my dagger and slide it into my thigh sheath, twisting the flint ring on my middle finger she'd paid no mind to.

*The Earth still spins.*

I root through my bag and walk closer to Ezra, kneeling to hand him the tin canister I'd collected last week. Deciding now is the time. If I'm brave enough to piss off a Bear, he's the least of my worries.

"Can I tell you something?" I ask. "I know you don't like me talking about myself and personal stuff, but this is important." Ezra nods robotically, holding the tin as if it's a ticking bomb. "The only thing I've ever smoked is a cigarette. And I hate them."

"Why'd you do it then?"

"You were right about one thing. I've never gotten invited to a party. Sam said all people do is vape and pretend to be drunk off shitty bottom-shelf vodka." I smile slightly at the memory. "So, we had our own. Begged Vincente to buy us a pack of cigs and a bottle of the nicest wine in the grocery store. He agreed because I would have just paid someone sketchy to do it, and it was *very French of us.* But he also said it would teach me a lesson."

"Is being French cool?" Ezra ponders aloud.

"I was entirely uncool about it. Got caught behind a tree in my backyard." I blow a raspberry. "Dad was pissed off. If only he knew that was the *least* of his worries." Ezra frowns, dimples popping out as I add, "But I did a research paper for him as an apology and learned there are ways to curb the cravings. And now I'm glad I did that because I have a feeling you don't love it."

"Why do you think that?"

"You grimace when you light a new one. Every time. And, smoking is an oral fixation so I got you cinnamon sticks to hopefully fill the gap. I bite my nails, so I know the feeling of needing something for anxiety. I started painting them to help me stop. It's not full-proof, but it works sometimes."

Ezra's face pales, pulling at strands of ink as if he might yank them from his own head. "Did you slap Nox to get me to stop smoking?"

"I slapped Nox for Sky's benefit," I say. "But knowing it would surprise you was extra motivation."

"Not at all for yourself?"

"Despite your belief that I'm evil incarnate, which, whatever, I can't really dispute. *No,* I didn't want to hurt him, and I'm getting a handle on making sure I don't hurt anyone else." Ezra's eyes fill with something even deeper than regret as I add, "Still seeking the butterfly you insist is worthless."

"Stars above. I... am so sorry. There's been a—"

"I hope the cinnamon sticks work." Unvoiced questions swim within his eyes as I rise, looking toward the stadium exit. "See you around?"

"Wait."

"It's no big deal if you throw them out. At least you're trying."

He doesn't acknowledge what I've said as he stands. "There are things I need to apologize for. Things you don't—"

"Josephine!" I blurt.

"What?"

"She has no right to be as mean as she is, but you were about to—"

"I broke up with her before I ever laid eyes on you. Her tongue is a whip she doesn't ever control."

"After the things *you've* said and done to me, you have no room to judge her?"

"You're right. But there are differences. Things you don't understand."

"I think most people you're cruel to because of your own issues don't understand it, nor should they have to." Ezra scratches the back of his head, olive face flushing maroon. "But you say she's not the way that she is. Just how I know how you've treated me is not who you are. Go find that woman again. Even if it's not as your partner, she could use someone's friendship."

"This isn't about Josie? I'm saying I want to explain myself to *you.*"

"And I'm saying I don't want your explanations." There's a beat of silence before I say, "Sorry. I'll follow your instructions and class assignments, but I only want Sky to teach me from now on. I trust her."

"Because you don't want the truth, Dreamer?"

"The truth is, I forgive you. But I don't forget."

"No. The truth is, there's a web being spun, and you're letting yourself become entangled in it by refusing to hear the full story. *Exactly* like I did. My mother, she—"

"No matter how stupid you assume I am, I hold my own scissors."

"I told you I never thought that?"

"When was I supposed to think differently? Each time you decided to talk down to me? Or every time you told me to shut my mouth, or you'd ruin my life? Take your pick."

"That wasn't—"

"It was enough to know how you treat your captives. You weren't cautious, you were cruel. Basic rule of war? Humiliation is off limits."

Ezra inhales sharply as I pass him, grabbing me until his hand wraps my upper arm. Hold firm, but gentle, as he says, "You don't really know me. I made a mistake."

"That's the thing. I don't want to anymore." I slide myself from his grasp, and a shudder racks through my body, walking away to the quiet shuffling of cinnamon sticks. A whirlwind of thoughts swaying my resolve until I can't quite pinpoint where I land.

# CHAPTER 23

Nox meant what he said by one lesson. Though I didn't know any interaction between us was limited to that night, too. Since our training, he's returned to his broody mood. The only tangible evidence that I hadn't imagined him are the smoothies that show up around the clock, prepared and delivered by eager kitchen staff at all hours of the day. Plus, the way he eyes my plate at mealtime, silently waiting to eat until I've finished a few bites of food.

Sky says it's a sign of respect from men in Hiemsternum.

That Solara and her fill up quickly so that *he* can begin eating.

If I were still hungry, it would only be right to give me his plate before acquiring food for himself.

On the flip side, I've realized how patient Sky is when I give up my fear of fighting her. How informative and intentional she became when her words wouldn't be wasted on me.

"My bruises have bruises." I groan into the grass as Sky picks up my arm before allowing it to flop back down. "Ouch."

"Come on, Cub. Let's finish this mile."

*"Noooo. Let me rot hereeee."*

Sky drags me to my feet, slinging one of my arms around her neck as hers wraps my torso.

We jog side by side, and she sets the pace for us both, tickling my ribcage each time I slow down.

Where Nox's defense was a crash course on survival, Sky's is beautifully brutal with each swerve and dip, every jab and maneuver a work of art. There's no need to use brute strength if you know how to play with your prey and let *them* make the mistakes.

By November's end, her words become a stock of information I store in my muscle tissue, hearing her voice in my head each time I stand on my toes.

"Bears grow roots in battle," Sky quips, hands gripping my hips before she pulls my boots to the ground. "We own the field, we're no visitors." She presses my left leg forward with her thigh, tapping her fingers on my abdomen until my muscles jump beneath a flattened palm, feeling the Earth through the rubber in my boots.

As sturdy as Sky demands me to be, she's just as demanding that I be soft and languid. Avoid her hits *before* they're fully thrown. Examine every match like a dance, a meticulous tango to avoid death. Each day, she's a little less inclined to push me, knowing I'll return the shove twice as hard.

I still lose more than I should. A fact I note when Sky forces my head under freezing river water. Our persistent punishment for losing the last round of the night.

Or rather, *my* persistent punishment.

There's not any part of me that wants to know what pneumonia would look like on the Bear, so we agreed she has to carry me home when *she* loses. I re-discovered I'm lazy and really don't like to work out, even if I'm halfway decent at it.

Sky doesn't seem to mind her punishment much. Unless I decide to discreetly check her vitals while she's walking.

Apparently, it's never quite so discreet when I'm timing her heart rate because she bites me in retaliation.

And by *bite,* I mean the feral animal leaves full teeth marks and bruises on my wrist.

I sputter as she yanks me upright by my shirt collar, huffing cold breath in the chilled night air.

Sky rocks backwards to escape the freezing droplets I shake from my mane, pulling a pink microfiber towel from her backpack so I can use it to dry my curls.

"Aw, you switched to the floral ones again? These are my favorites."

"You're mentally deranged." She frowns. "You know that?"

"If *d*-deranged means *b*-badass for lasting one *m*-minute, I'd agree." I cough out the last bit of water, teeth chattering from the cold. Sky takes over towel drying my hair, because apparently, I *never do it right.*

"I'm thinking up a different punishment from now on."

"Why? I *n*-need something that keeps me motivated. Avoiding a nightly ice *b*-bath is pretty *m*-motivating." I poke her armpit while she squeezes excess moisture from my hair, and Sky releases a noise somewhere between a hiss and strained chuckle. "Sorry. Intrusive thought."

"What's with the burst of energy? I'm of half the mind you get off on being drowned."

"Are you *k*-kink shaming? That's not *c*-cool."

"You have kinks to shame?"

"Teacher's desk...? I've imagined it a few times."

"With the Professor?" Sky rubs warmth into my trembling shoulders, cold hands warmer than the chill from the rushing river nearby.

"Hear me out, the Professor steps out of the room for a minute, and you have to be *s*-super quick. Lab notes go flying, and it's *s*-steamy and forbidden, and you pretend you weren't getting stretched out on his desk when he gets back. Does that not sound kinda..."

"*Stretched out?*" she asks. "I thought you'd be more reserved about this stuff."

"Probably, but I'll never have to act on it. Plus, Mom says my mood swings are like different people, and *Silly Shiloh* is inappropriate, talks too much, and needs rest. Now, what's your fantasy?"

Sky's suspiciously silent as she tosses the towel back into her bag. "New question, Silly Shiloh."

"But—"

"New question."

"New answer," I mutter.

"Jason?"

"*Noooo.* Even in some Universe where Suede and him weren't desperately in love, our differences would lead to World War Three."

Sky roots through my tattered backpack for an additional layer of clothing. Body shaking like a leaf as she slides it over my head, bundling me in the warmth of a stowaway sweater.

The design includes a punny ghost quote Henry thought was entirely too hilarious as we handed out full-size candy bars and bumped *Thriller* on a loop last Halloween.

Sky stares incredulously at the image of the baby ghost at the doctor's office. She's getting a bandaid on her limb, the ghost doctor's word bubble reading, *Oh no! You have a boo-boo!*

"Want to borrow this one?" I ask, piling my damp curls into a top knot, the cold shakes gone as I rise to my feet.

"Don't insult me." She scowls, following me to lie in our spot in the middle of the bridge and looking to the moon like we own it, boots pointing to opposite ends as we position our heads side to side. "And I wasn't insinuating he's the love interest in your... *desktop fantasy*. In fact, it's the opposite. You seem to like irritating him."

*"Me?"* I gape, fingernails digging into the scratchy wood panel beneath us. I stare at Sky's side profile, glaring at her silver helix piercing and the salt and pepper diamonds studding her cartilage. "You don't think you're wildly projecting?"

"At dinner tonight, you suggested he start *letting me speak* again."

Ever since the yelling match I wasn't privy to, it's been an unspoken conversation that she's not welcome at his table. Sky's stopped insulting Russ and Suede to their faces, but now, even the smallest disagreements with either of them earn her a Jason Honestus stare-down.

"Everyone should get a say. He can't ice you out because you don't like Suede. She's not innocent either, so I think it's pretty even if you both agree to play nice."

Sky turns her head to glare back at me. "Which leads me to my issue. Your wholehearted belief in democracy when interacting with the future Sovereign."

"He should still work to earn his votes."

*"Work* to earn votes? The Sovereign's only child hanged herself decades ago. His niece will take a seat in Ardengris one day, my brother in Hiemsternum, Veggie Boy in Leonusver, and Jason will be King. I am under no pretenses as to how the future of my country looks, Cub."

"It could be different. Things change."

"Not here, they don't. And for good reason. Democracy is the world's greatest lie."

"So we'll do nothing to make it true? We'll live our entire lives accepting... benevolent dictatorships that serve no one but the privileged?"

"Yes. The disadvantaged aren't really in a position to be making demands, and most of them are unintelligent."

"That is *mean*, Sky Sapienti. Not just unkind. It is a horrible, awful thing to say, and I know you don't think that way."

"I do. Once you haul in enough deer, you've shot dead yourself, you realize how much lighter the haul would be, how much shorter the hours of work, if the people waiting to be fed just... up and died. But you don't want them to die. You know they can't hold a bow to save their lives. You understand that it's not their fault they can't walk to the woods. So, you start breeding chickens because they're easier to manage. The coops are closer to your family, butchering them is less strain on your back, and collecting them saves you time in the day. It's a win-win situation. You think, surely everyone can be happy now!"

Sky shakes her head back and forth, a scoff escaping her lips. "Couldn't be further from the truth. Because eventually, when they begin to think they deserve your handouts, you start getting feedback in return. Some of the most entitled requests you've ever heard. *I liked venison better,* or *poultry upsets my stomach.*"

"What if poultry really upsets their stomach?"

"Then those useless cows can snack on some grass like Veggie Boy," she sighs. "Stars above, you know what's even more upsetting? Putting in work every day of your life to provide for someone, knowing they'll still find something to complain about. Working yourself ragged to meet their ceaseless demands until, one day, you realize something that sets you free of their expectations. Starving people's only job, is to shut up and eat. Their complicity is how they repay you. They don't get a say about the way I hunt. They don't get to tell me they'd have preferred the turkey I brought for my family. In fact, they shouldn't so much as look me in the eye unless it's to express gratitude that I exist."

"Sometimes you're born with more and have to give more than others do," I whisper.

"See, that's the thing about privilege, Cub. I don't have to do anything but enjoy it." Sky sits up with a flourish, saluting the stars, then flipping off the souls waiting in earnest. "We're here because we're here, and the grand purpose for existence should have been left in writing if the Universe wanted me to follow the righteous path. It'll have to settle for whatever the hell I choose to make of my life."

"That kind of nihilism only belongs in war trenches."

"The human race has never crawled from those pits. So, belong it does. Everyone outside those borders can kiss my ass, and everyone inside these borders can kiss the ring."

"No." I shake my head. "You can't believe anything you're saying right now. You're too good a person."

"Who are you to say what I believe? I told you about the cost of empathy. No one piques enough interest to acquire mine."

"Then why, when I was a *stranger,* did you twist your body to catch me before we slid down those stairs?" I ask. "You purposely took the brunt of the fall that day. Your reflexes are too quick. Don't deny it."

"You're exactly five feet tall. I thought you were someone's child when you ran into me. So, yes, I instinctually twisted."

I raise my shirt and pretend the ghost is talking. *"You're upsetting my mother."*

"I know, Gertrude. One of us has to."

"You named my baby *Gertrude?"* I frown. "She's gonna get bullied by the other ghosts for that name."

"That should tell you something. Even post mortem, people suck."

I scramble to my feet, making it a few steps before Sky catches my wrist. "Shiloh—" I twist my arm from her cold grasp and shiver, stepping away from the bridge and back onto the mainland of campus. "I don't want to have this conversation again."

"Then don't have it!"

"Jason Honestus is someone you need to keep in good graces with. Stop questioning him, or I'm done talking to you outside of training."

Any annoyance I've accumulated washes away in a flood of confusion. "Seriously?"

"I promised you loyalty, not friendship."

"Right. I just wasn't aware our *friendship* could be revoked for sticking up for you."

"Well, it can. And now you know my boundaries. So tell me what you want in exchange."

"That's not a boundary, that's an order. And it isn't an exchange, it's an ultimatum and a concealed apology because apparently Sapientis are incapable of saying I'm sorry."

Sky squares her jaw, glaring past me as if the chrysanthemum bushes nearby have personally offended her. "Tell me what you want, Cub. I'm tired."

For a fraction of a second, I consider leaving without a response, but instead I blurt, "Stop by the stables with me."

"Why?" She frowns. "New Bloods don't have access to the stables."

"I know. I tried to go in once, and a stable hand stopped me. But founders' kids don't get in trouble, so I'm assuming you don't mind breaking me in to visit my actual friend."

Sky rolls her eyes, staring down her nose until I raise my chin in defiance. "Fine. We'll go this weekend. It's empty on Sundays."

"Fine."

"Fine."

*"Fine."*

"You don't have to have the last word."

"Yes, I do. You're being a jerk and... you're not my Mom! Matter of fact, don't walk me home!"

"Shiloh, we're in the same building, and it's dark out. You're not walking by yourself."

"Yes, I am. Sweet dreams."

"I—"

"I said sweet dreams!" I brush past her, and she sighs, following a few yards behind me in complete silence for once, a stark reminder that she's a huntress too.


WHEN THE WEEKEND ARRIVES, I wait for Sky on the front steps of our dorm, shivering in the early morning chill as she bounds down concrete steps with heavy thumps. Eyes and lips still puffy from sleep, while her two violet plaits make her look about sixteen years old.

For once, she's not clad in tight leather. Wearing a brown long-sleeved thermal and cream colored overalls, holding a camo hoodie so oversized it can't be hers, and throwing it at my head without a greeting to be had.

I sniff it cautiously, registering her brother's scent.

By the time my head peeks out of the hole, Sky's already marched down the steps without me.

"Hey! Wait for me!" I shove my arms through the long sleeves as I dart after her. "What's wrong?"

"Nothing."

"It doesn't seem like nothing."

Sky's gait slows while we pass bustling staff members rushing to early morning posts. My knuckles grazing against her shirt sleeve until she folds her arms across her chest.

"My Father ordered Caveman and Sol back to Hiemsternum for Yule. They're staying for the entirety of Mid-Year Break."

"You love Hiemsternum?" I frown. "Why wouldn't you want to visit?"

"Where was I included in that, Shiloh?"

"You don't need an invitation to go home, do you?"

"When I left, my father didn't say goodbye, he said find another name before you graduate. I'm not crawling back there to have him look at me as less than until I marry." Sky kicks a nearby trash can with her steel-toe boot, pounding the metal with every word and hanging on so it doesn't go flying. When she's done beating it into deformity, she releases a few coughs from the exertion. "Born a few breaths behind my sister, and I get this to thank for it?! I'm a Sapienti! Sureblood or not!"

"Who cares? Your—"

"Who cares?!"

"No, I meant about being Sureblood. I—"

"You're a low name girl who surrounds yourself with the founder's blood to get through life, and you're talking about how it doesn't matter?"

"You of all people don't get to throw that in my face," I choke out.

"But fine. If I'm so beneath you, and you're this upset about the promise you made me, then break it."

"I was incredibly clear about the type of person I am. From the start."

"That doesn't mean I'm not going to be concerned when you act like this."

"Can't say you're not entertained when you keep coming back."

"I'm not, in the slightest! I didn't come for a show!" This seems to bring her up short, lips parting to say something nasty before I add, "I'm here for *Sky*. My friend who doodles constellations on my shoes when she's bored."

I twist my ankle, showing off the metallic stars on the heel of my boot that she rolls her eyes at. "Are you? Or are you here for whatever the hell it is you're attempting to morph me into, to fit your standards?"

"My *standards* are seeing everyone be true to themselves? That's it. And finding that person isn't conditional on you being perfect, but—"

"I'm not going to change, Shiloh. I *like* who I am, and what you see is what you get. So take what I've got to offer or see yourself out."

"Wanna bet? By the end of the year, you're going to stop acting like a 2-D robot when you're cranky." Her eyebrows skyrocket at this, attempting to step past me as I block her. "And I'm going to call you out even if you hate me for it because *that* is what you do when you truly care for someone. You tell them when they're wrong. You disagree, and you fight and compromise and still hug them after. So let's do that now."

"I'm done with this conversation."

"No, you're not." Sky attempts to walk past me, and I dive for her leg, holding on as she drags me through the grass for several yards.

She curses me out until I manage to stop her stride, yanking me to my feet with bared canines, hands fisting in the strings of my hoodie.

"What is wrong with you!? You're such a... such a...."

"Bitch?" she offers.

"Yeah! Exactly that! So tell me the reason because this isn't working for me anymore."

"This?"

"This *cycle* where, eventually, everyone I care about decides not only do they get to dictate my life, but they get to do it without any ounce of respect." My voice cracks, and Sky releases me. "I'm strong. I don't need your protection. I've survived by myself just fine. So you have one more chance to tell me what's really upsetting you before I walk."

Sky releases a shuttered breath. "I'm not an early riser. Twilight is a cruel time to exist. It's horrible. Neither the stars nor the sun are out. Nothing but blue." I peer towards the horizon. The sun barely makes its way up as she speaks, blue giving way to a vibrant wash of orange and yellow that streaks the clouds above. "Unfortunately, if I'm having a bad week, so is everyone else. Usually, everyone consists of Caveman and Sol, but now you're here. So, I suppose I wanted to ruin your morning too."

"The sun is rising now, so there's no more desire to ruin my morning. Right?"

"The need has greatly diminished," she mutters.

"And you'll stop threatening our friendship to control me?"

I scoff when she sucks her teeth. "It's not personal, Cub."

"Your threats are always personal," I mutter, tugging on Sky's sleeve until she follows me, leaving the severely dented metal trash can and her tornado of anger in our wake.


THE STABLES ARE CONTAINED inside a domed building fashioned like an observatory. A hole in the roof large enough for the stallions to fly directly into.

Our boots echo in the thirty-foot-wide hallways, no staircases to be found. There's only a long winding ramp that carries us up several flights, passing dozens of closed-off suites containing sleeping pegasus.

The windows to each private room are eight feet high, so I climb on Sky's shoulders to peek into every one of them for the white-coated mare. Half an hour of searching aimlessly and shushing complaints, until we find Sunny on the top floor.

I shout in excitement, and this time Sky shushes me, gaze zeroed in on a white body lying in a pile of hay in the corner of her dimly lit living quarters.

Sunny curls into herself, vast wings folded over her face as if meant to block out the small streams of sunlight making their way into her room. She moves them at the sound of my voice. Eyes droopy. Wings twitching so much it looks painful.

"Sky." I pat her cheek, and she slides me to the ground, checking that the coast is clear before we sneak inside, sliding shut the steel door until only a small crack remains.

"Hi, Sunny." Her ears perk up as I whisper, but when our eyes lock, they pin to the side of her head, legs trembling as she rolls her body and rises to her feet. "Do you remember me?"

In answer, she turns in the opposite direction. Attempting to stretch her wings as her tail waves us away.

I step forward, and Sky fists the back of my hoodie, giving me a curt glance before she steps forward instead. "Let me try first. She might kick if she doesn't want company."

Sky inches toward the twitching creature, and I hold my breath.

She gives Sunny's hind legs a wide berth while approaching her head, extending her hand in offering.

Sunny sniffs her thoroughly, allowing Sky to pet her side after some consideration.

Sky waves me forward with her free hand when it appears safe.

As I approach, Sunny chomps her teeth down as if in search of a carrot, and Sky narrowly escapes with her fingers intact.

When I back up, the pegasus relaxes, allowing Sky to touch her again. "You're sure she's who we came for?"

"Yeah. She still has my hat." My gaze falls to my chewed-up beanie, buried in her hay-bed.

Sunny's wings droop, thudding heavily against the ground in response. For reasons unknown to myself, the sound induces a clench in my belly.

"Did you know the Honestus family invented the pegasus? It's where Veggie Boy got his namesake." I shake my head no, and Sky nods to herself. "Some centuries ago, Icarus spliced genes through blood magic and hatched pegasus. They all started out like her. Now, she's one of a kind."

"What darkened their coats?"

"He passed away." Sky beckons me forward, and I take a small step toward them. "They went crazy. Broke free from all around the kingdom and created a hole in the wards when they took to the skies searching for him. His soul went to the great morning star."

Sunny is enraptured, and so am I, tilting our heads as Sky stifles a grin. "How did they know?"

"All children retreat there. Beings whose life experience was fragile and unfinished, yet have established enough connection to wait to find the light. Their loved ones feel their energy come the next sunrise." Sky grasps my hands when I near her, rubbing in her scent until my teeth chatter. "But it's not only for children. It's a holding place for the gentlest souls among us."

"You believe that?"

"With all my heart. They wait in peace, and love, and warmth, and light. The Universe is protective of them, Cub. The sun resides by itself in the sky every day, and yet, you cannot look directly at it. It burns so brightly for a reason. Waiting there is considered the greatest honor possible after death. A blessing for your work in the lifetime before."

"That's beautiful. And they all returned with black coats?"

"Um. So, the little ones..."

"Wait, stop, you're lying." Sky clenches her jaw in annoyance, biting into her cheek when a tremor shakes my body. "Sky?"

"They were just too young to know better."

"All of them? Do you... think it was painless at least?" Sky steadies my swaying form, and even though I know I shouldn't, I cling to her like glue. A slow trickle giving way to a flood of poorly stifled sobs. Fingers clawing at her back like a life raft in an endless sea. *"S-s-sorry."*

"I don't think it makes sense to apologize for how the body evolved to regulate itself. I shouldn't even have brought it up."

"No, I'm glad I know. It's *j*-just, Sunny's *n*-not that old. She's just a *b*-baby."

"And she's safe. Okay? This was so long ago."

There's a brief silence before Sky presses her mouth to my eyelids.

The action's jarring enough to dry up my tear ducts. Soft lips and cold nose brushing away lingering remnants before her tongue sweeps the taste of salt off her lips.

"Please *t*-tell me the rest *m*-made it *h*-home?"

"The strongest ones survived. And their offspring were born with black coats, even more majestic than before."

Sunny huffs in annoyance, and I turn around with a blotchy face in an attempt to soothe her, "Not more beautiful than you."

Sky wipes my nose with her shirt sleeve before placing me between her arms, flattening my hands on the mare's side until they're pressed between silken hot fur and soft cold palms.

Sunny bristles with indecision, an erratic heartbeat pulsing under my fingers.

When I emit a sound of upset, Sky's fingertips slip between my own to check the heartbeat for herself, eyebrows furrowing as Sunny shuffles her hooves. "She's still nervous."

"Keep talking. You were calming her down."

"Okay." Sky moves our clasped fingers to smooth down Sunny's fur. "Do you want to know one more secret?"

"I don't know. Is it as heartbreaking as the *f*-first one?"

"Icarus was a Korovk when he lived, but history remembers him as an Honestus. Earned his name only in his final days."

My jaw drops, and she releases a chuckle, laughter reverberating against my back as I ask, "How do you know all that?"

Sky's warm smile fades, and I instantly regret my line of questioning. Eyes flicking back and forth to make sure we don't agitate Sunny.

"Icarus has a library full of his ancestors' journals. His father lent him a couple when he agreed to start getting into politics. To show him why a Lion must always be seated in Terra Australis. Why duty comes before all else."

My eyes threaten to squint, but I control my facial expressions.

*Icarus.* Not, Veggie Boy.

A tone so personal that it creates an odd stir in my gut. Focusing on Sunny instead of asking the question on the tip of my tongue.

"For centuries, pegasus have been born with mourning in their blood. She's different." Sunny flutters her wings, attempting to pick them up from the ground in response. "Lucky for you, Sunny, Shiloh Benson is a great friend to have when it comes to being the odd one out. She's odd too, but more than worthy of your friendship nonetheless."

Sky removes her hands and steps back, letting me pet the pegasus by myself now.

Sunny tenses, but allows it.

"Different is beautiful," I coo, giving the white stallion a soft kiss near her twitching wing. "If your mourning was over, that's okay. You're here for a reason, or you'll find a reason to be." Sunny's ears perk up, and I make sure to throw in a few good scratches as I say, "Sky?"

"Yes?"

"You know I don't care about Sureblood, don't you?" I glance back, and her mouth is set in a hard line. "What?"

"You're... an enigma."

"I don't think anything about me is mysterious."

"I studied a map of Addam territory, because you... so *mysteriously* informed me your middle name is plastered on a city," Sky insists, hand pressed to her abdomen, nose crinkling with irritation. "Is it Georgia? You look like a Georgia."

"Your information here is severely skewed. Georgia is a state. My middle name is Brooklyn."

"Shiloh Brooklyn Benson," Sky murmurs, testing out my name and seeming to appreciate it. "Maybe Gertrude can be Georgia instead? A *compromise,* as you call it?"

"Okay." I can't help but smile, cheeks extra tight from dried tears. "Have you ever ridden a pegasus before? Maybe we can show *Georgia* the clouds. Jason offered to take all of us on rides."

"I prefer my horses firmly on the ground."

"You're afraid of your namesake?"

"My *namesake?* Stars be damned, Cavemen told me they knew what the hell was coming and coined it in my honor?"

A laugh bubbles from deep within, and we back up to give Sunny space. I blink away a lash that's been slicing my eyeball until Sky notices, her thumb sweeping my lash line, revealing the pokey culprit for my inspection. "I think this means you get a wish, Cub."

"Hmmm, I think I wish to know *your* middle name."

Sky wets her lips, releasing a breath that caresses my cheeks and smells of spearmint and sweet almonds. "It's—"

"What are you two doing in here?"

# CHAPTER 24

We jump at the interjection. Heart skyrocketing from my chest as Professor Laroche clucks her tongue, leaning against the slid-open stable door with agitation.

Her ring glows, steel slats parting down the middle until a window-like panel opens between two stalls.

"I've told you New Bloods time and time again. You're not allowed in this building and especially not without a handler."

When Laroche opens the skylight, intense sun rays flood the dimly lit space. Eyesight adjusting until I note how sick Sunny appears.

With red-rimmed eyes and slightly yellowed fur, she's beautiful, but different than before. Sunny's not nearly as muscular as she should be and hasn't grown much at all.

A black pegasus sticks its head through the opened panel, and Sunny instantly gallops toward the sound of his huff, rubbing her muzzle against her neighbors, whose coat is shinier than any I've seen in passing.

"I'm sorry. This was my idea."

Sky shakes her head with exasperation, but doesn't appear surprised I've folded so quickly under the pressure.

Sunny moves back to her food trough, munching ravenously on a mixture of corn, barley, and oats before turning to lap up water.

"What was your idea?" Laroche frowns, exchanging a look with the black stallion that appears as if they're communicating.

"Visiting? I wanted to check on her."

Sunny nudges her empty food trough, insistent on more. Sky brushes past us to fill it up again, and Laroche turns to me with narrowed eyes. "You knew she wasn't feeling well?"

"Not really. Actually, kind of. I don't know how to explain it."

"Try."

"So, I look for Sunny in the sky every day to see how she's doing, and I've never been able to spot her. But I felt drawn here. Like, we had plans, and I blew her off, or something.

"That's because she hasn't flown since... since you... ordered her to drop me off at the stables." Laroche sinks onto a turned-over apple crate, rubbing her face as if massaging out a blooming migraine. "Stars above."

"Do you think—" Sky nears me as Sunny stomps her hooves, urging her to finish her thought. "Has Sunny chosen a rider?"

No. That can't be right.

It takes weeks, *months*, for a pegasus to want to bond with someone.

One ten-minute ride with Laroche and I? It doesn't make sense.

Though Sunny snorts in satisfaction, eyes saying everything I need to know.

*Took you long enough.*

"This is a predicament," Laroche murmurs.

"I didn't try to do this."

"Ms. Benson, the predicament is that Sunny's mate has been bonded." Laroche gestures toward the black pegasus peeking in the stall. "That's Jupiter of House Honestus."

Sky's face drains of all color. "Motherfucker."

"That has nothing to do with me though, right?"

"You and Mr. Honestus are not *necessarily* bonded. At least, not with a soul tie."

"*Oh.*" Sky and I instantly turn to each other. "How screwed am I? Be honest. Is Suede gonna arsenic my soup?"

"If she's agitated, she'll get over it. Sunny made a claim to you first."

"But you said—"

"I changed my mind. It was unfair to ask of you. Especially how I went about it." Sky nudges me toward the white pegasus with a proud grin that unbinds my nerves.

Sunny stretches her wings, and it clearly pains her.

Appendages slapping back down with a harsh echo in the vast stall, whinnying for help until I reach her.

"You'll need to go on the first flight to solidify your ownership. *Immediately,*" Laroche murmurs, rising to pace back and forth. I can practically hear her frantic thoughts as I reposition Sunny's wing to a more comfortable position.

"Can I ask what this means for Jason and I?"

Sky kneels at my side and holds Sunny's wing, taking over so gently that more tears are in danger of leaking from my eyes as I rise to adjust the other one.

"That there will be intense discussion moving forward with where the pegasus are going to be kept. Unless you live together, neither of you will be able to have them full-time. A schedule will have to be worked on."

"A *custody* agreement?" I wince. "I don't know if he'll—"

"Ms. Benson, I would normally caution you with the time and space to think, but for me, this has become a no-brainer. Sunny's health has rapidly declined from not being airborne during her growth period. She doesn't eat, she doesn't sleep, and if she doesn't fly soon, she will *never* fly at all. I can't promise you he will react well, but I can promise you that." Laroche wrings her hands before straightening her spine, voice as bold and assured as the day I met her. "As her current handler, I'd be doing her a disservice to not argue for the best course of action for her health. She's made her choice. If you would like to give her a shot at the sky, now is the time."

"I'll do it," I breathe.

Of course I will? If the choice is to either Earthbound Sunny or piss off Jason Honestus, well, he'd better prepare to be furious with me for the rest of his life. Because we've just become co-parents.

"What do you need from me?"

. . .

As much as we try, Sunny won't let us saddle her. The straps too uncomfortable after months of being grounded.

Laroche says that she'll take saddles again once she's ready. They're better for her back but the importance today is her wings.

We're flying to regain their strength, even if she might always be a bit smaller than all the others.

I whip off Nox's weighted hoodie in preparation, handing it to Sky.

"No, you're going to be cold up there," she insists, attempting to hand it back.

"Maybe, but her wings are atrophying. She needs as little weight as possible."

Sky seems to sense my guilt as she shakes her head. "This isn't your fault. You can't help that a stubborn ass horse with wings laid claim to you. No one would have believed you. I would think it was impossible if I wasn't seeing the proof of it firsthand."

Sunny emits a dissatisfied huff, and I stand on my tiptoes, covering her pinned ears. "Don't call her a horse. She's sensitive and has gone through a lot recently."

"What she should go through next is a bottle of purple shampoo."

"Jerk." I scowl as Sky smirks. "Are you going to watch?"

"Why?" She fashions her hands into a foothold, and I step my boot into them before Sky hikes me upwards. I swing my leg around Sunny's back, fingers fisting in a silky mane. "Afraid you'll fall and need someone to save you?"

"You're insinuating you'd do the saving?"

"No." Sky whistles air through her teeth. "I doubt you need any more white knights. I know you're in love with Veggie Boy. Mrs. *He's done it to me.*"

My cheeks tingle as I say, "He and I... That'll never happen, you know? I just don't like when people tease him."

"I'm aware."

"Plus, I'm pretty committed to the thing we have going on." Sky raises a brow. "The platonic thing, um, Russ and I have going on."

Laroche mounts her stallion, Shu, a pretty speckled pegasus—all black with a few white spots around its nose.

"Are you ready?!" she calls over her shoulder.

"Yes, ma'am!" I yell, steeling my spine and tightening my abdomen and thighs.

Jupiter brings up the rear end of our flock, intent to fly riderless like a wild stallion today. Apparently, there's no way he's missing his mate's first flight with her rider. "Ready, Jupe?"

He rears his head, bobbing with excitement, and I can't help but feel connected to him, too.

"Mind yourself, Ms.Benson. She may have chosen you, but on the first flight, you must get her to submit herself completely."

"How do I do that?" Sunny's muscles bunch against my calves. Huff after steaming huff leaving her nostrils, silken coat heating up little by little in preparation for our takeoff.

"Hang on tight and tell her you're her master."

With that, Shu gallops off, Sunny darting like a bolt of lightning behind him. Hooves thumping heavily against the concrete ramp, having started at the bottom floor to give her time to speed up.

Around and around we go, my thighs clenching with each increase of speed—our bond a radio station.

A buzz inside my chest, and a frequency I try to get in tune with.

The solidification of a partnership that's attempting to knit itself with each jerk of my body and each leap of her legs.

There's a specific rhythm to her gait that I memorize, feeling each heartbeat like the thrum of an engine. Hands shaking in her mane, and boots digging into her sides.

Sunny stretches her wings.

Once.

Twice.

Three times.

Releasing a mild grunt of discomfort with each attempt.

We reach the top floor, and I think she might skid to a stop until they unfurl out to catch the wind she's created.

There's a final push and thrust beneath me, and at once we've taken flight through the open ceiling. A brief feeling of weightlessness racking through me as we ascend, before gravity glues me to her back, insides bottoming out as if I've dropped on a rollercoaster.

I emit a shriek of elation, each steady flap of her wings thunder in my ears. An instant swell of excitement for my girl who soars higher and higher, understanding immediately why Sky attempted to get me into a jacket.

Sunny ascends rapidly, having gone nowhere near as high when Laroche was transporting me. As if she's deciding to test where Earth's atmosphere ends and space begins.

"Now order her to stop. Be firm and be assertive, Ms. Benson!" Laroche instructs us as we vertically travel upward, perpendicular to Sunny's mate.

They circle one another in our incline, realization coursing through me as Laroche's voice fades.

Shu and Jupiter are fast.

But Sunny, even injured, is *faster*.

"Stop!" I command, teeth chattering and body shaking from the intense chill.

I repeat the order again and again, but Sunny doesn't listen.

The only thing that keeps me from falling back to Earth is my death grip on her mane and my thighs that have strengthened considerably over the past few weeks. Stomach churning as I try to master her, attempting to bond with no clue where to grasp to solidify it.

The air grows thinner at this altitude, and Shu and Jupiter skid to a hovering halt when they've ascended as high as they dare. Laroche cursing the stars, situating herself below me in case I fall in our ascension.

A thought occurs to me as my hands become too cold to function that there's a lesson to be learned.

Who am I to be anyone's master?

Maybe killing me will free her to bond with someone stronger.

Someone she has to respect. Someone who won't force her into danger, or make stupid mistakes that stunt her.

My hands slacken until a hazy memory unfurls from the base of my skull. Aware almost immediately that Sunny attempts to shove her thoughts down the half-formed bond.

The image falters and dissipates before I can grasp it, but I don't need to see it through her eyes to remember how we met. A stark reminder that I fell into Terra Australis, the weakest I've ever been, imbuing a last push of strength within me.

The first time Sunny saw me, I was splayed across concrete after materializing from thin air. If she cared about *submitting* to strength, she wouldn't have begun the connection in the first place.

She chose me when I was a drunken girl, hopping up and down to reach my own hat.

She chose me when I didn't know how to fight or stand up for myself.

She chose me when I was seeking kindness from a mythical being to feel less lonely in a whole new world.

She chose someone who saw her as unique, not an animal to be controlled.

Sunny didn't choose a master the day she claimed me.

She selected a companion.

She found an equal.

She agreed to be my *friend.*

"*P*-please *s*-stop?" I ask through chattering teeth.

Like the words are magic, her ascension slows. A neigh of recognition in her tone as she levels out, flapping steaming wings against the bitter cold atmosphere.

We hover in place, and I fall forward, snuggling my body into her hot skin. Relief coursing through me as I shiver.

"I won't let you down again, Sunny. Where we go from this day *f*-forward is as much your decision as it is mine. Okay? On everything I love, I'm not your master, but your friend."

With my promise to her, I feel an instant shift.

A sudden stillness to her body that prompts me to crawl forward, nearly hanging off to catch a glimpse of glazed eyes.

I reach for Sunny's muzzle to soothe her sudden twitches, and she catches my hand in her teeth.

Screeching as the bite stings and burns through my body. Boiling my blood as a rush of energy blazes through my veins, and Ichor drips from her teeth. My wound bubbling and skin knitting itself up—a dull ache and a faint crescent moon scar on my left hand.

There's a click and tug at the invisible rope that's yanked me towards her until it pulls tight, locking in place like an electric thread that binds us.

My vision fogs and clears until I'm finally on the right station.

A sudden awareness, that the only thing that could snap this connection is death.

I feel every single emotion Sunny's had in my absence.

Hurt and anger.

Abandonment and foolishness.

Her tug toward Jupiter and her bewildering amount of adoration for me. Her innate worry and fears, and her love and her joy.

Everything she has, she gives me through her eyes, and there's no question that she's always been mine.

When I let her into *my* head, she flinches, dipping and cringing until I ease up. "Sorry."

I don't ask her to lower her altitude. She knows where I want to go, soaring down to warm me up again.

"Good job," I coo, receiving a flood of warmth back from her end.

Even talking to her feels unnecessary now. As if I'm speaking out loud to myself. A repeated echo of what my body already clues her in on. But she likes my voice anyways. Preferring that I speak to her because the sound calls her home.

Sunny zooms past the golden gates, and I let her go where she pleases. Exploring the acres of the surrounding forest and skimming the tops of coast redwoods with a fervor.

Shu and Jupiter are on our tail now that we've lowered in altitude. Neighs of excitement emitting from my pegasus with each turn and swish we make together. Every twist and movement solidifying the chain between us.

"Professor Laroche!?" I yell behind me as Sunny begins to tire all too quickly. "Her wings can't take air time right now. She needs rest."

Relief un-bunches her features as she looks Sunny over. "Take her down then, Ms. Benson," Laroche says.

Sunny descends at my insistence but pushes her luck with a long arc back to the stables. Aiming for the circular dome ceiling that opens as we lower in altitude, diving headfirst without care for the laws of gravity.

We make it through, and she lifts her wings, catching air to slow our descent.

Sky stares up with silver-saucered eyes, and standing beside her are Suede and Jason. Both tensing as Sunny and I touch down.

In the strained silence that follows our descent, I lock my arms around her neck and swing around, dropping two feet before landing on my toes—my friends in various degrees of shock as Jupiter lands behind us. Then, shortly after, Laroche and Shu.

Jason and Suede greet Jupiter, who stretches his wings in a show of strength for his rider. Suede kisses Jupiter's nose, and he nuzzles her shoulder, his wing cocooning her after her face falls.

Laroche motions me over, and I bend to give her a hug. "That was fantastic, Ms. Benson. Now all that's left is to rename her."

"*Rename* her? Why?"

"Pegasus take names from their riders. It's a sign of respect."

"Oh." My pegasus grunts in annoyance. Apparently expecting me to have prepared something as she attempted to kill me. I sigh at the natural superiority complex I feel brewing on the other side of this bond. "Can I take some time to think of something?"

"Yes. Though she's never particularly liked Sunny. It doesn't bode well with her... *unique* personality." Suede and Jason exchange glances as I back into my pegasus, staring at Sky until she walks over, icy knuckles grazing my own.

"What is the meaning of this?" Jason asks, biceps bunching as he crosses his arms.

Laroche brushes dust off of Shu's leg. "Sunny chose a—"

"I'm not blind."

"I've known you since you were a nameless seed in Amara's stomach. I'd encourage you to give me time to speak *before* barreling through." Jason scratches at his stubble but motions for her to continue. "It had to be done. Sunny's hurt everyone who's tried to approach her, and you've known she's been deteriorating. You cannot be surprised that I encouraged this."

"She hasn't hurt Suede? She enjoys her company."

My pegasus huffs in disagreement, and I silently will her to quiet.

"Jason, we've been over this." Laroche's eyes fill with pity. *Jupiter* enjoys Suede's company. His mate has decided to respect your soul tie, but unfortunately, respect is not a bond."

"Suede, you never said you were trying to bond. I would have told you first if—"

"You should have told me first, anyway? Mated pegasus live together?" There's an uncomfortable shift in Jason's stance, and he squeezes Suede's trembling fingers. "You said you were my friend."

"I am?"

"Yeah. It's *really* friendly to permanently tie yourself to my boyfriend."

I shuffle closer to Sunny, who tucks me under her tired wing. "I'm s-sorry. I was just—"

"Play innocent all you want, Arsonist, but you knew how I'd feel about this. It's a violation of my boundaries."

"Don't talk to her like that," Sky sneers. "You're making this entirely about yourself. If you want a *boundary* set, say that. But otherwise you're being cruel. Shiloh didn't do this for anyone but Sunny, and deep down you fucking know it. So lay off her, Audere."

"It does no good for Sunny to be Earthbound for the sake of comfort," Laroche adds. "There were no options left, and this stress is not good for her. She has a long road to recovery."

"There's another option now. Since she's no longer Earthbound, Shiloh should instruct Sunny to let Suede be her handler from here forward. It's the right thing to do."

My eyes narrow, red hot rage bubbling inside my stomach.

Sunny senses my burst of anger and rears, releasing a rough neigh to show her clear disagreement.

Everyone steps back, and I near her again, patting her leg as she gives Jason the evil eye.

Jupiter nears his rider, the mates huffing with irritation, steam puffing from their nostrils simultaneously.

Sky curls her lips in disgust. "You're suggesting Shiloh gives up her pegasus because your girlfriend's *jealous?* Suede can't bond with Sunny unless she dies."

"She doesn't have to bond with her," Jason says. "She has to be a handler. Which lets her ride indefinitely if Shiloh gives the orders as her master." He meets my eyes, his softening slightly. "Think about it, okay? Sunny stays with me, and in exchange, there's a lakefront property I'm entitled to. It's in Ardengris, and it's yours if we can work this out. Full staff included."

"You're out of your fucking mind. Who the hell does she know in Ardengris?!"

"This isn't any of your business, Sapienti. You speak of jealousy, but if your feet were held to the fire, you'd soot up all the same. I suggest you watch what you say next before the conversation gets honest in a way you likely won't enjoy."

"Okay," Sky chuckles. "Sure! Bring to light what you must, but allow me to go first."

"Stop, let's all cool down," I insist, tugging Sky backwards as Jason scratches his jaw. "We'll talk it out later."

"If anyone should be *ashamed,* it's you, Jason. You fucked up your brother's life to be universally tied to a spineless bitch. Your father now takes all his anger out on Icarus when you're the one who acted selfishly after preaching *duty above everything* for years! In that position, I'd grow to hate myself, too. I advise you to get out while you still can before the mother of your children makes your daughters hate themselves and you her stupid accomplice!"

Suede gasps, and a choked breath falls from her lips, looking at me accusatorially as I shake my head back and forth. "No! I didn't—"

Sunny shields Sky and I with twitching wings, scooping us against her warm body when Jason's eyes fill with rage, ring glowing as Sky begins to cough.

Air whirls around the stables, blowing the ribbon from my hair and popping everyone's ears. We clasp our hands over our eardrums as they ring, tinnitus drowning out the sound of everyone's screams.

"Jason, stop! Her lungs don't work like everyone else's!"

No matter what I plead, he doesn't seem to hear me, so I beg for

Suede's help instead. She pauses as Sky stumbles, banging on her chest while I hold her upright.

"Suede, I swear! I'd never break your trust!" My heart sinks through the concrete below our feet at the sight of Sky's blue lips, an innate clawing at the center of my chest as she gasps my name. "Please!? P-please I–*Fuck,* be the handler. Anything you want! Just make him stop!"

Suede swallows roughly, pulling off Jason's ring and wrapping her arms around his waist, murmuring that she's fine until her voice sinks into his head.

The airflow is gone in an instant, and it takes but a second for anger to course from my belly to my bloodstream as I bear Sky's full weight.

"You didn't have to—"

"She's no different from Tristain. She speaks like that again, and she'll cease to have a tongue in her mouth."

Sunny lowers her wings, and Jason's anger wavers when he sees the Bear's trembling frame.

I drag her body to the nearby trash bin and tilt her head into it as Sky gags, attempting to hold it in.

"No, Sky, let it out." I pat her back, and everyone flinches when she's unable to control the vomit, emptying her stomach contents before she works on her lungs.

Suede's lips form an O, appearing as if it's the first time she's ever witnessed the action in her life. And after a few seconds of calculation, I don't believe the observation is far off.

"Don't look," Sky sniffles, my fingers scratching her spine as she expresses sputum.

When it's over, Laroche hands me a water bottle, and I help Sky rinse out her mouth. My body shaking as I work to blink away the red tinging my eyesight, fingers digging into the metal bin and leaving faint impressions on its edge.

"Sapienti, I didn't—"

"Shut. The fuck. Up. You've all said enough. It's time for me to talk." I bare my teeth toward his pity-filled gaze. "Sky and Suede are done interacting. Since there's nothing nice to say, nothing will be said at all. And, you're wrong. She's different from Tristain because if you *ever* harm her again, you and I will have a permanent problem, Jason Honestus. And I swear that on more than just my name."

Laroche rocks back on her heels, breaking the heavy silence that follows. "I advise Ms. Benson to keep riding Sunny every day. As break is coming up, they'll have all the time in the world to get her flights in. Young man, I recommend you leave Jupiter here or stay on campus."

The fight saps from Jason's shoulders as I dab sweat from Sky's brow, her body depleted of energy as she rests her forehead against the chilly metal bin. "I'll leave Jupiter over break," he murmurs.

Sunny's wings droop and drag as she nears me to check on Sky.

I pat her twitching wing, my concern flickering between them both with no room for acknowledgement of Suede's apologetic glances.

"Wash her up," Laroche orders. "And tell her to allow caretakers, the stablehands will come in to inject her for the inflammation."

I nod, walking down the ramp and wincing through the sound of dragging wings on concrete.

Sky trails along, and I wait to speak again until we step into Sunny's stall, filling up a bucket with warm, soapy water.

"So, what did you think?"

"It was decent," she rasps, popping a mint into her mouth and staring right through me.

"Do you maybe want to help me wash Sunny?"

"Did you not observe my lung falling into the waste bin a few moments ago?"

"No...? Didn't see it."

Sky keeps a pinched expression until I splash her with water, gasping before proceeding to splash me back. We wrestle over the hose and soap jar until every surface, but my pegasus, is covered in suds. Declaring a truce before we collapse in a heap among the hay.

Sky's chortle soon shifts to groans, stomach gurgling until she curls into herself against the concrete. "What's your pain scale? One to ten?"

"Six," she pants, pressing her forehead against the soapy cement.

*Sky would never admit she's in pain if it wasn't already level eight.*

"Shiloh, can you get Nox?"

"Can I try something first? Just roll onto your back."

She follows my instructions without complaint or commentary, and it chills me to my core.

I scoot closer and unhook her sopping wet overalls, rolling down the corduroy material until they hang low on her hips.

When I raise her waffle knit to get to her belly, the chilly skin is bloated and rock hard beneath my palms.

Sky attempts to cover herself when I touch her abdomen, and I push her hands away, circling and massaging the area, following the natural flow of her intestines with my hands.

I press down ever so slightly, rigid pants morphing to small whimpers until she slumps into the concrete and hay.

"I don't know what's happening," she admits with a small gasp. "It's never felt like this."

"I suspect your mucus is affecting your pancreas. Blocking digestive enzymes. Have you, um, been taking your medication?"

The honest answer is no. But I give her the space to lie anyway.

"Fuck."

"And, to be clear, this'll give you relief, but you're gonna have to ask for laxatives or an enema." Sky squeezes her eyes shut, jaw tightening ever so slightly. "If you don't want your doctors to know, I can—"

"Stars be damned! You're not giving me an enema, Shiloh!"

"Okay?! Sheesh. I just wanted to make you feel better."

"If you want to make me feel better, don't look at me like... *that.*"

I frown. "Sky, I have no clue what you're talking about?"

"Neither one of us would like to be here right now. It's fucking gross, and I don't need a performance that says otherwise."

If Sky didn't look so devastated, I'd find it almost laughable that *she* could be the repulsive one between the two of us. Instead, her lower lip trembles in a way that fills me with rage. How dare anyone make her feel like things that she can't help would be disgusting?

"Well, my friend, you might not be in the optimal position but I'm pretty much exactly where I want to be. So stop making me feel useless."

Sky tugs at one of her braids, fingers twitching as if she's about to redo the perfectly woven plait. "I'm also not your charity case. I'm—"

"The coolest, strongest, most badass person I've ever met?"

"You say that now..." I push down on the center of her belly until she expresses trapped gas. "But there are scents that just came from my body that are not to be ignored. You can't pretend things haven't—"

"Fine, you're right! Okay? Things have changed." Her eyes peek open, and I whisper, "I have a new fetish."

"You're not being funny. In the slightest."

"I'm not joking? Give me what I want." I swoop down and rub my nose across her face, releasing a moan against her piercings as she curses me out, pushing my mouth away from her cheek.

"Stop! Stop inhaling! I'm going to vomit again."

I continue to sniff around, and she places a hand over my face, pulling away with bite marks and a red-cheeked scowl.

"Sky, bodies do things. Do you want me to pull out my tampon? We could have a clot party. Compare our current conditions down there. With the cramps I'm having, you'll lose."

My hands paw at my waistband, and she grips them with bulging eyes. "Time out. What the hell is a *clot* party? Because I can assure you, we don't have those here."

"Only one way to find out. Sunny, baby, close your eyes."

Sky shrieks, clenching my hands tighter as I attempt to show her the string. "Mentally. Deranged. You're going to undress me, rub me down, *moan* in my ear, then attempt to whip out your bleeding vagina? What's next on the list of this unsolicited seduction?"

"Unsolicited?!" I gasp. "When did the world get so fragile you couldn't sniff a woman after you've massaged out her gas and induced an impending bowel movement. Tristain's right. You females, need to tighten up. It's hard out here for the rest of us." Sky gapes, propping herself upright and allowing me to button her overalls as her jaw hangs to her chest. "Close your mouth. I heard there's flies around."

My pegasus snorts as Sky and I banter back and forth, heavy waves of amusement flooding my head that haven't stemmed from me.

I dig deeper to find the source, and there's a sharp sting in my temple as she swiftly tugs her emotions away.

I thought this bond was an open book, and at least on my end, it is. But it turns out my pegasus has a few secrets she plans to keep to herself.

# CHAPTER 25

"Watch out!" Jason yells. Jupiter and Sunny nearly collide mid-air, and I swerve to the right, avoiding a collision in our upward spiral toward the clouds.

I yank at Sunny's reins and signal for her to slow, teeth chattering the higher we rise in elevation.

It's the last day before break, and we've woken up early each morning to run flight drills, my hamper piled high with punny crewnecks that now reek of pegasus. At this rate, I'll need to start riding in the thick white puffer coat I'd arrived in.

Jason shows me another loop, hooking his riding boots in his stirrups and flying past me upside down.

"Are you using magic?!" I yell.

Jason twists right-side up, flying with a shit-eating grin as he scratches at the stubble he's yet to shave this week. "You wish."

He nears with Jupiter, the black stallion bumping noses with Sunny until Jason grunts, yanking back his reins.

The subjects of his ire are clear as day. Our pegasus are obsessed with one another, flying as close as possible unless we instruct them otherwise.

Things have increasingly grown more awkward between Suede and I. In large part due to what transpired between Sky and Jason.

It doesn't help that Russ picked my side, even after assuring him there are no sides to be taken.

"Bonds with your pegasus are bone deep. Only in death do you sever the ties." Jason scratches Jupiter's neck affectionately. "Living only a hundred years, they usually only bond one rider. Us, on the other hand? We live long enough to have a few pegasus if we're lucky."

I want to physically give Sunny my years.

Nauseous imagining a silver coat and wings that cease to glide through wind, this love so thick it's hard to swallow.

Jason panics as my face falls.

"Don't be upset. We'll be entitled to Jupiter and Sunny's offspring, and so will our children." He visibly cringes. "Our *respective* children. They're still young now. It won't be an issue for decades."

Sunny's ears perk at the thought of Jason and I one day bonding to her babies.

"Maybe Suede can bond their first offspring?" he suggests.

Jupiter's ears stay perked while Sunny flattens hers. "Come on, you've put me in a tough position..."

I tune out his rant because I know it will make no difference until she decides it does.

"Shiloh, *listen.*"

"I'm listening!" I insist, cheek twitching as he raises his brows. "What were you saying?"

"I can do tricks because I trust Jupe. If I fall, he'll catch me."

To prove his point, he soars upward, and Sunny circles around to give us a better vantage point. My fingers fisting in her mane as Jason dismounts, standing on top of Jupiter.

"What are you—"

I scream as he closes his eyes, throwing himself into a free fall, a skydiver with no parachute or attempt to slow his descent.

"Now!" Jason roars.

Jupiter darts after him, swooping underneath Jason's body and catching him several hundred feet from the ground.

Sunny flutters her eyes, undeniably smitten with Jupiter's talent, and something tells me she wants to prove she can do better. Perhaps the insistent push of a challenge down our bond, her flaps growing stronger, turning to side eye me with clear orders, *You'd better jump, bitch.*

"If you insist."

I dismount, crawling forward to kiss her head. Then, without hesitation, I throw myself off too.

And this time, Jason screams.

I spiral and twist into open air, unaware of which way is up or down. All I know is that Sunny is coming. The blurry glimpse of her barreling toward me, a flash of white hot lightning in the early morning sunrise.

The thunderous flaps of her wings pick up speed, and I close my eyes, not anticipating the harsh jerk of air itself catching me. Jason's ring shining from above as he slows my descent himself.

Sunny neighs, blowing straight past me in anticipation of catching me near the tree line.

I hover in the air while an invisible rope bunches around my waist, struggling against Jason's hold as she circles back around.

Air releases me once I'm mounted. Or rather, *Jason* lets me go. Landing in the saddle with a thump that will surely bruise my ass for the foreseeable future.

He rears Jupiter's reins to avoid a full-blown collision, catching his breath before he yells, "That's a move I've been practicing all semester, Shiloh! You could have gotten yourself killed! That was only a demonstration for your upside-down barrel roll."

"Jason, I'm fine?"

When he's assessed that my words are true, his shoulders slump.

"You're—"

"A grown woman," I remind him. "Thank you for being concerned, but I knew Sunny would catch me. She's faster than Jupiter already, and she's still building up her strength."

Our pegasus grunt for different reasons.

One in satisfaction, one in aggravation.

"Sorry, Jupe." If a pegasus can scowl, he's giving me one now.

"You have to think about things, Shiloh."

"I do?"

"Sunny is new at this. She can make mistakes and miscalculations. You could have died, and you don't even care." I chew on my cheek, and his voice softens. "We're done for the day. Get your flights in over break and don't do shit like that when you're by yourself."

"Is it that serious?"

"Yes. You guys are going to give Jupe and I a fucking heart attack. I suddenly have a small girl attached to my side who, at every turn, wants to waddle into a pool with dumbbells tied to her feet. Don't be insolent to prove a point."

He stares me down, and I mutter in agreement, flipping him off when he turns his back.

I don't care how beautiful he is, or what Suede promises he does in bed, Jason Honestus is a demanding ass.

Sunny agrees, annoyed with Jupiter in solidarity as we veer to the side, flying an appropriate distance from her mate.

"WHAT'S YOUR FAVORITE COLOR?" Sky asks as we head toward the cafe for dinner, braiding her damp hair as our boots clobber the pavement.

I massage the base of my skull to keep my focus, head still aching from my Formulations Exam. I took it by myself, and without Suede's help, the math did me in.

Though Professor Agarwal assured me my elixir was the most stable concoction by the end of the hour. As evidence of this, my hands are still stained violet, taking longer than I'd like to return to golden brown.

"White."

"Why?"

"Because it's all encompassing and the color of Sunny's coat."

"White's a shade, not a color."

"Then I guess I don't have one. What's yours?"

Sky ignores my question. Constantly picking my brain for menial information about myself and expertly avoiding answering questions in return. As evidence of this, she moves on to her next complaint.

Sunny's soon-to-be name.

"No. Something else. I compromised on Gertrude," she insists, pointing toward her chest at Georgia. Sky's doodled horns and a mustache on the baby ghostie. In fact, she's defaced my whole sweater with obscene drawings.

"Cleonia is a beautiful name."

"For the rest of her life?"

"You come up with something then."

"Simple, Cub." She slings an arm around my shoulders, freshly showered yet still smelling like spicy citrus from whatever it is she's doing in her personal time. "Name her *Sky.*"

"That's ridiculous."

"What's wrong with that name?"

"On days you're both pissing me off, I wouldn't be able to look upward. You know how much that happens? I'd get a crick in my neck and be stuck staring at the ground."

"And you're going to get a kick in the ass when she finds out she could have shared a badass name and you gave her Chlamydia."

I tickle her ribcage, and Sky leaps away as a soft tap lands on my shoulder. We're mere feet from the busy cafe when a gray-haired man with deep crows' feet extends a silver tray. Not moving until I take the familiar cream colored envelope.

"Thank you! Edmund, right?"

"Yes. Thank *you*, ma'am." He blushes, chin to his chest as I open it, gone by the time I lift my head up.

"What's that?"

"Dean Alvarez summoned me." I wave the note in the air, and Sky's eyes tense. "I'll see you in a few?"

"No. I'm coming with you. That cunt can't be trusted with a fork near a freshly birthed baby."

"Okay, drama queen." My stomach rumbles, and Sky sweeps her bag to the front, pulling out a clear package of sweets that are black and shaped like fish. "Whaaaat? For *me?* I couldn't possibly. Unless you insist? I don't wanna be rude or anything."

"Just take the damn sweets." She hands them over, and after another rapid scramble, produces a milk chocolate bar. "Hiemsternum also makes the best chocolate. Our cows are brown, so it comes pre-mixed. None of that vegan shit Icarus forces down your throat." I blink rapidly, and Sky sucks air through her teeth. "That... was a joke. They don't actually produce chocolate milk."

I grin, plucking a fish from the bag and popping it in my mouth, lips puckering when I realize the candy tastes of red wine and isn't actually coated in sugar.

Sky places a hand below my chin until the half-chewed gummy falls into her palm.

"Sky...?"

"Yes, Cub?"

"Someone's trying to poison you. We need to alert the authorities."

"Salt licorice is an acquired taste," she laughs, popping the spit-soaked sweet into her mouth as mine falls clean open.

"Really?"

"You thought I was going to let you waste my favorite candy?"

The Bear reaches for the bag, and I step back, hiding it behind my back. She narrows her eyes, chasing me toward the Dean's office as my feet pound pavement.

"Sorry! Excuse me! Sorry!" I weave through irritated Silver Stars as thunderous footsteps make their way up the spiral steps behind me.

I manage to outrun her, crouching behind a corner and popping out when Sky arrives, already making work on the chocolate. "I love it! Brown cows really are something special. None of that *vegan* shit."

"You love that vegan shit."

"What makes Russ happy, makes me happy." I pop another choco-late square in my mouth, wriggling the melted candy on my tongue and mouthing, *"Is a rim job also vegan?"*

I'd confessed to Sky my teasing taunts toward her brother, and luck-ily, she found it as funny as she does now—vicious giggles escaping both our mouths.

"Give me back my licorice, you ass eating thief!"

She reaches around me, pale cheeks flushed pink as I hide them behind my back, abdomen tense from the laughter that expels when Sky attempts to wrestle the fish away.

"I'm not a thief! You gave them to me!"

"You're going to let them get stale at the bottom of your drawer!"

"Untrue! I'm going to acquire a taste for it!"

"You're going to acquire a taste for candy you clearly hate?"

"Mark my words." I pop another licorice in my mouth, chewing without tasting and sticking out a clean tongue to clear my name. Sky's face goes slightly pinched the longer she stares at me. "You're stressed out. I can tell."

"How?"

"Your teeth are going to grind into dust." I prod at Sky's clenched jaw, and she relaxes it slightly, peeling up her lip with my thumb until she bares her sharp canines in response. "Are you still sad about break?"

"I was never sad, I was remembering my father is a douchebag," she sighs. "Honestly, this might be my most enjoyable Yule yet."

I keep a smile off my face even though I want to start jumping with excitement. Two whole months of *this*. No lectures, no magic, no sparring. Just my best friend, my pegasus and candy in my belly.

"Will you wake up early with me and wear ugly pajamas on Christmas?"

"How early are we talking?" Sky groans.

I flash her a toothy grin, and her forehead falls on my shoulder until I pat her back. "There, there, you'll get through this."

She grumbles some words I can't quite understand, but sound a whole lot like, *Not unscathed*—pinching my side until I jump.

"Ouch!? You know you only have a few more weeks to make the nice list? I know a guy."

"Tell him I can't be held responsible for my actions. Dimorphous expression's a bitch."

Sky sweeps past me into her aunt's office with a lopsided grin, several stunned moments before I manage to unglue myself from the wall.

"What the hell do you want?" she asks as Dean Alvarez sifts through papers on her desk.

"Hello, Dean Alvarez. Sorry. She gets rude when she's hungry." I toss Sky another fish, and she catches it in her mouth. "We were on our way to lunch when I got my summons letter. I'm sure my friends just arrived at the cafe. One of them was probably *right* behind us."

Sky audibly swallows her licorice half-chewed.

Dean Alvarez nods with squinted eyes. "I don't recall summoning the both of you."

"Somehow, I bet you expected it," Sky says, plopping into one of the angular armchairs and propping her muddy boots on the edge of the spotless desk.

I slide into the chair next to her, pulling her flaking boots into my lap instead. "Sorry. *Again.* We're working on her greetings."

"Ms. Benson, this subject matter is sensitive. You might ask your friend to wait outside."

"It's okay. She won't leave even if I ask."

"Then I'll make this quick." Dean Alvarez crosses her legs, cool eyes gleaming with amusement. "As I'm sure you're aware, we expect full participation in all of our classes for students."

"Yes, ma'am."

My stomach knots and I know I'm about to get busted for Russ and I's system during my first few weeks of Professor Martin's class. Preparing myself for punishment until she says, "So why have you not been taking part in First Year Casting?"

I jerk my head back. "Wait, what?"

"You've been sitting out of First Year Casting for the majority of the semester."

"Oh," I say, shoulders sinking slightly. "My Imaginifer instructed me to complete my lessons separately. And I have been. Every single night." Which is even more training than First Year Casting gives students, but I don't input that so as to not sound like a smart-ass. "I learn better by myself, so it's worked for me. Less distractions." And less bullies. But I don't say that because I'm not a snitch.

"It's a matter of not being capable of keeping up with the curriculum?"

"No? I just need time with things. I always have. My teachers can usually accommodate that."

"Maybe that's appropriate for humans, or people like you, but you have not been up to par with Alchemist standards, Ms. Benson."

"People... like... me."

"Yes. Addam's children may expect to sit on the sidelines and be passed, but we don't make special allowances here."

"I was instructed to do that by my Imaginifer." My palms sweat, head pounding with a blooming migraine as Sky sits upright, pulling her boots from my death grip. "He decides my grade and how I earn it."

"Unfortunately, I can no longer allow that. It'd be unfair to the other students who have actually done the work. A concerned Imaginifer alerted me that there's been some type of relationship to develop between the two of you. As his mother, I have to be strict about this and set an example. You and my son are not above the rules."

"What about him demoting me points for no reason? Is that not inappropriate?"

"All cases of point demotion have been well documented and confirmed by several eyewitnesses. Your peers have said you've been causing disruptions in the Fire quadrant since day one."

"That's bullshit," Sky says. "And I want to know why neither I, nor my siblings, were asked to speak on this? I've seen her work hard all year."

"I didn't need to ask the first son. He explicitly asked for her to be expelled. I took that into account, Ms. Sapienti, I can assure you."

"He'd say differently now? Ask him again!"

"Your sister wouldn't. She was called in and gave glaring details about Ms. Benson's insolence." Sky's face pales, and she avoids my gaze. "Not just her. Dozens of first years were pulled in and questioned on record about the shenanigans to take place this year."

"Yes! There were shenanigans!" I blurt. "Because you raised a pussy, so my non-participation is really on *you.*"

"That's certainly a new one," Dean Alvarez says, laughing until a dimple pops out in her cheek.

"Sorry." I wince. "Sometimes my mouth opens before I give it permission."

"It's alright, dear. I was informed before you came that you had trouble controlling yourself." Her face takes a false mask of pity while folding her pale hands on the desk. "To be blunt, I tried to give you grace, and you ignored my summons weeks ago. Can you honestly tell me you deserve a free pass?"

"I deserve a second chance, Dean Alvarez. Addam was clear about what they expect on my record. I've been on top of my grades. I've never skipped one class or assignment. I— This —It's not *fair.*"

"You know, I understand your anger and your difficulties assimilating into our culture, and I'm nothing if not reasonable. So, there is an alternative method that I feel will truly prove what you've learned."

"An... alternative method?"

"Competing in Ludi Bellorum. If you bring your team a win, I'll have no problem giving you a complete for the year."

"Are you *insane?!*" Sky hisses. "You cannot give her a task completely out of her control!"

Dean Alvarez taps red-painted fingertips on the desk, pressing the plunge of her pen in a pattern that liquidates my guts.

*Click. Click. Click.*

"I am not a babysitter, Ms. Sapienti. The truth is, I want her to succeed here. Perhaps more than anyone. If you believe nothing else I say today, believe that."

"What do you really want?" I whisper, staring at her thumb as it circles the plunge yet again.

*Click. Click. Click.*

She appears to consider my question thoroughly. "For you to leave my office. I've given you a gracious alternative today. One that the other students will feel is comparable to all their hard work this year. Figure it out, or frankly, you don't deserve a place here."

"The pen. You're—"

"Remove yourselves from my sight."

*Click. Click. Click.*

One breath. Two. Three. Then four.

Something inside my head snaps, and I launch upright.

Sky grabs my hand as I take a step toward the desk, nails digging into her palms so hard I smell a tinge of sweet iron. An incendiary rage searing and grinding anything in sight. Shredding all I know until my sanity is held together by the grunt of pain Sky releases.

*Click. Click. Click.*

Sky tugs at my hand, pulling lightly until I back away from the desk.

"Looking forward to your performance, Ms. Benson." Dean Alvarez slides her silver pen into a cup on her desk. "If you've been working as hard as you claim, I'll be happy to pass you and write a glowing letter of achievement." She looks Sky up and down with a skeptical sigh. "Ms.

Sapienti, I have to say you've surprised me, and it's not often that I'm surprised."

"Your soul will see a black hole one day," Sky deadpans, tugging me into the hall and kicking the door shut behind us, her voice a mere echo in my brain as red rolls in my mind.

I'm brought to attention by another grunt of pain, wiping at the red crescent moons I've left behind in her hand.

"Oh." My eyes widen as the anger in me wavers. "I'm so sorry."

"It's okay."

"No, it's not! None of this is *okay*. They gave me orders." I repeat everything Creen told me on the jet as Sky places her hands on my shoulders, inhaling and exhaling until my body follows suit. "At first, I was asking questions, but I stopped pushing you because I know how you feel about loyalty, and I don't want to put you in danger. I just thought if I did good enough, my work would speak for itself. And I don't want you to be—"

"Shiloh, I'm not upset with you?"

"You're not?"

"Over half-hearted espionage?" Sky's hands fall away, and she leans against the wall with a resigned expression. "If I thought it'd keep you safe, I'd spill state secrets myself."

"I don't know what to do. What I did was bad, Sky. I *hurt* people. Exactly how I hurt you. I need to make it better, and I need to see my parents. I want to know why they lied to me."

"You didn't hurt me. I made the choice to twist instead of dodge as you so kindly pointed out," she sighs.

I lean my head against the wall, storm clouds peering into my soul until my cheeks prickle. "If you want to leave, we'll figure it out. The way I see it, we have two good options. Murder or war."

"I think I'd like a third, please."

"And I think you'd be adept at both, but a Bear never walks away from a brawl." Sky's lips go lopsided, and I can't help but smile too. "Let's go, Cub."

I don't remember much of the walk to his table, only that when we arrive, it falls silent.

Ezra has a half-chewed cinnamon stick dangling from between his lips, Bridger and Mai on either side, and Josephine still nowhere to be found.

I clip out a recounting of the meeting I'd just had, the three Imaginifers exchanging incredulous glances.

"She has no say in your grade?"

"Astute, Cousin. And yet, here we are," Sky says.

"I'll handle it."

"You want to know how?" Ezra stays silent because he's aware my question is rhetorical. "You're going to put me on the team for Ludi Bellorum. I'm going to play this stupid game, and then we're never speaking again."

"And me," Sky murmurs.

"But—"

"And me."

"And Sky," I agree begrudgingly. "But, she's not using magic under any circumstances. So, you'll need to figure that out."

Sky grumbles under her breath but doesn't correct me.

"I don't know who'll be selected as captain," Ezra begins.

I hold up a hand, leaning over the silent table and plucking the cinnamon stick he chews from his mouth. When I throw it on his empty plate, it breaks into bits. "I didn't ask what you know, I told you what I need done."

"In that case. Sign me up," Bridger grins. "You and I can practice one-on-one."

"You're shameless. You know that?"

"You've pronounced aroused incorrectly."

"You're... a deeply unserious person."

"So, we'll take your last name then? B.O.B. are some interesting initials, but I could make it work." I bite back a laugh, focusing on anything but the scowl to my side.

"You've fucked me, so you will fix it. Make sure you're captain."

"Really?" Ezra rises, leaning down until our faces have a breath of separation between them, hands side by side on his table top. "Recount the act in detail, Dreamer. That's not something I'm likely to forget."

I swallow roughly, leaning back to cross my arms over my chest. "Not the time for jokes."

"Why? Is there anything funnier than realizing the scissors you hold are timed to close?" Ezra laughs, but it's completely humorless, popping open the tin canister I'd given him and sliding a fresh cinnamon stick between his lips. "Consider it done."

When I turn away from him, Sky frowns, the two of us strolling side by side toward the lunch line.

"What?" I ask.

She purses her lips. "I don't like him. Or the way he thinks of you."

"What should people think of me?"

"That you've got a scale and some ostrich feathers on hand."

"That's terrifying. You should run while you still can."

"I think I'll take my chances."

# CHAPTER 26

Mid-year break with Sky is a flurry of weeks spent goofing off, and as the only students left on campus, we take advantage of our free time with new lessons that don't involve sparring. "How is this a daily occurrence for you?"

I sit on the floor of my bedroom, attempting to weave six violet strands together until my pulse thrums through my fingertips. Sky's silken hair slips out of the plait every time I don't pull tight enough.

"You should visit one of our hair salons," she says. "My cousins get patterns that put my braids to shame. I used to watch them for hours through the window when I was small."

"I don't know if I could take it. I was tender-headed as a kid, so whenever I got my hair braided, I'd sob. My hairdresser whacked me with a comb for ruining her parts once. Dad had to hold Mom back, and by *hold,* I mean physically restrain."

"A good whack builds character. In Hiemsternum, we don't have tender heads, we have bitches."

"An eight-year-old can't be a bitch?"

"They *absolutely* can, Cub. In fact, most of them are."

I whack Sky with her comb, and we burst into laughter. Though seconds later, her statement spurs a stray thought that leads me to blurt, "That nickname. It feels like you're calling me a child sometimes."

Sky frowns, turning toward me until we're adjacent on my plush rug. "You don't like it?"

"No, I do, but I'm only two years—"

"Seven."

"What?! You're *twenty-five?*"

"I turn twenty-five on New Year's Day. I know, practically decrepit, Cub." Sky laughs as my cheeks burn. "We waited to start school until my body was ready. Caveman and Sol were taking system suppressants. Little blue pills that—"

"Tastes like chalk."

"How do you—"

"Okay? *Seven.* Not so far off? That's... one year in dog years."

Sky rolls her eyes. "Yes, it is. *Especially* in this developmental stage."

"We all have toddler brain. How am I any more childish than the rest of you?"

"Shiloh, that's not what I'm saying."

"What are you saying then?"

"I don't fucking know. What do you want me to be saying?"

"The truth."

"Well, the truth is those soul suckers are as terrifying as they are youthful." Sky bends her head to put herself in my sightline when I lower my gaze. "Shiloh, there are certain types of people society regards as mirrors. When a passerby looks upon them, there's a primal urge to glance while aching to shatter them to bits. Even if they admire the frame, inside is a thin piece of glass that begets self-reflection. Overweight, malnourished, beautiful, grotesque, it doesn't matter. Anyone peculiar gets to be shiny, and you are incomparable."

"I'm a... *unique* mirror people want to break?"

"Two-dimensionally, but we can spin the coin if you'd like."

"I thought society lost that ability."

"We won't dance for anyone but ourselves when we're alone."

"Am I a disco ball the rest of the time? Shining on people who take to the dance floor but never getting to dance myself?"

"If you want a turn on the floor, ask the closest Bear. Caveman does a mean waltz." A giggle escapes her that's like bells in a gentle breeze. The chiming gone much too soon to fully know where it came from, but lingering long enough to wish desperately that it remained. "You're spinning, and in front of me is a woman who refuses to be jaded enough to abandon curiosity. People see themselves as the adult for telling you to shut up. Or say, *Because I said so* when you ask why. You question constantly and do not accept pacifiable answers. You think of a better world and see a path there so clearly, that sometimes, you live in it already." I stiffen at this, and she shakes her head back and forth. "Being a visionary does not mean you lack awareness of the world around you. In fact, you're so in tune, so *rooted* in reality, that I worry."

"Why?"

"I like mirrors. Some call me vain, I say blondes do it best." I finger coil a dark spiral, and Sky whistles air through her teeth. "Well, redheads are outright lethal. You guys should be locked up for societal safety."

"Redhead?" My teeth dig into my lip as I pluck invisible lint from my tank top. "Are you, um, thinking about someone else?"

"No?" Sky flushes, sounding oddly defensive as she adds, "When you're in the sunlight, your hair has a red glow."

I hope Sky knows what she's talking about. Partly because I'd take after my mother, who is the most beautiful woman I know, and mostly because I've never felt lethal in a way that excites me.

Sky squeezes my knee cap when I've been silent for too long. "Can I ask you where you go when you get quiet?"

"Somewhere that lets me think."

"About?"

"That I wish this break would last forever. I feel like I can breathe for the first time in maybe my whole life."

"Shiloh, it's okay to show the face that protects yourself. You don't have to give people your shine."

"If I don't, then what's left to give?" I ask, our fingers intertwining in Sky's lap. "I feel like the apathy in this world keeps getting worse, and it's feeding this... *cataclysmic* blizzard. People say it's a cloudless sky as long as they don't face the brunt of it themselves. They have homes to retreat to that allow them to sleep through the storm, and I want to scream and ask what they all need so much rest for. Because they never step outside, Sky. Not really. They watch from a window or turn on their TVs talking about how bad the weather is with their families as they ride it out, and I'm so fucking stuck in it. My family gives, but it'll never be enough for how fortunate we are. We donate, and volunteer, and the needle *never* moves. It's getting to a point where throwing our money at charities is a paper thin bandage over gaping wounds. And there's always someone around the corner ripping them off. I can't even take pleasure in material things, because I feel like *I* rip bandages too."

"It helps no one to bear the brunt of a system that you didn't create and are actively trying to level. Are you annoyed when Icarus shows up in another fancy watch? Or upset that Jason has never worn the same thing twice?"

"I don't really think about it."

"Because they don't flaunt it in people's faces like assholes. The Honestus brothers may piss me off for personal reasons, but they are entirely integral to the well-being of my country. No one should be comfortable in a world ruled by Tigers and Bears that didn't also have Lions. So take your parents' success and your commitment to opening doors, as the beautiful things they are. Eighteen years of life, and you care more in each breath than some do in an eternity. This weight you hold, it's a compulsive need to be morally perfect, and the world takes advantage of such kindness. Twists the narrative until you believe you should have reinforced your skin so they could throw stones in peace."

"I'm only metaphorically made of glass. I'll be okay. You can treat me the same as you do everyone else."

"You're not everyone else."

"Neither are you. You've walked with me in the bitter cold, even when you haven't wanted to, and in comparison, holding your hand feels warm."

"Never give me that credit. You've built yourself up to survive the blizzard. And even in such harsh conditions, your greatest dream is to carry a stranger's child toward the finish line at the expense of never arriving there yourself. You flourish with hope while others wither with bitterness when they realize they won't live to see paradise on earth. So much so, that they sabotage the journey for everyone else. That is why we made a collective here to have reached it quicker as one. You're an anomaly of everything the world has lost."

"I'm scared I'll lose it too. Wolves don't slide into wool. They're born inside sacrificial lambs and claw their way to the surface."

"What is lost can always be found, and I carry belief in your inherent goodness in my soul." Sky lifts up my chin so I don't lose track of her gaze. "And guess what?"

"What?"

"You're more than a kind heart. If that went away, I'd still think you were unreasonably funny."

"Really?" I grin. "I do have some jokes."

"And you're super fucking weird. In a way that's fascinating."

"I'm *weird?*"

"Being weird isn't a crime that needs punishment. Frankly, I crave your company."

"Even more than your last apple slice?"

"Suddenly you want to eat healthy?!"

"You forgot my spoon."

"Ever heard of using your fingers?" Sky scoops a heaping glob of salted caramel with her index, and as she brings it to her lips, my head dips to intercept her hand.

A breath of surprise escapes her, and she yanks her sticky finger from my mouth.

"Why get my hands messy when I can use yours?" I create a drum beat with my mouth, and Sky blinks rapidly. Cleaning off what's left on her finger while glaring at the half-empty container between us. "So... maybe you shouldn't have told me I was funny. I got too confident."

"No. I mean, I forgot your spoon. So, it's only fair, right?"

Sky dips two fingers in the glass bowl, scooping caramel and extending them forward in challenge.

"Oh. Okay?"

"Shiloh, I'm fucking with you."

"Because you think I'm a *bitch?*" I crawl forward until my hands rest on Sky's kneecaps, lips parting as our eyes meet.

My teeth graze slender fingers, dragging from the knuckle to the tips until caramel pools on my tongue.

I hum, bobbing my head back down and swallowing the taste that's ten times sweeter than a spoon.

Sky stills as I move my head, tongue stroking the underside of her fingers, parting them to suck off every drop and then some until I pull away with an audible pop.

I wipe off my mouth, and she abruptly turns away. "You know what? We've been inside too long. We should... go on a walk. Get some... *air*. Air's nice, right? We should... get some. *Air,* that is."

"Okay?" I survey her blank expression in the mirror and talk through the whooshing in my ears. "Should I finish your hair first?"

"Okay."

"Okay. We're... okay?"

"Yeah!" she breathes, hand pressed to her abdomen. "Any more questions?"

"Who did your hair for the Welcome Ceremony?!" I blurt, cheeks burning when our eyes connect in the mirror.

"Caveman."

"Seriously?"

Sky's reflection morphs to one of longing, and my heart drops. "A braid is for the strong. Each strand by itself, weak and easily plucked. But together, unbreakable. Better when united as one." She pulls her knees to her chest, deep in thought. "Each morning, fathers braid their children's hair to lend them strength. Caveman learned how to fishtail braid when he was eight with a piece of rope. Said I couldn't walk around without my hair done any longer. Not when theirs looked so perfect."

"Your Dad only did Nox and Solara's?"

She answers with only a jerky shrug of her shoulders. "Until they reach twenty years, my people do not cut their hair. To honor us. When they finally do, they throw it in a bonfire and offer it to our ancestors. Soldiers keep it long. Always. It holds strength and memory."

"I'm sorry for what I did, Sky." Honor may be a dead concept, but cutting her hair was probably as dishonorable as one can get with a Sapienti. "It was disrespectful."

"It was meant to be? And I'm never apologizing for spitting on you, so call us even."

"How is that even? I didn't mind." A maniacal laugh bursts through her lips, and she shakes her head free of wherever she's about to say next, motioning for me to focus back on the braiding lessons. My fingers comb through faded violet as I say, "Fine. I know your hair is special to you so therefore, it's special to me. I'm braiding it from now on. Lending *my* strength."

Sky doesn't acknowledge I've spoken, but she never shows up with a braid in her hair again. Silently hovering close until I choose a new hairstyle for the day. The first I manage is a fishtail, but soon enough, I'm able to do a bastardized version of her Welcome Ceremony updo.

She claims she likes it just as much as the original.

THE MORE TIME we spend together, the more aspects of Sky's personality float to the surface. Noting that she only pretends to hate it when I do her nails, and can't help herself but to clean my room as soon as she steps through my door.

Little by little, the Bear reveals her hard-ass demeanor is only the smallest part of her. And as December blows by, Christmas Eve is by far the most illuminating glance at the other side of Sky's coin.

"They're bored," I whisper, squeezing Sky's knee as we watch Meesa scrub at the same invisible speck of dirt for the fifth time. "I think they miss the students."

Sky grimaces, swirling red wine as she leans back in her chair. "I don't see why? They don't have to work for nearly two whole months?"

"And yet, they still do, and it's going to waste?"

Every station has made food for Sky and I, as well as the handful of faculty who remain over Mid-Year break.

Ever since I saw them toss out large vats of soup, I've made it a point to try as much as I can for every meal. Tonight's final dish is a spicy pork curry that's heavenly, yet has me fetching tissues for a runny nose.

"I was thinking we should make them thank you cards. I'll write, and you can draw pictures."

"*Or,* we could go lie on the bridge and look for shooting stars?"

"Fine. I'll make them myself. But you have to sign your name, they'll feel special if it comes from you, too."

I rise to my feet, and she groans, tugging me back into my chair.

"Shit. Okay, just... wait here."

Sky mutters obscenities under her breath on her way out of the cafe. And she's gone for so long, I finish my food, twiddling my thumbs as I consider there might be a possibility I've been blown off.

Nearly half an hour passes before she returns with a roller cart stacked high with boxes, coming to a stop before me with cheeks flushed from exertion. Sky opens one with a flourish, and I peek at a collection of noise makers and trinkets, a few pairs of heavy boots thrown on top with bells and clackers attached to the ankles.

"What's this?" I frown.

"What does every faithful audience want?"

"They want to be—Hold on, you want to give them a show?"

"Tell anyone, I will deny it."

*"She has a heart, and it's melting!"* I whisper-yell, pinching Sky's cheeks until she gnashes her teeth, nudging me toward the workers.

It takes everlasting patience from me, and some heated demands from Sky, until the staff are gathered around in chairs. Dozens of them perched on the edges of their seats as I pull a ruffled skirt over my pajama shorts. Sliding into an extra pair of boots two sizes too big for me, double-knotting them, and hoping I don't twist an ankle.

Meesa's the most reticent of the bunch. Wincing at the old man next to her who blows into his harmonica and drops it.

The small metallic instrument clatters noisily to the ground before his gaze sweeps side to side.

I offer her a clacker, and she takes it in white-gloved hands, holding the object with upward-facing palms as if it might bite her. "Ma'am, this is lovely, but we're at work. This isn't an appropriate way to spend our time."

"What's your name?" Sky frowns.

"Meesa," she whispers, chin touching her chest at the clear irritation in the Bear's voice.

"You being happy makes this one happy, Meesa." Sky motions for her to look up. "Because of that, I'll get fewer headaches. Fewer headaches make *me* happy. Can that not be considered a good day of work for the staff?"

Meesa curls her hands around the clacker and shakes it with rhythm, the staff falling silent as loud jangling noises ensue. "Music?"

"Only one part," Sky insists, turning to a red-haired staff member I've come to learn is named Cian.

She teaches him drums in a few minutes flat, head-banging as she throws a percussion mallet and catches it mid-air.

My lips fall open when Cian copies her movements to a T, keeping a steady beat and holding a wide grin on his face while doing so.

Over and over, Sky helps each with their instruments until the cafe is so loud my eardrums ring.

When it's nearly unbearable, she motions for them to stop, stepping onto the tabletop and offering me a hand.

I take it, climbing on the heavy oak alongside her.

"Okay, Cub. You're the conductor." Sky kneels before me, picking up one of my feet and shaking it in her hands.

The bells create a deep jingle that echoes in the sudden quiet surrounding us, the staff patiently waiting to be led in their ragtag orchestra. "You didn't think you were in the audience, did you?"

"I'm not really good onstage. What if you danced with me?"

"No. That's not a good idea."

"But you promised me a spin on the dance floor?"

"With *Caveman.*"

"Sky, you said a Bear. Not Nox. And I'm sure you're every bit as capable of a waltz. Shouldn't *I* get to choose my partner?"

"I—"

"Please?"

She hesitates, but bobs her head in agreement, sliding on an extra pair of boots and motioning for me to follow her lead.

We circle one another on the tabletop, her face so pinched that I immediately make a run for it, fisting the ruffles of my skirt and leaping from table to chair to table.

Sky's just at my heels, wrapping me in her arms and tickling my sides until I wave the white flag.

Laughter rings out among the staff when she wags her finger and throws me a stern look, bells jingling wildly to signal the end of our match-fixed game of cat and mouse.

She places me back on the table, and the bands of our rings clash together, morphing sparks into butterflies that escape our clasped hands, flitting about until the air around us is filled with floating micro lanterns.

The staff clap and cheer, but the world narrows down to the woman in front of me until we may as well be alone.

Sky tugs me closer, an incredulous look on her face as she whispers, "How has no one taken you dancing before?"

"Didn't even go to prom. It's a travesty, really."

"Of monumental proportions." Sky dips me, and my curls brush the table top, lips grazing the shell of my ear when I rise. "They'll hold regret for the rest of their days."

Sky's soft in her instructions and meticulous with each brush of her fingertips. Positioning my hips and tilting my chin up until I meet her gaze, as in sync as in any of our sparring matches.

She twirls me in circles, no care for how close we get to the table's edge as my skirt billows in the winds at our feet.

The tiny creatures distract Sky by playing in her braid, landing on her nose like a kiss. Emitting embers and inducing giggles each time she swats them away.

When her hands slide from my hips to the small of my back, all at once, they dissipate. Icy fingers fluttering against the hyper-sensitive skin on my bare spine until my concentration is dead in the water. The final remnants of them singeing my skirt.

Sky's hands tighten as if I may slip through her grasp, and we hold a small eternity between us. It's a peculiar thing to have someone respect your proximity so completely. To skim your curves and imagine them an hourglass, your body the sand they tip to prolong the moment.

"Shiloh, for too long I've denied myself the full scope of human emotions because the performance of strength calls for someone without soft feelings. But, I feel as if I've been cheated of time before I knew you. It's astronomically unfair."

"What are you saying, Sky?"

She exhales raggedly as if I've handed her a loaded gun. "Just that I'd be doing the world a disservice to not scream from the rooftops and tell the Universe it did one thing right."

My heart snaps and lances to the point of pain, and Sky turns me around to see what we've begun, resting her chin on my shoulder and wrapping her arms around my waist.

The staff members have created their own beat in the absence of our footsteps.

"*You* did this."

"No? You—"

"Opened my heart because the more I give, the less you have to. This blizzard will not take you, Cub. You lead the way, and I'll follow blindly."

Meesa has a new light in her eyes, shaking her clacker with glee. And the harmonica man blows at random, until it occurs to me that he may be hard of hearing.

I touch my temple with my index finger, twisting my thumb in front of my palm before pushing my hand forward with a smile.

He returns the hello, teeth forming a gaping grin big enough to be everlasting.

In truth, it's not great. Or in tune.

In fact, it's the worst band that's ever been made.

But our symphony is comparable to none.

Time escapes us, and I'm unsure of how long we watch them enjoy themselves. But when it's over, there's something I've never heard before in my many months here. Excitement and chatter amongst the staff as they clean up their work stations. As they talk about the fun they had. As they hope we get another *party* before break ends.

"Come with me," Sky whispers.

"Where?"

"Does it matter?"

I shake my head back and forth, and Sky helps me off the table.

Staff members yelling their goodbyes as we run away hand in hand, giggling like madmen and twirling our way to the bridge.

"You should be a teacher," I say when we're all danced out, plucking a white chrysanthemum and handing it to Sky.

She smells it, pulling petals off one by one and whispering to herself.

When there's a singular floret remaining, she frowns, chucking the entire flower into the rapids.

"No daughter of Fenrir Sapienti is becoming a *teacher.*"

"What about the woman behind the thorns?" Sky pulls her knees to her chest, and I turn my back to the water. Going still as she plucks a stray petal from my hair. "Penny for your thoughts?"

"My thoughts are not something that can be bought. Especially not with Addam's money."

"That's a shame. Now you have to share them for free."

"I've shared more than enough today," she sighs. "Do you have anything to add?"

My hands dance along the frills on my skirt as she scrunches her nose. "Do you believe in Karma?"

"No."

"Me neither." I wet my lips, eyebrows furrowing as I admit, "But there are things people do that are so bad, they wait for punishment they feel suffices to move on. They remember how they hurt someone, and when their favorite pair of shoes goes missing, they think, well, this is appropriate. I shouldn't be upset, because one time I gave Ximena Acevedo a soft-bristled toothbrush to help her receding gums, and she cried. Even though it was probably their Mom not understanding that they didn't wear the shoes because they wanted to pull them out on special occasions. They were bright yellow."

"You gifted a girl a toothbrush for her receding gum line?"

"Well, only because I overheard her talking about it in the hallway. I wanted to be her friend."

"Shiloh, you can't look how you look and gift someone you hardly know a toothbrush. It doesn't come off well."

"I mean, I don't think that had anything to do with it? Because she said 'not everyone is from *uncanny valley* and has *chiclet* teeth.' Sam called her ra-cede-da-vedo for a whole year after that, which wasn't really nice either. Anyway, I should've minded my own business."

"I don't know, I'm with Sam. I hope her gums bleed daily from her hard ass toothbrushes."

"Sky—"

"Do you feel like that for me?" Sky blurts.

The tip of her nose pinkens and all I feel is the urge for a sedative.

I haven't touched a drug in weeks.

I made the conscious decision never to use around Sky, and so far, I haven't crossed those lines. I think that's as much as I can do for her until I find the strength to quit.

My only hope is that she can forgive me for abusing what she craves.

"Do I... feel like I should buy you tooth brushes?"

"Shiloh, you know what I'm asking you."

Sky's gaze lingers on my mouth and I can't hear, or think, or breathe. I can only scramble backwards as she leans forward to brush her lips against my own.

One moment, my fingers claw at the wood below us, and the next, I tumble into open air.

Unaware that I'm falling until she shrieks my name.

I crash into the rapids, and my skirt soaks in an instant, sinking like a boulder caught in an unyielding current.

I grab for anything in reach, catching fistfuls of rock as I'm drug across the riverbed for what feels like miles, using up air supply I don't have to scream Sky's name in return.

For the first time in years, perhaps my entire life, I fear death.

It's selfish, really.

I never cared about the possibility of a laced pill, or thought about the pain my absence may cause Sam or my parents. I danced with death willingly and, at times, even begged it to embrace me.

But Sky's horror-stricken face as gravity stole me away is a stark contrast to the pitch black darkness that envelopes me now.

I kick my legs, and my ruffled skirt gets caught on a jagged tree root, fighting my way out of the poofy fabric because I haven't had enough time. Because I think—*I know,* that if I claw my way back to the surface, there's something worth fighting to reach.

My arms grow sluggish, and I'm pelted with stray ice chunks each time I move a limb, electric shocks in my muscles that grow stiffer with each passing second.

With one final push, I break the surface of the river, hand clasping around a low-hanging tree limb as I bellow her name.

Water pours from my nostrils, and I blink ice out of burning corneas, getting a glimpse of Sky cutting seamlessly against the current like a sharp blade once she spots me.

"Shiloh?! Shiloh, I'm coming! Stay where you are!" I squeeze my eyes shut until slender arms circle my waist, and it's only when her skin's on mine that I sob my vision blurry. Frozen limbs wrapping around her body while she croons my name. "I've got you. You're okay."

"*N*-no. Your *l-l*-lungs. *Y*-you'll get *s*-sick. What *d*-did I do?!"

"Breathe. Just breathe." Sky presses her forehead to mine and fights against the current, one arm crushing me to her torso while the other clings to the tree branch. "I'm fine, Shiloh! This cold? It's *nothing* to me. You're having a panic attack!"

*Inhale. Exhale. Inhale. Exhale.*

Sky helps me find a rhythm again, lips kissing my forehead until I croak, "You're fine? You're okay?"

"I am," she breathes. "So, let me help you now. Your lips are blue."

Our fingers knit together, and we wade back to shore side by side, collapsing a mile away from the bridge on a small patch of grass.

Sky coughs up a storm, blinking ice-flecked lashes, and instead of being angry, her first words are, "I'm sorry."

I flinch, sitting upright and scrambling to my feet. "I need to get out of here."

"I'm so sorry, Shiloh," she repeats, reaching for me as I raise a hand to keep our distance. "I completely misread what was happening."

Sky steps forward, and I stumble backwards, twisting away from her accusatory stare.

For once in my life, I don't ramble, I don't beg, and I certainly don't attempt to justify my actions.

I run, and I run, and I lose her pursuit—a gaping canyon expanding between us where there'd just been no space at all.

# CHAPTER 27

My door creaks open, and I go still as heavy footsteps pad around hardwood. Minutes go by as Sky cleans up the mess I've made, the clunk of an empty wine bottle hitting the wastebasket before she peels up the corner of my blanket, exhaling a sigh of relief. I make room under the comforter, and Sky kicks off her boots, sliding in alongside me until our legs tangle together.

"Merry Christmas, Shiloh Benson."

"Happy Yuletide, Sky Sapienti."

Sky flicks her fingers until candlelight pools from her index, rolling her eyes as I press mine against it and keep the flame going, leaning forward to blow her finger until hers flickers out. Our heads nestle against my silken pillowcase as a single flame remains to fill the space between us. "You have to stop doing that."

"You're letting me."

"I wish that were the case," she grumbles.

"Well, we could both stop. Forever? I'm okay with a hundred years."

"And what exactly would we do with a meager century?"

"Doesn't really matter as long as we're together."

"But only on your terms?" Sky's lips twitch downward, and I notice for the first time her eyes are swollen and red-rimmed. "You left me. I thought you'd come back and you didn't."

"And you still woke up in the blue."

"It's your favorite holiday, Cub," she says this with some exasperation, as if the idea of disappointing me is preposterous.

My hand runs over the front of Sky's shirt, and I wonder at what point in the change will the need to cry ever fade.

It only gets worse when I realize she's stolen another one of Dad's sweaters—a gray crewneck reading, *Climate change is snow laughing matter,* featuring a melted snowman frowning on a beach. As it turns out, she thinks wearing puns is hilarious. The same ironic sense of humor as Henry, that's half because they make sense and half because it's fucking ridiculous to wear statements on a t-shirt. "Last night, when you asked me if I had anything to add, I should've said, 'The blood of the covenant is thicker than the water of the womb.'"

"What?"

"My Mom saw that phrase spray-painted on the side of some dive bar, and it changed her life. Used to say it about my best friend Samantha and I when we were on the playground and would fall and scrape our knees. Sam would demand she kiss our ouchies."

"Who'd solicit a kiss from a beautiful woman? Sick fuck. I told you kids are bitches."

I can't help but laugh as Sky puffs air into her cheeks. "Mom said growing up like that would bond us for life. And she was right. The bonds we made through mulch-covered playground wounds made Sam my sister as much as Solara is yours."

Sky crinkles her nose. "You're saying I'm your sister too."

"I'm saying we've shed blood together, and if we make a promise, it's special. It's something we commit to, not because of chance or circumstance, but of *choice.* I trust you with my life, Sky. What is that if not family made? Family chosen. Our covenant in action?"

She shakes her head back and forth. "I don't know if I can do this."

"But I thought—"

"I just think that a break would be wise until I can get my head on straight. I want you to be comfortable around me."

"But I don't *want* a break?"

"What about what I want?" She pauses. *"Need."*

"Fine." I press forward, and Sky's breath stutters in her chest. "Whatever it is, we'll do it. Just don't leave me."

Her hands slide into my hair, fingers massaging the base of my skull so methodically that I almost forget I'm waiting for her to speak. Eyes fluttering closed as my lack of sleep catches up to me. "Please?"

"Okay... I accept your covenant. *Family.*" Sky slides out from beneath my blankets, and this time, I allow her distance. "But I want to go back to normal. Immediately."

"Well, I have a present for you. Is that normal enough?"

"If you put some clothes on." Her cheeks redden, and I cross my arms over my skimpy tank top and briefs, running into the closet and tossing on the sweatpants and puffer coat I'd arrived in. I even managed to get my beanie back from Sunny with some struggle, the staff having to stitch a hole closed from our tug of war.

As I slide the hat over my curls, I step out of the closet with a small twirl, and Sky snorts.

"What?"

"You look like a marshmallow."

"I want you to remember what you said ten seconds from now." I grin, walking to the window of my room and sliding it open to perch on the windowsill. "Because you decided to roast me, I've become goo."

I fall backward, and Sky screeches in a pitch I've never heard before. Running to see me lying across Sunny's back two floors down, giggles racking my body as she goes beet red in the face. "What the fuck?! You didn't look to see if she was there!"

"I felt it in my bones! She's been thinking about some company."

"No." Sky bares her teeth, fully awake now. "Get that look off your face."

"But Sunny would never drop you!" I crawl forward until I'm a few inches from her stubborn gaze, arms folding over Sunny's eyes as I rest my chin on her head. "And I'd sooner throw myself off with no hope of being caught than let you fall."

"If you think that's comforting to me, you've read this all wrong."

"Shouldn't it be? I think there are very few things to be scared of when we're together."

"Very few," she agrees.

"Exactly. So get on the damn horse. Or else."

My threat makes Sky cackle and eventually concede, pointedly ignoring the cheese grater in the base of my skull as I help the princess on my annoyed pegasus.

The Bear seems much smaller than usual as she shakes like a leaf, crawling into Sunny's saddle with her eyes clenched shut.

"Sunny, be gentle," I caution.

When Sky settles behind me, I turn to check on her. "Not bad at all! Now, you just open your eyes."

"No," she whimpers, white knuckling my puffer. "I changed my mind. Put me back."

"One short flight?"

"No."

*"Please?"*

Her face goes green as if she might hurl. "Five minutes. That's it."

"Ten." I squeeze her hand before pulling Sunny's reins, flapping away from the window, and gliding over campus so Sky gets used to the elevation.

To her credit, Sunny doesn't go as fast as she normally does. Hooves skimming the river as she presses her worry down the bond, showing me she felt my fright last night.

"I'll explain later," I whisper, "Just stay low and slow. She doesn't like heights."

Sky catches our reflections in the water and seems to enjoy it if we remain close to the ground. Pink lips curling upwards as she points out several mackerel and dragonfish for me among the ice chunks.

Apparently, Bears enjoy fishing, and her level of interest compels me to pretend I know what a *wiggler* is.

We fly miles downstream at low altitude. Going into winding, steep-sloped mountains until Sky is comfortable enough to attempt an ascension. "Okay, don't look down anymore, look up. It's the same thing but a little higher."

She doesn't seem to agree, burying her face in the crook of my neck as we rise, body shuddering against my back.

Sunny keeps a steady pace, gliding through clouds like a slow dip into still waters, our visions fogged by huge puffs of cumulus.

My thighs squeeze the saddle as I hold both arms out, wind dancing through my fingers like an old friend.

We come to a wide open patch of air, and I feel a touch of warmth on my face, the beginnings of morning sunlight kissing the tip of my nose.

Sky refuses to look as I twist, side saddling to get her reaction to the view before us. "You can open your eyes now."

"No!" she shouts over the wind. "I will refrain! Ten minutes have passed."

"Ten minutes will have passed when you open your eyes."

"That's not how time works."

"Up here, time ceases to exist at all." I coax her eyes open by lightly tapping her lids until she meets my gaze.

When I turn Sky's head to take in the sight to our left, her ragged breath evens out. Dark lashes fluttering in disbelief of the endless stretch of orange before us. A spellbinding sunrise that paints the air and stains the clouds golden yellow. Shining over distant mountain tops and bathing the forest and rushing river below in its enchanting light.

There's a specific pinch in my insides when she nods in approval.

Gray orbs drink in every bit of sunlight that soaks my skin as she places a hand on her abdomen, lifting her shirt up when she sees me eyeing her hand.

I prod Sky's stomach while she takes in the view, lips curling crookedly as she says, "Caveman taught me how to give myself an enema before he left, Dr. Benson. Then, he forced a shot of olive oil down my throat."

"But, I could have done that? And not have forced you to drink olive oil like a jackass. You know, I've never even seen him eat a piece of candy! That's why he's always grumpy. And... not as fun, I bet."

"Stars above, between the two of you, I'll get away with nothing else in this lifetime. Who needs a father in these conditions?"

"Why don't you trust me?"

"It's not for lack of capability. You're an undercover freak who's talked about ass play one too many times for it to be a joke. I can't let you prep the area. You'd be tempted to slip a tongue in my hole, and then what? I'd have to upkeep the regimen when you enjoyed it? I can barely manage to shave down there."

There's a moment of silence before laughter erupts from us both, clinging together until Sky wraps me in her arms to enjoy the rising sun.

My ear presses against her fluttering heart until I'm sure I understand life more than I ever have before. This small and mighty barycenter between two celestial bodies keeps us in perfect orbit as the need for the why fades away. "Ubi tu, ibi ego. Semper et in perpetuum."

*"You're getting better,"* Sky whispers in Latin. *"You sound like you were born here."*

*"I've been practicing saying anything other than, 'Were you made in a cool person store' when I'm at a loss for words."*

Sky releases a shuttered sigh, coiling a curl around her finger and showing me auburn strands brought out by the sun-rays. "This right here proves Karma is real."

I swallow roughly, left without the courage to ask if I'm her punishment or her reward.

I'm unclear whether I could survive either answer.

WHEN OUR FLIGHT HAS FINISHED, Sky decides she'll clean up Sunny by herself, kissing the mare's muzzle every so often because she thinks I can't see them.

I peer at the pair from Jupiter's stall and feel like a third wheel, perched atop his wing with sudsy fingers while I scrub the topside clean.

If there's one thing about my pegasus, it's that she loves being admired, and Sky gives the little attention seeker all the love in the world. Hooked, ever since Sky put a matching braid in her mane and got her coat brighter than seems possible—emphasizing to me that I'd better take note.

When an adoring smile lights Sky's face, I know she's in such a good mood that I take the opportunity while I have it. "You've been hooking up with Russ."

Sky's brush clatters to the ground, and she turns to survey me with wide eyes. "What?"

"You've been having sex with Russ."

Jupiter extends his wings so I can crawl to the window, pulling myself up before hopping into Sunny's stall, dropping the sponge to soak in a stray bucket.

"He told you that?" Sky asks, rubbing her chest as I dry my hands on a towel.

"He didn't have to. You were waiting for him when we tripped down the steps. That was his *secret meeting?*"

"It... didn't start that night. I met you instead, remember?"

My jaw drops, and everything goes still. Even though I'd suspected it, having registered their scents on each other for months, hurt floods my system. "Does it even matter when it started if it's still going on?"

"Give me a reason I shouldn't, and it's done." Storm clouds brew within her irises, and Sunny tilts her head, nudging Sky forward.

"Russ was celibate!"

Sky squints her eyes, and it stirs my stomach. Wondering if, to her, it's just scratching an itch. And if so, why choose to scratch that itch with *him?* "So, you're okay with me being with whoever I want as long as it's not Icarus?"

"What you do is your business."

"And if it's yours because I said it is?"

"I... see no issue aside from the fact you lied to me."

"I'm not doing this," she scoffs. "Stars above, sometimes I think your only goal is to drive me batshit crazy."

"I could say the same? You *lied* to me, Sky!"

"No one lied except you right now! You see no issue?!" Sky covers both eyes and aims them towards Sunny. "Well, I see no pegasus!" She nears me, and I stumble into the wall when only a foot remains between us, her fingertips digging into the steel slats on either side of my head. "I'm contagious now?"

To put it mildly.

Sky Sapienti has infected my every thought. Every experience is tinged in violet, and she refuses to say anything to heal the pain that makes my heart beat to a different rhythm.

Her lips skate across my jaw and rest against the shell of my ear until I gasp. "Last I checked, you don't mind my spit."

Sky slides down the zipper of my coat, inch by inch, until my over-sized jacket falls to the cement. She plucks off my beanie next, tossing it in the hay before fixing my curls.

My nipples pebble as chilly thumbs swipe along my hip bones, tugging me forward, skimpy tank top rising above my navel and appearing thinner with each movement.

Traitorous arms twine around her neck, and soft curves mold to my own like a missing link.

Sky backs us into the wall, and everything feels impossibly tight, like a guitar string pulled taut, on the verge of vibrating within her fingers.

I can count every dark lash as her eyes narrow with decision, intense storm clouds blocking out all sense of self. There's no Heaven, or Hell, nor Earth below my feet. This cage I'm in, this mind that bends reality, opens up until I'm floating, and only Sky exists.

"In your fantasy—"

"Don't go there."

"Somewhere you've already gone?" Her eyes grow big enough to pluck the chord and make it hum inside my chest. "Who's with you when the lab notes go flying?"

"Sky."

"Who's. With. You?"

"You," I whisper. "You're always with me."

The words appear to melt her last bit of control, feeling as if I've been stripped bare when Sky's mouth latches onto my throat.

My head lolls back, and she grazes my carotid with razor-sharp canines, baring the most vulnerable part of me to the jaws of a Bear. The bone-deep instinct that no one should be so close eviscerated by my desire to let Sky protect what I'm entrusting to her.

Her canines sink into the base of my neck, a knife to butter as fire floods my veins, limbs loosening until I'm buzzing from inside out—emitting soft noises that prompt her hands to tighten until I see stars.

Sky's tongue laps at the pouring wound until the flow becomes a gentle drip, tasting my essence like an aged red wine until our bodies release vicious shudders in response.

She releases my thumping pulse with a searing kiss, and every nerve burns under her touch. Bloody mouth scorching a pathway to my breast, biting through the thin cami and sucking on a peaked bud until another flash of heat floods my core.

"You're perfect, Shiloh. Every. Damned. Part of you."

I clamp my thighs around her leg as tension pulses and throbs at the apex between them, tugging at the strap on my shoulder with a desperate whimper.

Sky pulls away for the briefest moment before her mouth suckles on bare flesh. Legs wrapping her waist as her tongue swirls my nipple, eliciting sounds that cross between a purr and moan, needy hips pressing forward while Sky holds me upright.

Every minute movement is fire and ice, and I'm unsure who will melt or extinguish first. Or, if this may be a perfect dance. A delicate balance that's as inevitable and ancient as Earth's rotation.

Sky's plush mouth kisses a pathway to what I know she's saved for last—my swollen lips that I've gnawed, teased, and bitten to quiet my cries. That ache to be soothed and explored, but turn away before the last puzzle piece connects, a sudden stillness and suspension of gravity between us.

Sky steadies me on trembling legs, and I push her away from my body, pressing my spine into steel. Mouth watering while my ears fill with the sound of an irregular heartbeat, fluttering and thumping as if it may leap from her chest with each step away from me.

Sunny cloaks Sky in her wing, masking her scent until it's bearable to inhale.

"It takes two to tango, and you've known how to dance this entire time. Yes or no?" My gaze falls to the ground, and she inhales sharply in surprise. "Answer me!"

"That's not fair."

"And the way you look at me is?! The romantic gestures, the flirting, the *touches,* it's all what exactly?! A game?" When silence stretches between us, Sky turns her back to me. Hands fisting by her sides as she says, "You're right. The Universe didn't hand either of us a fair life, so leave this be or take off your damned blindfold, but I'm done playing."

"None of this is a game."

"It never feels like it when you're the winner, does it?"

My pegasus swishes her tail and nuzzles Sky's cheek until she picks up the dropped dandy brush and gets back to work. White knuckling the hard-bristle piece of wood as if her life depends on it.

Her trembling shoulders are an automatic beacon, and I stumble toward them, realizing I forgot to braid her hair this morning.

Sky drops the brush when my fingers coil a silken tress, darting past me and escaping in a brilliant blaze of violet.

Sunny tilts her head to watch her leave, staring me down as a flood of annoyance creeps through my skull.

"What? You have something to add? Because this is grown-up business! You and Jupiter are separated for a reason, ya know?"

My pegasus whacks me with her wing, and I fall into her hay-bed, making her chosen side known as she kicks the hay to cover my body, and I lie in silence until I'm buried alive.

By NIGHTFALL, Sky pretends this morning never happened, surprising me by having spent all day cooking a feast with Meesa.

It's an entire spread of the things Dad would make for dinner, and she instructs the kitchen staff to put down their pans and share our table, all of them fawning over the Bear with gratitude. Sky's made us greens and buttered cornbread and mac and cheese and sweet potatoes and the juiciest turkey I've ever consumed.

The staff boot-stomp in her name, rising to dance with full bellies and bells tied to their ankles.

Sky's somber face is at odds with the joyous mood she's brought to the Cafe. I place my hand on her kneecap, and she eyes my flint ring, a lopsided smile tugging at my heart. "You never asked for it back. Why?"

"Because I like knowing you can demand something for yourself and not apologize for wanting it." Sky shrugs. "Every time I see my ring on your finger, it makes me happy."

"Then I'll never take it off."

She swallows roughly, thumb circling the gems on my castor ring until it glimmers under her touch. "I know you've been waiting for the other shoe to drop, but there's no ultimatum, Shiloh. I've seen firsthand how people treat you and I refuse to be another person who feels entitled to take from someone so eager to give. You said you didn't want to go there, and I did."

I shake my head back and forth rapidly. "That's not even close to the full story. You know how much I care about you?"

"Then answer me honestly. If I had asked to touch you first, would you have let me? Yes or no?"

"That isn't a simple yes or no question."

"It is for me. If I were a secret your whole life, then so be it. But I'd never forgive myself for accepting an invitation to your body, extended solely because you want to keep me around."

Sky sucks on her bottom lip, and I can feel her pain as clearly as I feel Sunny's pushes down the bond. Even more so. And to know I've caused even a fraction of it squeezes my chest until I can't quite breathe.

"Don't be sad."

I kiss both cheeks that flush, and her chin that wobbles, and her sweet little nose that scrunches every time she squeezes her eyes shut, taking several deep breaths before my eyes land on her mouth.

"Shiloh," she whispers, face twisted as if everything hurts. "I've already made my decision. Kissing me now won't change that. It'll just upset us both."

"Sky, I just need some time to think. Okay? We can figure this out."

Sky rubs her face until it's relaxed, the hilts of her hands pressed against closed lids. "Walking the blizzard alone isn't optional, but the only way I can hold you tightly is for both of us to let go a little. And I need you to say okay. For my sanity, I need this to be done. And if you care about me, I need you to respect that."

"Okay... Whatever you *n*-need. Whatever you want, it's done."

She stands with a curt nod, kissing the crown of my head before retreating to stomp her boots with the staff.

By the end of the night, Sky's boundaries are made clear.

In fact, for the next few weeks, she doesn't welcome any physical contact at all. At least, not initiated by me.

And as students arrive at the tail end of January, she spends the final days of break with her siblings. Leaving me to note that letting go *a little* feels a lot like a fractured covenant that barely bridges the gap.

And I can't so much as blame her.

# CHAPTER 28

Russ shifts his head in my lap, eyes flicking back and forth over the pages of a leather-bound journal he's brought back from vacation. Two months away, and a second puberty has hit him like a brick wall. Always boyishly beautiful, but now, he's devilishly handsome. Sweater vests and slacks replaced with a deep green hoodie and denim jeans, no fancy ties to be found.

Suede groans my name, and I focus on the task at hand, careful not to move as she pours a thick neon paste into the beaker.

When a drop plops on Russ's book and begins to smoke, he rises to avoid spilt chemicals, cracking open another shake from his backpack before throwing me a shy smile that's uniquely him.

"You're staring again."

"Sorry."

Admittedly, it isn't just his change in appearance. Each time I catch a whiff of Sky's scent on his clothes, I register the reality that neither of them address. It seems to coat him more frequently now as if there's a point to be made.

What I don't understand is how everyone can't smell it on them?

Are they all *pretending* to be oblivious? The secrets never end with these people!

Russ adjusts his glasses. "Is it that big a deal?"

"Girls are starting to talk to me to get to you, ya know?" Suede rolls her eyes, pitching her voice up higher. "*Isn't Icarus single?* Name chasing whores."

"Suede, that's daisy territory."

"My bad, Arsonist. Forgot the truth is unpopular these days. I'm sure they're in it for true love."

"They're interested in me?" Russ asks, looking almost pleased with himself. "Really?"

"Guys, too. Let me know if you wanna dabble. Men are always easy to get in bed. Dick slinging sluts. See? I'm an equal opportunist!"

Russ coughs, protein shake going down the wrong pipe as he bangs his chest to free his lungs of liquid.

"They should've seen all that before! Not because of... new developments!" I say.

"You mean my weapons of mass destruction?" He flexes his arms, biceps popping through his hoodie, pulling up the hem to show off a ripped six-pack soon after. "My guns are almost on par with yours, Shi." I pull down the hem of his hoodie until his V-line and happy trail are safely stowed away.

Russ chuckles as he throws an arm over my shoulder and kisses my temple, confirming his hardened exterior is still gooey to his core.

"What's going on here?" he asks Suede. "Or is it still top secret?"

She claps her hands together with excitement. "It's nail polish!"

Russ deflates in an instant, leaning against my bedpost with exasperation until I poke his side. "You said it was a scientific breakthrough?"

"It is." Suede pours black goop into an empty container, shaking it as she explains. "Each person has their own distinct scent markers, lost to basic senses. Emitting releaser pheromones—"

"They're not lost to my senses," Russ says.

"Let me finish before you start peppering us with braggy commentary."

My eyebrows furrow at this. "Wait, I want to hear about his thing first."

"Of course you do," Suede mumbles.

"Suede, that's not what I—"

"It's fine. Just get it over with."

"We've all evolved," he begins. Reiterating the changes Alchemists go through when we begin using magic. Along with healing, touch has become more stimulating, colors more vivid, the world far clearer, tastes richer, smells stronger, and feelings all-consuming.

"But the purer your blood is, the better your senses get. It's why the Sapienti's are so good at hunting. For instance, someone down the hall has *just* opened a pack of nuts."

I inhale sharply, managing to get wafts of cashew in my nose. Suede keeps sniffing and eventually gives up, shoulders sinking downward.

"How do you know it's about pureness of blood? What if your families are mixing up the punch to seem... You know?"

"I have no clue what that means, but sure. I know a few Loyalists who were born bloodhounds. Low names, I'm doubtful."

I rub sweaty palms on my kneecaps, and he sniffs again. "Stop!"

"Stop what?"

"Stop *surveillancing* me. It's rude."

"I don't—"

"Seriously. Promise you won't do it, Russ."

"Okay?" He frowns.

"Well, since the rest of us don't have that, what if someone created a substance that reacts to the pheromones you release? What could they react with?"

"Bodily secretions?" I ask, crossing my arms over my chest. "Sweat, vaginal fluid, semen, urine, saliva... the list goes on."

"Exactly. One thing that's overlooked, one thing I think about frequently as my manicures peel, is that we have natural oils on our nail beds," Suede says. "Over break, when Jace was working, I got bored. I created a nail polish that turns colors when you see someone you're attracted to. Based solely on the natural pheromones you release."

Our response is unison. "Whoa."

"I know. I'm a *genius*. Who wants to test it?"

"Not me!" I yelp. Suede narrows her eyes, and I raise my freshly painted red fingertips.

Russ shakes his head firmly. "Count me out, too."

"Come on you guys, it's perfectly safe!"

"Then you do it," he says.

"I have? I want to make sure it works on other people's pheromones too."

"I'm not wearing nail polish," Russ insists as she uncaps the wand, waving the brush near his nail beds until he yanks his hands away. Russ leaps to his feet, and Suede launches upright, chasing him around our room with the nail brush.

"Keep your weird sex paint away from me! Heeeelp! I'm being harassed!" Suede and I burst into giggles, and I hop on Russ's back to slow him down.

He keeps up the same pace, hopping from desk to bed to floor with me in tow, room spinning from all the jerking around. "Baby, I know we broke up, but I never expected you to betray me this way."

Just when she's about to land a dab on his finger, the door bursts open, all of us frozen in place. The black paint drips from the wand onto Suede's fingers, instantly shifting to a bright yellow.

Jason stands before us, eyebrows knit in confusion at the scene surrounding him.

"What's wrong, babe?" Suede asks.

We slide off of Russ, who's become our personal jungle gym in the struggle to paint his nails.

"The banners are up for Ludi Bellorum."

"Did you check them?!"

"No? I ran here first. Hurry up!" We scramble to follow Jason, momentarily stuck in the doorway when all three of us attempt to exit at the same time.

We fly down spiral staircases and across stone walkways, heading toward the announcement banners hanging on the front of the school. The crowd grows thicker the closer we get, weaving through hundreds of people to get a better look.

To none of our shock or surprise, Jason isn't listed on the golden banner, though Suede still huffs and puffs about it.

I slip through the crowd to survey the brilliant red banners next. Names written in a cobalt black that are easy to read. The top banner is full of people I don't recognize, and twice as long, with ten participants per team. Filled to the brim with third and fourth years, I haven't had the chance to meet yet.

The lower banner names are all too familiar.

**Bridger Emerson.**

**Mai Black.**

**Shiloh Benson.**

**Sky Sapienti.**

And toward the top of our team of five, the Captain's name is none other than **Ezra Alvarez.**

A finger hooks my belt loop to tug me toward them, nose scenting sweet almonds and burying in the crook of a cold neck.

"Congratulations, Cub." Sky hugs me tightly, but I don't mind it one bit. Sometimes I miss her when she's right next to me, and the only thing to soothe it is to squeeze her. Never seeming to get close enough to sate the feeling, just enough to make it hurt a little less.

I shiver, and she retreats in an instant, burying her fists under her arms as if they're on time out.

"Congrats to you, too. I don't want to sound like an attention whore, but I kind of wish you weren't on that banner with me."

A scoff escapes a crooked mouth. "Funny. My father sent me a letter this morning saying the exact opposite."

"Did he also say he misses you and apologizes for being a raging douchebag?"

"No. He's going to be at Ludi Bellorum. Wants to talk if we win. Says he might have been too abrupt with me when I left."

"Oh my God. Sky!?"

"There's no guarantee he won't change his mind. What's important to me is that we *will* win. You'll get to go home." Sky's smile turns bittersweet, and my stomach fills with rocks, her thumb smoothing out the line forming between my eyebrows. "Home, right? That's the goal?"

"Yeah, I just figured—" Sky drops her hand as my friends approach, Tristain and Osira in tow, screaming with elation.

I take turns hugging everyone, drunk off their excitement, but settling on a concrete goal that's sobering. While Sky fights for me to have choices, I'll do the same for her.

"Okay!" Suede yells. "We're all going to make signs for Shiloh!"

"And Sky," I add.

"Why would I do that?" Sky flips Suede off, and I pull her hand down. "You hate me. Bedazzled posters are for my friends."

"I don't... *hate* you, Blondie. Where did you get that idea?"

"You told your sister I have the emotional intelligence of a lizard. In front of me."

Tristain chortles, and Osira side-eyes him.

"Have you ever encountered a bearded dragon?" I narrow my eyes when Sky adds, "Some say they're highly intelligent creatures. Not me, but that's neither here nor there. Shiloh likes them."

"I'll make Sky's poster," Russ declares, his cheery interjection whirling my stomach.

"Perfect!" Suede claps, jumping up and down with glee. "You know, I've never rooted for the Fire quadrant before! But come May first, we all bleed red motherfuckers!"

There's a beat of silence before everyone bursts into laughter, and Suede's smile drops.

"What? What's funny about that?!" Jason composes himself, and Sky sucks in her cheeks when I poke her side. However, Tristain, Osira, and Russ cannot stifle their reactions.

Suede swivels on her heel, managing to escape a few yards before Jason catches her, immediately sinking into his embrace. I can't help but eavesdrop as he whispers, "I'm immutably in love with you, Suede Audere."

"Even though I can't ever do anything right with anyone?"

"You do it right with me. No matter when, no matter what?"

"Where you go, I go. It's always us." Her freckled cheeks flush beneath his gaze. "But I don't deserve to be laughed at."

"You're being..." Jason trails off as she gapes.

"I was being *supportive*, babe?"

"And *funny*, my love. Why was that your Earth-shattering, revelatory cry to a group of black people?"

"Well, when you put it like that!" She groans, nuzzling herself into his sturdy arms. "Fine. I won't make rudimentary statements of kindness. Since apparently that's an issue."

"You're not going to hear me when you're embarrassed. So, take a moment, and we'll discuss this later, yes?"

"Okay," she whispers. "I'm sorry. I love you?"

I have to turn away because they're tonguing again. Not long before Jason approaches, and I notice Suede looks a little disheveled and dazed.

Our friend group falls silent when a heavy stare prompts the resounding jokes to quiet.

"You heard her. We all bleed red motherfuckers! And come May, we'll sit in the fire section and watch Benson and Sapienti burn it all to the fucking ground!" Jason roars, banging his fist over his heart.

This scream is different from the one of rage a Bear releases.

A Lion only roars so viscerally out of pride for his people.

My friends cheer as Jason hoists me on his shoulders and Russ swoops Sky onto his, pink nails fisting in his coily curls as our friends scream our names.

I can't help but grin over the small group chanting below, the surrounding students joining in.

My hands cover Jason's eyes while I steady myself, and he continues to dance, paying me no mind, spinning and throwing me around until I'm dizzy.

When enough celebration has been had, I tap on his shoulders, and he relents, setting me back on my feet before ruffling my bangs.

"Put me down, Veggie Boy. Or you'll end up with cracked frames."

Russ twirls Sky to the ground and dips her until her braids sweep the grass. A raspy laugh flies from her lips when he pulls her into a hug that goes on for an uncomfortable stretch of time. Straining my ears to try and hear them over the cheering crowd.

*Seriously? Who the fuck hugs someone for that long?*

I send a spark off my ring to flick the back of Russ's neck, and he releases Sky, swatting at his nape as if he's been bitten by a mosquito.

Tristain's more than happy to talk my ear off while I inspect my nail beds for chips that don't exist, refusing to look to my left because anything going on with them is not my business.

At least, it shouldn't be.

# CHAPTER 29

I bank left, soaring over the heavily wooded area as Sky peers down at the ground, hands white-knuckled in the hem of my shirt. Sunny tends to glide, wings fully extended, instead of flap when she joins us. A smoother journey for our not-so-friendly companion that's still deathly afraid of heights. "Your hair."

"What about it?" Sky pants.

It's woven down her back in a messy fishtail again. The quickest way for me to do it when we're low on time. The once violet tresses are now a bright white I can't help but stare at, snow colored silk dancing in the wind with each minute shift of her head.

I've always thought the Sapientis' hair takes the quality of moonstones when they bathe in sun or starlight. And unfortunately, since she'd surprised me this morning, Sky's had a knack for standing in the shade whenever possible—more self-conscious about the color than I understand. "I don't know? I just feel like you're hiding less now."

"Icarus said something similar."

"Oh. You showed Russ?"

"He stripped the color," Sky mutters, wiggling closer to me as if she's attempting to glue us together. "Land this horse. Now. Or we're going to have an issue."

"Don't call her that!" I caution as Sunny begins our descent.

We rise and dive, my preferred landing if only I rode her. But Sky shakes like a leaf, releasing small whimpers that I attempt to soothe. "Sunny, don't be mean! You know better!"

My thighs tighten, booted feet tensing in the stirrups to keep us firmly seated while my pegasus controls her temper, gliding down in a slow spiral instead of nose diving to be softer with her landing.

I pat Sunny's neck when we touch Earth again, aware that the two will be in an argument within the next few minutes that I have to de-escalate. "Sky, it's fine. You can look."

She pops her head up from my neck at the sound of Sunny's hooves against cobblestone.

My pegasus clobbers through the entrance tunnel, vast wings curled into her sides as we break into a gallop.

The moment Sunny comes to a halt in the fire quadrant, I dismount, sliding down her lowered wing that's made a full recovery the past few months—despite her smaller size being a permanent attribute.

I land a few feet from Ezra, who seems to be the first one to arrive. The grass below my feet squelching with each footstep closer to him.

"Hi," he starts. Two months on the islands, and away from his mother, has done him well. Ezra smells of oranges and cinnamon, no hint of tobacco left on his breath. His olive skin has a deep golden tan, and he seems utterly relaxed, almost happy to see me. So happy that I turn around and check he's talking to me. "How was your break?"

"Hi? It was fun."

"That's good."

"Yours?" I ask.

"Clarifying."

"I can see that. You look... rejuvenated."

He smiles through the awkward silence, both dimples showing with little effort. I get the same feeling as I did when I first laid eyes on him, but less intense this time, mere remnants of the quiet warmth of candle-light when our eyes meet.

Ezra Alvarez is still angelic, but he's fallen down to Earth.

"When did that happen?" he asks, pointing behind me.

Sky's still working on dismounting the left wing, muttering profanities at my pegasus that have me emitting a giggle. "You know, I asked Sky the same thing. They spend more time together than *I* get with her. I think they fight to keep things interesting."

Ezra frowns. "I'm just talking about the pegasus, actually."

"Oh." A flood of warmth prickles my cheeks. "The week before break. Laroche told me you're able to include pegasus in the games, and Sunny basically ignored me when I suggested she sit out. So, here she is. At our use."

"That's—"

*Boom.* A harsh thump sounds behind me.

"Motherfucker!" Sky releases a string of expletives as she lies in wet grass. "Shiloh!? Come here, you fucking thief!"

"One second." I wince.

"Yeah. Okay?" Ezra runs a hand through the back of his hair, and I turn on my heel, tugging down the hem of my t-shirt.

Sky's fallen from several feet in the air, smack on her face, left nostril oozing blood. I turn her jaw to get a better look, and she nips my hand in sheer aggravation, wiping blood away with her shirt sleeve.

"What did you say this time?"

"I told that *horse,* since I'm no longer using my hair dye, if she didn't stop twitching her wing, I'd have plenty for her tail."

"And you don't see why she's upset now?"

"No!" Sky snaps, grabbing my belt loop and tugging me forward, stooping to glare into my eyes. "Did you take my daggers?"

"Maybe," I say. "Or, maybe not. Quick question, are you planning to use them on a mare in our vicinity?" She searches my person, hands skimming my sides and finding one silver-hilted blade in my waistband, the second one stuffed in my boot. I wrap my arms around her torso, pulling her back when she steps toward Sunny.

"In her defense, you can't call her a horse, then threaten her because you didn't want me to help you down!"

Sunny swats Sky's head in agreement, and I snap at her next, a three-way argument that comes to a halt when a throat clears from off to the side.

We turn our heads to two slack jaws and one wary pair of irises.

Sunny shifts backwards until I swear my nine-foot-tall pegasus is attempting to shrink herself behind us. Their momentary squabble saved for a rainy day when she tucks her large appendages into her sides, nuzzling into Sky's shoulder and licking her cheek.

We like to call this mood, *going baby on us.*

Acting innocent of all wrongdoing whenever she wants her tantrums forgotten. Sky cups Sunny's muzzle in her hands, throwing me an almost embarrassed glance as my pegasus cuddles into her side.

Because yes, unfortunately, going baby on us always works.

"Hi, Little One."

"Hi, Bridge."

"What did I tell you guys?" he grins, throwing his arms around Mai and Ezra. "I know a rider when I see one."

"How?! I've only been flying a few months!"

"Wasn't talking about the pegasus."

I narrow my gaze. "Then... what were you talking about?"

"We could discuss it over dinner tonight?" he offers, eyes twinkling with golden energy.

Mai rolls her eyes, but I don't mind.

Bridger's the only person on this planet who could be so direct and still always feel safe. So overwhelmingly friendly to every person he meets that I want to wrap the large man in bubble wrap, even when his mouth should send him to timeout.

"We had a two-month break, and you didn't manage to get laid?"

"I was waiting for you! Can you blame me?"

"Yes. No one should be *waiting* for me. I'm an objectively uninteresting person."

"I find immense pleasure in being bored."

"No one likes being bored."

"I'd like anything you'd tell me to like."

"Barking?"

"I've never turned down doggy style." Sky sizes him up with squinted eyes, a minuscule shift in her stance that Bridger stills from. "On second thought..." She brushes past him as he mouths, *"Am I in danger?"*

I bob my head yes, and he gives Sky a wide berth, the five of us moving to the Imaginifer platform without further discussion.

Ezra unfurls a map of the Arena while we huddle to watch a projector, parsing through old footage of Ludi Bellorum as he draws lines and plans for attack, giving each of us our assignments.

I lean over the map with furrowed brows, and Bridger pauses the tape. A frozen image of a charred, burned-down battlefield before my eyes. Students running away with singed hair and third-degree burns.

"What's wrong, Dreamer?"

I point at the Earth quadrant, various areas marked with X's, where Ezra says they've been secretly sprouting seeds in advance and will likely grow thick foliage to hide away. He's circled where we should set fires to have the spread be most effective.

"I think they're going to expect us to sweat them out."

"That's fine. Everyone has a go-to move," Bridger says, lying down and staring at the clouds, head propped up on his pack. "Water affinities bring in the boats every year. The first game I ever saw, a guy from the Fire quadrant drowned when they flooded it."

"They aired that on *TV?*" I ask.

"They air everything," he mutters.

"Which is why we need to get the Earth flag before we're flooded out," Ezra says, twitching his fingers and throwing a fireball into the damp grass below.

The flame lands, but flickers, his fire not spreading as quickly as it should.

"Then, we destroy the boats. Water may not burn, but wood and people sure as hell do. All that's left after that is fighting the Air quadrant. They don't ever do well in hand-to-hand combat."

"But look at the burns they're coming out with." I unpause the tape as Earth affinities run out of their forest like startled fawns, shrieking and patting out flames from their clothes with soot-covered faces.

"These wins aren't pretty, but they won. They're also Gold and Silver stars. Our game isn't ever so hectic," Ezra says.

"And that's what we're here to do," Mai says. *"Win."*

"It's still a game at the end of the day. We should focus on minimal injuries. It isn't worth anyone's life."

"Its outcome affects your life," Ezra reminds me.

"I don't care. There's a way to play, and this isn't it."

"What's your idea, Cub?"

"I'll case the Earth quadrant from above, drop down and swoop in, hand to hand combat."

"You don't want to use fire at all?" Sky asks.

"We don't need to decimate them to win. We carry the weight of daggers for a reason. Fire, it isn't *destruction,* it's light to guide us." Mai scoffs, and Ezra appears mildly wary, my eyes darting back and forth between Sky and Bridger, silently begging them to bite.

"You want to go into the Earth quadrant by yourself?" Ezra asks. "You realize they'll have no qualms about hurting you when you're on the ground?"

"Riding with Sunny is in my blood. It's more natural than walking across a flat surface. Plus, I'm fast on my feet. I'll sneak in and out. I've had plenty of training."

"No," Ezra exhales sharply. "You take a second. Drop them in, hand-to-hand combat, and pick them up. You're our only pegasus rider, you won't touch the ground during the games."

"That's ridiculous! I'm not here to watch you guys fight."

"That's a direct order, Soldier."

"Then the second rider is me," Sky insists. "I'll be of use in hand-to-hand since I'm not using my fire."

"Because Benson said you're not allowed? I thought that was a joke?"

"Watch it," Bridger says. "Our titles aren't a shield, Mai."

"I've been watching! Clearly, more than all of you. And you know what I've noticed? A low name girl has got the Bears *and* the Lions whipped, along with the first son of the Alvarez family. Is this not raising concerns for anyone else?"

Sky's hands twitch for her blade, and my stomach twists. She's mellowed out this year, but I can tell there's one more snide comment before she snaps.

Mai turns to Ezra next. "We're going to war, and you're using it as an opportunity to make amends to someone who refuses to hear you out! Soldiers don't question, and perhaps you've picked someone who can't understand that."

Sky lunges forward, and I snatch her silver blade, icy fingers lacing with my own as she glares across the map—an overly satisfied gleam in the Imaginifer's eyes.

"Mai, you missed something in all your observations," I interject. Everyone holding their breath as the bronze star leans forward, elbows placed firmly on her kneecaps.

"Enlighten me, New Blood."

"I'd risk my life for any of my friends, and I know they'd do the same for me. But if Sky decided to punish you right now, we'd all sit here and watch it happen, even Ezra. He'd let her beat you half-dead for disrespecting the Honestus family without intervention."

She side-eyes her closest friend, and his jaw tightens.

"Mai doesn't need my intervention," Ezra sighs. "She's always understood the risk of speaking her mind and does it anyway. There's no expectation for me to fight her battles."

"There's no need for either of us to fight my battles," she replies dryly, a respectable steel in her eyes that I know will never die. "She's bluffing. She couldn't help herself but to step in."

"Am I?" I drop Sky's dagger in her lap, and she sheathes it with her free hand. "You know, I don't blame you for thinking I'm a punching bag. I waited way too long to ever stick up for myself and would've cut off a limb to have even one person show interest in knowing me a few months ago. But those days are over because I'm worth more than scraps of kindness. And this leash you insist I hold is extremely fucking long. Sky knows I'd forgive her for anything, so I guess just be glad that Sunny's softened her up today."

Sky's lips crook upward, and Ezra's words slice through the tension like a serrated blade. "Come on M.B., Good ideas are good ideas, no matter who they come from."

"What's that supposed to mean?" Sky asks.

He sighs, hands running through a wild spill of ink atop his scalp. "That all ideas are welcome. We shouldn't be fighting, we'll do enough of that when the games begin."

"Then we'll burn the boats still. No use flooding the Arena if they have to swim," Sky says, using her free hand to etch Mai and Bridger's names near the water quadrant, everyone eyeing her precise right-hand calligraphy skeptically.

"Make sure those boats are unoccupied," I add.

Bridger nods as he sits up, and Sky writes Ezra's name into the Air quadrant. "If there's one person's flames they won't snuff out or manipulate, it's yours."

"We can't send our Captain into the air quadrant by himself if he's holding the flag. They'll ambush him," Bridger says.

"He won't be." Everyone pauses as Sky meets my eyes. "She'll have it."

"For fucks sake!" Mai exclaims.

"Give it a rest," Bridger sighs.

"I'm a member of this team, too. And I'm not playing around with my life to spare feelings and small injuries!"

"*Small* injuries?" I unpause the tape, and several frames flicker. Less than a minute before someone trips and impales themselves on their own knife when attempting to escape the blaze.

"It's not unheard of. I saw the little one flying on my walk over. She's good."

"We don't need *good,* we need excellent. We should..."

"Will you drop it?" Sky asks, tuning out Mai's rant and squeezing my hand.

"No," I promise, squeezing back until she smiles.

"Perfect. Shiloh will carry the red. I'll obtain the green, and then we'll be air-bound until the game ends. Swoop in to get the other flags when we see you've acquired them. Whoever else has a pegasus, they'll never catch us on Sunny. The only thing we'll be on the lookout for is wind currents affecting her flight. We can practice with Jason Honestus. If we can go up against his wind, then the ones in the game are nothing." She points at the white lightning above, everyone in awe at the streak bounding through the air.

"You're not..." *Scared?* I want to ask, refraining from spilling her secret.

"There are few things to be scared of when we're together. Right?" My eyes widen, and I turn to Ezra with a pleading gaze.

"If I say yes, and they catch you with all the flags, we're done for."

"They won't," I promise. "I can do this."

He blows a raspberry, everyone waiting with bated breath. "Fuck it."

"That's a yes?!"

"It's a get on your pegasus and show us what you're made of."

"Yes, sir." I grin, whistling for Sunny until the blur above stops in its tracks, a flash of curiosity spilling into the base of my skull.

# CHAPTER 30

I triple-check that the red flag's secured to my belt loop, boots digging into the grooves of Sunny's wing as I bound up her side, sliding onto worn-in leather. Everyone but Sky scurries away from scalding steam and spit, Sunny's coat shaking slightly until I realize the mare holds in a laugh, raising her hoof so Sky can bump it with her boot. "Don't encourage that? She and I already discussed the spitting."

"I thought you didn't mind spit?" Sky smirks, and the two of them exchange a knowing look as I raise my middle finger. "Your rider's stressed out. We'll talk later."

Sunny lowers her muzzle for a head scratch, watching the Bear stroll away before she sends a shot of annoyance towards me.

"We can't be attached at the hip," I protest. *Boundaries. Find some.* Sunny presses images of Sky and I into my head that are tinged with disbelief, cheeks burning as I blink away memories of burning skin and ragged breath. "That—We—You're basically a teenager! You shouldn't even think about that stuff."

My pegasus snorts, twisting her head until I receive the side-eye of all side eyes. "Fair point. Sorry. No more blood-sharing in your room. Or... anywhere else. Now, can we focus on the task at hand?"

Sunny stomps her hooves, ears pinned back as more steam puffs out.

"I'm aware. But you wanted to be on the team. If you still want that, you need to audition."

A wave of confusion floods her mind, Sunny's natural superiority complex reaching a boiling point.

Telling a pegasus that she should audition for her place anywhere is as absurd as it sounds. But I explain Ezra's reasoning, my mare weighing the decision in her mind until I add, "They doubt me. And unfortunately, it makes them doubt you for choosing me. Can we show them why? That you didn't make a mistake?"

I don't have to ask her twice.

Sunny bursts forward, barreling through where the group once stood in front of us.

"Sorry!" I yell as they collect themselves off the ground, wind whipping and burning my face as if with a heated blade. I yank my feet from the stirrups and crouch on Sunny's saddle, standing slightly in preparation just before she takes to the air.

Sky roars like a Lion, fists banging her chest while she yells, "Let's go, you fucking Bear!"

I squat on pegasus' back, surfing clockwise around the Arena as Ezra takes off toward the Earth quadrant.

Sky counts to three before she begins her pursuit, boots clobbering grass and making up the deficit until she's right on Ezra's heels. Gaze zeroed in on the green flag looped near his belt buckle.

She slides across wet grass on her knees, slicing at his Achilles tendon and narrowly missing when Ezra tucks and rolls.

Sky makes up for the blunder in her next breath, throwing her second dagger and hitting her target, a grunt of pain released as silver impales the meat of her cousin's forearm.

They rise, and Ezra rips the weapon from his skin, tossing it aside before his forehead connects with her swollen nose.

Red rivers stream down Sky's face, Ezra's knee connecting with her abdomen hard enough to draw out a shriek of pain—my stomach doing cartwheels as the Bear shudders in a breath.

Ezra traps Sky in the crook of his elbow, cutting off her air supply.

She scratches at his forearm, dislodging it just enough to swing her lower body upwards. Slim thighs locking around Ezra's neck, squeezing with every ounce of strength until they slam to the ground together.

They exchange a series of punches and blood splatters on the grass, the scent of iron heavy in the air as I order Sunny to the ground.

My pegasus offers no resistance, skin hot enough to burn as we make our descent.

I throw myself off her wing before Sunny fully touches down, rolling into a crouch behind Ezra.

Sky tears into his stab wound with her canines until he releases her, pink lips dripping red as she rises with several staggered coughs. A smile finding her mouth as I wonder how someone could look bewitching with blood-stained teeth.

"Jesus Christ, are you—"

"Not now. Hop in the ring, Cub. You can lick my wounds after."

I roll my eyes, fingers twitching to fashion a light whip before snapping the weapon at Ezra's heels.

Sky and I work as a unit. Two against one, and no need for conversation between us. We've sparred and danced enough to know each other's movements like our own.

Ezra's good enough to avoid serious injury but has not nearly enough eyes to see Sky coming when she slashes the flag from his waistband.

I whistle the moment it's shoved into her pocket, and we take off side by side. Ezra's long legs moving twice as fast as our own in his pursuit.

Sunny dips low, and I mount with ease, reaching out a hand for Sky just before Ezra tackles her. "God Damnit! I call foul play!"

"No rules, baby! Now come and get me!" Sky ducks and dodges each swing of Ezra's fist as sweat coats her temples, staying calm and collected until I have no choice but to do the same.

Sunny and I circle back around, my weight pressed down on her gossamer appendage while I hang off its edge.

My light whip snakes around Ezra's ankles, dragging him several yards away from Sky.

He scrambles to steal my flame, singeing my palms until I release the rope before rising to his feet for another attack.

I order Sky to run, and she coughs and stumbles towards me, wiping sweat and blood from her lash line. An iron fist gripping my intestines while I ready another whip.

Ezra catches Sky's shirt, and I lash it forward, slicing through the small strip of fabric between his hand and her body.

The back of Sky's shirt ashes as she dives for Sunny's wing, scrambling up the lowered appendage with one arm due to a dislocated shoulder blade.

I dismiss my fire, shoving Sky into the saddle while Sunny gallops away, scrambling up after her and getting seated just before my pegasus leaps upward.

We rocket a hundred feet in mere seconds, red dots screaming and shouting from far below.

I pull the reins, and Sky gags, hovering in the clouds by the time her lips open and the green flag falls from her mouth.

I stuff the piece of fabric in my pocket before gravity takes our win, shoving Sky's shoulder back into place and fending off a retaliatory slap.

She simmers down after rotating her arm a few times, sinking against my chest as she wipes the front of her face with her tattered t-shirt.

"What if you had choked?!" I yell, forcing her to turn her head after she catches her breath. "I'm serious, Sky, what the fuck was that?!"

"That, Cub, was a good round one," she pants, sitting upright with a slight wheeze. "Don't worry. Emerson will give me mouth-to-mouth if I need a little kickstart."

"I thought we agreed we weren't arguing in front of Sunny? Her brain is a sponge. She gets bad ideas."

"You're right. Let's table this before you defend him, and Sunny and I decide to whoop his ass."

"Oh."

We descend, and I help Sky dismount, facing off with our team members in anticipation of Ezra's decree.

She yanks off her tattered shirt, and everyone's eyes widen at the revealing lingerie underneath, sheer pink lace hardly leaving room for the imagination.

A smug grin finds her mouth when Bridger takes off his sweater, handing it over in an instant. "I've changed my mind. All three."

Sky slides on his top with a raised brow. "You're barking up the wrong tree, Emerson."

"Am I? Peanut butter and jelly balance better on bread. I usually go for wheat or rye, but I don't mind that it's white."

"Shiloh?" Sky asks curiously. "Any input?"

"I wouldn't want to *s*-spoil my dinner." My voice cracks slightly, and they tilt their heads. I'm not sure what it says about me, but there's a certain level of acknowledgement between the two of them. "He's not serious! All jokes!" I finally manage.

*"Jokes,"* Sky repeats.

"It was! Tell her, Bridge! He's got a—" Bridger throws me a scowl as Mai and Ezra eye him. "Sorry. I'm a reformed over-sharer."

I present Ezra with a perfectly intact red flag and the tattered, damp green one that he grimaces over. "It was our first attempt! We won't destroy them on game day."

After a minute of stony silence, he breaks into laughter—a throaty chuckle I've heard rarely, but enjoy a lot. "You've got yourself a deal."

"Really?"

"But stay off the field. I mean it. Sapienti can hold her own down there."

In evidence of this, he rolls his arm that's just stopped bleeding.

"Yes, sir!" I nod, walking towards Sunny to reset for round two of practice with Sky in tow. "F.Y.I., If you need me, I'm dropping in. I blatantly lied."

"I don't need your help."

"Oh. You're lying too?"

She narrows her eyes, and I scream for Sunny to lower her wings right before Sky catches me, tumbling into the damp grass. She pins my wrists above my head with a furrowed brow. "You seem to forget that I'm not as soft as I seem, Cub."

"Consider me... informed." Sky's throat bobs as my thighs wrap her waist, bucking my hips and twisting our bodies until I straddle her. I flutter my lashes on her eyelids, narrowly escaping gnashing teeth. "Come on! I learned from the best! You thought I was that easy?!"

"What the fuck did I tell you about letting me win?!"

"Cap's going to take everyone to the whipping posts if we don't run it back," Bridger says, approaching from the congregation of Imaginifer's several yards away. "He's over there grumbling about your little wrestling match."

"Tell him I need five minutes. My back hurts from carrying the weight of this team."

"Don't tell him anything. I don't need a break, Cub. You're acting like Caveman."

"I would hope Nox isn't this close to you."

"We're being Silly Shiloh, right now? Can I get... Sweet Shiloh back?"

*"Nope. That bitch is dead,"* I say, voice low and rumbling as one side of her mouth crooks upwards.

"You know what? Yes! A break *is* necessary." Sky scratches my spine until I yawn, her breathing pattern returning to normal as my ear rests on her chest.

Ezra gives us exactly three minutes to ourselves before he pulls Sky to the side for a discussion.

Bridger helps me adjust the straps of Sunny's harness, the large man oblivious to her side-eye as we watch the cousins yell at one another from afar. "Bridge? What do you do if the person you want is with someone else, but you still want them?"

"I'm not the best—"

"The someone else is Russ."

"Wow, okay. That's some deep shit." He stares at Sky thoughtfully, rubbing a hand over his fade. "This *person,* they're not leaving him?"

"No. So, what did you do when...?" I tilt my head toward Ezra, and he winces.

"I got creative quickly. And I don't recommend that you do the same. You're much better than I am."

"Am I?"

"There's something about you," he says earnestly, only deep admiration where his normal flirtatious lilt would be. "I think you're out of this world. *Special.* You deserve more than second fiddle."

"But I'm not? I'm just someone who wants what she wants, and asking you if you regret doing the same?"

"I don't think you can regret holding something priceless. It's a matter of not having enough value to keep it in your hands," he mutters, slinging an arm around my shoulder as we walk toward the team. "The price is hefty, little one. So I hope you know what you're doing."

And so it goes.

Every meeting that follows is a chance to improve our plan. Know it inside and out, until more often than not, I don't have to dismount.

My main jobs are to make sure Sky gets on my pegasus and secure the flags on my hip. And as promised, I don't let her fall once. Slowly but surely, her trembling is replaced by roars when she mounts, holding her hands out in the air instead of death gripping me for dear life.

As the weeks bleed together, I wonder why I'm working so hard to go home when I've found one here. When my friendship with a teeth-baring woman is the only thing that keeps the night terrors at bay, and the waking hours something to look forward to.

While the first semester at T.A.U. was a fight for survival, this one is a taste of what life could be when I'm focused on living.

Despite a Valentine's Day toothpaste incident, that I've committed to erasing from my memory, mealtimes have become crowded—our table packed to the brim when the team from the Fire quadrant joins us.

Ezra and Russ are thick as thieves, while Jason and Bridger butt heads whenever he flirts with his blushing bride-to-be. It's one of the things I truly admire about the Bronze Star. Bridger Emerson never changes for anyone, not even the first son.

Suede tells me sex with Jason is hotter when he's jealous, so I have to believe he doesn't mind it all that much.

The only ones who don't budge and make conversation are Nox and Solara—Nox, because he stares out the window, completely uninterested in small talk with anyone aside from his sisters. And Solara, because she uses all her energy to glare at me. If I brush against Sky, she sneers. Outright leaving if we touch.

Eventually, Sky's sister stops showing up to mealtime at all.

And as any opportunity for me to win Solara over crumbles to dust,

Jason and I come to an understanding, lingering hard feelings worked out over Ludi Bellorum practices with Sky.

He's kind to her when we go up against his winds, no matter how many expletives she hurls his way. Another olive branch extended between us when I convince Sunny to let Suede take a ride.

It didn't go as planned.

My pegasus refuses to tone down her erratic movements for anyone but Sky. So, I'm not completely shocked when Suede storms into our room with tangled hair and raccoon eyes, declaring that she wants to wait to try flying again until next year. Jason and I exchanging a nod as he grinned like a lovesick fool.

And as the weeks tick by, whether they like it or not, our group begins to melt and mix as I've dreamed, and March too goes by in the blink of an eye.

"I DON'T KNOW who you're hooking up with in the kitchens to make you special treats, but ask them to bring me one of those next time," Suede moans from the floor, clapping when I offer her the other half of my banana cream pie milkshake.

Since I've gained my full appetite back, the smoothies are sort of an overkill, but I always scramble to answer the door for my dessert.

"Seriously. I've never seen more variations of ice cream in my life!"

"I think the redheaded one likes you," Russ muses. "He lingers when you shut the door. As if he wants to say something."

"His name is *Cian.*" The amusement in his eyes dies pretty quickly, and I'm not sure what to make of it. "You guys should make an effort with them. He's not much older than we are." Russ glances at Suede, who shrugs in return, spooning a stray cherry into her mouth. "What? What's wrong with being his friend?"

"Nothing," he mutters, squinting at the golden watch on his wrist that's probably worth more than a Ferrari. "They're at work, is all. You might get him in trouble if he's goofing off on the job. These positions are hard to come by."

"You guys aren't being—"

"Can we talk about this some other time?" He winces.

"Why? Hot date?" Suede wiggles her brows as he scrambles to his feet, straightening his tie and adjusting his glasses in the mirror.

"Uh, it's sort of a longstanding thing."

"So it *is* a date?" Suede gasps, slamming down the shake and licking her lips. "Icarus Amias Honestus, do you have a girlfriend?"

"Ask me after Ludi Bellorum, and I'll have more than that." He shrugs, saluting us on his way out the door, a harsh thrum in my bones as it slams shut behind him.

"More than a girlfriend?!" Suede yells. "Stars above, I hope it's Osira. No offense to Tristain, but if I can't have you for a sister in law, she's obviously the best choice."

I feel ill all of a sudden, and it has nothing to do with the steady stream of milkshakes I've been consuming for months.

"I'm going for a walk."

"In your pajamas?" she asks, waving a hand over my tank top and frilly shorts. "Are you having a secret relationship too?! Honestly, fuck you guys for not telling me! I may be in a committed relationship, but I care. We could be *triple* dating, you know? And I've—"

I escape outside so quickly that I forget to put on shoes.

Unable to fully inhale until I'm sitting on the cool stone steps leading up to the first-year dormitories, picking at my polish as flecked pieces fall around my feet.

When simmering rage spots at the edges of my vision, I take Mom's advice a year too late, but still early enough that I don't take a hammer to Russ's watch collection.

There's an odd sense of Deja Vu as I approach the Dean's office.

Henry's Song playing with slight changes made in the tempo, the tune far more soft and sweet than the rushed frenzy I play with. No surprise when I push open the half propped door to Ezra Alvarez locked into the piece.

If he hears me come in, he doesn't acknowledge it. Eyes closed as long fingers fly over ivory keys. I sit beside him and watch his face more than his hands. A frown emphasizing the dimple in his left cheek.

When he's done, his eyes remain closed. "We have to stop meeting like this."

"You changed my composition. Why?"

"I have different questions than you do," he says.

"Did the Universe answer you?"

"I thought we'd come to the conclusion that the bastard Universe doesn't answer questions to lowly Alchemists."

"Then did it help asking yourself?"

"Sort of... I'm sorry, Dreamer."

"Ezra, I don't want to go down this rabbit hole again."

"Then just let me say what I was actually thinking the moment I saw you." He turns to straddle the bench, long legs on either side of my body. "Your eyes."

"What about them?"

"They're peanut butter whiskey, and I'm an addict with no desire to stop drinking them in. I was a fool for not telling you I found you breathtaking. I was a *fool* for not saying you've stolen it every day since. I—"

"You know what I've been thinking?" I meet his gaze, dimples popping as his mouth twists into a grimace. "Why do you get to treat me like shit and decide that once you want me, it's time to show basic human respect. And now I'm supposed to hear you out, or else I'm a heartless bitch?"

"My mother—"

"I don't know how much clearer I could be, Ezra. I'd rather bite curb than listen to your woe is me, I'm a little man-child whose mommy didn't love him enough sob story. I mean it. If I have to listen to you tell me why you've *never let anyone in before* and how that should make me feel *so* special and different from other women, I'm going to leave. Right now."

"Fuck," he mutters. "Fine. Sure. I deserve that."

"You don't even deserve the breath from my mouth, but I'll gift you a little advice. Go find some other woman whose wet dream is to hook up with their bully. I'm sure someone's foaming at the mouth to hear you out. The market is bleak these days, and dimples are in."

Despite my rant, Ezra laughs as I finish. A fiery glint of determination in his eyes. He nods his head, taking each jab like fuel instead of the killing blow I thought I'd dealt.

"You're right, Shiloh." I straighten my spine and eye him warily as Ezra taps his hands on the piano, deep in thought before finding the right words. "What I'm asking of you is selfish. You've embraced my friends and been willing to give me some sense of civility these past few months, and now I dare to ask you for more. Dare to request your friendship too. Even knowing how much I hurt you."

"You really want to be my friend? Because I feel like guys say that when they're secretly still trying to fuck you."

"The you that you are today is the only type of person I want to be friends with. I couldn't truly respect anyone who won't stand up for themselves. Who'd let someone walk all over them with batted eyelashes in return. No, you're not different from other women. You're the epitome of what a woman is to me. *Strength.* So to hell with words. I'll spare you the details. I'll stop attempting to justify what was, and just show you what is. My actions will prove the man that I am."

My hands flex on the piano bench while I release any thoughts about what, or who, Russ may be doing in this given moment. Forehead leaning against the flats as I deflate before him.

"Are you okay?" Ezra asks.

"No."

"I—"

*"Friends.* I'm not open to anything else with you, Alvarez."

"Okay," he says. "What you offer is what I take."

"Then why am I sensing a but in there?"

He chuckles to himself. "Fine. Friends are honest with each other. Right? So I have to admit at least once that I'm playing the long game, Dreamer. You may feel for her, but you felt for me first."

"Oh. So you're playing a dangerous game then, not a long one."

"I'm not asking for a promise on your end. I'm not asking for you to make it easy on me or to tone down what you have with anyone else. But if you're okay with knowing that's what I feel, I'm okay with keeping it to myself. I've never been afraid of starting with a detriment. Slow and steady wins the race."

He squeezes my hand, and after a moment of debate, I squeeze back. Falling into a silence that's not exactly uncomfortable, but not steady either. A million unspoken words between us and a relationship that doesn't quite make sense.

"Will you play me something?" he asks.

"Yes, sir."

Ezra repositions himself, scooting the piano bench closer for me to use before my fingers fly into Auld Lang Syne on their own accord. To accompany the tune, I sing. "We're hereeee because, we're hereeee because, we're hereeee because, we're here..."

He says my voice might be more beautiful than my eyes are. And twenty minutes later, after I've shown up at Tristain's door, I briefly wonder if the game has begun.

PART FOUR

# METAMORPHOSIS

# CHAPTER 31

If I'd been able to predict where I'd end up on my 19th birthday, wrapped in a slinky black micro mini would've been last on the list. It's barely long enough to cover my ass. Modest cleavage spilling from the cups of Suede's gift while I spin in six-inch stilettos, surveying my reflection from every conceivable angle.

She squeals from beside me, hair and makeup half-done and in rollers, sporting a white dress similar to mine with a bit more coverage to it. "You've come a long way since the oversized sweats, Arsonist."

I twist to take a look at my butt once again, and I'd have to agree.

For one, there's definitely something back there now.

I shake it as a knock sounds, and Suede attempts to replicate the movement, practicing in the mirror with a frown.

When I open the door, Tristain is the first one to speak, the scent of pine permeating my nostrils. "Happy—Stars above."

Jason and Russ stiffen at his words, but he's oblivious to the tense atmosphere, digging into his pocket and tossing me a bag of sour worms. *"Oh.* Thanks."

"That's your last treat," he says. "Too much of a good thing is bad for you."

"She flosses twice a day," Suede replies.

I stuff a few gummies in my mouth before tying the bag off, chucking them onto my bed as she adds. "She's a creature of habit."

"Well, I'm not feeding her habit anymore. It's unhealthy."

"Maybe he's right. You've been kind of sluggish this week. You can't eat candy for every meal if you want to keep the…"

Suede shakes her hips, and I wince.

"I ran into Nox earlier," Tristain adds. "The present's from both of us." The Honestus brothers exchange a confused glance, but I'm more than certain he's being serious.

Tristain nurses his casting arm and has some slight bruising on his neck, a once crooked nose, swollen and seemingly straightened now.

Jason shifts uncomfortably, taking in our outfits. "Are you guys going to that party down the hall?"

"Maybe," Suede teases. "Do you like my dress?"

He pulls off his crewneck, kissing her hello before he whispers something in her ear. When Jason retreats, Suede slides it on with a small sigh, thick sweater hanging to her mid-thigh as she ogles his muscled chest like a platter of treats.

"Do you want a jacket, Shiloh?"

"No?"

"You're going to be cold." I raise my eyebrows before Jason adds, "So you should put on a jacket."

"No, was the full sentence."

We appraise one another in a wary exchange that doesn't end until Russ pulls a fistful of seeds from his pocket.

One second, sixteen buds crack open in his fist. The next, the most beautiful bloom of roses I've ever seen.

"You cautioned against presents, so I hope you'll accept these."

I gape, pressing the red blooms to my face. "We're already doing a whole day together tomorrow?"

"You should be celebrated daily," he proclaims, pulling me into a hug as he avoids messing up my full face of makeup. "Happy birthday, Shi."

"Thank you, Russ." He kisses my temple, and my tongue becomes weighted sandpaper in my mouth.

Jason shuffles a box from underneath his arm. "Courtesy of the Honestus family."

"He and Jupe flew to Leonusver last night." Russ grins, clapping his brother on the shoulder. "It was his idea, but I'll take some credit."

I open the wooden box, and a gasp escapes me, warmth inside my chest that's mostly due to the edibles but definitely a little bit because it contains a hand-stitched Lion.

"Seriously?! This is beautiful, Jason."

Suede's eyes narrow.

"My mother made them for us as children. She made one for Suede too, and then Russ said that you are like a sister to him, so she insisted we had some leftovers from what should have been."

My gaze darts to the stuffed elephant on Suede's bed, having watched her snuggle with it on nights she doesn't sleep at Jason's.

"I brought mine from home," Russ interjects against the growing tension that even Tristain can now glean. "I don't sleep with it, *obviously.* It's on a shelf, but it's sentimental."

I whisper thank you to my friends, inhaling the scent of waterfalls, lilac, and freshly trimmed grass—exactly what I imagine Leonusver to smell like. A single teardrop escapes down my cheek, and Suede shoos the boys away. "Enough! It's supposed to be girls' night, and it's illegal to make a woman cry on her birthday."

She shoves them out the door, giving her boyfriend a long goodbye in the hallway.

I cradle my lion close, made of oranges and browns, with a pink tongue and white paws that are much too big for its teeny body. Blotting under my eyes and putting it on my bed as Suede returns.

She yanks off Jason's sweater and chucks it in her hamper, retreating to the bathroom to take out her rollers with a pinched expression I wish I knew how to fix.

As another knock hits the door, I'm greeted by Osira's warm hug and energetic shriek.

"Happy—Stars be damned! Why didn't you warn me? I've been looking for an appropriate time to show out."

I shrug because, as always, she looks cooler. Wearing high-waisted black jeans and a green tube top. Wavy braids parted down the middle with white beads placed in a few, clacking together each time she sways her head.

"It's a surprise for me, too."

"Now, if your answer was to say, 'It's because I'm going to ditch you losers and get my insides rearranged,' I'd be perfectly okay with that."

My cheeks heat. "Nope. Just Suede's doll for the night."

"Alright, well, I found this in Tristain's room, and Icarus said to give you something useful, or you'd be weird about it."

A flood of relief nearly knocks me over when she reveals my back-pack I've been searching for since yesterday.

The tattered bag's been sewn up and restored by Osira herself. And more importantly, it still has all of the drawings Sky's done for me throughout the year.

I hug Osira extra tightly, trying not to tear up for the second time today. "Okay, let go, Skinny. I have a shitload of Alch in my bag, and it's not going to drink itself."

We take shots and organize the bottles on my dresser just in time for a familiar soft rap to hit the door. Heart doing a flip as I run across the oak hardwood and skid to a stop, hand hovering over the handle and glancing at my skimpy dress.

I creep toward the mirror to give myself a once-over, checking my teeth for red lipstick and confirming that Osira has gone into the bath-room with Suede before running to answer the second knock.

Sky's eyes widen as she takes in my outfit, stuffing something silver into her shorts pocket.

"Hi," I say, stepping into the near empty hallway with her as a stir of dismay grows in my chest. "Solara isn't coming?"

"Huh?"

I repeat my question.

When Sky doesn't answer for a second time, I step around her to put a braid in her hair, swirling together a few strands and leaving most of it free-flowing. "You look so beautiful," I whisper.

"*Me?*" Her voice is incredulous as she looks down at Georgia.

"Who else?"

My skin and veins are tingly, and the world's hazy as Sky cases the hallway, twisting to twine her arms around my neck. We're nearly eye to eye as I grab her waist, leaning forward to nip below her jaw where her pulse flutters like moth wings.

It's inappropriate and thoughtless, and I no longer care as I walk us into the corner of the hallway and out of sight.

"Wait," Sky breathes, eyes glazing as I bite her earlobe. "I just—I need you to be sure about this, Shiloh. I can't keep doing this."

"I am?" Two words are all it takes for every movement between us to become a desperate scramble.

Here's the thing about being the way that I am.

If she'd told me she needed me to have a doctorate in Chemistry before putting my hands in her pants, I'd have shown her Dad's degree and claimed it as my own.

Anything to get the drug that I need as fast as humanely possible.

Sky hooks her leg around my waist to give me access to the bundle of nerves between her thighs. Head falling into my neck and attempting to stay quiet while floorboards creak and feet shuffle nearby.

Another unfortunate side-effect of taking drugs?

My responses aren't the only thing on autopilot.

I know what I'd feel if I were sober.

The physical desperation and the mental ecstasy that come with being close to her.

I know that I'd appreciate this more. Say something more romantic than, *You're mine. Right? You don't want him?*

I know I'd be a lot gentler, a lot more present, and maybe even someone worthy of sharing your body with.

But, there's Silly Shiloh, and Shy Shiloh, and Sky's Shiloh—*which is by far the most important part of me*—and none of them are present when psychedelics hit my system.

In this moment, I'm not *anything* but high.

I won't remember shit about the next few minutes, but how disgusting I feel to let her do this with some twisted version of myself.

Suede and Osira shout my name from down the hall, and I leap away as if soaked with frigid water.

Sky stumbles to stay upright, doing up her shorts with hyperventilated inhales and silver-saucered eyes. Gaze sweeping the hallway and landing on incredulous staff members with O-shaped mouths.

They abruptly scramble away with their cleaning carts, and when our eyes meet again, Sky's are narrowed to slits. Cheeks rosy as she wipes at her lipstick-stained neck with her shirt sleeve.

"Um. I didn't mean... I wasn't—"

"Fuck. You."

"Sky." She sweeps around the corner with a pinched mouth and the fury of a hellhound. Catching the door she slams shut as I run after her into the den of the beast.

On the bright side, Sky's mood seems to improve with each beer she downs. Not complaining when Suede makes her take pictures of us in our dresses. Or when she gets pictures of Osira and I shotgunning seltzers. Or, when I demand we get some together, too.

We dance to artists I've never heard of before, and mix our own face products with Suede's careful, but drunken, instructions. Suede and Osira deciding to put on a show with their magic. Showing off the things they're learning in the Earth and Air quadrant by the fireplace while Sky and I nurse our drinks.

Our first semi-private moment of the night since I'd dove straight into her panties more awkward than it's ever been between us.

Halfway through their demonstration, I can no longer ignore the glances. Downing my glass as her eyes dart to my outfit with energy so disgruntled I cross my arms over my torso.

"Do you have a problem?" I hiccup, ears popping as there's an instant change of air pressure around us, the sound of the demonstration going silent.

I know the feeling like clockwork. Gaze darting to Suede, who gives me a thumbs up behind her back without turning around, a faint yellow glow on her finger.

She and Osira guffaw from the other end of the room without noise. Backs facing Sky and I as Osira takes one of my flowers and changes its chemical structure. Blood red petals seeping to a pure white.

Sky looks toward the ceiling in prayer before turning to pluck at my thin spaghetti strap.

"Do I have a problem?" She traces her finger underneath before she snaps it. The fabric stinging my shoulder and raising several goosebumps. "You laid out a fucking bear trap tonight, and you're asking *me* if *I* have a problem?!"

I stare directly into her eyes, my stilettos a savior from having to glare upwards. "Stop being mean, or I'll hang out with someone I know will be nice."

"It appears we've run our course, so by all means, go ahead! Just allow me to make a toast to the birthday girl before she leaves." Sky raises her wine glass with a bitter smile. "Cheers to Shiloh Brooklyn Benson. She'll soak in anyone's interest like a petal deprived of sunlight as soon as they offer it. I'm sure there are lots of men who will throw you a bone like the good little bitch you are."

"Okay." I nod, vision tinged red as I meet her eyes. "Your cousin's first. Then, I'll knock on doors and entertain anyone who lets me in on the way back, because I'm such an easy slut."

I turn on my heel, and Sky catches the back of my dress, yanking me towards her. Touch an ice burn that soothes my feverish anger through the fabric.

I push her away, hands clenching and unclenching with every hot thud of blood swirling in my chest. "Stop. I'm just frustrated, Shiloh! Solara didn't want me to come, and—"

"*Biiig* shocker, your bitchy sister who abandoned you for weeks on end didn't want you to see me?"

*Hiccup. Hiccup. Hiccup.*

"She lets your Dad *w*-walk all over you, kick you out of your fucking home, and didn't call you once while she was away. *I* was here. Not her! *Me!* Who was with you on your birthday? Answer that! Then, explain why you decided to ruin mine!"

Tears spring to Sky's eyes, and she swipes them away with her shirt sleeve before they can fall. "Shiloh, what's going on?"

I rub my forehead, attempting to focus my blurred vision, skull pulsing as I bat away the memory that almost broke us and bury it deep.

*Hiccup. Hiccup. Hiccup.*

"What's going on is, I've outgrown you! I'm an adult!" I pick up a bottle of vodka, slurring my words as I point. "So leave. Go *b*-be with Russ, since you're *soooo* unhappy. They're all at Jason's right now."

"I'm not leaving? Not when you're like this." Two versions of her reach for me, and I'm unsure where to look. "I didn't mean it."

"Yeah? Well, I don't need this shit. You think I need this shit? We're done! I'm bored just looking at you."

Sky steps forward, and I hold up my hand, taking the whole vodka bottle with me instead of my drink.

I push against the barrier until Suede notices resistance against her magic and drops her shield, going wide-eyed as Sky sniffles into her shirt sleeves.

*Sky doesn't leave.*

She spends the rest of my party being comically nice to Suede.

So friendly, that eventually, Suede asks her if she's feeling alright.

When we show no signs of slowing down, Sky cuts off my drinks, ordering a flood of food and desserts that are delivered in no time at all.

We sit in a circle on the floor bingeing the fancy spread as Osira fills us in on the loyalist drama I had no clue was going on.

Turns out, the founders are tame compared to their loyalists.

"Are we okay?" Sky whispers while I'm nibbling on a chocolate-covered strawberry and in a considerably better mood.

"No."

Her nose crinkles in response.

"But, I didn't mean what I said." Sky wets her lips, and when I remain silent, whispers, "Please?"

Suede and Osira appear as if they've been watching a tennis match for hours, eyes darting back and forth nervously amongst the tension.

They're only mildly confused.

Suede's been a bit *too* good about giving me privacy tonight.

"Okay. But only because I'm too full to argue." I rub my stomach that's bursting with food. A noticeable bloat to my belly filled with seltzers, pasta, and snack cakes.

Sky eyes me, and I yank down a blanket from my bed.

"It's freezing in here. Is there room to share that thing?"

I nod, and Sky slides in behind me. Teeth chattering as ice-cold skin brushes against my own, swaying in a raging sea, and attempting to find my anchor.

Sky rests her free hand on my bloated abdomen, and I sigh, snuggling closer as the hem of my dress rises. Wishing my actions reflected how much I crave being her peace instead of the reason pain now streaks her face.

"What's wrong?" I ask.

*Hiccup. Hiccup. Hiccup.*

"Nothing."

"I'm not making you happy? Is that why you need both of us? I'm never enough for anyone, am I?"

"Shhh." Sky pulls down the hem of my dress before she covers my mouth.

"Please don't be mad? I didn't mean it, either."

"I'm not. We'll talk about this tomorrow."

"No. I *live* for you. You know that, right? I hate existing, but never with you. Never ever ever ever." Her eyes grow wet, and I boop her nose with my fingertip, kissing away the tear that slips down her cheek. "Don't be sad."

"I'm not," Sky rasps. "Just sleep, okay?"

"So..." Suede starts as Sky rocks me, shaking her head at something Suede's about to ask. "What's new in—"

"It's the best birthday ever," I slur.

"I'm sure it is, Skinny." Osira raises her shot glass with a wink.

"Yep. And I love you guys and the friendship you've given me. Juuuust friends. Right, Sky?" *Silence.* "This is when everyone says they love my friendship too!"

Suede and Osira rush to agree while Sky goes still, sliding me away from her as gently as she can.

I wrap the blanket around me like a shield when she stands to leave. "Wait."

And, the thing is, she does.

Sky never breaks eye contact. Waiting for me to say something, anything, that doesn't embarrass her.

When I don't, she nods in defeat, scooping up the disposable cameras filled with pictures.

"Get some sleep, okay? We'll talk tomorrow night."

"Fuuuuck," Osira moans as the door slams closed. "I hate drama."

"You love drama," Suede says.

"*Other* people's drama. Not my friends?"

Osira's eyes are half-lidded from the sour worms, and I lean forward, stuffing another handful into my mouth.

Suede yanks the bag away from me, jamming her fingers between my lips and outright scooping the wad of chewed gummies off my tongue.

She'd realized they weren't regular candy when Osira had popped a singular gummy. Words slightly slurred still as she asks, "Stars above, when did you get so strong?"

Suede huffs, a wild look in her eyes as she deposits the half-chewed candy in the wastebasket, throwing the bag away too.

*Joke's on her! I'm not above going in the garbage.*

"Are you guys... insane?! This is *exactly* why I don't do things without my man! Everyone acts like an idiot when he's gone."

"That *was* brutal," Osira murmurs. "I'm embarrassed, and I'm not even sure for who."

"I do feel kinda vindicated." Suede frowns. "Jace and I have had our suspicions. Plus, I didn't think Sky could be nice to anyone, and I just watched her be a personal servant and offer to hang out with me. You should use your prowess more often as far as I'm concerned."

"I think I messed up, you guys." I hiccup, picking up a water bottle and talking through a mouthful of liquid. "So badly."

"Good news, I know someone who is *definitely* waiting for an apology right now," Suede says, tilting her head towards the door.

"But, she said tomorrow?"

"Korovk had it wrong, Skinny. Speaking from lived experience, women forgive the dumbest behavior when we're in love. So go find out if that's the case." My eyes widen, and she tilts her head too. "But be safe. Sober up. Seek your pleasure first, and *never* act too tired to eat box. If a man does that, he's on my do not bang again list. I assume it's more valid in this situation, but we'll debrief after. She seems... like the type to *really* know how to rearrange, if you know what I mean."

Suede visibly gags, and I roll my eyes.

The both of them cheering me on as I scramble to grab my things, bolting after Sky as if my life depends on it.

Because it does.

# CHAPTER 32

"It's freezing out here!" I've been sitting on the floral welcome mat outside of Sky's front door for the better part of an hour, talking every few minutes to assure the Bear I'm still here.

Luckily, the founder's floor is the penthouse level of each dormitory. Their rooms spread out like private apartments with thick walls to drown out excess noise. Anything else, and I'd have made a fool of myself by my fiftieth time knocking.

On the fifty-first, she moans, "Go away, Shiloh."

"No. I'm not leaving until we talk."

"Then you'll be sleeping in the hallway."

"*Pleaseeee?* I'm going to—*Ooof.*" Sky yanks open her door, and I tumble backwards, staring directly into mournful gray eyes. "Okay, before you kick me out, I'm sorry. I was a jackass. I pulled trig in that plant back there, and the staff brought me a toothbrush, so I'm functionally sober and prepared to kiss you."

I scramble to my feet when she doesn't respond, toes wading across a fluffy white throw rug, instantly aware of why Sky's never allowed me inside her den.

And it has nothing to do with *Chewy* not being ready for visitors.

Her room is that of a fairytale princess.

Behind her white oak headboard is a blush-pink accent wall and frilly curtains with sage-green stitching.

There are images of a sweet-faced little girl dancing in white tulle dresses that share her face, and the pictures fill me with an urgent longing for a future where I'll never disappoint her again. Curious if this small sweet grin will appear once more. Certain that I'd take a bullet for her and she'd feel a whole lot like my own.

A cracked framed image of her arms wrapped around a tiny blonde prompts me to chuck it in the wastebasket nearby. Muttering about their matching fur coats as the image of the girl kissing her in front of a roaring campfire sears the edges of my vision.

Among it all, there's a single photo I linger on.

One of Sky atop Solara's shoulders, and Solara atop Nox's. All of them inside a steaming lake surrounded by snow, clawed hands held up like roaring bears toward the photographer.

An instant lump forms in my throat thinking about the harsh things I'd said about her sister, who only looks up at her with love.

My hand trails over the glass top dresser in the corner, examining the rose quartz knobs and delicate paintings hung over its surface. Eyes drawn toward the massive bed with sheer curtains around its perimeter and a crystal chandelier hanging above.

Her cat has a playground here. A vast setup of cream colored climbing equipment on the far wall, as toys galore spread through the room—bells and feathers laid out for Chewy at every turn.

There's a soft purr, and I notice the squished face animal at my feet, rubbing her head on my ankles before I stoop to pick her up.

Chewy sounds as if a motor runs inside her chest, pawing gently at my face until I give her attention.

I kiss her cheek and rub away the lipstick imprint I leave on her fur when Sky nears us, leaning her hip against the dresser as Chewy wriggles out of my grip.

The cat hops onto my shoulders and presses white mittened paws to the crown of my head in an attempt to get a better vantage point.

Sky reaches upward and plucks Chewy from my hair, an unmistakable meow of protest when she sets her on the ground again.

"So, is she all you dreamed?"

"I love her, Sky." The kitten half-heartedly paws at my leg to be picked back up. "Shared custody? I think it's only fair."

"Sure. Though I have the sneaking suspicion I'll end up cleaning her litter box and you'd get to cuddle her all day."

"Not true."

"Who shovels for Sunny?"

"That's not *my* fault. She's potty shy around me."

"She's not. She knows I clean up better, and she's sparing your feelings."

"Really?" I frown.

"We all have different strengths," Sky insists as we wait for Chewy to stop zooming around. Eventually, she curls into a loaf shape on her cat tower, clearly unbothered by the tense atmosphere around us.

Sky tugs me toward a cream colored loveseat placed near the balcony, a chilly breeze blowing through the propped-open double doors as we curl into the couch. Our fingers knit together, chestnut and ivory entwining before she brings them to her lips, pressing kisses to each knuckle. "What's going on, Cub?"

"I don't know," I whisper.

"You *don't know?*" Sky extends my arm to examine my inner elbow, and I snatch my hand from her grasp.

"Nothing!? Nothing's going on!"

"Babe—"

"Don't call me that. Russ *s*-said you'd be more than his girlfriend soon. You're in love with him? Enough *f*-for marriage?"

Sky and I have steadily avoided all things Russ in the past few months. Walking a clear line of plausible deniability that anything else exists outside of us when we're together. So her eyebrows skyrocket when I ask her openly for the first time.

"In love with him?!" Sky presses her palms to her eyelids. "Okay, first off, I'm a Lesbian."

"Wait, what?"

"I thought I made that abundantly clear? Let the stars fall before I put my mouth near a fleshy turtlenecked dildo. In fact, I frequently starfished until it was over."

"What's clear about you having sex with Russ, then marrying him?"

"Okay, sure. He proposed to me. And when you leave, I'm going to say yes, but it's not *love?*" I laugh without humor, and she cringes. "My marriage would be a contract."

"You guys hooking up is not a contract to me."

"It's what we agreed on before you and I were... anything. He and I stopped having sex after Valentine's Day. Now our talks are strictly business, and I can do as I wish outside of him as long as I fulfill my duties."

"In what world would Icarus Honestus be fine with you sleeping with women while you're married? His family is tradition—" She avoids my gaze, and it all comes crashing into place. *"Oh."*

Sky shakes her head in warning. "I have nothing to say about his motivations."

"Then is there anything left to say at all?"

"We haven't even scratched the surface."

"Really? Because I think we've just fallen through the surface and hit rock bottom."

"No, rock bottom was a few hours ago when I let you part my legs with an audience like I was working a pleasure house and open for business."

"But the staff are discreet?"

"There was a party down the hall that was taking frequent peeks. Realistically, I'd give it 'til Monday night before everyone knows."

"Oh my God."

"Stars above, I embarrass you that badly?"

"What? You've never embarrassed me! Do you really not see a larger issue here?"

"No! I don't! Veggie Boy means nothing to me. I mean—Yes, there's a budding friendship, but that's neither here nor there."

"*I* love Russ. *Me.* And you're his fiancée!"

Sky's cheeks flush ruby red. "We're not engaged yet. And if you didn't want me to be with him, why didn't you tell me to break it off?"

"Should I have had to? If I'm not worth exclusivity, then why lose him in the process? What else was I supposed to do?"

"This is not on me! You made me think I was a stand-in. Why would I embarrass myself by asking you to take this seriously, after you accused me of the most heinous shit imaginable? Was my forgiveness not enough for you to see how devoted I am? Or are we going to pretend I haven't given you all of me a thousand times over?!"

Sky's bitter declaration is a guillotine, memories spilling out of me like Pandora's box at her words.

The toothpaste incident on Valentine's Day was my doing.

Making advances while I was high as a fucking kite, and guiding Sky into my bed until I'd come undone in her hands. When the fog of desire lifted, and the reality of the situation set in, her big gray eyes gazed at me in wonder. Whispering that she'd never felt like this before.

I'm not proud of how I reacted. I said vicious things I can't even remember now, and she cried so hard I snapped back like a rubber band, Sky's keening an instant beacon to my mind, running straight to her sister and bringing her back to my room.

Solara punched me square in the face when she saw Sky balled up in my bed. Actually, she'd obliterated my body worse than Nox had until Sky threw herself in the middle.

The week that followed drove me to places so dark, that eventually, I had to confess to Bridger before I did something stupid.

He told me I was wrong, he told me to give Sky time to herself, and then he held me as I wept.

Being away from Sky was the worst withdrawal I've ever known, and it came to an end in Professor Agarwal's lab. When her slender arms wrapped my waist after he'd stepped out to have dinner with his wife.

Most of that night is still hazy. Because frankly, when you're riding a manic high for a week straight, and the girl of your dreams plays out your biggest fantasy to make up for her absence, you're going to crash pretty damned hard.

But I remember Sky arguing in hushed whispers as she carried me home, later finding out Solara had given her an ultimatum.

Me or her.

Sky chose me, and I've tried my hardest to be worth it.

Tried my hardest to not have an addiction come before she does.

So, after she'd given me a second chance, it was all on her pace and time. A feeling of relief with every dark corner Sky pulled me into. Holding me close as we talked around the fact that her berry-flavored chapstick began to permanently coat my collarbones between classes.

Our secret afternoons were nothing compared to the nights we'd stay late from practice to lie in the damp grass.

Talking for hours about everything and nothing. From philosophy, to art, and even Sky's love of lamb stew—I made it with Cian, and she pretended not to mind the burnt bits too much.

The memories throw my brain through a spin cycle, one after another. And the truth is, if it were anyone but Russ who was caught in the crossfire, the guilt would cease to be at all.

I'm not sure it necessarily existed in the first place. At least, not nearly enough to stop. And that's what spirals me down the drain, deflating the energy in the room like a popped balloon.

"You're right," I whisper. "It's me... I'm hurting you, and Russ, and I deserve Solara's hatred, and I—"

"Stop." Sky brushes her thumb along my ankle because she still won't fault me. Not then, not now, not ever. She'll always bear my pain and take it as her own. "Breathe. Your mind's not clear right now."

"Why do people say that to me? You told me I live in reality."

"A mirror can see everything but itself. Your first instinct is to swallow blame, but you're not wrong because you empathize with everyone else's reasoning. You know how to spin the coin, Shiloh. That's a gift most people lack. Don't automatically flip it whenever it lands in your favor against people you care about."

"What's real then?" I sniffle. "Please help me, Sky. My head's all over the place."

"My anger," she declares, right before the Universe stands still. "I'm angry that my body fails me. I'm angry that my Mother's dead, and my Father's never loved anyone but himself. I'm angry that I was horribly unkind to my siblings as a byproduct, even though they are the only other people who will never turn away from me. And most of all, I'm angry that I've contributed in any way to this idea that you're always at fault by refusing to talk this out for fear you'd deny me still. Because I'm so in love with you, it is *painful.* Every part of me aches for you to feel the same, and it was easier to believe that I was being led on a string and not that we were tugging at opposite ends."

"You're in love with me? Even though I—"

"You think you've tricked me into my affections, but trust me when I say I know every inch of the woman I fell for." Sky motions toward the sky, its glistening stars and moonlight twinkling down on us like freshly shone diamonds. "Even on nights we fight, *especially* on nights I thought I hated you, I come and kneel and tell the Universe how grateful I am to know you. When everything feels like too much, I admit aloud that this life of sickness was my trade-off, and I feel like I can keep going."

My heart skips a beat in my chest before finding its new rhythm.

"Your trade-off?"

"Maybe the Universe said, to pay me for this gift of being close to her, you will never be able to catch your breath. And I signed my life away without a second thought before ever opening my eyes to this world." Sky shrugs. "Was it even a choice? Without you, it wouldn't have been worth much. From afar, breath would have been stolen from me anyway."

"Don't say that."

"Shiloh, I need to stay in reality from now on. There's no going back for me."

"I don't want to go back. I wanna walk with you, but I'm not worth that trade. The Universe would not ask suffering of you to know me. I would not want to live in a world where that is the case."

"Life requires everyone's suffering as payment, and for you I'd pay any price." Sky meets my eyes and takes my hands in her own. "I've made mistakes, too. Maybe the ultimate one. I've loved you selfishly when what we are is much deeper, much truer... This invisible pain you carry every day is no less than because you internalize and hide it away. I'm leaving everything on the table now, because this time I will love you as you need, no matter what I want. Let this be the most sacred vow I ever swear. Above blood and name, above honor and country, the performance is over, and I'm going home."

"You're not talking about Hiemsternum," I murmur as her thumbs swipe my knuckles.

"No. You've forever been the destination. For me, it's only you. Unconditionally. In any way you'll have me. I'll wait at the door as long as you need me to without complaint because you're worth weathering any blizzard for. And when we've rested, I'll walk with you each morning. We'll get where you dream of. Together."

A sudden warmth floods through my chest, a deeper sense of knowing, and like a complete dumbass, I say, "*Oh.*"

"What does that mean?" Sky asks timidly.

How can I explain that it means a thousand things?

That in this instance, my soul has cracked open irreversibly—a sacred piece of it exchanged. Reserved specifically for this woman, and this night, and this moment, in a way it will never be for another.

"Right now it means I need to kiss my girlfriend, or I'll never forgive myself."

"*Oh,*" she whispers.

I scoot closer, pausing a few centimeters away as Sky releases a gust of air, the soft and sweet scent dancing on my lips. So unique to her, it makes my mouth water.

The urge to sink my teeth in and taste it, dizzying.

She cups my face before I can withdraw, hands like frost as they cradle my burning cheeks. "Was that okay? No pressure, for, like, labels, or anything. I'd take whatever you give me, too."

Sky guffaws, and the bells return in full force. "Pressure? Baby, I willed this shit into existence."

Since my secrets are coming out tonight, I admit, I've imagined kissing her quite often too. *Definitely* longer than I had good reason to.

Along with many other assumptions, I figured if the event ever arose, it'd be rushed and frantic.

That the built-up tension would be an inferno burning quickly and without caution. That she'd tease me and kiss me silly to brand herself in my heart even deeper than she already has.

But reality is different than my fantasies, and when her mouth presses against mine, it's nothing like I dreamed.

*It's so much better.*

Sky brushes her lips back and forth against my own to the barest degree. A cold sting in the full pressure of them as I intake the sound of two distinct heartbeats.

A butterfly that finds her home in my chest. And a hummingbird that nests inside of hers.

Then, only one, as Sky and I sync to one fluttering being.

Her hands slide to the small of my back as my fingers tug at her hair, lips blooming open in response to her tongue—a budding flower stroked by fresh morning sunshine.

Sky asks a gentle question in each flicker of movement. Even as my tongue twines with hers, she is overly careful with me.

Every slight touch shaky.

Every firm pressure rescinded to something soft.

I crawl into her lap, knees straddling her waist, before I bring her hand to my breast.

Sky moans in response, pulling me closer before she deepens the kiss. The motions of our mouths a slow, languid dance with her taking the lead. Nipples budding against the freezing grip of the huntress, rubbing against the soft, slinky fabric.

Sky lifts her arms for me to tug off the shirt I paw at, emitting a hitched breath as my eyebrows momentarily knit.

She's the most lovely thing I've ever seen. Slender and willowy, encased in lacy lingerie embroidered with honeysuckle flowers.

When my lips move to capture hers again, she avoids them slightly.

"What's wrong?" I whisper, thumb tracing the outline of Sky's lower lip. Her mouth is stained red and bee-stung from my kisses. A crime to leave untouched for long.

*Mine,* my thoughts insist with a hyper clarity that stills the planet we spin on, seeking to reconfigure gravity and give me a new tether.

The word *need* seems pale in comparison to this vicious desperation that claws from the depths of my being.

Sky's eyes soften, and I know I'm doing the thing she once cursed me for. Looking at her in a way that is wholly unfair. Talking with glances and leaving breadcrumbs that ask her to follow the trail without a guide every time her beauty stuns me into silence.

"If you regret me in the morning, leave before I wake up, okay? I won't be mad."

At Sky's desperate plea, every last illusion I have shatters.

She's not otherworldly, or out of reach, because there's no other planet a woman so perfectly made for me could exist.

So beautifully spun with silver thread and a bleeding heart she barbs with thorns—massaging out my tense spine until I whisper, "I haven't been the best at affirmation when it comes to you."

"It's okay."

"It's not. Every time you've tried to kiss me, I knew if I let you, that we'd be irrevocable. Something would click and... there wouldn't be a future for you, where you wouldn't always be mine. A future where I'd let you walk away from me. And I needed you to be able to walk away."

"I've always been yours?" She frowns. "From the moment we fell down those stairs, it was never going to end anywhere but this."

"But I needed to know I wouldn't take you and not cherish what I've been blessed with. I wasn't okay then, and I know I'm not okay now. But I've stored my faith in our love, and you're worth getting healthy for. Anything it takes, I'm doing it. I want to feel everything that filters through this heart you rebuilt. The good and the bad, and for you, I find strength to do it. I find peace. Find reason. Find *hope*. Find everything I ever need. Loving you is my purpose. There will be no ounce of regret because it's always been you, Sky."

"You swear?" I press her hand over my fluttering heart, both of us grinning as her ring catches its beat and shimmers.

"I swear you own this. Understand that this is not about surviving the blizzard. I ache for you in the eye of the storm and after it's passed me by even more. My partner in the home I'm building to escape it all. In every happy moment, I look to you first and want to experience it as one. I don't want you to wait at the door. Come inside. Stay forever."

"And Icarus? I won't ask you to choose. I love you enough to—"

"What is the opposite of love?"

"Hate."

"No. It's *fear*. Fear is the weed we'll rip from the soil, and we will not have it root between us. Not when we're giving love air to bloom. Don't you see there is no choice? There's no me or you, it's us now. It's the path I choose to walk, no matter how hard it'll be. You're my destination, too. Let me reach you."

"Ubi tu, ibi ego," she promises. "Semper et in perpetuum."

"Semper et in perpetuum," I vow just before our mouths crash together again. Magnets fulfilling their inevitable destiny, a rabid frenzy of lips and teeth and smeared lipstick between us.

My tongue attempts to memorize every inch of her until I could describe Sky's taste in death. Bits and pieces of myself breaking off in bow scarred fingers as friction consumes my every thought. Unhooking her bra as a rolling wave floods my core, building and lapping against shore while I beg her to save me from drowning.

Sky jerks away, panting and gasping for breath. Lungs working overtime to catch up to her body.

I hold on tightly, massaging her back as she wheezes against me, wrapping her arms around my waist while I rub out soothing circles—a coughing fit distorting her face and tensing her body with pain.

We recuperate in silence, and she nuzzles her face into my neck, head tilting to the side as Sky sweeps her nose across my fluttering pulse.

"I'd like to be in your bed now." Her heart thuds against me as I add, "But there's a list."

"What's on it?" she rasps.

"First, I want you to clear your lungs. So you're feeling better. Second, I want you to teach me how to check your blood, so I can take over the night watch from now on. And third, I haven't been as giving as I should have. So we will figure out how to compensate for my bad, *bad* behavior." She raises her brows, and I rush to add, "Sorry. The sexy talk is a hit or miss. It sounded better when I imagined that before bed."

"Shiloh, your idiosyncratic behavior has always done it for me. It worked the first time."

"Thank God, I have nothing else going for me." Sky rises, and I cling to her, legs wrapping around a narrow waist as she cradles me close to her slender frame, walking us towards her bed. "Just so you're aware, this was number three on the list. You're jumping ahead."

"Am I? I'm sorry, baby."

"Well, we can mix and match to retain spontaneity. And, after one and two, I'd be happy with number three a few more times. It's my birthday after all." Sky lies me in a cloud of pink, climbing on top of me with a wry grin. I undo her braid, a halo of white silk curtaining around us. "Please and thank you."

"No. Thank *you.*"

# CHAPTER 33

I'm stirred from sleep by a plush mouth pressed between bare shoulder blades, tender sentiments licking my spine in an attempt to wake me. I have no intentions of the sweet nothings coming to an end, but my ruse is only as strong as my willpower, traitorous body emitting a sigh of contentment. "I woke up, and you were gone."

Sky's lips curl upwards against my shoulder blade. "Forgive me?"

The crackle of freshly lit logs and patter of kitten feet on her dresser are the sweetest symphony to ever play as Sky's room fills with a soft golden glow. "Nope. It's over."

"Fine, then your nipples *are* crude."

She licks my nipple, and I palm her forehead away, pressing down on the instantly peaked bud with tingling cheeks.

"Will you forgive me if I say last night was the best night of my existence? That I promise to wake up to you for the rest of forever?"

"Hmm. You drive a hard bargain, but I think I could forgive you if you said that."

"Then I said that." My heart's surely ready to burst through my rib cage and into her roaming hands. Fingers tracing the plastic tubes coming from Sky's nose, hyper-aware that they lead to an oxygen tank off to the side of her bed.

"Are you okay?" I finally work up the courage to ask.

"I'm better than okay."

I brush a thumb behind her ear, tracing where I sank in and went into a frenzy, leaving bites and bruises at her pressure points.

Sky covers them with her hair, and I feel for her clawed-up back, shakily stroking the path I'd dragged down her spine.

"You were trying to protect me," she insists, stretching out her wrist until I register a slight change to her scent. A sudden relief within me that I can't explain. There's an endless war raging within my mind between satisfaction and disgust, and neither of them wins. "For you, that's as natural as breathing."

Sky places her hand over my heart and snuggles closer, fluttering her lashes against my cheeks until I turn her against the pillows, taking special care of her nasal cannula as I feed my newfound addiction.

The sun rises with each labored breath we share, and by the time we're through, my fragile psyche has been glued back together, and I've managed to leave no more bruises.

Sky does a reverse striptease, sliding her leathers up her hips and bundling herself in a cream turtleneck and oversized hunting coat, chattering a rapid string of consciousness as she plays with Chewy using some feather-like toy.

She loves green apples because her brother once told her they keep the doctor away. *Only* the green ones. She never had a doctor's appointment the day after she ate a green apple.

Her siblings don't make her skin her kills. She loves animals too much, but she's the most accurate shot in Hiemsternum. It's been said that her arrow is always right through the heart, and it makes sense how she's pierced mine.

I knew Sky was funny, opinionated, strong, and temperamental. All of the things I've grown to love about her public-facing persona.

But she's also... everything else I'd suspected she was.

*Silly* and feminine and sweetly shy about her interests.

She journals daily and practices calligraphy in her notebooks. Never missing an important moment in all her life.

Hell, I may be the villain in her diary. She'd had *a lot* to scribble in it as I slept beside her.

Sky's desperately curious and ridiculously smart.

Seeming to spill every thought in her head until it's incomprehensible to see how many thorns she's barbed herself with to avoid wilting in this world. Understandable why her brother turned this woman, who currently snuggles her once feral kitten she'd nursed back to health, into a teeth-baring warrior outside the walls of her own room.

I tug our Georgia sweater over my naked frame, and something she says gives me immediate pause.

"You what?"

"I have to tell you something." Chewy purrs from where they sit on the loveseat, clawing to get to me when I walk over to braid Sky's hair.

Silence falls around us, and not the easy kind we normally fall into. A strained quiet as I tie off a fishtail and kiss the crown of her head, unable to take it any longer. "What is it?"

"I need you to keep an open mind." When my brows furrow, Sky sucks on her cheek. "This place, the things they teach us are..."

"They're what?" I whisper.

"Shiloh, you know what. I may not have explicitly said, but you've seen."

"So you've been lying to me?"

"Never." Sky rises, and I take a singular step back. "Omitted things I shouldn't have? Absolutely. I'm... not the people I come from, and I don't stand by the things I once did."

"A lie by omission is still a lie."

"And I refuse to do it any longer. We'll sneak away on Monday to the outskirts. Once you see for yourself, you can ask me *any* question you want."

Our eyes meet, and hers are filled with agony. Chewy meowing until Sky scratches between her ears.

For a fraction of a second, I wonder if she waited until she had my heart to reveal what lay behind the curtain of their society.

If I'm stupid for trusting her blindly, exactly like I trusted my parents. More so, because I *chose* to give myself to her.

Sky catches my hand, and fear melts away in an instant, remembering our promises.

The glasses I put on aren't rose-tinted.

They're a permanent, gleaming filter that shimmers like moonstone. Regardless of what she shares, the secrets she's withheld, I won't go back to a world of black and white.

Not when Sky's shown me how to feel in color.

"Okay." I nod.

"Okay," she whispers. "Come on. I'm running late, but I got you presents. One now and one when you get to your dorm."

Sky roots through her shorts pocket from last night and hands me a silver trinket, guiding me towards a white oak chest by the door.

I insert and turn the key until there's a soft click, a ragged breath of air falling from my lips when the box falls open. "I got my uniforms tailored to your size. Now, the arctic tundra wouldn't even phase you."

"Is this even allowed?"

"I earned them, and I've served this country for over two decades. So frankly, whoever has a problem with it can kiss my ass. Plus, I had them take off all my medals first."

"But you could wear this stuff? I have my marshmallow coat."

"I donated your marshmallow coat this morning."

"Stars be damned, I was sexually fondled for the first time wearing that coat! It held sentimental value!"

Sky rolls her eyes at my dramatics. "One. That coat was on the ground when I fondled you. And two, I checked for yellow shoes. Anything you haven't worn in months, I gave to the kitchen staff."

Honestly, I'm incapable of being mad at the replacements and the giddy way Sky eyes me for my reaction.

The most beautiful sets of leathers and furs are contained inside the chest. Befitting a princess, because they were originally made for the one beside me.

My eyes are drawn to the heavy cloak folded carefully and placed directly on top, not one fray or seam out of place. It's composed of black wool and grizzly fur trim. A singular Bear medallion leftover that's stitched into the lining of the hood. Her full name placed right beside it.

"Your middle name is Aelia? That's so pretty."

Sky leans over to peck my lips before I snuggle her cloak. "It was my mother's name."

"Did she name you?"

"No. She died during childbirth. My father just called me *Girl* for years."

"What?"

"Caveman realized I didn't have a proper name like him and Sol when we were four years old," she chuckles, and my face falls. "It's okay? It could have been worse. Nox is Dyslexic, and his favorite color back then was *bwurple.* Imagine moaning that in—"

"What if we left Terra Australis after Ludi Bellorum?" I blurt, a prickle down my spine that grows stronger by the second. "What if I don't care to know what you've lied about, if you come to Addam territory with me and give up magic?"

"Leave everyone behind?" Sky picks at the fluffy rug beneath us. "Just like that?"

"We'll visit if they let us."

"But my doctors are here?" She frowns. "My magic heals me."

"It also drains you. We can't pretend that you haven't needed my help." Sky grimaces as I add, "That wasn't a complaint, I don't mind."

"You'll mind it when your whole life becomes managing mine. I've seen what it's done to Caveman, I won't allow it with you."

"You *are* my whole life, and it wouldn't be *just* me. My parents own one of the largest drug companies in Addam Territory. Money isn't an object." From my impromptu lessons on human society, Sky has an inkling of certain levels of wealth, but I'm certain she doesn't grasp the concept of what I offer. "I'll have more than enough to take care of your needs."

"With all the work we've done on transmutation, my cells haven't responded to anything but magic use. Nothing out there is better than where we are here."

"If Henry hasn't taken a look at your charts, then they haven't been looked at properly. Sky, my Dad will find a cure, and none of this stuff matters out there. We'll leave it all behind us. Just be human together."

"There's no come and go, Shiloh. I'm too high profile. If I forsake my country, I can't return." Her eyes fall to the floor. "If you get bored of me, I'd have nowhere to go. I'm not even sure how your parents—"

"I could never be bored of you?" I shake my head back and forth, nauseous over words I'd hurled in rage and burned in her brain. "I'm asking you to elope."

Sky's cheeks flush, and her eyes grow larger than I've ever seen. "You're crazy, Shiloh Benson. You know Blondie explained *post orgasmic euphoria* while she helped me pack up your closet this morning? And now, I think you're sex hazed! Happens to the best of us, I'm afraid. You got me locked down with just your eyes."

"Sky—"

"You can't ask to marry someone on a whim," she says, laughter slightly strained. "They might actually take you up on it, and then what?"

"Then we'd kick ass in Ludi Bellorum and high tail it out of here? Sky Aelia Benson has a ring to it. No?"

"I don't understand," she whispers, voice soft enough that I may have imagined it. "You're... I— What happens when we're wrinkled before all of our friends? Would you still want me as a human? Will that version of me even satisfy you? The lonely housewife who relies on her partner's inheritance?"

Sky's hands tug at her braid, and I take them into my own.

"I don't want you to be lonely ever again. We'll take my inheritance and make a real change for people. And you could go to school to be a teacher! And we'd get to do normal things like raise horses and fight over the TV remote, and it would excite me just as much as you throwing daggers. And sure, we'd get old. Faster than expected. But then there's wrinkly old people sex to look forward to. When I get a cool cane because my wife blew out my back the night before."

"Clinically insane. Exactly as I suspected. And, hypothetically, how many whiny bitches would be in our home? Aside from us, that is."

"Two?"

"Three," she challenges. "And they all come from you."

"We might have to compromise on a two-for-one. I planned to see your face again, and I refuse to give that up." Sky inhales sharply, entire body going stiff before she calmly removes her nasal cannula, turning off the valve of her oxygen tank. "Now you know. I'll be crazy enough for the both of us, and you'll just say yes along the way. Run away with me."

There's a strange shift in her expression as she rises to her feet, and I scramble up after her.

Without a word, Sky backs me against her door, thumb pressing into my jaw so hard it may bruise. Her castor hand wraps my throat, and she viciously sweeps into my mouth. Biting and sucking the blood that beads on my bottom lip, pillaging with her tongue, and branding me in a way that leaves me lightheaded. Brutal and unforgiving. So passionate and demanding it feels a simultaneous punishment and reward.

Sky stops as abruptly as she began. The both of us panting as resolve fills her gaze.

"I have to go."

"Wait, can we finish getting engaged first?!" I'm brushed aside with half-lidded eyes, grasping at her sweater as Sky darts out of her room without a look back. "A simple yes, no, or maybe would do!"


I REMAIN in a hazy stupor on the way back to my dorm. Almost walking past Meesa, who sits directly across from my door, bundled in my marshmallow coat and dozing off until I kneel to tap her shoulder.

"Stars above!" she yelps. "Hi, Ma'am."

"Hey Meesa. What are you doing here?"

"I ran into Ms. Sapienti this morning and offered to pick these up. The least I can do! I'll miss you both so much when the year is over. You're all I talk about at home these days." She grins, looking side to side before adding, "Everyone from the cafe is doing a small gathering to support you two for Ludi Bellorum."

"We'll miss you too. I don't know where we'll be, but we'll send you letters. All of you."

Meesa sighs happily, swooning about young love as I slide to sit beside her. Opening the wooden box and flipping through pictures Sky got developed from last night.

My favorite is one of us dancing as I sling one arm around her neck. Sky narrowly touches my poked-out tongue with her own, eyes crossed in a moment of silliness.

I don't realize I've been tuning Meesa out until she says, "Sorry, I don't have your morning smoothie. Mr. Sapienti was too busy to come in."

My heart sinks, and the box clatters to the hardwood floor. "What?"

"Mr. Sapienti is taking the day off. His sister has not joined them on a hunt in—"

"Nox?" I guess that explains the pause over break, but I'd assumed they saw me overeating all their food and knew I was being fed properly. I hadn't questioned it once. "I thought he asked you guys to make them?"

"No, Ma'am. He comes in every morning to grind your vitamins and pick out the proper supplements. And once after dinner for your desserts. He asked us to deliver them at certain—"

"No." I shake my head back and forth, wondering if banging my head against the brick wall will erase the knowledge from my mind.

"I'm telling the truth," she says, cringing away from my gaze.

"I mean, I didn't—" I pick up the box and cradle it to my chest. "It needs to stop. Today."

"Are you sure? It appears to be working. You look so vibrant and—"

"Meesa."

"But—"

"Meesa!" She presses her lips together while I rub my temples. "I don't want them. Tell him he should've known to stop a long time ago."

"Okay?" She frowns. "I'll catch him before he departs for the day?"

"Thank you." I shudder.

"You're welcome." I turn to meet her gaze, mine widened in pleasant surprise as she smiles the fullest grin I've ever seen. "What? I'm doing you a favor, aren't I?"

"You're damn right you are."

She bumps my shoulder with her fluffy new coat, and I bump her right back.


RUSS INHALES DEEPLY, speeding ahead to clear our path. He pushes a low-hanging tree limb out of my face as we head towards his secret grove, nose brushing the crown of my head before I swat him away.

"Dude, you said you wouldn't scent me!"

"It's not an everyday occurrence!" he sputters. "It feels like ignoring a buzzing fly a few yards away. Or, tuning out a passerby's conversation. I focus on myself, and it only insists on my attention every once in a while. Your scent is... potent. It's not always up to me."

I sniff my own shoulder. "Can I ask what I smell like?"

Thankfully, I'd scrubbed myself clean before I built the courage to head to breakfast.

Skin raw and red as I'd slid into my chair, catching a fist bump from Bridger, who'd repetitively barked until I blushed maroon.

Russ, by some miracle, has been oblivious to the gossip being spread around school. And by another, his late birthday extravaganza included a full day of spa treatments away from all other students.

I've been waxed, prim and proper. My hair finger-coiled to perfection, and my body now glistens with fancy massage oils.

What remains is the smell of fruit and eucalyptus soap. Pulling a curl under my nose and sniffing mango conditioner every few minutes.

"There's this flower we call nature's candy. People drizzle its nectar on fruits before eating," he sighs. "Reminds me of home."

Another flood of guilt sears through my core. Each time I've attempted to confess, my tongue gets tied by Russ saying something sweet. It's enough to send anyone to the insane asylum. "To be fair, the sniffing is your fault for wanting to finish out the day with a hike."

We're still a mile away from Russ's favorite thinking spot on campus. Smack dab in the middle of the nearby forests. The Sapienti's must be somewhere in this vast canopy of multicolored foliage, or heading back to campus now. Though Russ promises we shouldn't encounter anyone on our trek.

"You suggested the location. I just said we should walk."

"We could've flown." He points to my pegasus that soars above, casting shadows every now and then from the fading light rays peeking through tall oak trees. Sunny escorts us to Russ's private sanctuary for the sake of some extra flight time. "Did you make the girls do a four-mile hike too?" he jokes as I slow my gait. "Or did you finish out the night with a secret blood pact I don't know about?"

When I'd entered my room, Osira had popped up from my bed, half asleep and hungover. Screaming in elation, jumping up and down in her blue silken bonnet.

After our morning debrief, the girls had been especially tight-lipped at breakfast, but Jason alluded to having heard the rumor after he'd gotten up to corner me at the muffin station—suggesting that nineteen is too young for a serious relationship. I'd *suggested* that he should fuck off and mind his own business.

He'd left breakfast early.

"I kissed Sky," I whisper as Russ trudges forward without me.

"Huh?" His face distorts as it swivels over his shoulder, pinched expression a clear indication he's heard me.

"By kiss, I mean, we had sex. A few—More than a few times."

His eyes squint behind golden-framed lenses. For once, seeing a large jungle cat before me instead of someone who couldn't swat a fly.

"Define, *Sex?*"

I rear my head back. "I don't like the way you asked that."

Russ throws me a glare so lethal my stomach flips. I give him a few feet of space to unpack whatever it is he's feeling about the situation, crossing my arms and holding my breath for the explosion sure to ensue.

What I don't expect is for him to turn on his heel, continuing our path through the thicket of trees, hands clenching and unclenching as his ring glows bright green.

The first crack is subtle, as if he's stepped on a twig.

But like dominoes, the path before us clears.

Hundreds of years-old trees falling to the left and right. Booming, splintering, and ripping from their roots in the tightly packed soil. The ground shaking beneath every step he takes.

"Russ!"

He bolts forward through the freshly built pathway, long legs putting him far ahead of me.

"Icarus!" I shriek, dodging a fallen limb as I stumble through an earthquake to the cadence of his erratic heartbeat.

"Wait! Let me explain!"

Bushes and branches snap and wither around us, and I follow him until we've broken into an open clearing, which can't be anything other than the secret oasis he's been building.

It's a vast field of flowers. Organized row by row in every shade and color the world has to offer.

In the center of it all, stands the prettiest hanging willow tree I've ever seen. The wood is a pure stark white. Tall, thick, and sturdy as if it's been growing for centuries and not one school year.

The leaves that hang from it are not leaves at all, but long strands of lavender that match the Honestus house colors.

Russ bolts for the tree, only stopping his escape when his hand touches it. Ring no longer glowing, and the ground no longer shaking beneath our feet. He slumps into the hanging willow, sliding down its side while warily watching my approach.

Twilight surrounds us as Sunny touches down beside me. I caution her to stay back with my hand, and she seems to understand, traipsing off through the flowers and nibbling at one she thinks will taste good.

"What is wrong with you?" Russ whispers as I kneel before him and sit cross-legged, as close as he'll allow. "There's no way Sky didn't tell you we've been hooking up. Why didn't you ask my permission first?"

I swallow back bile in my throat. "Because it wouldn't have changed my decision."

"You don't care about how it affects me? You're just doing it?"

"I'm begging you to forgive me for doing it."

"And if I said it's either me or her?"

Hurt morphs his face when I don't respond, my heart physically shredding in my chest. I know that even if he forgives me, I won't ever forget this feeling. He won't ever forget my silence.

"You're important to me, too. I love you, Russ. So much."

"Icarus," he sneers. "Icarus. Amias. Honestus."

"Okay. If that's what you want."

"Where is this coming from?! Alvarez didn't work out, so his cousin will do? Actually, *he* had a girlfriend too, so this is a pattern now. Wanting what's shiny and already spoken for. I thought I'd be safe, but there are never boundaries with you!"

"It's not like that," I whisper.

"No, it's not. Because I'm not calling off my betrothal for a single night of drunken sex." When I avoid his gaze, he scoffs. "It wasn't a single night?"

"Do you really want to know?"

He clenches his jaw and shakes his head, coily curls bouncing on top with every rapid bob. "What explanation could be good enough? You're not even into women. You like boys!"

I stop myself from the obvious snarky response sitting on my tongue.

"Well, actually, I'm capable of attraction to men, but my tolerance grows shorter daily." Russ rolls his eyes, so I add, "Fine. I've thought long and hard about my sexuality this year."

"And?"

"It's confusing. I feel like there's a colorful scale of attraction where people consider how they fall in love, and why they fall in love, and who they prefer, and who they'd never even consider. And after enough self-exploration, everyone seems to find a shade that feels authentic to who they are. Something that perfectly encapsulates their desires. But I've considered and picked it apart and slid around so much that I've become an... indistinguishable, non-spectral, blob."

"You think you've changed your mind too much to settle?"

"I haven't settled. I've finally been seen in my entirety. Sky said that when she let herself look outside of bounds, I was instantly ultraviolet." My heart flutters in my chest, and I wet my lips before adding, "She told me I don't have to show up as anything but myself for love to find me. It'll meet me where I am. As long as it doesn't abandon the person giving it on the way there. And we're together the whole way. We are."

"Where are you two exactly? And where are you going?"

"Russ, time and space couldn't contain this feeling. A human life together will be where we start, but it's not our end."

"A *human*—"

"Sky's inordinately beautiful and ridiculously attractive, but it wouldn't matter how she came to me."

"So, you're Pansexual," he offers dryly.

"Russ."

"Is Bisexual more appealing?"

"I'm not doing this with you. Or, anyone but her, actually."

"That's bullshit, Shiloh. Have you ever denied it when someone assumes you to be straight?"

"No. Because frankly, it took a lot of self-reflection, and a year cut off from the internet to learn being straight isn't a default setting. It's a shade people label themselves, so society better understands their feelings and decisions. I am a straight man, therefore I'll only date women. Even if there's curiosity buried within me! I am a straight woman. I will only tie myself to a man, even if there have been moments of longing, I won't ever feel the need to unravel. Yes, sometimes labels *are* absolute, but it's not a catch-all. It's an identifier for how you'll move through this world. And if you're brown, there are other labels that far exceed society's perception of you unless you intentionally make it so. There's nuance, Russ. I will deny it now that I know, but a detailed explanation isn't owed to anyone but my partner?"

"Except we don't exist in a vacuum, Shiloh? Labels matter. Even if they're not all encapsulating. They're how people make sense of the world, and it sounds like you're avoiding them to avoid the truth. I deeply care about Sky, and if you want my honest opinion, I think you love that *she's* in love with *you*. Because you don't have the best track record with the men in your life, and you just admitted you were confused!"

"This conversation... is over," I whisper. Russ stops me from rising with a tug at my wrist. "No, don't fucking touch me!"

"I didn't mean—"

"I know what you meant, Icarus, and I never once asked for your opinion. You rolled your eyes and had your thoughts, so I tried to explain myself the best I could. And I understand why it's annoying, and infuriating, and unfair. You think the way I experience the world will allow me to dance through life. While actually, it just feels like I'm hanging above you by a fucking thread, spinning too fast to catch a breath. I understand I'm not owed your sympathy, and I don't really expect it, but I *refuse* to be your shattered reflection. I'm a person who fully realizes who she is for the first time in her entire life, and I will be damned if I let you warp what I've built with her to make sense of how I operate."

"I'm not trying to be hurtful? I'm just protective. Of you both!"

"Thanks for your concern. I'm sure you've already told your family and citizens, you like men. Since it matters so damn much and the world needs to know."

"Shiloh, it's different for me, and you know it. I'm Gay! I'll only ever be Gay! And you have taken my *only* chance at a marriage without betrayal, when I am positive you had every opportunity to choose differently! To walk away from her so that I could have just one single thing in my future, I've decided for myself. Do you have an inkling of what I've just lost!? Do you even care?"

My face crumples, and his anger deflates in an instant, replaced by a detached numbness. Slowly but surely, our fingers meet, lacing together so intimately that I know we'll pull through this.

Even if it leaves us jagged around the edges.

"I'm sorry. It's okay, I want to be a father. More than anything else, even. My children will be the loves of my life. I will choose them."

"No."

"No? What more should I give up in this deplorable life of politics?"

"Russ, I'm saying this life is yours. You can have that and still take a husband."

"I cannot afford to have kids with a man. I was already pushing that with Sky, but I figured..."

"Tristain."

"He's in love with Osira, so it didn't seem a big deal to arrange their marriage."

Russ once confessed that his family has never *technically* committed incest. But, for the Honestus family, to marry outside of heritage means your children are obligated to marry within the Korovk line.

Since Jason chose Suede, Tristain's older brother will marry from an approved list of brides, committing to the same amount too. Tristain was born a few weeks after Russ as *his* counterpart and waits for Russ to choose his future so he can understand his purpose.

"You're a founder's son. If you can't decide your own path with all that power you hold, what's the point? Who else gets to?"

"The Universe decides. It put me in this mind and body that—"

"Stop." I cover his mouth with my fingers. "Stars can only be held together by love for whatever lives inside them. We're not bound by anything but people's perceptions of our reality."

He kisses my hand before moving it away from his lips, patting the back of it in a soothing motion. "Perception is all there is."

"It's not all there will be when we shake these people awake. You're a goddamned Lion named after the great Icarus Honestus. You'll write your own story."

"You sound like Jason," he muses. "If he knew, or could accept what I am."

"Your brother loves you. *Unconditionally.*" Russ grasps my hands so tightly they might burst. "And your mate's gonna find his way to you. *That* is your future. The only one I'll accept."

He pulls me into a hug as darkness falls around the clearing. Sunny nearing us to curl up next to the willow tree, white body glistening in the moonlight. "That's a nice sentiment."

"It's a promise. And an I'm sorry."

"Shi, I reacted too harshly. I said things I didn't mean."

"I was sneaking behind your back for months. I don't think you reacted harshly enough."

"If I'm being honest, I'd be remiss if I said I hadn't already known her feelings. The issue is that I was willfully ignorant about yours." Russ pauses briefly. "Last night, you said there was supposed to be music and —Was it perfect?"

*Was it perfect?*

No words can explain the feeling of someone touching your soul and wiping away the cruelty in this world. Last night, while Sky cleaned me up and kissed every part of me that was tender, I knew with absolute certainty that I'd never forgive myself for touching her in the dark, using her for pleasure before I could love in such pure, radiant light.

Though I know one day there may be a time and place where recounting the entirety of last night will make sense, I'm keeping it close to my heart for years to come.

"Russ, whatever future you choose, I'll always be in your corner. But there are things to be experienced that are worth more than the lie of perfection. When you truly love someone, you get to worship their flaws too." His big brown orbs are glassier than normal when I curl against his chest.

"It's time for your final present," Russ says, chin resting on my head as he folds me into his arms. "And you have to be quiet, or they won't show us."

We fall silent and, little by little, they make their appearance in his secret garden.

Tiny lanterns fill the open space. Thousands of lightning bugs making themselves known, twinkling and giving us the most amazing light show I'll ever witness in my life.

"Oh." I lift my hand, and a luminescent bug falls into it. Blinking rapidly before flying to flit across Sunny's stretched wings, disappearing amongst the others.

"They started coming when I finished the meadow. I think they've made a home here."

"I love you, Icarus Honestus. You're the strongest man I've ever met, and it's a blessing to know you." He appears skeptical, but doesn't deny it.

"I love you more, Shiloh Benson. The blessing is all mine."

# CHAPTER 34

After leaving Russ at the stables, I run to Sky. Light as a feather, as a thousand pounds of stress slides off my shoulders. I yank the do not enter note off her door and crumple it in my grasp before I bang. *"Mrs. Bensooon!"* My words come out in song, and I can't seem to conjure the slightest bit of embarrassment for my behavior.

"You'd better be naked with only the nasal cannula on!"

I'm so in tune with Sky's scent, I can smell how close she is. A mere foot away and directly on the other side, yet silent in response to my advances. "Hello...?"

"Go away," she demands, a reply so monotone my smile fades a bit.

"You know I was kidding about the nasal cannula. Right? Unless you don't want me to be kidding. In which case, I wasn't?"

"I said go away, Shiloh." Sky's voice has hardened to ice. "Caveman and Sol will be back any minute now, and you shouldn't be here."

I turn the handle on her door, but the lock is firmly in place. "Is this your idea of a joke?"

"No. You need to leave. I'm not saying it again."

Sky's footsteps patter away from the door, and some part of me snaps at her words. The little deranged bit that's always felt like a barrier in my own mind. Glued together by her touch this morning and fractured instantly by confusion and heartache.

I slide my dagger into the flimsy lock, going to work at it with a vicious red haze clouding my vision.

After some trial and error, it clicks open and I rise, storming inside her den like a category five hurricane and melting the lock shut behind me so we're trapped inside until she sees me.

I catch a glimpse of long white tresses before Sky locks herself inside her bathroom. The loud thud of a thick oak door branding itself in my eardrums. "Get the fuck out of my room!"

"Have you lost your mind?!" Chewy meows in distress as I stalk past her, banging on the bathroom door with clenched fists. "What part of 'will you marry me,' led you to believe you could break up with me without *any* explanation!? That's not how relationships work!"

"You don't know how relationships work! We had *one* night together. You're crazy."

I laugh without humor, an integral chunk of my sanity shredded as anger brews in my belly like I've never felt before. Only overshadowed by the swell of pain that keeps me from setting her room ablaze. "No. You don't get to do this to me."

"Go away," she whispers, releasing a dense cough.

"Face me like a fucking Bear!" I yell, kicking and attacking the wood with my steel-toed boot until I make a crack in it.

"Shiloh... *Leave.* Please?"

"No! What did I do wrong?! I'm trying to be better. I'm sorry!"

Somewhere amidst my screams, Sky begins to sob, my swell of rage washed away in the flood.

She cries as if someone has died.

*Has someone died?*

Crazed wails that scare me half to death, wane and repeat.

Agonized croaks stifled that make me claw to get through the door for an entirely different reason.

I lean my forehead against the splintered wood, resorting to begging even faster than I'd resorted to violence. I'd rather do this with her than nothing at all. "Want to know something? I'm declaring for the Bears. I won't question you about leaving again. We'll fly to Hiemsternum tonight, and I'll kneel for your father. I'm giving my honor and name to House Sapienti."

"No," she moans. "Shiloh—"

"We'll stay in one of those cottages you were talking about. Drink wine, watch snowfall, and dance every night. And I'll win Solara over. Maybe she can come for dinner this summer? I'll learn to cook, and I'll be more mindful... I'll be easier to love. I won't make it hard ever again."

Muffled sobs answer me.

"Sky, just give me a chance."

"It's too late."

"It's never too late. Anything that's broken, I'll *f*-fix *f*-for the both of us. I choose this. I choose *you.* Again and again and again. As long as you keep choosing me, too."

At this, the door cracks open.

A smidge.

Then an inch.

Then a foot.

Then all the way until a dreadful chill spreads through each nerve ending, watching her struggle through ragged breaths that don't fully fill her lungs.

My girlfriend unleashes a wet cough that prompts her to double over from pain.

When Sky straightens her spine, the distance between us is only several feet. Yet, it may as well be worlds apart.

Her corneas are bloodshot red. Black tears streaking her face.

She sobs, and my body stumbles toward the sound like a beacon, cupping scorching cheeks that were ice cold and blooming with a healthy pink glow just this morning. Now filled with an angry red flush that's clammy and feverish under my palms.

"My knife." I scramble for the dagger on my thigh, and she shakes her head. "We'll cut off your finger."

"No."

"Sky, we have to. I'll do mine first so you won't be scared. Okay? I'll do my whole fucking hand because we're leaving anyway. This stuff doesn't matter out there."

"It's... too... late."

"Don't say that shit again!" I snap, pulling out strands of my hair as I pace before her. "Wait here. I'm getting your brother. He'll call your doctors. We have time to figure this out."

"Stop." Sky grabs at my waist weakly. Gray eyes still gorgeous even when surrounded in a sea of veiny red, glancing at the overflowing stack of envelopes she's left on her dresser. "You should go. But to find your friends. To be with them. Nox will help me."

"Help *kill* you?!" She's silent, and I nod my head. "Over my dead body."

"Nox would sooner take a blade to his own throat than strike you again," she sneers. "Did you honestly think there was any lifetime where I wouldn't have been promised your safety?"

"I'll fight him until he has no other choice! Or, I'll do it myself!" My fingers launch toward my dagger, and Sky places her hand over mine, shoving it back in its sheath.

"If you kill yourself, I'll run to the light alone."

"You wouldn't do that to me."

"I would. How could you truly love me and take away my reason for being with your last breath?" Her threat is stern and certain, a sob hurtling through my chest as I attempt to catch breaths that keep slipping away. "Do you understand what I'm saying?" Sky grips my chin, and I yank it away from her hands. "We will *never* know one another again! I will make sure of it!"

The unwavering certainty in her tone is the only thing that stops me from moving my knife. "How could you?"

"You asked me to be your wife. That meant something to me."

"In sickness and in health! It meant, for the rest of our lives, we'll make decisions *together!*"

"If you can recall, our vows are much deeper than earthly promises." She places her cracked ring over my heart, and it still catches its erratic beat, wiping her bloody nose with her sleeve. "Ubi tu, ibi ego. I will be there when your heart takes its last beat, but that will not be today."

"Sky—"

"I've made my choice," she whispers simply. "Now take me to my bed, Cub. Or leave. That choice is yours."

My brain pulses, and my vision blurs. Legs and body on autopilot as

I guide Sky into her bed. Somehow, knowing a part of me will remain in this moment, her grave gaze, for eternity. And the other half will hang above it all, permanently detached and unaware of the reality before me.

I comb my hands through her platinum tresses. Braiding the silken hair with trembling fingers as I try to memorize the exact weight of each strand. The end result is something like the intricate crown she wore at the welcome ceremony. She swears instantly she likes it better, without a mirror to be found except my own gaze.

"I've *n*-never been cold before." Sky shivers as I attempt to rub warmth into her already burning shoulders.

"Sky?"

"Yes, baby?"

"Our souls are tied. Did you know that?"

"Took you long enough." She smiles crookedly, sweeping my over-grown bangs from my eyes. "Sunny and I stress about it whenever you leave us on our own. Our girl is impatient."

A fractured laugh sounds in the air—a cross between a sob and moan I'm unsure I knew could ever escape me.

"Mate me then. We'll never part again. She'll be so happy." Sky shakes her head back and forth, shredding what's left of my heart into tiny, irreparable pieces. "Why?"

"Three hundred years is a long time." She offers me a lopsided grin, and my mouth goes dry. "I don't expect—"

"Fuck. You. I *f*-fucking hate you." Sky chuckles, coughing into her elbow as sweet iron permeates the air. "Did you hear me? You're a coward, and I *hate* you! If you don't mate me right now, I will hate you for as long as I live! I will *never* forgive you. I swear on my name!"

"You couldn't care less about your name, Shiloh. And not even your mate will keep me from claiming your heart in the next life. Understood? You and I transcend magic, and a Bear doesn't lose a fight. We will get another chance." A pale hand reaches for my hair. Tugging white ribbon from my ponytail until curls spring free, entwining the silken fabric through slim fingers as if she's seeing something that's not yet there. "Now tell me you love me or you'll regret it."

"Mate me first." I blink tears furiously from my gaze, each blur of her face a sin against me. "It's my only wish. The only thing I'll ever ask for again."

"My answer will remain the same. I refuse to leave you in agony, but I don't leave you on your own. Your happiness will never hurt me. It's all I want, all I've ever wanted."

I clutch at my stomach, and it feels as if my insides might spill out, begging and using every trick in the book, anything that will convince her to bind herself to me.

The most vicious words spew from my mouth. Teetering between love and hate and weeping and pleading, and Sky denies my every attempt, capturing my lips with her own to stifle my unbecoming sobs.

Feverish mouth still tasting sweet, the satin ribbon threaded through her fingers soothing against my skin.

I pull her into my lap and try to avoid messing up the intricate braids I've woven into her hair. Fingers clawing desperately at Sky's back as she curls into me, so frail and shaky that I'm terrified of hurting her.

"Tell me you love me." Her hands are a tangle in my curls, grabbing fistfuls that should hurt, but everything is numb aside from the soul that fractures within my chest.

"Mate me first."

"No!" she yells. "Don't do this to yourself! Tell me you love me! It's time, Shiloh!"

There's a weighted silence between us before I whisper, "I'm eternally in love with you, Sky. There is no limit. No end. No reason. Our love just is and will always be. I— Please? *Please, please please.*"

I repeat the one word she's never denied me, begging as she hurls up impossible amounts of blood onto her pink duvet and claws at the soft fabric in her hand.

Chewy scratches at the door, attempting to get help as Sky screeches into her blanket. Banging her hands on her head over and over again until I catch both wrists, willing her to keep it together.

Her cracked ring glows softly. Skin burning my palms like a branding iron. I don't let them go. Even as my hands begin to sizzle, blistering at her touch.

"Come on, Sky Aelia. Stay with me." She inhales raggedly, and the burning ceases. Her cloudy eyes momentarily sane again, darting to the dagger strapped to my thigh.

Sky finds strength to rip away one of her wrists and pushes me into the mattress, pulling my blade out and turning the sharp end toward her heart. "You could never hurt me. You know that, right?"

"I'm scared."

"There are very few things to be scared of when we're together. Remember?" Her whole body shakes as she struggles to stay inside her own mind. Sky flips us until I'm on top of her, sharp knife pressed to her chest and unable to fully inhale below me.

"No. I can't, Sky. I can't."

"This will not last, and it will *not* take you. There will be everything you dream of when you reach your end. My people just have to meet you first. Know you, and they'll rise."

"You think I will help a world that has done this to you? They're animals. I see it now. They deserve every bad thing that's coming to them. They will do it to themselves, and I will watch and be glad to see this planet rid of such hatred that masquerades itself as humanity. I will see it burned to the ground and reduced to ashes, remaining solely to kill the phoenix that *dares* to rise and rebuild!"

"Don't...let them... take... your heart," she gasps.

"You *are* my heart."

"Then want it for me. Your dreams have become my own."

"I—"

"You can do anything, you know that? You know how strong you are? You know how much I love you?" Sky begins to hyperventilate and repeat herself, and I know I've done the unforgivable.

I've frightened her.

I've shoved her my own fear in her final moments.

So, with a shuddered breath, I do what she's taught me to.

*I perform.*

Sucking every emotion into a little box until a complete numbness spreads through my veins.

"I'll fix it now. You're gonna be okay. I promise."

"You promise?" Her voice sounds almost childlike as I shudder.

"I swear on my name." This seems to relax her completely. Leaning down, lips brushing hers to erase the fear. "Just kiss me, and you'll feel better. No pain at all."

Sky kisses me back hungrily. Fully. Passionately. Using every bit of strength inside her as if my lips are the lifeline she hangs on to instead of the cruel embrace of death.

I pour as much love as I can into her. Every ounce I have inside me, I give as I drive my dagger through her chest. Tuning out the sickening squelch and kissing her through bloodstained lips, a soft gasp leaving her as blood gushes out around my blade.

"You're right, Shiloh. There's... no pain... at all," she rasps, a deep wet quality to her words. Pretty eyes losing focus beneath me, flickering back and forth in search of my own. "It's just love."

*"Exspecta me in astris. Cum iterum convenimus, ad lucem simul curremus."* Sky's hand goes limp, and I press it against my cheek. "It's going to be so beautiful up there. I know it." I clear my throat of its rasp. "I love—"

There's an intense buzzing in my ears as the last struggling thump of her heart comes to a stop. Sky's ring disintegrating to dust beneath my blistered hands.

I'm unclear how much time has passed before I close her glassy eyes. But it is only when I'm sure I cannot frighten her lingering soul that my emotions unleash from the box.

Only now does my careful hold on reality slip as I scream my vocal cords bloody.

Everything happens in bursts and flashes.

In fragmented memories, as my world melts around me.

*"Shiloh?!"* someone roars. *"Where are you? Shiloh!? Shiloh, hold on!"*

After several loud bangs, the door bursts open in a rain of fire.

I shield the body, splinters cutting the back of my arms as Nox bursts through, pupils scanning the room with imminent death in their core.

Solara must have been at his heels. The both of them covered in blood and mud, holding freshly skinned pelts.

The woman I once thought was a wall of ice shatters apart when she sees me covered in black sludge and rocking her sister's limp frame, wails keening and intertwining with my own.

Nox holds her against him as her legs lose function. Making no sound at all until his own kneecaps hit the floor with a heavy thud.

Russ finds us next, running towards where he believes he may be able to help.

But Russ doesn't help.

*He harms.*

Attempting to pry me away from a stiffened body.

"Come on, Shi. Let them take care of her."

So much blood.

So many scents.

*How can they take her from me?*

*Where will she be safe aside from my arms?!*

"She wanted *m*-me to take care of her."

"And you did, Sweetheart. Now she'd want you to come with me. Okay?" Russ cradles a slashed-up arm, gushing blood from both nostrils and blinking rapidly behind shattered frames.

"What did I do, Russ? Oh God, what did I do?! Please—"

I begin to argue aloud to no one but myself until he scoops me up.

I try not to hurt him.

I don't think I do.


IN THE HOURS THAT FOLLOW, someone showers and changes me, scrubbing blood free from my body and hair.

Someone else carries me to the fireplace. Wraps me in a blanket as I stare into the flames while disembodied whispers float around me.

*"My people are coming to... I requested... It's not possible."*

*"She shouldn't travel."*

*"...can't... in her state."*

*"... might bring her comfort... sent every day..."*

*"I'm so sorry, Nox. I'm so sorry."*

Somehow, someway, sleep is worse.

I clutch my hands around my skull, and each time she's in more pain. "Make it stop! Please, make it stop!"

"You're having a nightmare, Arsonist! It's a nightmare! Wake up!"

I don't know what is real, but in rare moments of lucidity, I've come to realize Jason is.

He keeps me in a bubble that smells of lavender. He stops the sirens.

"I've got you. You're safe," he murmurs as we ball together by the fire. I'm aware at times it's not me taking in air but him pumping it into my lungs.

Jason sings sometimes.

He stops.

He begins again when I eye him.

Hours and days.

Suede and Russ.

Osira and Tristain.

Jason. There's less shine when he's singing.

Suede says he's sleep-deprived.

That he's using too much power to contain me.

He says he doesn't care, constantly asking if I'm inside somewhere.

I try to assure him I am.

Answer him when he begs.

It doesn't seem to help.

I can do nothing but scream her name.

# CHAPTER 35

I'm woken up to Chewy curled in the crook of my neck as my head lifts from Jason's chest, Suede patting my cheek until my swollen eyes peel open. "We're going to Sky's send-off, okay? Her people are here to get her."

Suede guides me to the bathroom, slipping me into a heavy black dress, brushing my teeth, and washing my face. All I can do is stare into the shattered mirror as she ties my hair back with a black ribbon. Her face is battered and bruised—a blood vessel popped in her right eye.

"This batch should be strong enough," Suede whispers, attempting to give me more shiny medicine. I shake my head, refusing hazy memories if this is my last time seeing her face.

"Apple," I croak, sitting on the toilet as she slides black heels onto my feet.

"Apple?" Suede breathes. "You want food?"

"Apple."

Suede races off, and I note she does not leave me alone. She passes me along to Jason. And I have no idea when he changed. When he'd found the time to run back to his room.

Then again, time is different now.

It's all so... *endless.*

*Has it been three days or three years?*

Jason adorns a distinguished military uniform, locs pulled back into a tight knot. He wears a black undercoat with golden tassels. A lavender and white sash across the front of his suit, as golden Lions hang in various places, white gloves covering his many rings.

Before everyone arrives, I head to my dresser. Opening the top drawer and stuffing its contents into my pockets until they bulge. Lastly, finding my favorite picture with Sky.

On second thought, I tuck that one away. Selfishly taking out my second favorite picture instead. A candid of Sky sitting on my desk as I stand between her legs. The two of us laughing so hard our eyes close as she examines my stuffed Lion.

Russ arrives in the same suit as Jason. Osira and Tristain in all black.

I can't look any of them in the eye. I've seemingly brutalized their bodies, and it doesn't appear that they've once hit me back.

Suede returns breathless with a handful of apples. I survey them all, grabbing the green one and stuffing it into my dress pocket. She frowns when I don't eat it, but says nothing.

We walk downstairs in pairs, following Jason, heading to the front steps of the school where crowds wait.

Hundreds of students are lined up, the section of students dressed in the furs of Hiemsternum seem to be doing the worst when we arrive, crying and weeping for Sky.

I stare at them as I pass. Trying to be glad people miss her.

It does not work.

I am *angry.*

Maybe it is unfair. But life is unfair.

We stand in the front. Rows of Honestus Loyalists lined up behind us, heads lowered in silence.

The Ouroboros flag is lowered at half mast. A brown and black flag waving above it, a silver Bear's head roaring over stripes.

The main staircase to the school is lined with faculty. Dean Alvarez at the end of the steps, her face devoid of all emotion as Ezra stands at her elbow, chain-smoking cigarettes.

As drums begin to beat and the golden gates to the school are pushed open, Nox and Solara exit the main building. Every head on campus turning to survey the two.

Black and brown leather plates are strapped to their chests. Hands clad in black gloves and silver medallions dangling at odd places.

I recognize their cloaks. Similar in fashion to the one Sky gifted me. Slightly different and made especially for them. Nox's hair is braided down his back with brown straps woven through. Solara's in the updo I'd given Sky in her last moments.

They reach the end of the stairs as carriages, hooves and cars approach. Thousands of feet marching in unison as Hiemsternums' army swarms through our gates. Boots stomping against the ground with the thunderous promise of homecoming.

It's when they bring out the pure silver casket that Russ weeps uncontrollably beside me. Jostling my shoulders with every sob as four soldiers unfurl the Terra Australis flag. The crisp white sheet billows in the wind before covering the entire thing.

I imagine Sky standing in front of him.

On her toes to kiss Icarus softly.

*Tough shit, Veggie Boy*, she'd tease with a lopsided grin. *The Earth takes back. It is why I hunt and love animals more than you do. It's the circle of life. Don't tell me you don't fuck with maggots because they're not as pretty as I am. They have a purpose too.*

"Raise the flags!" Nox thunders. Someone sounds a horn, and several soldiers lift wavering poles at forty-five-degree angles.

Her people load her into an empty carriage, and I feel a wave of nausea, stumbling forward as Russ attempts to grab me.

My ribbon falls from my hair. Curls whipping in the winds as I run toward the soldiers who move in a blockade to stop me.

One grabs me too roughly, and I hiss, kicking the side of his knee in until an audible snap follows.

At once, several soldiers lunge. Russ and Jason leaping forward until Nox raises a hand.

Everything stops in an instant.

The drums, footsteps and even the breath of his men.

He fists his hand. Fixing them all with a glare that promises retribution upon returning home. They move back into formation with lowered heads, and I can't find the will to care that they'll be punished.

Only an enemy would keep me from her.

The man I kicked moans and whimpers at my feet, hand twitching for his dagger between grunts of anguish. "Touch me again, and the arm's broken too."

"You dishonor the—"

"Honor is a lie!" I heel him in the face, and when I cock my foot back for a second time, Nox picks me up, heel landing on open air. "All anyone does is *lie!*"

"How's the leg, Druskson?" Nox asks, holding me in the air as I refuse to so much as breathe.

The young man hisses when rising to his feet, putting all his weight on one leg to bow to his first son. "Broken, sir. Along with my nose... Permission to leave formation?"

Nox gestures toward the cars at the front of the procession.

The swollen-nosed man hops on one leg, hobbling uncomfortably until Nox signals for another soldier to help the man get there. Lowering me to the ground and nudging me forward.

I take no offered hand as the carriage is opened. Pulling myself up and scrambling beside her casket. Nox hops in and shuts the door behind us.

Drum beats and footsteps resume outside upon Solara's insistent demand, and I waste no time. Taking out my green apple and gnawing at the skin, swallowing without tasting as I eye the Ouroboros.

If Nox thinks it's odd, he doesn't say it. Sitting on a wooden bench and observing me eat. A gurgle echoing in the silence with each chunk that hits my empty stomach.

When a considerable amount of it is gone, I push back the crisp sheet and open Sky's casket, looking at Nox in surprise.

"Suede Audere came and did her makeup last night. She said you'd want to open it."

"Hi, Baby."

Sky's beautiful.

Unbearably so.

Her makeup is soft, bringing color to her face again as dark, thick lashes fan her cheekbones. Body swathed in a pure white cloak lined with polar bear fur, resting on a bed of white silk as if she's sleeping in a cloud.

As if when I kiss her, she'll awaken, and it really will be fine.

"I only owe you half an apple because you shouldn't have pissed me off in the first place, okay?" I open her hands and wrap them around the half-eaten fruit. "And I know you're scared of heights, so… I've prayed so hard that you're not alone up there. Wherever you are, I hope they're being kind to you. You're too gentle to be surrounded by anything but love."

I kiss the tip of her nose that would have crinkled if she were still inside this body. I kiss her cheeks that would have blushed. And I kiss her lips that would have cursed me before pulling away and sliding Mom's red lipstick out of my pocket. Tucking it into her cloak along with all of Dad's blocks.

"One day, when they deserve to know you, they will."

I tuck the picture of us laughing directly over her heart. "And if you're ever sad, know the covenant still remains. With every breath, I'll miss you. *W*-with every *b*-beat of my heart, know it will only ever be yours, Sky Aelia."

Nox shifts around the casket to better view her face, rivers of tears streaming down pale cheeks, eyes holding a vacant stare that tells me he's somewhere else.

"Do you want to leave anything with her?"

He nods, removing his glove and sliding off the ring of the first son. The token is too big for her thin fingers, but he slips it on anyway. Minutes before he's able to speak again.

"There won't ever be a day—" His breath hitches. "Where I don't wish to have taken your hardships. When I won't go to bed dreaming of a life where we switched places. Sky, I am the luckiest man to love you… You are my own." His voice cracks, and a sharp pang of agony floods through all the numbness. "Exspecta me in astris. Cum iterum convenimus, ad lucem simul curremus."

Nox kisses her forehead, shaking as he works to bottle his grief. Seconds to fall apart and forever to stitch himself back into a cold wall— into the soldier he has to be in the days that will follow.

Eventually, we both know it's time to be done. Closing it together before we seal the hinges shut with fire.

Nox gathers himself to solid blankness before I ask, "What do you do at funerals?"

"We burn our bodies so the remaining bits of their soul can reach them with the smoke."

"Don't leave her until the embers have gone out. Okay?"

"Until the ash has gone cool," he agrees.

When I have nothing further to ask, Nox pops open the door to the carriage and hops out, making sure I don't fall while I climb down by myself.

I land roughly as a large man about his height approaches. He's middle-aged and brown skinned. Ringlets white and eyes of crystal blue.

"Uncle," Nox says sharply.

The man bows his head. "My boy."

"Father's nowhere to be seen. I assume he'll be able to make it to Ludi Bellorum? Or am I expected to come back?"

"No. He demands we march faster on the return so we can get through the pyre in time for his trip."

My eyes sweep the crowd. Murderous when I register that her father has not come for her remains.

Nox's gaze meets mine, and I hold it.

The only acknowledgement of this heinous act between us. This unbelievable and unforgivable disrespect.

His voice is as frigid as a glacier as he says, "Then get back in formation. Let's get my sister home so he can arrive in time for what matters to him."

His Uncle nods, sliding back into his spot near the carriage.

I bow to Nox, and he bows back. Walking back to Russ's outstretched arm as he tucks me beneath it again. Jason on my other side, hand smoothing down my curls that wave in the wind.

Everyone stands at attention, and Nox weaves through each unblinking soldier. Wind whipping his braid while he checks that not a thread of clothing is frayed or misshapen. Not a foot placed outside of its mark, back perfectly straight and stiff, as everyone hangs on his every move.

Solara follows a step behind him, head held high—eyes bloodshot. An expressionless face that is so similar to Sky's, I have to look away.

*"Your daughter, born of wise men, returns to the land of eternal winter!"* Nox roars in Latin. *"Pay your respects! For her journey has reached its inevitable end, and she has served faithfully!"*

We kneel row by row, bowing our heads as the procession begins to move.

The drums and footsteps are not many people marching, but one combined force that shakes the ground they walk on. A single entity as they leave and take her with them.

All I can think is that the sun hasn't even risen. It may as well be night time still, and Sky would not like this very much.

Suede gives me more shiny medicine when I beg.

Shininess is better.

It is all that's left in this blue.

THE NIGHT BEFORE LUDI BELLORUM, everyone crowds on the floor of my dorm, munching on the special dinner that Meesa has delivered.

I asked her myself on Tristain's behalf.

"The kitchen staff has been inconsolable as fuck. All they've made is mushy oatmeal and pea soup. This ginger poured it *directly* onto my tray when I asked him about it. Said there was *not enough* for seconds. I didn't want the first serving! The fuck did I look like going back for seconds!?" He'd informed me one day. "I can only stomach the food they make you. Tell me when you want a bite. In the future, though, I already ate everything on your plate."

"Korovk!"

"Sira, I have *two* more fake teeth than I had a week ago. It's fine." She'd kicked him out, but I think it's the first time I've smiled, so they let him come back soon after.

A heavy rap hits the door, and Jason answers it, breaking into a hushed argument with whoever else decided to come and give me their condolences.

Since someone has dared to argue with the first son, the list of people who it could be grows to one.

When it becomes apparent he's not going away, I rise to my feet, padding over to the door until I'm face to face with Ezra Alvarez.

A haggard look fills his eyes, ink black hair springing up at odd angles. "Hey, Dreamer," he murmurs, breath reeking of cigarette smoke.

"What?"

"I'd like to talk to you."

"I already told you no, Alvarez."

"Twenty minutes?" Ezra asks, peering around Jason's broad shoulders.

"Does she appear capable of carrying on a conversation?!" Jason bares his teeth, and Ezra takes a step back.

"Twenty minutes," he repeats. "That's all I need."

Jason glances down at me, gauging my reaction. When I nod, he drops his shoulders. "Twenty minutes. If she tells me you have upset her, you're dead. There will be no questions. There will only be executions."

Ezra sizes him up, but I don't have to. I know his threat is serious.

I slip my feet into someone's much too large boots, throwing my friends a tight smile that's meant to be reassuring before I follow him.

I think I scare them all.

We wind up at his mother's office, sitting in silence for minutes on end until he asks, "What's the deal with Jason?"

"The *deal* with him?"

"Sky was the daughter of Fenrir Sapienti."

"So?"

"In times of mourning, it's required to bring her partner peace. It's why the soldiers who made to grab you were taken to a whipping post. Beat within an inch of their lives." I flinch, a wave of shock breaking through the numbness. "It was televised. They haven't done that in years."

"Nox?" I ask timidly.

"Don't look at the footage, you'll be sick."

"And?" I croak, sensing there's more to the story.

"Sapienti loyalists are unhappy. They wanted to take care of you in the first days. Things have been... *tense* around here. Jason's typically more diplomatic than this."

I'd grit my teeth at the number of bouquets and treats we'd waded through on the way out the door of my room. All of them piled high like some sort of fucked up shrine. I feel an overwhelming rush of defensiveness for my friend who's been without sleep since her death and reprimanding every person who's felt entitled to my time. "You have five minutes left."

"Ludi Bellorum is tomorrow," he blurts. "You need to show up and play the game if you want to pass the year and go home."

"I don't care where I end up."

"I care," he insists. "I thought maybe you could ask your questions again. That it would make you feel better."

I examine the instrument that used to be my salvation. Playing the high C over and over again as Ezra presses his boot to the sustain pedal. With a simple twitch of my fingers, the piano is encased in flames.

I've made it halfway out of the room before he shouts, "Her purpose was to love you! Can that not be called a grand existence?!"

The notion stills me in the doorframe. Anger ballooning at the very core of my being. "Where do you get off suggesting that someone so... unfathomably brilliant, had nothing more to offer this world than to love me? I should fucking kill you where you stand. Better yet, Jason should, because then I'd get to watch. Know there's an inkling of justice left in this world."

"You've lost faith, Dreamer. That's all. You've lost faith, and you can find it again."

"*Faith?!* Ezra, I've lost everything!" I clutch my skull, feeling as if I might fall apart at the seams. "You were right. They clipped her wings, put her on display, pinned her to a board and stripped *everything* good away. This world takes pure things and ruins them because it can. That is the horrible condition of mankind that cannot be healed."

"They couldn't have taken everything good, because you loved her? So much that you willingly destroyed yourself to set her free."

"It doesn't matter."

"Then would you rather have *never* met her?" Ezra asks. "Tell me you would rather have *never* met Sky and I'll believe it."

He picks up a chair and throws it through the windows of his mother's office, glass raining down until the night air kisses my skin.

"Swear it to the stars! Scream, you'd rather *never* have loved her than feel like this, and I'll believe you!" I shake my head as he catches his breath. "Her time here was worth it. She'd want you to fight."

"She can't want anything anymore! You didn't know her, and you no longer have the chance to because she's *dead*. We're born, we die, and that horizontal line between two inconsequential dates tells the whole truth. *Nothing. Matters.*"

Ezra digs in his pocket, raising a crumpled letter. Her pretty loopy scrawl is on the front—lingering traces of sweet almonds wafting to my nose and sending my heart to my throat.

"She wants the same things now as she did in life. The woman who's on these pages is someone who spent her last hour doing everything she could to protect what matters most. And that happened to be you. So this doesn't end with you wasting away or living an inconsequential line when you have the destiny of a tremendous existence. If you love her as much as she did you, you'll show up and fight tomorrow."

"In case you didn't get the hint, the first, second, or fiftieth time, it was *never* you. And it will never *be* you. So stop trying to save me because I am not yours to save. You're embarrassing yourself."

When I leave, Ezra lets the piano burn. In fact, he lets the entire office go up in flames.

All that's left to do is walk.

I walk and walk until my legs buckle beneath me, tumbling into the grass with no more miles to go, but the destination isn't much farther.

In this blizzard, sounds a rushing river nearby.

Just a few more paces and the stars need not be so far.

I crawl across rocks and grass, temples pounding and brain stretching as it pulses between my ears.

I make it to the water and manage to slump my head inside the river before my body gives up on me. Face hanging inside, relentlessly pelted by ice chunks—torso slipping into the current as I hope Sky was bluffing.

As I wonder if she'll let our souls touch before the light catches us.

As I pray she'll forgive me for not being strong enough.

My vision spots and darkens.

I suck in lungfuls of freezing liquid, a feeling of peace as my insides buzz with warmth.

There's a levity to my body, a brief feeling of... weightlessness?

Floating.

*Light.*

And then, a hand yanks me out. Banging on my back as frigid water and drool pour from my airways.

*"Sky?!"* I cup cold cheeks, and for a brief, glorious second, it's my baby who wipes away snot and weeps for me.

For half a breath, the blonde is icy and not sandy. The nose ski sloped and flushed pink instead of elven and freckled.

When my vision focuses once more, she's gone.

Ripped from my hands as I scramble to catch a violet butterfly, accidentally crushing its fragile wings in my firm grip.

Suede calls for Jason as I thrash in her arms, fighting against being dragged back to my room and clawing towards the river.

We compromise by lying on the bridge. Russ curling behind me like a blanket and a guard. One arm flung over my waist as my fingers repetitively stroke a scratchy panel, thumb pads tracing a whittled doodle I twist to examine.

My eyes widen, noting the shape is an arrowed heart containing the initials *SS+SB*. Scribbled over harshly with jagged strokes of a blade in an attempt to hide it.

A flicker of understanding tears through me along with another stab of pain. How many memories are forever half-baked? How many times had I been too wound up to notice? It's enough to be dumbfounded that she'd taken me anyway. Enough to hope that that amount of devotion could never truly be erased.

I turn to the stars with an unrelenting gaze, and I search.

Once they understand my mission, every so often, my friends point out an especially bright star. But the truth is, none of them feel like her.

None of them *are* her.

My search bleeds into hours until night and stars roll into twilight. The last star blinking away as warmth kisses my face and washes away the blue.

I bolt upright in an instant, heart lurching in my chest.

"Shi? What's wrong?!" Russ stirs, half asleep but reaching for me on instinct.

I point, rising to my feet and dragging him up.

My friends watch in awe as the sky is painted for us. More pink a morning sunrise than ever before. Sunshine blazing in earlier than it should logically arrive.

I've hidden away from any sunlight since I took her life. Which means, I've hidden away from *her.*

"I found her, Russ! She's there!"

Suede gapes, hazel gaze widened on the horizon. "The Great Morning Star?"

Russ blinks rapidly. "For... the purest of souls to reside in."

"All together," Jason whispers, tilting his face toward the rising sun. "She's not alone, sweetheart."

"I'm not crazy. I promise. I feel her."

It's the first true moment of sanity I've managed to scrape together since I knocked on Sky's door.

"We believe you," Tristain says.

"What a beautiful star she's picked," Osira whispers, leaning her head on Tristain's shoulder. "What a wonderful wait she'll have."

"She's there," I weep, eyes staring straight into the sun, uncaring if my retinas burn.

At least she's the one doing it.

*"Ubi tu, ibi ego,"* a voice whispers through the wind, the morning breeze gentle kisses upon wet cheeks.

"Semper et in perpetuum," I finish softly.

"What was that?" Russ asks.

"A vow."

Because I know now, with absolute certainty, Sky will continue to wait until I join her.

To *be.*

In every sunrise I ever see.

I'll never walk alone again as long as I have her light to guide me.

# CHAPTER 36

I slide into the battle suit Ezra's left at my door while munching on a tasteless protein bar, pulling up the matching cargo pants, and slipping my dagger in its sheath. It reeks of bleach, and I gather someone was aware enough to sanitize it before leaving me on my own.

When I tie my curls up with a shiny satin ribbon, the entire uniform, from head to ankle, is as red as the blood that flows in my veins until I lace up my black steel-toed boots.

I decide to get ready as Suede taught me while watching the newscast of Nox whipping his soldiers. Anguished screams in my ears as I carve out each angle of my features until there's no softness left.

What was once a grief-stricken girl is replaced by a hardened succubus who shares my features. Button nose, high cheekbones, and a heart-shaped face shimmering with each brush of powder. Almond eyes slightly upturned, dark liner emphasizing the swirls of amber hidden within. Bottom lip coated in berry chapstick, the slightest bit fuller than the top as if in a permanent pout.

Countless deep breaths and a reserved greeting later, I'm in the sky again. Taking contentment in the feeling of wind on my cheeks as I soar through open air.

Sunny rises to new heights, stretching and warming up her wings for the day ahead. Our bond closed off because I can't stomach her grief, too.

I hadn't had to explain my absence. I plucked dozens of black hairs from her mane today before mounting, and I think the upkeep might be a regular occurrence now.

When we lower in elevation, I hear the roar of the crowd first. Breaking through tufts of cumulus to the view of hundreds of thousands of spectators buzzing from below, filing into the arena and walking in packs together.

It's the first time I've seen this many Alchemists in one place. A swaying sea with bursts of red, yellow, green, and blue below me.

A majority of the attendees have shown up in gray, and kids pick flags the color of their chosen team. Waving them with immense excitement in one another's faces like liquid gold.

Sunny and I skim the treetops, spreading her wings to maximum capacity until they bounce light rays on the audience below.

"Look, Mama! *Loooook!*" A toddler screeches and squirms from her mother's arms, chunky little fingers pointing at us. "It's white!"

They *ooh* and *aah* as Sunny gives them what they came for.

We create our own jet stream of wind. Blowing hats and scarves, and locks of hair as people scream and duck for cover.

Most rush to grab red flags from the stands at the sight. The soldier handing them out, barking at them to step back.

We dip and rise, veering in a J shape as I brace for our vertical climb, skimming the side of the arena and entering from overhead. I scan the fire section as I descend. Eyes wide open as Sunny touches down, sliding off her lowered wing on impact.

The arena is different today. Stages and raised podiums placed on the outskirts of the field. Elevated platforms centered on the east end, where four regal men sit. Players from each team surrounding them to pay their respects.

A Lion, two Tigers, and a Bear perch to overlook us all. Seats grown from the soil below them, made of trees bent and twisted into elaborate thrones.

An odd recognition burns in my bones, spotting my friends within their father immediately.

Cairo Honestus is disturbingly beautiful, familiar in the strong nose and jaw he's given to his sons. Not one gray hair peppers his beard. Not one crack or abnormality in his flawless skin, except for a lone beauty mark on his right cheek. Though his eyes tell me he's seen several decades longer than he presents.

I catch only small glimpses of him as he squats near the end of the stage. Bending to shake hands, bearing straight shiny teeth.

His locs are waist-length, midnight black, and flowing free. Cairo's deep brown skin glowy from years spent under a gentle spring sunrise, almond eyes crinkling around the edges as he laughs.

He wears the same regalia his sons had. The addition is a lavender cape flowing from his shoulders and a golden Ouroboros with shiny scales resting on his head.

Its purple gems for eyes seem to follow me from his forehead.

Next to him are two orange-haired men with ocean blue eyes that may as well be twins. Short in stature and well dressed with emerald green capes and stark white uniforms.

The heavily freckled one adorns a copper Ouroboros, bouncing his legs while shaking Mai's hand. Her lips pressed together uncomfortably as she bows her head to Alasdair Chalybe.

He smiles back with tender eyes and hangs onto her hand far longer than she appears comfortable with.

Despite the odd exchange, his energy is nowhere close to the steel-spined man I thought would hold dominion over Ardengris.

Yet, King Chalybe looks exactly as I thought a Tiger would.

The Sovereign's eyes are hardened. His orange mane streaked with white. Skin holding only a soft smattering of freckles, while still extremely pale, even more so than the bears.

As aged as the man is, I wonder if he's ever stepped off his throne into the sunshine.

He adorns a crown made of gold, silver, and copper. Three glistening snake bodies interwoven into one sparkling coronet. Blue eyes glazed over as he shakes hands without meeting irises, deeply uninterested in anyone who approaches.

My feet stop in their tracks as I lay my eyes on Fenrir Sapienti. White hair splashed with silver and braided tightly behind his back.

On the top of his head rests a silver Ouroboros. One side of his lips twitching downward when the person before him tears up.

I walk closer, taking the next spot in line, even as people complain behind me.

"Excuse me," I interrupt. The student he converses with quiets midsentence. The blue team member glaring when I hold my chin high, responding with one of my own. "Leave."

After a hesitant moment, the student cringes from my gaze, bowing his head to the Father of Hiemsternum. And when Sky's father gives me his full attention, my vision tinges red.

*He wears her eyes.*

Bile rises in my throat as an exact replica of the beautiful silver coins, that once stormed and burned, now cut through me like blades.

So much of a mockery that I wish to claw them from his face.

"Well, aren't you the most stunning creature I've ever seen," he grins. When I don't so much as smile in return, Fenrir raises an eyebrow.

"I'm sorry for your loss."

Fenrir extends his castor hand, and I hand him my right instead.

His practiced smile doesn't falter.

He lowers his dominant arm, grasping my hand with his right and doing the thing all weak men attempt at least once in their lives.

Overly direct eye contact and a too-tight grip.

A tilt of his wrist in comfort to himself as he positions our handshake closer to his body to regain his perception of control.

"How peculiar," he says while staring at my ring.

The Sovereign glances at me with some interest. As does Alasdair and Cairo.

"I'm sorry for your loss," I repeat. Some small part of me hoping he'll have any visible reaction. Give off any indication that he's as torn as I am. His life just as incomplete without her.

"Yes," he replies, face contorting uncomfortably. "It's a difficult time for my people, but I must continue my duties in service to my country. This is an important day to many." He turns my hand in his frigid grasp, twisting it to better survey my ring. "Your name is?"

"Of course. I understand." I plaster on a smile that doesn't meet my eyes, feeling a certain type of comfort in this anger. In the animal instinct, I have to rip out his throat. Wishing to carve into his face and erase every shared feature he carries with his offspring.

Why should I see what was pure in something so evil?

The reason she'd pushed herself past no return, before daring to live a human life with me.

I may have driven in the knife, but he's the blade itself.

He and his unreasonable demands and expectations are the true sickness that spread inside her.

*He* is the reason this world is a darker place.

"Did you know my daughter? I've been informed she had... eccentric taste."

"Not well, no. Solara is a private woman." His brows furrow, eyes narrowing as I let go of his hand. "Enjoy the show, your highness. I'm aware of what a priority it was for you to make it here. So much so, that you dipped out early on the funeral services for the most amazing woman this world had to offer."

There's a sharp intake of breath from the side. *Cairo Honestus.* I spare one glance toward the man who's gone completely still before I turn back to traitorous gray eyes.

"Truly. What an honorable man you've proven yourself to be."

He chuckles in response.

"You know, while I haven't been able to make acquaintance with your daughter, I'd like to think I know a thing or two about your son. He's not anything like you. Isn't that interesting?"

"An interesting assessment indeed. I admit, I disagree. I've trained my boy well. He's my spitting image, some would say."

"You'd think so, but it's astonishing really. Your legacy will be yours alone. It will be one for the books, and no one will dare question the type of man you are when they know how deeply you hold your values." A warning bell goes off, signaling audience members to their seats. "I'm glad we've met today, *sir.*"

I walk down the steps with eyes boring into my back, no bowing to be done. And as I stroll away, all I can think is that a father names you.

He gives you a shiny pink bike and teaches you how to ride it.

He makes sure you're always full before he eats.

He braids your hair every morning for school.

He checks on you *so* frequently that you leave notes on your door to ease his worries in the middle of the night.

A father loves *unconditionally.*

A father grieves *eternally.*

And a father marched with his soldiers to Hiemsternum until his feet bled and blistered in her name.

As Sky-like as the creature's eyes appear on the surface, I'll be content to never look into them again until it's to bring them to a permanent close.

When I make it back to the Fire quadrant, my team has begun to gather. Ezra's eyes flooding with relief as he walks toward me, tone gentle as if I may shatter with a few words. "Hey, Dreamer."

"Hi, Ezra." I cross my arms over my chest as I tilt my face upward. "I should say I'm sorry. Last night wasn't one of my better moments."

"I don't care. You showed up." His shoulders sink in relief, and my gaze darts toward the setting sun with worry.

I have to remind myself that the sun's always there. But for the world to keep spinning, it has to circulate and shine its light elsewhere.

Ezra's fingers swipe my overgrown bangs from my eyes, desperately in need of a trim. I allow it because it's harmless and sweet, and he knows better than to linger. Dropping his hand to his side, fingers clenching and unclenching against his pant leg.

"I hope you leave," he whispers. "I hope you leave and don't come back."

"Because I'm not cut out for games?"

"You're above the board, and I think... I think you deserve that much." Ezra tilts his head toward the team. "Let's finish this?"

"Let's finish this," I agree.

Mai and Bridger are arguing in hushed voices as we approach. She wears the same outfit as me, navy fringe swept into a slicked back bun. Bridger wears the same cargo pants, but his shirt is short-sleeved like Ezra's, small knives strapped to each of his forearms.

"Little One," he sighs. Our eyes meet, and he extends his arms until I walk into them, smelling of soft cedar-wood as he cradles me to his chest. "You okay?"

"No."

"One day," he promises, grabbing my shoulders and pulling back. "As for today? You tell all these assholes to kiss the ring. I'll brag I was first to the corpses of those who deny you."

"Thank you, Bridge. For everything."

"Low names have to stick together. We're one and the same, baby." He cups my face and kisses my cheek sloppily.

"Not too much." I shove him and wipe away his wet kiss. "I have a knife for little Emerson that I'm not afraid to use."

"Trust me, your girl bared her teeth enough times for me to know my place. Came to the conclusion that there are other things you'll make me fall to my knees for in this lifetime. Regrettably, none of those includes us naked. Unless you ever want a quickie when you're healed up. Then, forget what I said, use me at your discretion." I twist and tug at his nipple until he yelps, "Sorry. Too soon."

The sound triggers a pained huff of air that masquerades as a laugh from deep within my chest, sparking fire at the same time we raise our flaming horns.

A *'see you later,'* I hope is the truth.

Off to our side stands Josephine. Black hair plaited into two french braids and appraising us with apprehension. I expect a snarky comment as her lips part, but she only looks to my pegasus, who comes to stand behind me. "I'm your second rider today, Benson. I'm the only one who's taken flight this semester."

None of what she informs me of is a question, so I just nod.

Over the next half hour, the stands steadily fill, and the chatter of the crowd grows louder. Eyes drawn to the camera's getting situated from above, electronics recalibrating to catch every angle. In mere minutes, the broadcast will begin. Millions of Alchemists watching what they view as only the pregame for the major event to follow.

The five of us gather as Sunny nuzzles between my shoulder blades and Ezra enforces the plan under his breath. The announcer, Fraus Doluson, booming through the loudspeaker, letting players know to gather in the center of the Arena.

We walk together. Ezra pulling the red silken flag from his pocket, knotting it through my empty belt loop in front of everyone as we'd discussed.

Hungry eyes fall onto my side from all angles. Many of them Imaginifers from First Year Casting. Sunny taking stock of the other teams that have all managed to include pegasus in their ranks.

Three of the Air affinities, smirking from afar, have sizable stallions behind them. The captain from the Earth quadrant patting hers to calm it down as a Water affinity appears green near the steadily roaming stallion he's chosen to include in our game. I don't believe any of the pegasus are bonded, except the Earth captains.

The sun sets as trumpets begin to blare, a beast awakening inside me as the remnants of her light fade.

*"Welcome to Ludi Bellorum...."*

Fraus drones on and on via the overhead screen, naming each player who's partaking today. I don't understand why, but I've never had such an urge to rip off my own earlobes. *"We ask our warriors to kneel and our audience to rise as we recite the Vow of Fealty."*

As they did in all the tapes, we walk to the center of the field, joining our hands in a connected ring of twenty bodies, hanging on tight as our knees fall into the grass.

Audience members rise from their seats, turning toward the Ouroboros while placing a circle over their hearts. The entirety of the nation reciting its sacred pledge.

**I vow my life and liberty to the Kingdom of Terra Australis.**
**Let our flag carry the promise to place the collective above self.**
**Walking the path of those who built this great nation**
**In service and sacrifice, may we know peace with a steady hand**
**Guided by the Fathers and their Sons, United we all stand.**

Thunderous applause shakes the stadium, and we wait with our heads bent, hands clasped as one while the rulers take their bows. When everyone's seated again, a clock begins ticking on the screen. Counting down sixty seconds in my head with each click.

When it reaches single digits, Ezra throws me what's meant to be a reassuring smile.

*Click... Click... Click.*

"This blizzard will not take me," I whisper as a gong sounds and the teams break into four.

There's an odd moment of bated breath before every sprinkler in the field bursts. The Air affinity that had been holding Ezra's hand just moments ago diving for my waist.

Ezra slashes at the man's arm. Blood splattering the grass as Sunny yanks me backwards, biting the back of my bodysuit and throwing me onto her wing in one swift movement.

"I thought we were partners!?" I yell, crawling up her appendage and patting my hip to make sure the flag is still firmly in place.

She snorts as if to reply, *Bitch, please. I run the show.*

"Chlamydia it is." I shrug.

Earth affinities kneel in their quadrant, unveiling their pre-grown maze. Large cornstalks rising from the ground, inducing small tremors.

Josephine stumbles, climbing up Sunny's wing and sliding into the saddle behind me.

We launch forward, air-bound as we soar toward the North end of the Arena, where thick greenery has taken root. Row after row of corn bursting up below us. Sweat pouring down their temples while they work as fast as they can, crawling as if their lives depend on it.

Josephine shouts in my ear, pointing to the short-haired captain in green just before a leaf sprouts, covering her from view.

Sunny dives, landing smack dab in the middle of the Earth quadrant, tucking her wings into her side, hooves pounding against the wavering grass.

As fast as she is when airborne, she's slower on the ground than other pegasus. A noise of frustration sprouting from my lips each time we run into a sprung-up plant wall and have to change course.

"Burn a pathway?" Josephine suggests.

In response, my fingers twitch to form a flaming whip. Josephine's fiery orb allowing sparks to fall from her grasp, singeing Sunny's hair, who neighs below us. "*Focus!* Don't burn my pegasus!"

She grunts in concentration, the crowd and cameras buzzing by her face an added distraction until she manages to fashion a whip like my own.

Together we burn through foliage and clear the path in front of us, heavy plumes of smoke rising in our wake.

It may alert the Earth affinities to where we are, but we blaze through much faster this way. Eventually coming to a dirt pathway.

"Found her," I whisper. Sunny barrels forward, and we're on the captain's tail, narrowly avoiding the weeds that pop up to slow our gate. "Do you want me to dismount? You'll go up and come back to get me when I get the flag?"

"No," Josephine says, crawling onto Sunny's half-extended wing as we near the Earth captain. "You have our flag. Get up and come down when I call. It won't be long."

She makes the jump without hesitation.

It's as if in slow motion. Josephine soars through the air, releasing a roar of victory as her fingers grasp at firm leather, hanging onto the Earth captain's saddle before boosting herself up.

The minute she's seated and sparring, Sunny launches upwards.

When we rise, an Air affinity swoops from behind us—his pegasus' teeth chomping on my ponytail.

I unsheathe my dagger, slashing through the firm hold on my hair. Six inches of curls jaggedly sheared from the end by my own hand.

Sunny spirals and we soar upside down, kicking at the stallion's chest with her hooves.

The crowd roars as I make my escape, and white lightning kicks into gear. Multiple pegasus trying, and failing, to tail us.

One quick glance upwards shows we appear as a red and white blur on the screen until they somehow change the frame rate to keep track of me.

I feel Sunny's concern, but wear only a wide grin. "Call it dead ends. Call it Karma. Either way, I'll thank them later."

I realize that the camera buzzing by my head has microphones when there's a large portion of the crowd that laughs in response.

*Weird... And not nearly that funny. But, okay?*

We stay as close to the maze as possible. Ears straining to focus on Josephine while yells ensue from all ends of the stadium. It's only when I hear a shrill voice bellowing for my assistance that I dive back in. Sunny tucking her wings to avoid the thorny vines that reach to trap us.

Fire bursts from both hands, gripping the saddle with my thighs as we descend, disintegrating everything in a four-meter radius.

Bronze Stars shriek as a wall of fire descends on their maze. Sweating bullets as they run from the blaze, unburnt, but startled.

*Plants, not people,* I remind myself.

Josephine is scraped up but virtually unscathed. She runs from the Earth captain, green flag in her grasp, before switching it to her right hand. Using her castor hand to throw fire bombs, slowing down her pursuit.

Sunny and I slow our gate to a trot, and she unfurls her wings to catch wind. I crawl to her hind, hooking my boots in her harness before reaching down for Josephine. "Jump! I've got you!"

"You can't hold my weight like that! Have her lower her wings!"

"Jump, Josephine! You won't fall!" I practiced holding Sky with only one arm, upside down, for months. Surely I can pull Josephine up with two.

"Lower the wing!" she demands.

I release a string of expletives, crawling back into the saddle and instructing Sunny to stop. My concentration is already divided, making sure my fire doesn't burn people, there's no energy left to argue while smoke seeps into our lungs and makes us hack.

Josephine throws fire bomb after fire bomb until we come to a halt, stepping on the wing and climbing into the saddle behind me.

Sunny takes off once more to gather speed, vines tangling around my pegasus' legs as I roar. Fire morphing from red hot to bright blue, metal melting, heat.

I tone it down when a girl shrieks, a harsh burn forming across her back after a flaming corn stalk falls on her. A nearby Earth affinity dragging her limp body through mud.

We free Sunny, and the Earth captain catches up to us, her pegasus running side by side with my own.

Josephine urges Sunny's weak legs to run faster as we dodge blazing corn stalks, and the Earth captain unfurls a thick rope of weeds from her hip.

As we make the leap up, it shoots from her grasp and wraps around Josephine's wrist so tightly she releases a grunt of pain.

"Drop our flag!" The woman growls.

We're suspended in mid-air. Sunny hovering in place for fear that Josephine will be yanked off her back.

The only reason she's still firmly on the saddle is my arm wrapping her torso, keeping her seated as we hover a few feet above ground.

Josephine refuses, hacking at the vines on her wrist with a dagger. A camera flying so close to my face that I bat it away in aggravation.

"Drop! Our! Flag!" The woman snarls, voice so cold that everything slows around me, hair rising on my arms as a sense of danger shreds into my soul. "I won't say it again!"

I help Josephine hack through the vines that only thicken around her wrist. An odd sense of deja vu, hearing my own voice count down in my mind.

*Five... four... three... two...*

"Drop their flag!" I yell, right before a blood-curdling shriek falls from Josephine's lips, and the vines sprout thorns.

# CHAPTER 37

The thorns are harsh razors on her skin. Shredding through muscle, tendon, and bone until Josephine's right hand goes limp. Blood-soaked flag falling to the grass as Bronze Stars scramble for the stained green fabric.

The vines wither away, and I keep Josephine saddled while we ascend. Darting to the Fire quadrant as blood stains Sunny's coat, spurting from Josephine's wrist.

I call my team back, roaring our agreed upon emergency phrase as I help her into the grass, smacking her face to get her to do anything but stare silently into a void. It's only a minute until we've reconvened. Everyone horror stricken when Josephine cradles her nearly detached hand, attempting to keep the shreds of tendon in place.

"Josie!?" Ezra exclaims, falling to his knees beside her with a minor cut across his nose bridge. Mai and Bridger kneel forward until we're all in a huddle, drenched and smothered in soot but otherwise unscathed.

"I... dropped... the flag."

A wave of anger swells when I attempt to cut fabric off my bodysuit and cargo pants, knife making no dent in Ezra's special material.

Cursing, I rip the red ribbon from my ponytail. Another stupid drone buzzing close to my face that I elbow away, binding my ribbon around her forearm.

It's not the best choice for a tourniquet, but it's momentarily slowed the blood flow.

*Buzz buzz buzz.*

The drone adjusts its lens, zooming in on her hand while the crowd emits a collective wince.

I briefly consider cauterizing her wrist, but I hold out hope for her hand. Even though it looks as if it's been sent through a meat grinder and I'm unsure of where her thumb has gone.

Ezra cradles her to his chest as she weeps, shock wearing off when the bleeding slows.

"Stop! We forfeit! We're done!" I yell into the camera.

"We don't have any flags but the one on your hip, genius. You knew the rules. Don't start acting stupid because you're scared."

I want to smack Mai. So, I do. Backhanding her across the face hard enough for her to spit blood.

Bridger stops her when she leaps to strangle me—a scramble between the two of them until she resigns herself to a lethal glance in my direction.

"Would you look at that!" Fraus Doluson announces. "A cat fight's just broken out in the Fire quadrant. See folks? This is why you tune in to both games, the New Bloods get *spicy.*" The both of us glare towards the announcer's platform, Mai hurling a few choice words that prompt Fraus to add, "We also recommend informing your children beforehand of what horrors they may witness."

"These games go on for hours." Bridger winces, pulling off his shirt and shifting the wailing Josephine into his own lap.

He wraps the fabric around her hand, and she shivers into his side, calming down the instant she's in his arms.

Ezra's brows furrow. "We... can't leave until we unite the flags."

My gaze darts to the exits blocked by the guard, lips peeling backwards in disgust.

"Shiloh," Bridger says. In his eyes, I see a plea. For what, I do not know. But for some reason, he looks towards me to do something.

"I'm getting the water flag," Mai declares. "I suggest you make yourself useful if you don't want her to bleed out, Benson."

She takes off without looking back, and Josephine immediately clings to Bridger, begging for him to stay.

"You kidding me, Jose? You finally crawled into my arms. I'm not letting you out of my sight."

"Actually... you... pulled me... here."

"Shut up. For once in your life." She manages to laugh through her sniffles, and he leans down, pressing his lips to hers—tears streaking through soot on her cheeks. The crowd goes wild as Bridger comes up for air and Ezra cuts him a sharp glance of surprise.

Moisture gathers below our kneecaps as liquid gushes from hundreds of sprinkler heads, soaking my curls and plastering my bangs to my forehead. The Water affinities have managed to fill the stadium to ankle level, and the showers don't appear to have an end in sight.

Ezra and I exchange a look that lasts centuries.

According to the iron that persistently dribbles within Bridger's shirt, we have minutes before there's no other choice but to cauterize the wound.

I swallow roughly, rising to my feet as cameras focus on more action-packed areas of the game. The crowd's cheers a gong that strikes something sinister within me.

I understand Josephine, more now, than I ever have.

Relate to shepherds who blame sheep for the way they're sheared. Imagine them sustenance, upon glancing at the wool they've allowed to fall into their eyes. They've banded together to bleat instead of move mountains with the force in their hooves. What will get these people to stop if not the horrors of a senseless act?

I stifle my anger as the year ricochets through my mind on fast forward.

Every fight.

Every laugh.

Every tear shed.

Every lesson learned.

*Be the one to remember*, Agent Creen assured me. *You can't ever lose.*

A heartbeat goes by.

One.

Two.

Three.

I scream without a thought for what rips through my lips.

"*Damnatio ad bestias!*"

Heads snap and turn toward my cry. My face on camera and blown up for all to see—voice blaring through the surround sound speakers and back into my own ears.

Cairo's eyes widen as if he's seen a ghost. And yet, he doesn't move.

He knows full well what I'm asking, but he *doesn't move.*

"*Damnatio ad bestias!*" I plead over and over again, turning away from him and toward the bleachers.

There's hurried movement in the stands, the crowd parting in a sea of red for Russ and Jason as I glimpse Suede, Osira, and Tristain beside them. In Suede's grasp is a heavily bedazzled pink poster reading, **We love you, Sky Sapienti!**

She would've sneered at it in public. Then, hung it up tonight in her room. Staring at it as she insisted on being little spoon and complained about the crookedness of the letters. The lone flicker of our lost future would be enough to bring me to my knees if not for the matter at hand.

The Lions hop the barrier in unison, splashing into the bottom wearing white button-downs and vibrant red ties.

I take off running, and Russ and Jason come for me. Meeting in the middle and throwing myself into the both of them as they catch me. The shins of our pants soaked in frigid water from the rising flood.

Even amidst a trembling group hug, I feel sturdy.

"You answered."

"You called," Jason whispers. "We'll always come when you call."

"Tell us what you need," Russ says before they release me.

There's not one angle unaccounted for as I turn with both men flanking me. "I need to get Josie help. So we end this. *Now.* Order the Earth and Air quadrants to give up their flags."

We throw glances at the founders who are still as statues, deciding to let it play out instead of intervening.

"And the Water quadrant?" Jason asks, as we wade through a steadily rising lake.

"I have orders of my own."

I run across the field, and Sunny lowers her blood-splattered wing for me. I leap, boots making contact before she raises her wing, and I slide down into my saddle.

She takes off in a gallop, and I glance toward the monitors, cameras trailing me and the Honestus boys, cutting back and forth between the three of us to catch all the action.

Jason uses air to repel the water at his ankles, running across soaked grass as winds blow through the stadium.

Sunny spins through the cyclone that's descended upon everyone— yanking flags from people's grasps and forcing the founders to hold on tight to their crowns.

His locs escape his hair tie, floating around his head as he herds the Air affinities. Jason plucks and drags their pegasus from the sky as if with an invisible hand, bright golden light spilling from his ring.

Air goes still, and he stops his advance when they're hanging upside down before him. Swaying from invisible strings as three pegasus kneel, submitted beneath their bodies.

He doesn't steal their breath as he did with Tristain, but he doesn't need to. One look from Jason has made them fall silent.

The cameras cut to Russ, who has reached the Earth quadrant after wading through the elements. Although I'm now air-bound, I notice the ground shaking under each thump of his foot, water swishing back and forth near his calves.

Russ kneels, palms diving into the flooding grass as his ring shines a brilliant green.

At his touch, the freshly sprouted corn maze shrinks and withers. No place for Earth affinities to run when the soil they hide in collapses and sinks. Russ steals nutrients from the Earth itself, veins bulging in his arms as he intakes it with a guttural scream, murmurs of fright carrying over from the stands.

The ground beneath him blackens, dying beneath his touch as Earth affinities huddle together in a newly formed ditch.

Phantom arms tighten on my waist, and I crane my neck, lips forming a joke I know will make her laugh, words floating through empty air.

Sunny's flaps falter when my heart rolls in my chest—wings jolting as a wave of pain shreds through her mind, muscles spasming while she attempts to stay upright.

We're jolted sideways, and my eyes sting. Dropping several dozen feet before we level out, bursting upwards to avoid turbulence in a stray wind current.

"Shit, are you okay?!" I yell, slamming the bond shut as wind rips into my cheeks and dries out my eyes.

Sunny only huffs with impatience, pushing a flood of insistence down the bond until I twitch my fingers, flint ring throwing off sparks.

My hands burst with white flames, and her wings are set ablaze. The audience's eyes drawn over like moths to light as I crouch on Sunny's saddle. Gritting my teeth, we circle the arena to catch their eyes, roaring like a Bear and releasing a stream of fire from my palms.

The hungry flames consume everything in their wake—skimming across the vines and flowers decorating the barriers and newly built observation decks until they're incinerated. Moans of despair triggered as plumes of smoke and walls of fire rise to block the view of the audience.

Drones rain from the sky as I lash them with a whip, flying past each monitor, dragging my dagger across the newly installed screens.

They tumble down, and people dive to avoid them while I circle back to the Water quadrant with only one thought in mind. The screams and roaring inferno around us are the sounds and visions of the damned, and they will cede, or I will declare their hearts sunken.

Sunny dips lower as I slide down, taking my fire with me—her gossamer appendages warm to touch but unharmed.

Bronze Stars hop down from the boat docks to escape the blazing heat. Trapped in the ring of fire, I've begun to herd them in. Their feeble lake nowhere near enough to stop its spread.

A white viper twirls up my arm and around my neck, sliding down my legs as it awaits my orders.

"Yield your flag to me, or your life will not be lost for your land or for your fathers. It will be revoked because you have become cowardice prey. Allowing your own to be harmed for false glory and dead honor!

See how much the audience will blink as you bleed to death. The choice is yours!"

There's utter stillness in response until my snake begins to slither through water, completely unaffected.

*Five... Four... Three... Two...*

One by one, they drop to their knees like flies.

The last one standing trembles with the blue flag in his hands, taking a half step back as my snake wiggles against his boot.

"You don't want to cede?" I ask. The viper slithers around his ankle like an electric eel, traveling up his pant leg. Steam and scorch marks rising on the fabric as his limb begins to twitch. "Why? Haven't I given them something to watch?! Something to root for?! Enthralled them as they desired! What is left for us to fight for?!"

He shudders as it tightens around his neck, curling up affectionately and brushing his nose before dissipating in an instant.

*"Kneel."*

He falls to his knees.

*"Crawl."*

He splashes through water to get to me, hand trembling around the soaked flag as I kneel with him, eye to eye. Staring into brown irises that dilate from terror, then fall to the ground.

"Look at me when I'm talking to you."

The man raises his gaze and, in an instant, becomes a boy when I smell his piss. A long glance exchanged before I swallow the gulf ball in my throat, slipping the flag from his outstretched fingers.

When I rise, I catch a glimpse of Mai. She wields her dagger as if I might attack her next. I bare my teeth before I loop the blue flag into my belt loop, raising my hands to the sky.

The burning flames around the arena draw inwards as they're called home, a tornado of fire spiraling toward me.

The audience cheers. Their field of view cleared in time to see me roar my flames toward the stars. A beamed burst of light that illuminates from my mouth, flames licking through my vocal cords until the blaze is expelled into the heavens.

Everyone supporting the Fire quadrant bursts from their seats as I mount Sunny. Soaring above the Air quadrant as Jason stands in its center, floating up a golden yellow flag that I catch.

The screams grow deafening as we swoop to pick up Russ, who hands over the green flag until they're all in my possession.

We spiral towards the founders, and Russ stays on my pegasus when I dismount. Trotting with her out of the way while I unloop the remaining two from my belt loop, holding them above me in one fist as trumpets blare.

The other affinities gather around, hands united as one chain link before the founders' thrones.

I yell the words in Latin that are customary to claim our victory. *"My fellow Alchemists, the war is over! To survive, we must come together as one! For there cannot be an enemy among us, as long as we remain united beneath our righteous Fathers and their Sons!"*

The crowd goes wild as cannons shoot red confetti, a podium rising from the Founders' feet, that I place the flags inside.

The machine whirs, and another compartment pops out. Grabbing and unfurling the thick flag of the Ouroboros, holding it up as I'm supposed to for the photo op.

Cameras click immediately, and they've somehow managed to get the feed back up and operating amidst my show. Backup drones that are even more annoying, buzzing near my face, flashing neon warnings not to touch them.

I spare a glance toward Josephine, and my stomach churns.

Bridger and Ezra's shirts are soaked in her blood, Bridger smacking her cheeks lightly to keep her awake. Ezra uses his hands to grasp her forearm as tightly as he can.

We stand through the Sovereign's speech, and my vision tinges and wavers, fisting the crisp white flag in shaking hands.

I spare another glance toward Josephine.

Then, the absorbent material in my grasp.

Then back to her, a flicker of resignation in my mind.

"Dreamer," Ezra cautions. Seeming to understand what I'm thinking as soon as I make the choice to put the fabric in my mouth, biting down with my canines, and tearing it down the middle.

The harsh, slow rip echoes in my skull as I rush towards her.

Ezra curses, taking a strip of the fabric and getting to work on a tourniquet alongside me as the celebration and cheers fade to nothing. A heavy, all-consuming tenseness in the air following a collective cry and the held breath of thousands.

Josephine screams and jolts as we wrap one half of the flag around her hand, soaking up the blood before binding the other half around her forearm tightly until it stops leaking.

"It's okay," I whisper as Josephine bites into Bridger's shoulder to muffle her sobs. "Physical pain is temporary. Repeat it to yourself as many times as you need to believe it."

"Physical *p*-pain is *t*-temporary."

"Good. You'll be fine. We'll get you help." I tie a final knot and can finally breathe again.

*The blood's stopped at last.*

"Get her to the infirmary Bridge."

He doesn't hesitate, sparing one final look back as he bursts into a sprint.

Ezra's warm irises glance up as hostilities grow and people argue amongst themselves in the bleachers. A crowd divided as they debate my actions and seek to justify or condemn them.

"Help him, Ezra." He shakes his head, eyes squinted in the distance until I squeeze his arm. "Ezra?"

"They have each other, Shiloh. I'm worried about *you.*"

He wavers slightly, as if sure this is the last time we'll see one another. And really, it might be.

My hand grasps his as he swats away the camera from prying on our conversation.

"I can handle myself." My gaze trails toward the exit as Bridger's stopped by fifteen soldiers. "Keep him safe."

His mouth twists in a sneer. "He—"

"This isn't about you. Josephine needs our help, so prove you're who you said you are."

Ezra sucks his teeth with a sharp nod as Sunny's hooves thump down beside us. Our hands squeezing tightly before we let go, taking off with Mai right at his heels.

Russ dismounts beside me, and Jason arrives at my other side, narrowly concealed horror on the Lions' faces as people shriek obscenities.

Jason cocoons the three of us in a bubble, my ears popping ever so slightly as Sunny stretches her wings, continuously swatting cameras away with every stretch.

"Jason, can you have someone come for Josie?"

"Of course," he breathes. "But listen. What you did, it's—"

"I know."

Even though I know it, my shoulders sink in relief.

Whatever repercussions I face for debasing a piece of fabric have to be worth the potential of a life saved. Especially if that life is meant to be represented within it.

"I'm not sorry, Jason. She needed my help, and I'd do it again."

"Unfortunately, I'm all too aware." He sweeps me into a hug, squeezing tightly enough to prevent my next inhale. "Cry, sweetheart."

Jason pinches my side, and when that doesn't seem to work, he croons her name in my ear.

Not Sky Sapienti. But the one I wept to him. *Sky Aelia.* Over and over again until there's a flood of tears down my cheeks.

"You're proud you've won a game for your country. In your interviews, in your introductions, that is all you talk about. The fact that your partner served faithfully and was just *memorialized* with that flag. You respect each and every person who died for it. Don't open your mouth to say a damned thing else."

He plasters on a grin as he sets me down, and Russ follows suit. Sunny's wings furling into her side as Jason amplifies his voice, grabbing my hand and lacing it through his before thrusting it in the sky.

My eyes dart to the ripped screen.

Every eye in Terra Australis is on me as wind whips through my curls. As my name is displayed for every soul to see. Right next to Jason's until Russ flanks us too, his name popping up beside the two of ours.

I want to push him away. Protect just one person from any scrutiny at my hands.

"This is the point!" Jason shouts. "This is why we play the games of war! United, we're better against any threat to our peace and prosperity. For one to bleed, is for all to bleed!"

Russ takes my other hand, and the camera angle widens. Jason lets him continue for him.

"That is the meaning of our flag! To use it to help any of our own is something the founders would weep tears of joy for. The Lions will never let you stand alone or know divide again! It is the vow my ancestors died for, and the Fire quadrant won this year by showing the truth of that vow!"

Several silent breaths pass before their father rises.

All of us tense until Cairo's face breaks into a warm smile. Genetically infallible like his sons. A grin that spreads like golden sunshine, reaching nearly every inch of him.

Their father answers the call. *Late.* But he answers.

Eyes the only part of him that remain truthfully tense until they soften when a drone nears.

As the other founders remain seated, I realize the problem.

Cairo should've waited for the Sovereign to make a stand first.

His stance forces their hand.

Stand and rise with him, or show a clear divide to their people.

Cairo's ring flashes a brilliant green, and the entire stadium shifts and shakes. The dead soil in the Earth quadrant flooded green and filled with lush grass with a turn of his pinky.

The type of power that comes from decades of practice. No sweat broken as he bends to pick up a small bag bursting with seeds.

Cairo tosses them into the air, and they burst into vibrant purple flowers. Spreading like wildfire throughout the field until the ground is covered in a sea of violet and reeks of lavender. Nowhere to walk and not trample a flower beneath our boots.

As their scent wafts around us, the rulers stand. United together, clapping with wide plastic grins.

And only now does the entire arena burst into cheers as Fraus Doluson rambles off stats about our record-breaking win into the loudspeaker.

I can't hear anything but muffled shouts and blood rushing in my ears as Jason and Russ put me on their shoulders. My hands forming a circle above my head as the cameras catch the three of us roaring together, the audience copying my movements with glee.

My gaze falls over my shoulder, eyes meeting the Sovereigns for the first time. He smiles the broadest of them all, but his eyes remain cold to the bone.

And they never leave me.


An INFLUX of people want to meet me after King Chalybe finishes his speech. In intermission, before the real game begins, I'm flooded with admirers. Shaking hands like it's my job alongside Russ and Jason, recognizing the names of some of the top Loyalist families.

They drip with jewels, wearing symbols and family crests as I come to understand what autopilot can do for me if I let it. Especially when conversing with people who only want to talk about themselves.

On the outside, I appear a wide-eyed daisy. Gushing about how fortunate I am. How I really thought the best way to honor my founding family was to showcase its sons.

No matter what family they kneel to, they all feel the need to adjust my hair and touch me like a doll. Many weeping openly until I have to comfort them about Sky's passing.

I find myself dodging inappropriate questions about my newfound *single status* most of all. Immense curiosity if I will be the future Queen or Lady of Leonusver. Dragging Sunny away from the crowd when she begins to nip people on the ass for asking.

She's deeply unhappy with how many people I've let pet her, and she's making sure I know it. Josephine's blood still stains her pure white coat, too. A wing swatting my head as Sunny pushes her deep longing for my girlfriend into my brain. Wanting me to tell her how I lost our Sky.

I feel her burning grief like a fist around my heart.

*Why didn't you protect her?*

*You were supposed to protect her!*

Sunny's pain and confusion hits me like a truck, and I stumble into Laroche, mustering a smile seeing her in such close proximity to Professor Agarwal.

For once, she's dressed down, out of flight leathers. A hefty oval diamond on her right hand that she hides under folded arms.

And if that doesn't clue me in, the way he looks down at her with such adoration does.

"Agarwal, how did you pull Laroche?"

I'm in no way being facetious, but I am pretending to give a fuck as another unyielding wave of Sunny's hurt racks through me.

*Why can't she see that I can't bring her back?*

*Why can't she understand? I can't speak about her without wanting to follow.*

No matter what I attempt to show her, Sunny's tantrum balloons, and she yanks her reins away.

Agarwal's handsome face lights with a smile that can't seem to leave him in his wife's presence. "Prayers... *luck*... more prayers."

"I would've respected you twice as much this year had I known." They chuckle but can clearly tell I'm on autopilot. To their credit, they play along all the same.

"You make good points, Ms. Benson." Laroche nudges his foot with her own. "Listen to her, Hari!"

"I beg her to put the ring on," he grumbles in my direction. "It'd appear as if I'm lying! Never took my last name. Never says she's a married woman. I have my work cut out for me with this one! I can promise you that."

"My dear, the gloves are too slim."

"They're not, I've checked."

A twinge of something painfully bitter floods my insides as they banter, and my smile slowly falls—a dark emotion that I've never had access to before hitting me like a sack of bricks.

I want to say something vicious. Hurtful. Deplorable and downright cruel, even.

The all-consuming feeling makes my insides curdle.

"Here, allow us, Ms. Benson. I have a special shampoo for stains."

Sunny huffs, but at the moment would seemingly rather have Laroche ride her than me.

She mounts as if it's second nature. Professor Agarwal cringing as his wife holds out her hand, scrambling up Sunny's lowered wing and grabbing hold of the little woman tightly.

Agarwal smiles softly. "It's been a pleasure working with you in the lab this year, Ms. Benson. And a greater pleasure watching you shine today. My wife and I were inspired by your gameplay. Never a more valiant win in my lifetime."

They bow their heads to me, and I remember now what true guilt feels like. Pointed looks in their gazes that words cannot say. *They forgive my misplaced anger.*

"We've written letters to ascertain that your time here was well spent."

"Thank you, Agarwal."

"I hope to see you back next year. Your flight safety could use some refining." Professor Laroche declares sternly. "If not, take care of yourself, young lady. We are... immensely sorry for your loss."

"Thanks, Laroche."

She nods, patting Sunny as my pegasus launches into a gallop before taking off into the air.

I watch them fade into a small dot in the distance. Escaping the stadium as quickly as I can. Ready to scrub Josephine's blood from every inch of my body, and wishing for it to be the last time I ever see this place.

# CHAPTER 38

The infirmary is white and sterile. A brightly lit, echoey building that contains only the necessities of treating patients. And right now, it's barren aside from the best surgeons in the country, all dressed in scrubs and laughing at something their first son has said. Jason sits in their circle of chairs, thanking them for working on the holiday. Promising a dinner with him and Russ at the Honestus estate this summer. He's finally shaved his beard, and what little relief it brings me takes some weight off my shoulders.

I walk past them, clutching a plant in my hand as I spot a steel door with her name etched into the placard.

It slides open as I approach, and Josephine bolts upright, eyes widening slightly and shoulders sinking. Her ink black hair is parted down the middle and pulled into a messy ponytail, skin sallow, and under eyes purple. "What's that?"

She's referring to the cactus I clutch in my hands, the pot slightly cracked from where she once flicked it over. "Flowers die."

"Okay...?"

"So, I thought about this plant I've had all year. I haven't taken good care of it, but it's low maintenance, and it's been okay to look at before bed. I had Icarus add some flowers to it. They'll die, but the plant will stay alive, and they'll regrow every spring."

She eyes the yellow flowers blooming on the green and spiky plant as I approach, reaching forward to take it on instinct.

We glance at her right arm, gauze and bandages wrapped around her wrist, revealing a clean amputation.

My steps falter, and she lowers her arms back to her side, eyes filled with disgust. A slight crinkling sound as she flops into her pillows, paper gown irritating her as she struggles to get comfortable.

I place the plant on her side table, adjusting her pillows before sinking into the angled chair nearby.

It must have been recently vacated by Bridger because his scent lingers around me, and the seat is still warm.

In the silence, a maniacal laugh emits from Josephine's lips. "It's whatever. I'll be healed in a week or two. Fresh baby skin and a few pounds lighter. Castor hands fine."

"It's okay to feel upset. What happened to you isn't fair."

"War often isn't. It's mankind's wet dream. Soaked and showered by tears as the Universe weeps for its souls." She sucks her teeth. "But that's the point, right? I could have ceded. I'd still have my hand then. It was an expensive lesson, but a lesson all the same."

"The cost was too high. You're too young to have known what paying it meant."

Josephine crosses her arms, eyeing the cactus beside her. "Why are you here?"

"Where have you been sitting for mealtimes?"

"What's that have to do with anything, Skeeter Bites?" My brows raise, realizing this will be the longest conversation I've ever had with her, discounting when she'd broken into my room.

Josephine grunts in distaste when I remain quiet. "I eat in my dorm room."

I square my shoulders, nodding in confirmation. "I don't know what's happening next year, but if we're both here... you're welcome to eat with me. Or, Russ will take care of you. Just tell him I promised."

"I lost my hand, and you're worried about where I *eat?*"

"Yes."

"Why?"

"Growing up, whenever my sister wasn't at school, I'd eat lunch alone in the bathroom. It was the loneliest I've ever felt... Have you ever snorted a blend of molly and coke off a toilet paper dispenser?"

"Ahh. No wonder you're weird, slow, and skinny."

I choke out an off-key croak, and Josephine stills slightly. "There's not a day I went to school and didn't get made fun of by people like you. And maybe the world will never change. But, I found people who chose to eat with me at lunch, and I'm better for it."

"Fuck off, I don't need your pity invite. I hope the next pill is laced."

"My Mom would always tell me she used to say despicable things when she was hurting. She hated her life, hated everything, and wanted everyone to hate it all too. I didn't know what it felt like to be that bitter until today. Now I do." Josephine lowers her eyes to her amputation. "She's now the second kindest person I've ever met. She'd take the clothes off her back for the worst of people. She was just screaming she didn't want to be alone, and was scared she deserved to be. I realize I'm not your number one choice—"

"You're not anywhere on the list," Josephine says. "And for the record, I couldn't care less about where my ex sticks his penis. Consider this my concession speech. Bang the man if you want to." She shrugs. "That's why you're here, right? To release the guilt?"

"I don't feel guilty about what happened between you and Ezra. I'm only here to tell you, you can be whatever you want to be in this life."

"Is that so?"

"It is. A lifetime is so long and yet so incredibly short not to give a second chance."

"I didn't ask for a second chance. Especially not to hang out with someone who has the personality of paint and likely huffs it too."

"See, that's your jealousy talking. Because I'm pretty, and nice, and still have both hands. Meanwhile, you're miserable and terrible to be around, and *everyone* you love prefers my company. If I were in your place right now, they'd both be at my bedside still."

"Not very nice now, are you? Not after you stabbed your experiment through the chest and had a mental breakdown so loud everyone on campus heard it happen. Jason Honestus threatened anyone who speaks badly of you. I see who's next on your list. Moving closer to home this time?"

"Your insults are boring and wrong. I heard worse from my girlfriend when I was getting bent over Agarwal's desk in the formulations lab. *That* made me wet. However, this conversation fully makes me understand how a uterus can self-sterilize. You shrivel me."

"Why are you still here?!" she snaps.

"To take you as you are now. The holes you dig don't have to carry you down to hell because you think you're too deep to ever get back to the surface."

"You think anyone cares about change when they've made up their mind? Ezra didn't."

"You didn't change. You're violently aggravating, *obscenely* insecure, and one day we'll seriously have to discuss why you accusing me of molesting your ex is batshit crazy." Her sudden avoidance of my gaze speaks volumes. "You aren't owed anyone's forgiveness for what you do when you're hurting, but it's free as long as it doesn't cost you your soul. I find myself with the collateral to take a chance on you, and I'll pay the price if I'm mistaken."

"Is that so?"

"It is. You lost something that no one should have to lose for some ridiculous tradition upheld by men who sat and watched from their thrones. Refusing to act when they could have prevented what happened to you with a few words from their lips." Tears leak from her eyes, and she roughly swipes them away. "We can be better than they tell us, and I'll prove it. I forgive you. We'll break the habits together. One step at a time. All you have to do is say okay."

We spend so long in silence that I consider I may have been wrong until she whispers, "Okay."

"Give yourself a reason. Just one."

"I'd prefer not to spill crumbs on my carpet next year," she mutters, staring at the door as if someone may overhear her willingness to try.

Perhaps the man who'd carried her in.

"Then consider us friends." She gives me a curt nod of agreement. "Do your shoulders feel any lighter?"

"Of course, they feel lighter. I've lost a fucking hand."

"I didn't. *Lucky me.*" Josephine finds some type of amusement in this as I rise. "You can get in touch with me by—"

"No. I don't care to flick our beans, tongue kiss, or giggle about nonsense."

"I'd rather have my labia sewn shut than flick your bean and tongue kiss."

"My point still stands. Lunch is as much interaction as I'm willing to share with you people."

"Even Bridge?"

"Stay out of my business, Skeeter Bites. I agreed to try, but if you start playing matchmaker, you're going to piss me off."

I glower at the ceiling until I can relax my shoulders, aware of how unproductive it'd be to tell Josephine I wish on every star *she* were dead instead of Sky.

I do this not for my own benefit, but for the love of my life.

For the dreams that she left me.

For the hundreds of futures I can change by ringing bells and revealing a different path for one woman to travel.

"Ask Russ for my number when you're ready. I'll answer your calls. Even if it's to *giggle about nonsense,*" I say, pausing halfway out the door. "But, if you call me Skeeter Bites again, I swear on everything I love that I will let Bridger fuck me. So, the next time you come crawling back to suck his dick, because you decided a low name was *good enough* for your ambitions, you'll have to live with the knowledge that it was just in my cunt and I didn't let him wash it." Her lips fall open as I add, "Do with that knowledge what you will. Then again, I'm getting the feeling you might even prefer it that way."

"And so the lamb became a Lion," she chuckles. "This world's done a number on you."

"Or, it clawed its way out... Have the summer you deserve, Josie."

"You too, Shiloh." She salutes me with her amputated hand. "You too."

# CHAPTER 39

"Suede, this isn't working."

She groans as I twist her ring on my finger. Not one ounce of shine coming from the yellow heart-shaped jewel. "If you can set an arena on fire, you can float a damned flower! Air never denies someone help." I breathe deeply, trying to command it to my will, and the flower petal she holds doesn't so much as stir in her palm. "Maybe my ring is only left-handed? Try that!"

I toss it back to her before sliding my own back on, greeted with the low vibration of its familiar energy.

"It's not meant to be. Fire's all I've got."

"I, like, really don't believe that."

"Or, you're like, really procrastinating me leaving?"

She glares at the envelope containing my grades as if she might steal it. Below, are letters from faculty stating that I've gone above and beyond in their classes. All except Professor Martin, who had no interest in giving me anything but a passing grade. I cheated my way through the first semester of societal operations, so I can't blame him.

"Why are you leaving when we're all going to be in Leonusver this summer?"

I dismiss the fire in the hearth of our packed-up room with a shrug, sliding Chewy into her cat carrier as she releases a screeching cry.

She sticks her paw out of her cage, eager to be snuggled back up to me, and my heart breaks over her little shrieks—meows growing torturous as I tune Suede out.

I'd considered bringing her with me, but I'm no longer that hopeful.

I doubt they'd let me take anything from Terra Australis into Addam Territory. They'll probably fight tooth and nail against my return, and I was born there.

Amidst her wails, Suede grabs one of my old hair ribbons from the floor and opens the cage, throwing the white silk inside.

Chewy quiets immediately, swatting at the hair ribbon with glee.

"How'd you do that?"

Suede throws me a sheepish grin as she closes the latch of the trunk set Jason's gifted her. All matte black with golden handles.

"Animals need entertainment. They'll wreak havoc when they're cooped up."

*Truer words have never been spoken.*

The entire reason we've started testing whether I could bend air the past week is to give me something else to focus on. So I won't feel trapped in sadness as my mind and body work to function again.

Slowly but surely, the fractured pieces of my own psyche are pulling back together to resemble large chunks of who I was before. Others are lost to the Ether for good.

"I had a cat when I was a baby. Doesn't take much to distract one."

"Really? I'd think she's smarter than that."

I peer between the bars again. *Nope.* Chewy's thoroughly focused on the ribbon. But maybe it has nothing to do with her intelligence. Maybe the instinct is bred into her.

"No one's smarter than a good distraction," Suede says. "Jace walks by, and I'm in heat. I could sign my life away when he's kissing me."

Something about her sentiment fills me with caution. She's insisted *I* need necessary distractions each time she's dolled me up. Putting ribbons in my hair and painting my cheeks with blush. Not that I needed shiny ribbons in my cage. This year I've been perpetually distracted. Everything about this school is shiny, including the band on my finger.

I twist my castor ring, lips pressed together and eyebrows furrowed in thought.

For now, Chewy's distracted. Her cage safe and entertaining.

Will she cry out again and ask to be set free when she isn't? Would she want to escape if someone took her cage, tore it apart, and stitched it back together? Could she ever be distracted again if her world shifted and broke around her?

*Where would she go if her cage ever spat her out?*

*Certainly not with me.*

*My parents' deal with Addam was unheard of.*

"Suede?"

"Yeah?" She sits on one of her overstuffed trunks to jam her clothing inside, not paying attention as I eye her from across the room.

"Addam is the closest ally Terra Australis has?"

"Yeah."

"I was born there, and I don't even have citizenship."

She twists her head to look at me, eyes blinking rapidly at the territory we're approaching. "The islands serve under the same Sovereign as Terra Australis. They fall under the domain of House Honestus."

She cracks her knuckles, remaining silent while I rack my brain for any other mention of outside lands.

Suede, Meesa, and anyone I've ever asked has said this place is a choice. That they're free to leave whenever they want. Yet, none of my friends has brought up their alternative.

Not even Sky.

She'd wanted to lift the veil, but she hadn't had time.

My tongue dries up, but I keep my voice steady. "Where do people go?"

"What do you mean?"

I close my eyes, listening to her heart skip several beats as I say, "You know what I mean. If they quit, if the staff here don't serve, if they *choose* not to, where do you send them?"

Her lips part, then close again, a vague debate about whether or not to be deceitful flickering in her hazel orbs. "We don't send them anywhere? They choose to leave."

"Where? To another community?"

"It's not really our business, *where*. They step outside the borders. Just can't take things *we've* gifted them with. That's the only thing."

"Are you saying people step onto the uninhabitable surface of Antarctica with nothing but the skin on their bones?"

"Shiloh." She laughs in an off-key tone, and my face twists sideways, nausea rising in my belly as the contents of my stomach threaten to spill out. "It's not—We're not murdering people. They ice themselves out."

"Serve me, or freeze to death, is not a *choice*, Suede. It's slavery."

"No, it's not?" She scrambles forward in a hurry, and I bare my teeth.

"Yes, it is? These people are forced to serve with nowhere else to go but to the stars themselves. What about that is okay to you?"

"It's not as it sounds," Suede says matter-of-factly.

It better not be. She has to be telling the truth. Not my family, and especially not my Sky.

"No one would've invited you to Leonusver if we weren't planning to clue you in. But, it's things you should see, not be taught. That's why we don't speak about it in our studies. It would only radicalize people. Create division and dissent, and all we need to focus on are high-level jobs. We all know our places. And when we knew you weren't exactly informed of our lifestyle, Jace thought it'd be better if we all waited—"

"You let *Jason* decide for me?"

"Well, it's always been unspoken, but when we saw you interacting with the no name—"

"Call her that again, and we'll have a problem. Her name is *Meesa.*"

"Sorry." Suede's face falls. "When we saw you and... *Meesa*, we knew it was a deeper issue. Jace decided it'd be better to wait until the end of the school year. Sky wanted to, but after you hit Nox, no one needed any more convincing. We wanted to protect you."

"From what?!"

"Bellum omnium contra omnes fugimus. It's the natural state of man that our people have transcended!"

"I am a woman. War will never be my natural state."

"That is the way. It's the only path this world has ever traveled."

"Then I will create a new one! Because I've never aspired to climb a ladder to equalize the abuse that I want to escape myself."

"All of our ancestors chose this! Okay?! This new way of life needed to come under one head. The powerful provide what is necessary for everyone." I throw her a wary look. "It's not ownership, it's direction. Think of how this country is run. All year, we've been learning about how to protect our borders and improve our lifestyles. All of the necessary jobs are in the hands of people who yield the elements. The top provides! Do you really think someone who can bend Earth should be cooking our food? Scrubbing our toilets? Taking out our trash? They pay their way through acts of service."

I pull off my castor ring and drop it beside where she kneels in the same instant the words leave her mouth.

My stomach churns as I think of Meesa. Who's young but has laugh lines and crow's feet in a way the students and faculty do not. Who was pleased by an ugly puffer coat. Whose hands I've never seen under her white gloves. Who surely has no rings underneath.

"Human. *No names* are Human? What does that even mean?"

"They don't have a need for legacy. Why would they need last names?" Suede forms a circle with her hands, but I shake my head back and forth, shifting her fingers into a triangle before lifting the shape in front of her eye. "So say it is?" She flinches. "It's the most stable structure you can build."

"You think people spend so much time reinforcing the bottom of a pyramid for what's at the top to be most important?"

"There's a natural order to things?"

"Yeah. Okay. These people are good enough to organize your life, and raise your fucking children but they're *so* far below you? Wake the hell up, Suede."

"Stars above, you're acting like we tag them and keep them in barns. I'm open to progress, but—"

"Of course you're open to progress! You're okay with supporting things in private that benefit you as long as you don't have to use your voice to move the needle! Don't have to sacrifice an *ounce* of your privilege to do so!"

"I wasn't born with privilege? If you hadn't noticed, I'm not exactly used to luxury either?" She cracks her knuckles and rubs her tense face. "And what's the point of even debating this stuff? Not one person asked you to play savior. If you're not careful, you're going to leave these people worse off than you found them."

"By acknowledging their service and meeting their eyes?"

"By giving them an overinflated sense of self-worth that they hold the same functions and have earned the same things in this life! The world isn't some magical, *Shilohland,* where peace is given freely. Peace through strength is the only way to provide for everyone."

"Don't condescend me. You think anyone grounded in reality expects a world where everyone can balance on the same rung? That's impossible. I expect that the people who have scrambled to rise, don't purposely stomp out others on the way up. I care that they don't constantly enforce the idea that contribution equates to deserved respect. Fewer rights for playing a smaller role in society? That's greed! What would helping others cost you at the end of the day?"

"Shiloh, *you* want to help others, and it makes you miserable and depressed! And then they're awful to you regardless! So what's the point? I'm not ruining my future fighting for people who are content where they are and ungrateful when I lift them up!"

"That's the definition of what it is to be a queen? Sacrificing for people who fucking hate you, but doing it anyway because you see the way forward. If you only feel powerful when someone vulnerable kneels to your strength, you are no proper leader! Your throne is only a higher perch to overlook your people and see how best to protect them. If you cannot understand that, what are you doing marrying into royalty?"

"I'm marrying for love? I don't know enough about politics to even get into this stuff. But Jason's educated enough to make policy on his own, and I'll stand by it. I trust his decisions. We're a team."

"Are you... deadass serious? That's how you'll live this life?"

"What does that even mean!? You've known this and told me you wouldn't judge me, and now, you're being *judgmental!*" Suede's cheeks flush as I gape. "If you care so much about humans, don't leave. I know you grieve, Sky, but Russ floated the idea of marriage, and it makes sense to all of us. The Lady of Leonusver has just as much power as I would."

She tries to shove my ring into my hands, but I scramble backwards until I hit the bedpost, eyes staring at her widely. "Change takes time."

"That's the go-to line by people who are doing a whole lot of nothing."

"But it's true?"

"Of course it's true! I'm saying using those words to pacify me while admitting you're content with doing nothing to help is a steaming pile of shit." Suede closes her fist around my ring as I shake my head back and forth. "I honestly don't know what else to say to you."

"So you're not going to be my friend anymore because I don't agree with you?" she sniffles. "I'm not a bad person, Shiloh. This is just how things are."

"I never said that? I love you like a sister. Even in the moments you've made me look like an idiot for feeling this way."

"You're my sister too!" she pleads, "I would not allow the things I have allowed if I didn't love and trust you in return."

"Then tell me how someone capable of love for me and Jason and Russ thinks how you do? Doesn't accept any part you play in maintaining this system. I'm trying to understand what it is to feel so comfortable living in ignorance."

"Comfortable? I've been trying all year, and it's never good enough."

"Maybe you're right? Maybe just trying isn't enough anymore. And I wish it were, because I get shit wrong all the time. But if we can't learn to care for people we don't love, that we'll never know, that will *never* praise us for our help, we will not survive. The human race can't afford to continue on good intentions. The price is too high."

"Good intentions are all I have to give, and I don't ask for anything in this life but to love in return," she whispers. "I'm not like you, and I never will be. But I will dare to ask the Universe to give you strength, and I'll pray there's still room for me in your life when you find it."

"Okay. Well, in the meantime, I'm going to go give this cat back. I'll see you downstairs to fly to the transport pad. All I ask is that you don't reiterate this conversation to Russ or Jason. If I can trust you, wait until I leave."

"Are you ever coming back?"

"Promise me, Suede."

"I promise," she sniffles. We exchange a wary glance before I scramble to my feet, grabbing Chewy's carrier.

She returns to pawing at the bars of her cage. The entire journey upstairs, she screeches to be let out, asking why I won't help her as the truth weighs heavy on my shoulders.

The harder she cries, the worse the pain gets until the shattering of glass from Nox's room knocks my mind free of its spiraling thoughts.

"Nox? Is something—do you need help?"

There's no response.

Just another crash.

Then another.

Then another.

I tuck the cat carrier under my arm, hand wavering over the handle.

Glass breaks and grunts of pain follow before my body decides for me, turning it to the same resistance I'd felt right before the worst happened.

I bang frantically, croaking out his name over and over.

Heavy footsteps thumping in a rush as my voice cracks and waves of terror rush through me.

The door bursts open, and I stop, taking a step backward. Nox slips through the narrow space, brows slick with sweat that falls into a confused gaze. He looks me over for signs of injury before he takes the carrier from my arms. Shuffling his feet and debating whether to go inside his room without speaking to me or not.

After a sharp exhale, Nox sets it on the ground, pale knuckles bloody and bruised all over.

I don't ask what happened, but he understands I question it anyway. Raising his hands to the intricate silver knob and turning it without looking behind him.

His room's destroyed from floor to ceiling—reeking of charred leather and burning book pages. Large shelves are toppled over, and a four-poster bed is reduced to splinters, ash, and feathers. Not one surface within it that's left untouched or intact.

When I peer around his body, his arm blocks me from entering the space. A chandelier crashing directly behind him before Nox leans against the door jamb with resignation.

I retreat to the wall opposite him in the wide hallway.

Chewy cuts through the silence with her meows, and he frees her when she reaches through the bars.

The cat purrs, wrapping around Nox's leg in thanks before trotting over to me, pawing at my leg until I pick her up. She presses her paws against my cheek as if to prompt me to speak.

He's lost several pounds. His facial features are always sharp, but they're hollow now—gaunt and lifeless. A look in his eyes that doesn't just stir my stomach but tightens my chest.

I focus on petting Chewy until I settle on a safe question. "When did you get back?"

"Ten minutes ago," he rasps, voice raw and cracked. From screaming or crying, I do not know. Maybe from not speaking at all.

He turns abruptly, heavy boots crunching and dragging across glass.

Nox returns with creme colored paper, and my heart lurches forward. Amidst my fractured reality, I'd forgotten the dresser full of envelopes. The letters she wrote when she thought she was going to face death alone. These are her last words to me, and I'm nowhere near ready to hear them.

"What are you thinking?" he asks, obsidian eyes shutting as if too tired to remain open.

I step forward to take the letter, Chewy hopping onto his shoulders after pouncing from my arms. I cradle the unopened envelope to my heart and whisper, "I watched the broadcast."

Nox doesn't respond, and I didn't expect him to.

I'd watched his sister explain with cold certainty that she demanded justice for the broken formation at the send-off. Noticed the look in her eyes with each snap of the silver chain until Nox took over.

Solara wasn't planning to stop. They'd disrespected me, and therefore they'd disrespected her sister. And that wasn't a forgivable offense to her. Not anymore.

"How are they?"

"Alive."

"And Solara?"

"Alive." Chewy sounds like a car engine in his hands, eyes attempting to function as he adds, "I watched you on the television, too. She'd be proud. No longer a Cub."

"Is there another level to unlock?"

"Ursus Maritimus? When you finish your training, you dive head-first into the frozen lakes. The mug of ale you chug beforehand is your only coat."

"Do you earn the title after you get out?"

"You earn your title when you crawl out and hunt a grizzly. Cut out their heart and eat it raw. Then, you wear the pelt home and lay it at the feet of my father."

"You didn't make her, did you?"

"Unfortunately, it's part of the ceremony, and there are facilitators. It was the first and only time she skinned an animal."

"You're being serious."

"It's what they use to line our cloaks."

My hands clutch at Sky's cloak in panic.

Being wrapped in her uniform is like a large band-aid that keeps me from falling apart at the seams. "Please don't think we would make claims to things Sky gifted you. That is yours now. Earned all the same."

I cast him a look of gratitude as the fear rushes away from me. "Okay then... *Cool.* I don't need to slay an innocent bear."

His lips twitch upward. Lopsided, crooked, and hurting to look at. Swirling obsidian eyes containing specks of gray, a certain type of torture.

I play off the pain as I step forward.

After a hesitant moment, Nox thrusts his hand to shake my outstretched limb, the both of us flinching from the static. His grasp so icy it causes a tingle as I pull away, shifting the letter under my arm to massage my palm.

Chewy meows, swatting at his braid, and Nox ignores her unhappiness at my retreat.

"Where's your ring?"

"Suede has it for the foreseeable future."

"Oh." His brows raise in immediate understanding. "If you don't come back, I hope you continue to think yourself justified. In anything you endeavor."

"Nox, I just... *Hope* for you." We exchange one curt glance before looking anywhere but at one another. I stare at the brick wall, and I can feel him shake his head. "That was stupid."

"Wishing for hope isn't stupid. It is all that's left to do."

He swallows a sob, and something inside me cracks. Just when I was sure there were no more pieces to break.

Nox is one of three, maybe four, people on this planet who understands the sheer magnitude of what the world has lost. His entire purpose stripped from him in the blink of an eye.

I can't recall how many showers I sat through catatonic. Can't remember the amount of times Suede changed my clothes or Russ helped me brush my teeth. Or Tristain attempted to force feed me soup, or Osira readied my hair for bed. Or Jason just... kept me *breathing*.

I'd wanted to waste away, and no one would let me.

Before me is her brother. Her father. Her everything.

And I can't fathom that Nox does anything but step out of the window he keeps eyeing once I leave.

"Swear on your name that you'll remain alive," I say, trembling as I force him to hold my gaze. "Give me another friend to return to."

"Your sobriety?" Nox rasps. "Do I get to make stipulations too?"

"I don't know."

"You've been doing well. Relapses aren't cause for defeat."

"I never told her, Nox. She asked. *Begged* even. But I couldn't say it out loud. Making the choices that I made, when the person I'm in love with is sick, is— There's nothing more selfish."

His brows furrow. "Addiction isn't a choice? It is a disease. No different than the one she was born with."

"It's not the same thing. Sky would've *killed* for a healthy body. And if I had told her, how could the next words from my lips have been anything other than, you should leave me? To tell her, that in a million years, I could never be worthy of her love."

"Shiloh, when we went out to hunt, she sat Solara and I down and said she was engaged. That she knew you struggled and... was still going to leave with you. Because there was no doubt in her mind that you'd put your family first. That you'd done so all year."

"Nox, I can't—"

"No. You will listen to me," he says, voice rumbling as if a clap of thunder is on the horizon. "I'm telling you this, not to hurt you, or comfort you with falsities, but to set you free. You convinced my sister to live a human life. Something I tried all my life to convince her was worth living, in less than a year's time. You question if you were good enough when I know you were the best thing to ever happen to her. I believe you gave her time, brought *meaning* to it, and I hope one day you grow to believe that too. That I made a mistake not thrusting her in your arms from day one and telling you both to run."

A hitched sob leaves my throat. Releasing the overwhelming feeling that if I had pushed harder, done something different, that she would have left her father's pressures behind.

She had left them.

She'd learned to fly, but they'd caught up to her.

And for once in my life, I let the blame fall on shoulders that aren't mine, so I can hold the weight of grieving her properly.

"You saved her," Nox finishes simply. "And never in her wildest dreams would my sister expect you to focus on my well-being if the trade-off was your own. If you need my word, you have it. I'll be here waiting if you ever return. On my name."

Nox's promise releases me, his words a foothold in the abyss.

*It's okay.*

It's okay that there's not enough left in me to survive pulling the both of us from this darkness. The world will wait, it will spin without me, and I don't need to hold it.

"I swear. I'll try my hardest. For her."

"Do it for yourself," he demands. "And don't come back unless it's for yourself either."

"Okay... Bye, Caveman."

"Goodbye, Cub. Here's hoping."

With that, I leave this hallway and the nicknames behind for good. Bolting down the stairs and running as fast as I can with absolute certainty that letting go of Terra Australis will prevent my fractured soul from shattering.

Getting as far away as possible from these walls that haunt me and scream her name. Outside and down this new path, as the blizzard looms nearby, but the sun rays blaze bright, lighting a clear way forward.

# CHAPTER 40

I say goodbye to my pegasus on the landing pad as Russ unbinds my luggage, heart squeezing inside my chest. She knows I have my doubts about returning, and instead of making me feel guilty, she'd flown with only a blank look in her eye. Intelligent enough to understand that I leave now or I don't leave at all.

"Don't worry, you'll be with family." Suede clings to Jason's back atop his black stallion, my ring on a necklace around her neck. Clearly troubled but still having kept quiet about our conversation. "You'll let my friends ride you, right? You won't quit flying?"

She huffs in reluctant agreement, and I wipe away her tears, kissing her muzzle.

Russ rolls my luggage toward me, appearing slightly perturbed.

"Caelus will be gentle with you on the flight home, I promise."

"*Caelus?*" Russ asks.

My pegasus stills, head tilted to the side.

"*Caelus.* It's her chosen name. From this day until her last."

Caelus, formerly known as Sunny, flaps her wings up and down. As she once did when she chose me as her rider, she now agrees with this choice I have made, too.

I kiss her nose once more, stepping backward. "Treat her kindly and pluck the black hairs? She hates them."

"Of course. Until your return, she'll be well kept in Leonusver." Russ sweeps me into a fierce hug, lips landing on my temple as they always do. "I love you... Take care of yourself, Shi."

"I love you desperately, Icarus. Please remember what I said. About perfection?"

He releases me with a small nod, climbing up Caelus' wing before she steps off the landing pad and into the surrounding clearing. I walk past Jupiter to pat him on the side, squeezing first Suede's hand as she leans down for a long moment. Then Jason's.

"Where's your castor ring?" Jason turns my hand over, examining the flint ring left on the middle as his stallion radiates tense vibrations. I extract my fingers with a shrug, patting Jupiter's hind until he takes the order, walking backwards off the circular transport pad.

"I don't want Addam to confiscate it. It belongs here."

Jason's eyes tense, pulling Jupiter's reins and glancing to Suede for confirmation. She shrugs, resting her chin on his shoulder and patting his stomach in a soothing motion.

"None of us has fire to light the transport pad," he mutters with a searing glance downward. I pull the lighter Agent Creen gifted me out of my cloak pocket.

"It's okay. I brought it with me." I flick the lid open and kneel down, flame sparked and wavering above the glistening dark stone.

"Wait," Jason says. "You may not be my blood, but your heart is Lionborn, Shiloh Benson. I look forward to seeing you again. Join us at the estate as early as you feel inclined to make it back." The boys exchange a lingering glance as Jason's fingers knit with Suede's.

"Thank you, Jason. I'll miss you more than I can explain."

I brush the flame against the ground and stand upright, stuffing the lighter into my pocket and sliding on Sky's leather gloves. At last, I pull the hood of my cloak over my curls and grip the handles of my over-stuffed suitcases.

Jason waits for me to add more as orange leaves fall around us and the landing pad steams and glows. Fire catching. Stone melding and changing like hot lava beneath me.

A snake takes form. Spiraling from inside toward the pad's outer edge. Glistening red scales turning white, glowing brighter and brighter and brighter.

When I look up, I can barely see them anymore, but I shout anyway.

"I love you guys! I'll never forget all you've done for me!"

My eyes find Russ's through the bright light, and his grow wide with realization.

"Wait," Russ's voice fills with dread. "*Wait, wait, wait.* Shi—"

I bend my knees as reality bursts into an array of color around me. The world morphing and twisting on its axis. Swaddled in warmth and light, floating upward, and then given a harsh push sideways.

I'm shot out of the Arch of Maria and thrust into darkness as my boots skid across ice. Snow falls from the sky, and my cloak and fur-lined leathers keep me perfectly warm in the subzero temperatures, steel-toed boots crunching with each step forward.

No sun shines overhead. Most of the light coming from the fading fire of the arch and the headlights of a nearby helicopter.

A male figure stumbles forward, and I make out his face, running up to me with clear relief written on his features and crushing me in a hug.

Steven Creen pulls back to make sure I'm alright, and I wonder what he sees that puts him on edge. "Shiloh...?"

"Hi, Steven." I grab the handles of my suitcases, wheeling them toward the helicopter. The echo of ice crunching under my heavy boots rivaling the whooshing blades. "We need to leave as quickly as possible."

"Why?!" he shouts through the nipping wind. "What happened?"

I glance toward the Arch of Maria, cooled down and sealing off Terra Australis from the world. Finding I don't know which side I should be standing on anymore.

My whole life, I've asked the Universe a singular question, again and again. Too many curiosities encased in three letters to ever get the answers. But when I close my eyes, they appear in a brilliant blaze of violet and fade to white, vowing I'm done with Karma as I realize Sky was wrong about her pain in this life.

There is no Universe that spun her suffering to know me.

There is only a broken world that put someone so pure through an immense amount of torment to receive what was always meant for her.

A world that now demands I live with this grief to prevent it from taking others.

Yet, in knowing these atrocities committed against my love, I won't ever regret the price I paid to fall.

*I'd pay it a trillion times over.*

Because to never have felt this agony, means I never would've witnessed a hundred nose crinkles or heard a thousand raspy chuckles.

I'd never have known the feeling of dancing on tabletops in a glass-roofed cafe. Or known what it's like to stare into gray swirled orbs *just* before they darken, a pink mouth twisting as it says something vulgar.

I'd never have known what it is to crash into silk and have my body worshiped as if it's something holy. To have worshiped back and known I touched a piece of something divine. Held a fragment of the Universe and got to experience it so thoroughly.

There may be relentless hurt to pay for this tradeoff, but the sun will rise tomorrow.

As long as it keeps rising, the world keeps turning. *Life* keeps going.

Someday I'll find hope in some deep dark place and show it to the sun as offering for each weeping night I'll suffer through.

Sky Aelia is the answer to the unsolvable question of human existence.

*She* is what happened.

*She* is why I stepped through.

*Will she be why I go back?*

"Shiloh?" Steven prompts, breaking me from my spacey thoughts. "What's going on?"

"As usual, I made a mess of things." I shrug. "But I didn't forget."

"Go figure. I think I did too."

I'm unclear what he means until we make it to the jet.

Until I'm ripping off my gloves and my eyes land on Samantha. Inky hair held up by a pencil as she sifts through a box of legal documents, taking notes with an ankle monitor on.

"Sam?" I breathe.

"Hey, Bee." My sister throws me a watery smile before I bound into her arms, trembling because I know Steven's done something drastic to give me this gift. And with this bell to keep me centered, he's just become one of the only people I know I can trust.

THIRTY-SIX HOURS LATER, I stand in the lobby of Addam headquarters. Hair pulled back with a red satin ribbon. Dressed in the most frilly, white, non-imposing sundress I could find when we'd stopped to refill the jet.

Steven and I stand when my name is called. Thumb dragging over the flint ring on my middle finger as I walk into the room. Head held high as every set of eyes turns to observe me with varying degrees of skepticism.

I stand at the podium as the man interrogating me turns on a tape recorder. "State your name," he demands monotonically. So many different pairs of eyes on me, it's hard to count.

"You don't know my name?"

"For the record, Girl."

The lights in the room are blinding, but I feel not one ounce of fear. Definitely not from pawns in suits who have no right to deny me my place here. Not when they've dictated my life for the past year with no knowledge of me at all.

I fold my hands, leaning my elbows on the podium and clearing my throat. "For the record, my name is Shiloh Brooklyn Benson."

I get a whiff of hyacinth flowers, and in the back of the room stands my Mom. A smile finding my lips as her clenched jaw loosens to a shy grin, shifting eagerly as if wanting nothing more but to run over and hug me.

When she moves, I notice an ID clipped to her waistband that's identical to the one Steven currently wears on his hip.

*Of course.* In hindsight, everything is clear.

My smile fades, sucking my teeth as I turn back to the man questioning me.

"Tell us about your background, young lady. Start from the beginning. How did we all come to be here today?"

"Well, first and foremost, I'm an aspiring Ethologist. Green, but to no fault of my own."

"Ms. Benson, we are gathered here today to talk about your attack on our nation. Start there."

"No, sir. Because the story goes back much further than that. We're here today, because everyone I know and love is a habitual liar."

The man purses his lips. "Including yourself?"

"Next question, please. Let's try and keep it interesting this time."

***End of Chronicles of the Phoenix, Volume I***
***These events have been recorded faithfully by National Historian***
***S.S., approved for shelving in the Library of Veritas — certified via***
***signatories of House Honestus.***

# ACKNOWLEDGMENTS

I began writing *The Terra Australis University for Alchemists* in August of 2023, after months of typing middle-of-the-night brain sludge notes, recording incoherent voice memos, and leaving unintelligible scribbles on crumpled paper culminated into the skeleton of my debut novel. By December 2024, I'd finish what I thought was a final draft, submitting my first-ever query to the tune of *instant* rejection. Ultimately, deciding to put it out myself and just see what happens. (After about fifteen form rejections, and a few non-responses, sent me into what I'd describe as a calm but catastrophic meltdown.)

I know. Trust me, I know! I'm built for a lot of treacherous journeys, but the query trenches are a different beast. (One that trad authors are valiantly fighting, might I add.)

After several slaps of reality whooped my ass—I crawled out, dusted myself off, and took a leap of faith on a new path.

And look at that! We made it through another year of painstaking edits, trials and tribulations, several moments of panic, and countless days spent squinting at a laptop in confusion.

Perhaps you're a friend who's been guilted into reading for the first time in years, a curious individual who saw a spirited review, a cautious reader five years from now that stumbles across this at a yard sale, or maybe you're just someone who gambled on a decently priced doorstopper. In any case, I hope the novel's thick enough, and I thank you all for taking a chance on Shiloh's story, for sharing your precious time with the T.A.U. Crew, and for whatever strongly worded feelings you may or may not express after you've reached the end of this book.

Now that being said, with these big emotions at play, I don't have much space left. So, to my parents, Mom and Dad, I love you. It is an extreme privilege to have the space, time, and support to write a manuscript. I don't take it lightly. Without your help and encouragement, this story would've faded with other passing thoughts.

To my friends and family, I adore you. Sometimes it feels like our group chat is the only sane place left on the internet. And therefore, the world at large. *(Sidebar: I have so much to say about the desperate need for third spaces. More on that later.)* And shoutout to my brother for reading unedited sample pages. A year later, I'm horrified.

To my critique groups, you kept me on track when the self-doubt monster began to creep in. Special thanks to the #1 Skiloh fan, SM. You were the first person to read and love these messy, sometimes throttle-worthy characters, in their entirety. TikTok is a blessing and a curse.

Last but not least, I thank every other indie author who's put work out, in print or otherwise. There's a common saying when you're in the query trenches that it only takes one yes for success. One positive outcome, one needle plucked from a haystack, one extended hand from above to make it through the slush pile.

And unfortunately, and fortunately, if you've decided to self-publish, it takes a thousand yes's and a million, 'Okay, but how do I make that happen by myself' moments. Wearing a hundred hats at once, that may not fit, but shoving them on regardless—because you're your own biggest cheerleader. I'm blessed to have had the blueprint laid out for me. There have been countless resources available, so many writers willing to share advice, so much community and inspiration online that it never really felt like I was fully 'independent' in this.

So thank you, thank you, thank you.

We have reached the end of this book, and perhaps we will meet again soon. But if not, the Earth keeps spinning, and the Sun keeps rising. You'll look at yourself in the mirror while they do, and I beg you to be a little kinder to the person set to navigate this world with such uncertain times ahead. And hopefully, when you're nice and bundled, you'll step out into the cold and afford your fellow travelers a helping hand. Lighting small fires along the way.

All my love,
Jada Mckinley <3

# About the Author

*The Terra Australis University for Alchemists* is an explosive debut from author, Jada Mckinley. You can find more of her on Instagram and TikTok @jadamckinleywrites where she'll post the occasional Spotify screenshot or divulge her most recent hyper-fixations to anyone who will listen.

To catch up on the latest news, visit jadamckinley.com, or *The Mckinley Notebook* on Substack.

instagram.com/jadamckinleywrites
tiktok.com/@jadamckinleywrites